Hunting Diana
By
Doreen Orsini
Triskelion Publishing
www.triskelionpublishing.net

Triskelion Publishing
15327 W. Becker Lane
Surprise, AZ 85379

First printing by Triskelion Publishing
First print on February 2007
ISBN 13: 9781933874746

Cover design Triskelion Publishing.
Cover model: Andrei Claude

Publisher's Note. This is a work of fiction. Names, characters, and
places and incidents are a product of the author's imagination. Any
resemblance to a person or persons, living or dead, business
establishments, events or locales is purely coincidental.

"Hunting Diana by Doreen Orsini is a great read. The book offers you a really interesting twist on the Dracula Legend, and brings to life characters you would love to meet. Tall, dark, handsome, and definitely single Lucian, needs his soul mate, and what he doesn't know is she is just around the corner. Diana has been promised a soul mate, a lover, and the love of her life if she will just remain a virgin and wait. She has no idea why her grandmother is so adamant about this, but is tiring of the loneliness. She is tempted by the phantom lover in her dreams, teased and tormented until she feels she is going crazy. Then an encounter in a local bar leads her to think maybe Nana Lina wasn't so far off the mark after all. Meanwhile, the residents of Mina's Cove are restless, Diana is in more danger than she or Lucian know about, and it will all come down to love. Will Diana be made to succumb to the fateful drop of blood that will lead to madness and interment on Fentmore Island? Will Lucian destroy the danger to them in time? There are many questions for Doreen to answer in Hunting Diana. Vampire lovers will not be able to get enough of this thrilling paranormal, and they will be clamoring for more. I suggest you get to Triskelion Publishing and get your copy of Hunting Diana today. Join the residents of Mina's Cove, and learn what all the fuss is about!"
Romance at Heart Magazine

"Diana Nostrum always listened to her grandmother Lina about keeping her virginity and that she had a soul mate, and she would know him. Diana is twenty-five and desires to meet her soul mate soon, but it seems all she can find is a lingering shadow of a man in her dreams. That is, until she meets Lucien.

Lucien is a vampire, and actually a champion, but when his step brother is murdered by Frank Nostrum, the family and Lucien knows he has to be dealt with. They want Lucien to find out if his daughter Diana is leading vampire men to the slaughter, and if so, Lucien is to turn her. But what Lucien finds is an innocent, and one he is strongly attracted to.

As Diana and Lucien come together, they both know their feelings are strong and Diana is sure Lucien is the soul mate her grandmother spoke of. But Lucien still has a small doubt about Diana. Then the night of the bonding, something goes horribly wrong and increases Lucien's doubt about Diana. But there is someone evil who wants Diana dead. Will Lucien find the truth before it is too late?

This vampire romance will rock your world. From the beginning you will be drawn in by the characters of this tale and ensnared by the action, danger, and intrigue. Set at a steady pace; this story is loaded with spine tingling action, chilling adventure, and a twister of a plot. Exceptional dialogue and very steamy sex scenes are also entwined to this tale, then tied off neatly with a sensational ending that makes this reader think there will be more to come. An absolute must read." **Coffeetime Romance**

"I have to admit that HUNTING DIANA is the best vampire story that I have read. Even before I had reached the end of the first page, I was totally gripped. The initial chapters set the scene with haunting descriptions of vampires and clear explanations of their hierarchy and culture. Offset against this are the delightful descriptions of Diana. She is presented to us as pure and innocent, unaware of her beauty and tormented by the loss of her mother. By the time that Lucian comes across her naked in the moonlight, we are just as fascinated with her as he is.

With HUNTING DIANA, Ms.Orsini has shown off her glorious talent for bewitching the reader. To describe this tale as a simple vampire love story would be doing it an injustice. I found the secondary characters and storylines just as fascinating as the main characters. Lucian and Diana's story is the hub of the book and is fascinating to read. They have their own sets of values and beliefs; being able to watch them play out against the backdrop of their all-consuming passion is a gift. The web of intricacies Ms. Orsini wove was brilliant. Characters and story lines meshed and amazed at every turn. If you read only one vampire tale this year, ensure that it is this one. With powerful imagery, sensual descriptions and a totally mesmerising plot full of twists and turns, you will not be disappointed." **Romance Junkies**

"**Miss Orsini** has really outdone herself with *Hunting Diana*. With her intensely graphic description of not only the bonding ritual but the daily life of Lucien's people she brings the story to life. You find yourself pulled into the story deeper with every scene. **Miss Orsini** keeps her readers enthralled with every novel she writes. I found myself not only drawn to Lucien but to his stepfather Damien as well. If I had one suggestion it would be "Bring on Damien and Angelina's continuing story!" If you are looking for a hot and spicy novel with a tender twist then *Hunting Diana* is just the one I definitely recommend." **Fallen Angel Reviews**

He might be able to chain her, but
could he ever tame her?

Watch for

NO ONE BUT MADISON
By Doreen Orsini

Coming in June 2007

Dedication

For sharing her knowledge and instilling in me the confidence all authors need to write well, I thank Julia Fierro, author and founder of The Sackett Street Writer's Workshop. I'd also like to thank Catherine Chernow and Jan McAndrews, my critique partners and friends for their support and guidance, and Gail Northman, my editor. Finally, I thank my family. They put up with my endless hours on the computer. Natalie and Jesse listened and gave advice as I read and reread those scenes I felt did not work. Victor spent many nights sleeping to the sounds of keys clicking and papers rustling. Nicholas and Logan dealt with late meals and take-out. My parents kept their calls and visits to a minimum. For seeing the author in me so many years ago, I will forever thank my father.

Chapter One

Listening to the roars reverberating through the auditorium of Mina's Cove High School, Lucian feared his fellow night creatures had all reached that point where the beast inside reigns supreme – or as the younger vamps would say, gone over the edge.

Those old enough to recall Van Helsing's reign of terror and those years away from cutting their adult fangs cowered in the shadows in fear. The females, usually so adept at keeping their mates from releasing their inner beasts, shrieked and tore at their hair. The males bared their fangs, snarled, and roared as they clutched their children in their arms. Some even spoke of leaving Mina's Cove.

Up until now, they'd all felt safe living along the secluded, northern inlets of Lake George. Thanks to the combined powers of their elders, humans approaching by air, on land, or from the lake failed to see the vampires' village or majestic homes, failed to see the metal shutters descending over every window moments before dawn. The vampires' peaceful co-existence with the humans sharing this little slice of heaven might have gone on for centuries.

If not for Frank Nostrum. Now, for the first time since Dracula and Mina brought them to this haven, the vampires of Lake George, creatures capable of snapping a man's spine in two with no more effort than it took to pop open a beer, hid within the confines of Mina's Cove, too terrified to leave the protection of their elders. Lucian couldn't blame them. This morning his brother, Marek, Frank

Nostrum's latest victim, had merged with all their minds during his agonizing demise beneath the dawn's searing rays. His screams had ripped them all from their slumber.

"Silence," Tobias, Lucian's grandfather, commanded in a steel-laden voice. Dust floated down from the timbers rattling overhead. "For over a hundred years, we've lived here with only the occasional hunter to deal with, and you dare risk exposing us with this despicable display? I have watched over you, as I promised Mina and Dracula when they left on their quest, but I can not protect you from your own carelessness."

A hush fell over the crowd. Only the sound of a summer breeze whistling through the blinds broke the silence. Tobias' wrath could incinerate them all if let loose. His eyes filled with crimson tears as he met each terrified gaze. Lucian had never seen his grandfather so angry, so grief-stricken.

"I too heard Marek's screams at dawn. I too lay trapped in my home while he burned beneath the sun in Nostrum's pen. My daughter, Olympia," Tobias glanced down at Lucian's mother, "is right. It is time that Frank Nostrum pay for hunting and killing our kind. He has condemned so many of us to an eternity without our loved ones, an eternity of grief. It is only right that his punishment fit his crimes. That he face a future without his greatest love. His daughter, Diana."

"But the angels," a female yelled from the back. "What of the angels?"

"Their wrath could turn us all into Slashers," one of the females closer to the front shrieked.

The need for revenge churned in Lucian's stomach, but he was a Champion d'Angelique, a protector of all innocents. Those sent to watch the hunter had yet to prove Diana Nostrum even believed in vampires, much less helped her father hunt them. He knew he should speak up, be the voice of reason, but how could he not avenge his stepbrother's murder or those who perished in the hunter's pen before Marek? He longed to wipe Frank Nostrum from the face of the earth.

But kill his daughter? They hadn't killed an innocent human since the angels returned Dracula to Mina.

"Please, you must listen to me," Damien, Lucian's stepfather, pleaded. The other elders sharing the stage with him held up their hands for silence. "I beg of you, don't taint my son's memory with the blood of an innocent woman."

"I say an eye for an eye." Lucian's mother, Olympia, cried out knocking one vamp after another out of her way as she neared the stage. "Nostrum killed my son. I demand we take his daughter. As Marek's mother, I have the right to choose the hunter's sentence. I want his daughter's head!"

Damien bared his fangs. "You are *not* Marek's mother."

Olympia scaled the four foot stage in one leap. "I am more his mother than the human bitch that spit him out." Shoving Damien aside before her feet touched the floor, she fell to her knees before Tobias. "Father, Diana is the one luring our vamps into the hunter's pen. She's Nostrum's weapon. She bewitches them somehow. I say, let her taste our blood.   Just a drop, just enough to send her to Fentmore."

"Turn her into a Slasher?"   Damien's fists clenched. "Tobias, I beg you. Don't even consider this."

Olympia's eyes shone with hatred as she turned to Damien. Only Lucian knew that his mother would do anything to win his stepfather's heart, only he knew that she spent countless nights crying because Damien still pined for Marek's human mother.

Olympia touched her forehead to Tobias' knees then raised her head. "As the only mother Marek knew, I deserve to pass sentence on his murderer."

Tobias' eyes filled with sorrow. "Very well, Olympia, I'll send—"

"Lucian," Olympia cut in.

Lucian stumbled back as the vampires who had crowded around him shifted away. The Champion in him demanded he refuse. As he opened his mouth to do just that, he recalled Marek's screams. Their minds had merged so completely, Lucian felt his pain, smelt his flesh burning. The anguished roar lodged in his throat since dawn threatened to break free.

"But he's a Champion," Damien said, raking his hand through his hair. "Why the hell would you choose Lucian?"

"It's his right...as Marek's stepbrother." Olympia sat on her father's lap and cupped his cheeks. "Please, father. Send Lucian."

"You know that's impossible, Olympia. He'll never go through with it." Tobias stared pointedly into Olympia's eyes. "He's a Champion and you know as well as I that he's her—"

Olympia pressed her fingers over Tobias' mouth. "He'll do it, if you command him to, father." She kissed Tobias' furrowed brow and slid something into his hand. "Do it. Let the daughter of the hunter become the hunted."

Closing his eyes, Tobias raised his hand. "Take this, Lucian. Follow Diana Nostrum's scent."

A red strip of cloth floated from Tobias' palm towards Lucian's outstretched hand. It unfurled and caught the light of the overhead fixtures. Clenching his fingers around it the moment it landed in his palm, Lucian brought his fist up to his nose and drew in a deep breath. A strange feeling shimmered down his spine.

Tobias continued, "You have one week to prove Diana Nostrum's innocence. May the angels forgive us all if you fail."

Lowering his hand, Lucian barely heard his grandfather. Blood surged to his groin. A hunger he couldn't comprehend drew his hand back up to his face. His fangs shot down and sliced open his lower lip. Muscles and nerves quivered with the need to find Diana and...

Blinking against the pain and lust engulfing him, he opened his hand. A scant, strip of lace draped across his palm. The skin beneath it burned. He merged his mind with his grandfather's. *What spell have you woven into this?*

Tobias rose and turned to leave.

Grandfather!

Just when Lucian thought his grandfather would leave without answering, Tobias' voice filtered into his mind. *I have done nothing, Lucian. The cloth holds only her scent. Nothing more.*

"Lucian, don't do this."   Damien appeared beside him and grasped his arm.

"Mother believes our vamps follow Diana into her father's pen." Lucian fought to resurrect the rage he'd felt only moments before Diana's scent blindsided him. He crushed the cloth in his fist and held it under Damien's nose. "This is how she lures them. This is why they follow her."

Damien took the cloth and sniffed. "She smells no different than any other human."

"You felt nothing? Nothing?"

When Damien sniffed again then only shrugged, Lucian snatched back the lace that had incited his senses. Instantly, his body grew more aroused than he ever recalled. "What the hell is this, Damien? Some kind of trick?"

Damien blanched. "What did you feel, Lucian?"

Vampires patted Lucian's back as they passed on their way out. Voices both mental and physical offered condolences for the loss of his stepbrother and thanked him for coming to their aid.

"Answer me, Lucian. What did you feel?"

Guilt brought a lie to his lips. "Nothing."

Damien's fingers wrapped around Lucian's bicep. "Lucian, listen —"

Curling his upper lip high above his fangs, Lucian let out a low warning growl. "I feel nothing." He turned and shoved the cloth into the back pocket of his jeans. The desire to find Diana and mount her suffocated him until he caught a trace of her scent coming from outside. Yanking his arm free, he pushed his way through the door and followed.

Outside, he found the trail of her scent and began the hunt for Diana.

*****

"You've taken enough, Mother. Anymore, and you'll kill him."   Most summer evenings, Lucian relished the orchestra of his fellow night creatures—crickets singing their sweet melody, owls providing a soft bass, a raccoon's call to its mate adding the melancholy cry of a lone violin. Tonight he willed them to silence their clamoring so that he might hear the whisper of a breath, the soft thump of a heartbeat, the slightest sign that life remained in his mother's latest victim.

When his mother merely moaned in reply, he pushed off from the boulder he'd been leaning against and in one swift leap, crossed the yard. A toy shovel snapped beneath his feet. "Enough!"

His mother's head jerked up. Blood dripped from her fangs and splashed onto the tiny creature's glazed eyes. "I'll decide when I've had enough. What are you going to do? Bring me before the elders for killing a worthless animal?" Holding his gaze, she narrowed her eyes and brought the kitten back up to her mouth.

"Take another drop and I will."

With a toss of her head, she swept a lock of her hair over her shoulder then curled her tongue over her fangs and sucked until no sign of her deed marred a single, pure white tooth. "It's not like I stole it, Luc. The stupid animal offered itself to me." She pouted and kissed the kitten's nose. "Didn't you, sweetie?"

Closing his eyes, Lucian shook his head. One look and fully matured vamps who knew his mother, who had been warned and knew better, succumbed. What chance did an innocent have?

She held out the limp body. "Come on, Luc. Have a taste. There's no blood sweeter than a kitten's. Not even a virgin's."

"Touché, Mother." He kept his face devoid of emotion and shielded his thoughts. Her remark resurrected memories of the dazed virgins she had dragged before him in his youth, virgins she had held down while he'd taken their innocence and blood, virgins who had gazed upon him with revulsion, who had considered his kind nothing more than vile creatures more suited to dwell in nightmares than in the real world. He wished he could forget that time ever existed; yet, the memory of their faces saved him whenever the pure scent of virgin blood stirred a hunger he barely controlled.

"What's wrong, Luc? Still battling that addiction?"

Lucian released a low warning growl.

"Fine." She tossed the kitten over her shoulder. "You're just as boring as a recovering alcoholic."

He lurched forward and caught the kitten inches from the ground. The rich scent of its blood invaded his senses, mocking her claim that it could ever compare to virgin's blood. Baring his fangs, he glared at the woman he doubted would have shared her black hair and blue eyes if she hadn't been forced to pass them on in her womb. "Either tell me why you're here or leave and let me get this over with."

She glanced down at the kitten cradled against his chest. Rolling her eyes, she turned and stepped over a low hedge into the next yard. "You really disappoint me, Luc. How long has it been since you've indulged? Ten years?"

Following her only because Diana's scent would have led him that way anyway, he muttered, "I indulge."

"You know, damn well, I'm not talking about drinking some vamp whore's blood. Admit it. You miss human blood...the rush of adrenaline from their fear...the mind-blowing orgasms."

"That's where you and I differ, Mother. I find that fear during sex spoils the taste of blood." He gently messaged the fur over the kitten's heart and willed it to beat.

Snorting, his mother headed for the lake.

A faint heartbeat tapped into his palm. He let out a relieved breath and licked the kitten's wounds so they would heal before dawn. Carrying it in one hand as he picked fur from his tongue, he nearly bumped into his mother when she abruptly stopped and spun around.

"Aren't you getting a little old for pets?"

Bile filled his mouth. As a child he had poured his blood down the throats of the innocent refuse of his mother's ravenous appetite believing it would save them. Within days his "pets" had transformed into bloodthirsty creatures that attacked any vampire they encountered. Too many of his "pets" died before he realized they had lost their sanity to a hunger his blood had spawned, a hunger only his blood could satisfy. Too many before he learned how vampire blood turned animals and humans into Slashers. "Just tell me why the hell you're here."

"Impatient as ever." She pulled an antique lace

hanky from the back pocket of her jeans and delicately dabbed at the corners of her mouth. "You don't have to follow Diana, you know. The files the elders emailed you on her and her father have more than enough information. And my puppets are her dearest friends. They could tell you anything you want."

"Not according to Damien and the other elders."

"Damien?" she snarled, "Diana is *not* the innocent he described at the elder's meeting. You want a virgin, Luc? One lives right across the lake. A pure, sweet virgin just waiting to be plucked."

"Good bye, Mother." Lucian turned and leapt into the air. Below, a car pulled off the road on the other side of the homes lining the lake. Open windows released the perfumes and feminine scents of those in the car. Only one held his attention. Only one hit him with enough force to nearly send him plummeting to the ground. Following an older, lingering scent, that told him she'd come this way before, he soared over a dense wall of ten-foot high hemlocks and landed in the middle of a lakefront yard. Filling his lungs, he knew he'd come to the end of his hunt. Diana's essence permeated the area.

His mother alit beside him.

Ignoring her, he peered over the lake. Not a single boat disturbed the puddles of moonlight bathing in the gently rippling water. From a hundred foot wide beach, a well-manicured lawn sloped up to a three-story colonial mansion. The full moon consorted with a warm breeze which tossed aside the leaves and slender branches barring its way as it swept through the surrounding trees; a multitude of shadows danced across the white clapboard house and along the balconies wrapping around each floor.

Like many of the mini-estates nestled on the banks of Lake George, this one's borders were lined with towering hemlocks that insured privacy. Tilting his head, he mentally scanned the interior of the house. As far as he could sense, two of the three inhabitants slept while the third, an adolescent male, masturbated in his bed.

Not far from the shore, a rusty swing creaked as it swayed beneath the lowest branch of an old Weeping Cherry tree. A canopy of tear-drop leaves rustled from a sudden gust of wind.

Unbidden, the realization that his stepbrother, Marek, would have loved this place released the grief he'd managed so far to control. He took to the air and hovered for a moment above the yard that now shimmered beneath a crimson veil from the bloody tears filling his eyes. Soon, Frank Nostrum would share his pain; soon, the vampire hunter would lose a piece of *his* heart.

He soared across the yard and over the other hemlock barrier then cursed when he found his mother already waiting for him. "Don't you have something better to do than follow me around?"

"You want to know about Diana? There's no need to waste a week of perfectly good nights. I know more about her than anyone."

His mother's penchant for torturing him with tidbits of information irked him as much now as it had when he was a child. Years of experience, though, had taught him the benefits of hiding his impatience. He shrugged as if he could care less that once again she had piqued his curiosity. "I hate to admit it, but you're right," he said, absently caressing the tiny silken ears of the kitten. "Watching Nostrum's daughter for a week will be nothing but a waste of time."

"Of course, I was right!" She spat on the ground then groaned and slumped back against the trunk of a pine. A frown marred her flawless brow. She pushed away from the tree and, gripping his chin in her cold, slender fingers, stared intently into his eyes. "Listen, Luc. Don't talk to Diana. If you insist on following her this week, keep your distance. Then give her your blood and leave. I'd bet my fangs Diana's the lure." Her eyes shimmered. *Don't touch her, Luc. And, no matter what happens, don't drink a drop of her blood. It's cursed. It will infect your mind. Do you hear me? Do not drink her blood.*

At first, the fear and concern filling his mother's eyes revived the child who once foolishly embraced any sign of affection she cast his way but then he felt the tingling that signaled her attempt to control his mind. He yanked his head and heart from her grasp. Baring his fangs, he roared into her mind with enough force to knock down most vampires. *Get the hell out of my head!*

"Diana's a whore, Luc. I've watched her spread her legs to get her way since she was a teen. She'll seduce you and before you know it, you'll be facing the dawn in her father's pen."

The distant sound of car doors slamming caught his attention. Gazing towards the yard they'd just left, he asked, "How will I know which one is her?"

"You've never seen her?" His mother stumbled

back a step as if he had slapped her. She raked the fingers of one hand through her hair and shook her head. "But I thought...all these years...you've never once felt you should see what the daughter of Lake George's vampire hunter looks like? My God, Luc, you're our Champion. It's your job to protect us from the likes of Nostrum and his daughter."

"I protect the helpless, and you, dear Mother, are far from helpless."

She gaped at him. "You *must* have bumped into her."

"This new generation keeps me busy all night and leaves no time for checking out some little chit who may or may not have a hand in her father's crimes." He almost added that the elders had forbade him to go near the Nostrums the day Diana was born, but he'd learned at a young age that it was safer not to give his mother more information than necessary.

Back then, he hadn't questioned the elder's edict. Frank Nostrum had been nothing more than an annoyance, a harmless human mocked by vampires and humans for traipsing through the mountainside and along the banks of the lake each night in search of the ever-elusive vampire he claimed to have seen as a child. Lucian had no interest in Nostrum or his baby girl.

Back then.

But for the past several years, Nostrum had managed to kill some of their strongest vampires in his pen, and no amount of surveillance had revealed what weapon he used to lure and restrain them. In the last few months he'd taken down four.

The only preacher in Mina's Cove, Marek had

protected Nostrum from retribution for years with sermons on forgiveness. Lucian's indifference and the hunter's safety net vanished the moment dawn's fiery rays touched Marek's skin.

"This changes everything. Everything!" His mother brushed past him and paced along the hemlocks, stopping occasionally to peek into the yard. "Okay, just let me think a minute."

His mother suddenly stopped pacing and nodded. "I'll watch her this week. Then you could give me your blood and I—"

"*I* will follow her. *I* will prove she knows about her father's crimes." Lucian's voice shook. "And *I* will avenge Marek's death."

"Of course, she knows about his crimes! Any fool can see that she's the weapon."

"I swear on Marek's soul and all those before him, if she lured him into that pen, I'll pour so much of my blood down her throat she'll drown in it."

"No!" His mother clutched his upper arms. "One drop, Luc. No more! And wait the damn week. If you don't, they'll think I had a hand in it and banish us both."

One week. An eternity for a vampire intent on revenge. He despised Frank and Diana Nostrum, hated putting off their punishment, and prayed the week would pass swiftly. Diana's innocence meant nothing.

A soft mewl brought his attention down to the kitten struggling within the tight grasp of his hand. Cold fingers skipped down his spine when he realized how close he'd come to crushing the fragile body. He immediately relaxed his grip and compelled the kitten to sleep while he sped up its natural ability to replenish its blood. "One week. Not a day more. Whether I find out how Nostrum captured Marek or not, Diana pays for his death a week from tonight."

"Remember, not a drop of her blood."

"Just the thought of her blood makes me sick." Lucian watched his mother vanish. He couldn't shake the feeling that he'd just joined forces with the devil.

Striding a short distance into the woods, he carefully placed the kitten near the base of a towering pine. "I'll be back, little one," he whispered.

When he returned to the hemlocks, he was surprised to find Damien waiting for him. Lucian lowered his head in deference to his elder and stepfather.

"What's happened to you, son?" Damien asked, raking his fingers through his hair and mussing the bittersweet chocolate spikes falling over his furrowed brow. "How could you even consider punishing an innocent woman for her father's crimes?"

"Her innocence means nothing," Lucian muttered, wishing he felt as convinced as he sounded.

"That's Olympia speaking, not you." Damien's voice was calm but Lucian heard the steely edge of his rising anger.

"Mother's right, Damien. We're fools if we think the man hasn't brought Diana up to follow in his footsteps."

Damien continued to stare intently into his eyes.

Lucian mentally swatted away the doubt and guilt Damien's mere presence inspired. "Marek wasn't just my stepbrother, Damien. He was my best friend, my confidant, my only light in this damned eternal darkness."

His stepfather's rage slammed into him, knocked him down, and sent him skidding back into a tree. The impact of his head hitting the trunk was nothing compared to the searing pain from his stepfather's anger battering his mind. He raised his eyes and flinched; crimson tears streamed down Damien's cheeks, a heartbreaking contradiction to the rage twisting his usually calm face.

Damien towered above him, his fangs longer than Lucian had ever seen, his fists clenched at his side. *Your light?* He roared into Lucian's mind. *He was my son! My light! But I'm not blindly striking out at anyone who might be involved, am I? I'm not considering casting some poor, innocent woman into the pits of hell!*

Clutching his head, Lucian stood up, fell down to one knee, then with a growl, forced himself back to his feet. "Jesus, Damien! You nearly fried me."

Damien lowered his head. His chest heaved as he drew in one long draft of air after another. Lucian waited, wondering why his stepfather, a vampire who rarely showed any extreme emotion, had so easily slipped over the edge.

When Damien finally raised his head, desperation filled his eyes. He pressed his palm against Lucian's chest. "Look into your heart, son. You don't want to do this."

Lucian shoved Damien's hand away and pounded the spot where it had been. "I have no heart! It incinerated with Marek in Frank Nostrum's pen. I'm dead inside, Damien, just like Frank believes we all are."

"I hope, for your sake, you're wrong, son. Mina help you if you aren't." Damien sighed and looked up at the moon. He frowned as if he were searching, questioning, then nodded and spoke, his voice barely above a whisper. "They're here. She's a virgin, Lucian. Once again, your mother has set you upon a virgin. Remember that, tonight. And remember what you were. What you are, now. A Champion."

Before he could reply, his stepfather vanished.

He knew what he was. A Champion des Angelique. But he was off duty for this mission. Massaging his temples, Lucian peered through a slight breach in the hemlocks. A virgin. The red strip of cloth in his pocket felt as if it would burn through the denim separating it from his skin.

Three women in their mid-twenties slipped through an opening in the hemlock wall on the other side of the yard. Lucian focused his senses. Their voices, breathing, heart rate, and scent met with his scrutiny.

He recognized two of the women as his mother's puppets, identical twins with tall, model thin bodies and stunning faces that graced each equally. Their hair marked the only difference between them. Although both had soft brown curls, one had cut hers to rest at her jaw line while the other had streaked her waist-length hair with blonde. Hushed giggles mingled with whispers as they scanned the property before stepping free of the shadows.

Another beauty with piercing blue eyes and hair the color of wheat that streamed over her shoulders without a single ripple stood with the confidence of a woman who knew men found her irresistible and would do anything for a chance at her body. She sent a sultry gaze up at the house.

Lucian pegged her as Diana, the whore his mother had described, until she spoke. "Okay, so what's the big deal, Diana? Your grandmother was wrong." She pulled aside some branches and peered into the gap she'd just come through. "Diana?"

A fourth woman stumbled as she broke free of the hemlocks and landed face down on the dew covered grass. Lucian grinned when a string of muffled curses silenced her friends' laughter.

She ignored their outstretched hands and, scowling at the ground behind her, scrambled to her feet.

He drew in a hissing breath.

Petite compared to the others, not more than five foot three with breasts that would barely fill his hand, she brought out an instinctive need in him to protect. He watched as she drew up her shoulders and glared at the blond.

"Damnit, Terry, she's never wrong and you know it." The woman he now realized was Diana shot a glance at the house then shimmied out of her skirt. "If Nana Lina said I'd meet my soul mate tonight, then one of the guys I met tonight was him!"

Leaning forward, Lucian smirked. If her voice were any indication, Diana needed no protecting. He felt the strength of her conviction and her willingness to fight to defend it in each word. As she moved, muscles smoothly rippling beneath her skin revealed that her strength was not confined to her soul. He wondered if, like the female vampires, she would feel like steel encased in satin.

Terry rolled her eyes at the twins shedding their clothes beside her. "Did you guys see Diana's Mr. Right at Cabana's tonight?" They both giggled and shook their heads as she unclasped her bra. "Unless that nerd, the one you never would have glanced at if Nana Lina hadn't called—"

"He was not a nerd," Diana said with a soft laugh.

"Well, unless he's the love of your life," Terry continued, "or Mr. Right is some perv lurking in the bushes, face it, Di, you ain't meeting him tonight."

A wave of heat washed over Lucian. Watching the women went against every moral he possessed, every vow he'd made to the angels; yet, each discarded piece of Diana's clothing incited his body and, like a great mystery, insisted he remain and discover what had yet to be revealed.

He forced himself to close his eyes and reminded himself that this woman may have lured Marek to his death. The lump in his throat threatened to suffocate him. Why should she have another week of life? She already had one more day than Marek. Marek's wife and little girl didn't get another week with him.

Frank Nostrum didn't deserve another week with his daughter.

Compelling her to swim until she drowned would be kind compared to what Lucian had planned, but the idea of watching her slip under while her friends struggled against his mental hold was definitely tempting. Too tempting to ignore.

*****

Diana shuddered. One second the crisp night air caressed her skin, the next the air felt charged with electricity. A strange tingling that lifted her hair by the roots flowed over her head. She nodded in agreement with the sudden idea that she *could* swim across the lake but when she took a step towards the shore, the tingling returned, and she promptly forgot what she had been considering a moment before. She raised her hand to scratch her head, then froze. "Oh my God, Ter, I think there's a bug in my hair."

Terry immediately started sifting through her hair. "Okay, Di, don't freak out. It's probably just some moth."

Diana squeezed her eyes closed and forced herself to stand still while every muscle screamed that she run into the lake and drown whatever had crawled across her scalp. "Just get it out!"

"There's nothing in your hair. Wait a minute. Did you do that just so I'd stop making fun of Angelina's prediction?"

Diana glowered at her best friend. "The last time you convinced me to ignore one of Nana's predictions, I ended up losing my state title."

"Was that the year you puked all over my parent's carpet then passed out in our tub?" Cindy asked.

Unconvinced that nothing lurked in her hair, Diana bent over, flung her hair over her head, and answered as she combed her fingers through the knots and curls she could never seem to tame, "And woke up so sick and sore, I could barely raise my legs high enough to get out of the tub, much less kick some hotshot in the jaw."

Fingers parted her hair. Terry scowled through the opening. "Get over it, Di! That was in high school!   And how was I supposed to know the champion kick boxer from California had moved here?"

"Nana Lina did." Diana flung her hair back over her head as she straightened. She yanked at the buttons of her shirt then shrugged out of it. Emphatically shaking her head, she added, "I love you, Terry, but you're not screwing this up for me. Not this time."

Terry draped her arm over Diana's bare shoulders, led her away from Mary and Cindy, then whispered, "Girlfriend, you need to see a therapist. You masturbate nearly every night, and yet you wait for Nana's permission to do the deed just because she predicted your virginity would hold some power over your soul mate."

"Don't forget the warning that if I failed in winning his heart, I'd spend eternity in a living hell while you and the rest of humanity faced ravenous beasts unleashed by—

"The wrath of the angels," Terry cut in with an ominous voice. "Hello!" Terry held up a finger. "One. All old ladies believe men only marry virgins. And they all believe that women who give out before marriage will go to hell." She raised another finger. "Two. Soul mate? Ravenous beasts? Need I say more?" Not waiting for a response, she shot up a third. "And three. No offense, Di, but your Dad's whacked, and she's his *mother*!"

Diana's stomach clenched. "And I'm his daughter. Does that make me nuts, too, Terry?"

"No, but—"

Diana sighed. "Look, you come home every

night to a mother and father who miss you. It doesn't matter if you were gone a few hours or a few days. They missed you. You know they missed you." She glanced up at the stars and clutched the silver locket bearing her mother's picture. "I want that so much, it hurts. Someone who misses me, someone who's not too obsessed with—" She bit back her words and searched the dark windows overlooking the third floor balcony of the house for any sign of the boy who'd moved into town over the winter.

She could swear someone was watching, listening. She didn't feel it in her bones; she felt it on every inch of exposed skin. Heat washed over her body, lingering on her breasts, sweeping down her ribs, her stomach. She gasped and covered her mound even though she still wore her thong.

The shadows surrounding them seemed to press closer and closer. Her heart ached but she couldn't fathom why.

Her grandmother's prediction replayed in her mind. *I see you and your soul mate surrounded by darkness. And butterfly wings—thousands of butterfly wings—fluttering against your heart. You offer him a white rose that is so flawless, so pure its light blinds him long enough for you to capture his heart. Then you will have what you've always desired, Diana. Then you will know eternal love. But fail in winning his heart, and you will spend eternity in a place even worse than Hell, Diana, while the rest of humanity falls beneath ravenous beasts the angels unleash—*

"What's wrong?" Terry asked, squeezing her shoulder.

Diana bit her lip and glanced up at the house.

"Nothing. I'm just a little nervous."

"Look, sweetie," Terry said, "I understand how you feel. Really, I do. But you've lived your life by rules dictated by a woman who never leaves her house."

"In my family, we call that stability," she mumbled to herself. Her mother deserted her. Her father, obsessed with the idea that he was this century's Van Helsing, barely noticed her. A housebound grandmother who showered her with love and only asked that she wait for her go ahead to lose her virginity deserved her loyalty and obedience. "And I don't mind waiting."

"Yeah, right. I bet when she called and said tonight was the night, you nearly came in your pants." Terry let out a bark of laughter then covered her mouth and shot a quick glance up at the house.

Although the thought of finally being with a man terrified her as much as it excited her, Diana tossed her hair over her shoulder and Terry's arm with a flick of her head then grinned. "You've got that right."

When they rejoined Mary and Cindy beside their clothes, she slid her fingers under the straps of her thong and started to lower them. The hairs on back of her neck rose. Her hands stilled. She hesitated long enough to steal a glance at the windows before sliding her thong down her legs. The blinds and curtains didn't stir, but she still felt as if someone watched her every move. Dropping her thong, she looked up at the sky just as the moon disappeared behind a lone cloud. A cool breeze lifted her hair. The ends tickled her lower back. She stared up at the multitude of stars twinkling down at her and, with a mental wink at the moon, picked which star she'd dance for tonight. "Isn't it a beautiful night? It would have been perfect...making love under the stars."

"Been there, done that. The bugs kinda put a dent in the mood." Terry chuckled.

Cindy groaned. "Not to mention grass tickling your butt."

Diana giggled. She glanced over her shoulder and frowned. "Or unwanted onlookers. We'd better get swimming before our young voyeur wakes up."

Mary slid behind Cindy and peeked at the house over her shoulder. "Maybe we should find another spot. I heard Bobby has a website where he's promising naked pics of Lake George girls. Something tells me, he means us."

Diana crossed her arms under her breasts. "We've been skinny dipping here since we were kids. I'll be damned if some horny kid is going to make us leave." She stared at the lake. Stars twinkled on the ebony blanket of water. She watched them flow into each other, touch, merge. "I thought tonight I'd be here with the love of my life, finally giving this twenty-five year old body what it should have had with Rickie Lemax in twelfth grade."

Terry let out a short bark of laughter. "Yeah, right. Like you'd ever give in on the first date. Then or now."

Diana grinned mischievously over her shoulder as she sashayed towards the shore. "Girls, I'm so horny I'd probably tear his clothes off in the first five minutes." She waited for Terry to catch up then added, her voice firm, "*If* I was sure he was the one

Nana told me to wait for."

Terry ran in front of her and grabbed her arms. "See, you've got it backwards, Di. When I think I've met Mr. Right, he's gonna have to wait till I've convinced him I'm not a slut."

"Which you are!" Mary and Cindy said in unison as they ran past Diana and Terry into the water.

"I am not! Sluts have sex with anyone willing." Terry stuck out her chin. "I'm very choosey."

"Not!" Mary dove under to avoid the spray of water Terry kicked up.

Diana swished her toe back and forth in the cool water. "Well, I'm not totally led by Nana Lina's predictions. Her Mr. Right might not be right enough for me. It's not like as soon as she says go screw him, I'll let some stranger jump my bones. I'm not spreading my legs till I'm sure. That's really all she wants."

Terry leaned over and whispered. "Give up this crap about saving yourself for your soul mate, Di. Nana's old. Her predictions are probably as wrinkled as her butt. She said you'd meet him tonight, and you didn't. Doesn't that tell you something?"

"Man, I'll never get how you've held out so long, Di." Cindy said, as she floated on her back.

Terry licked her lips. "Especially with the last guy. The fireman? He had the kind of bod even I might go two nights with."

Diana closed her eyes, envisioning the washboard abs that had caught and held her attention for nearly a month. "Mmmm, he was tempting. He's still leaving me messages calling me a cock-teaser."

"Which you are." Cindy shouted from the water then dove under again when both Diana and Terry retaliated.

"I am not! The guys usually got more out of it than me. And Smokey the Bear left bruises all over my boobs, the creep." She poked a finger into the side of one of Terry's breasts. "Yours look and feel great, by the way."

Turning from side to side, Terry grinned. "They do, don't they?" She nodded down at Diana's breasts. "Well worth the money, honey. You could turn those Barely B's into Double D's by the end of the summer."

Diana ran her hands over her breasts and frowned. "I see nothing wrong with my perfectly full B's. If I had the money, I'd spend it on my nose."

"When you do meet Mr. Right, he's gonna be more interested in these than your crooked little nose." Terry flicked Diana's nipple and smirked when Diana gasped. "No, you're not too horny."

Diana rubbed her nipple, embarrassed by the way it hardened. "We'd better hurry. Our young Acteon," she whispered, nodding towards the house, "might wake up."

Terry laughed. "Then we'd just have to feed him to the dogs."

Chapter Two

Lucian felt like poor Acteon, the doomed lad the Goddess Diana had turned into a stag for gazing upon her as she bathed nude in a lake with her nymphs. He now understood why the young man had been unable to tear his eyes away from the virgin huntress and flee to safety. When he recalled how the goddess had punished the young voyeur, how she'd watched the hunting dogs tear him apart, a sliver of dread slid down Lucian's spine and demanded he leave.

But just as he was about to turn away, Diana hung her head back, grasped the locket dangling between her breasts, and closed her eyes. Her lips moved as if she spoke, but he heard nothing. The moon peaked out from behind a cloud and bathed her skin, set her pale breasts aglow then flowed over her slightly rounded stomach and muscular legs. He envied its freedom to spiral down the mass of amber curls that brushed across the pale curves of her buttocks with every move. Stark tan lines bordered the areas the moon held sole domain over, revealed just how much she enjoyed the heat of the rays he dreaded.

A gentle breeze carried the lingering aroma of the meat barbequed on a nearby grill earlier that day, but the hunger that gnawed at Lucian's insides had nothing to do with food. If Diana had been a vampire he would have already found some way to meet her, seduce her, bury his fangs in her neck while he buried his cock in her slick heat.

He shook his head and wondered how he could forget so quickly why he was there. Running his hand through his hair, he cursed Damien for turning his brain to mush when he'd slammed him with his rage. He willed the desire heating his blood to cool down. Thought he'd succeeded.

Diana began to dance, twirling around at the water's edge, lifting her face to the sky and singing in a hushed, silken voice the angels would envy. Her friends joined in the dance and, although they had bigger breasts and less muscular legs, Lucian could not tear his eyes away from Diana. Her body moved with the liquid grace of a ballerina. She looked like a fairy, a wood nymph.

A goddess.

His purpose there forgotten, he imagined his arms held her as she danced, could almost feel her naked body crushed against his.

She swirled around naked, illuminated by the moonlight for all to see, but from what he'd heard so far, Diana really was a virgin. Even if he hadn't heard it, he would have known. Knew back at the meeting by her pure scent clinging to the strip of cloth. Would still know without that clue. He had sensed her apprehension and seen the soft blush sweep across her cheeks when she had talked so cavalierly to her friends about her desires. He empathized with the fireman. Diana obviously had no idea what she'd done to the man when she had allowed him to touch, maybe even taste, but not possess. Damien couldn't have been more accurate. Diana was truly an innocent.

His mother's deception didn't surprise him. If

anything, he now understood why she'd wanted him
to keep his distance.   A virgin—one who'd never
totally given herself to another man, one whose blood
had no scent of another male marring its purity—
drew his kind like a moth to a flame.

Virgin's blood smelled and tasted sweeter than
any other. For years, Olympia had ensured nothing
else quenched his thirst, addicting him to the
lifeblood of innocents.   His fangs shot out as he
imagined Diana's blood sliding down his throat like
warm honey. So enticing, so damned addictive.

Too weakened by Damien's attack to deal with a
virgin, he moved to leave, but Diana and her friends
chose that moment to run into the lake. Entranced, he
watched Diana dive under then thrust her perfect
bottom above the black water. He wished he could
transform himself into water, rise up and lap at her
pert nipples, flow between her legs and slip deep into
her heat.

Diana gasped and glanced in his direction.

Then again, maybe his mother was right. How
could Diana, a mere human, sense his presence? Why
did he, one who had yet to relinquish his sexual
dominance to even the strongest female of his kind,
feel bewitched by this beauty?

She stepped onto the shore. Rivulets of water
trailed down her body, zigzagging to the very spots
his fevered mind had become obsessed with. Her
nipples pebbled, tempting him to taste. She shivered
then vigorously rubbed her hands up and down her
arms.

Before he realized what he was doing, he
warmed the thin veil of air surrounding her. She

stilled, took a step towards him, then shrank back into the warm cocoon he'd created. Laughter tickled his throat when she leaned her head forward and stuck her crooked little nose into the cool air then scrunched it up. His laughter died, his eyes focused on her teeth as she sucked in her lower lip and gnawed on it.

Passion and a bloodlust stronger than any he'd ever experienced seized him. White-hot pain streaked through his veins and brought him to his knees. Diana's virginity shimmered around her like an aura, a pure white glow that beckoned and promised untold delights. Thrust into the past where control succumbed to hunger, he felt the chains that had imprisoned his addiction all these years snap, one by one. Fearing the last would soon give, he threw his head back and roared in denial.

Diana and her friends screamed. Lucian watched in shock when, instead of taking cover behind a distant boulder like her friends, Diana crept up to the hemlock he hid behind. Instinct and years surviving amidst humans brought him back under control.

Muscles smoothly banding up her calves and thighs flexed inches from his face. Before she peered directly at him, he altered her perception so that no matter how intently she searched where he hid, she would only see a shadow. He decided to probe her mind for any knowledge of his stepbrother's death and looked into her eyes.

Spellbound, Lucian wondered if he just discovered Frank Nostrum's weapon. Huge orbs of verdant green splashed with gold like the mountains when the first rays of a new day kissed the peaks of the trees held his gaze. Dawn dwelt in Diana Nostrum's eyes, and its beauty mocked the photos and paintings covering the walls in his house.

Dawn. So deadly. So exquisitely beautiful. He couldn't tear his eyes away.

"It sounds like it's hurt," Diana called over her shoulder to her friends.

"Di, get away!" Terry yelled.

Diana spun around, unwittingly planting the soft white globes of her buttocks just above his head. The need to touch her slammed into him. Too many years, too many nights spent in the arms of beautiful vamps had left him confident that he could handle the effects of any female. Fangs, nails, everything grew in defiance of his will.

"Thanks a lot, Terry. Just leave me, here." She planted her hands on her hips.

Terry peeked over the top of the rock. "And let some wild dog sink his teeth into my tits? They cost me a fortune. Di, get the hell away from it. It could have rabies or something."

He tried to growl, but his clenched teeth and throat strangled the sound.

"It sounds more like it's dying," Diana muttered.

Dying? Oh, he was definitely dying. Did she have any idea that the bouquet of her sex filled his lungs, that he need only tilt his head up and forward a few inches to taste it? An unimaginable compulsion to mate waged war with his ever-weakening control; the need to feed upon her was so powerful that, for the first time since puberty, he feared he would not be able to stop until he had devoured her very soul. He squeezed his eyes shut, held his breath.

"It's all right. I won't hurt you," Diana crooned and leaned forward.

Lucian opened his eyes. The tender cleft below amber curls still damp from the lake hovered mere inches away from his face, exposing way too much to his hungry gaze. The growl that escaped this time sounded like that of a wounded animal.

Damn Damien. His attack had weakened Lucian more than he thought possible and left him defenseless to the effects of the hunter's daughter.

"Terry, we have to help it. The poor thing's in pain."

Terry leaned out from behind the boulder. "Diana Nostrum, if you get yourself mauled, I'll never forgive you. Just leave it alone! Please, you're scaring me."

He could smell Diana's mounting fear, a pungent aroma that called forth the Champion he'd put to rest for this mission.

"Come on, boy. I won't hurt you," she whispered.

The cinnamon of her breath and the tangy smell of her arousal ate away at his control.

Diana absently rubbed her hand between her legs and mumbled to herself. "I'd better meet this guy, soon. I'm getting horny at the sickest times."

Undeniable hunger reared its head. His fangs grew so quickly they nearly nicked his lower lip before he could adjust his jaw. He dug his nails into his thighs. If he touched her, he would definitely hurt her.

Run! He hurled the thought with a force she couldn't ignore.

Diana staggered back and shook her head. She glanced over her shoulder at the row of heads peeking over the top of the boulder and yelled, "Cut it out, guys, you're going to scare it."

Her friends exchanged puzzled glances.

She squatted down to his level, lost her balance, and nearly tumbled into the opening. She would have landed on him if he hadn't shoved a cluster of branches into her hand.

"Ow!" Diana settled onto her heels and peered at the tip of her finger. A bead of blood oozed out of a tiny scratch.

Lucian watched that drop of blood swell before her finger disappeared between her lips. The sight and the pure scent of her blood propelled him over the edge.

He did the only thing he could...for her...for him. He fled, moving with preternatural speed. His only consolation was the brief glance of her erect nipples across his bicep when he gave in to temptation and sped around her then raced back through the hemlocks and into the forest. He knew she only saw a gray blur, felt the caress of a slight breeze, but he felt branded, and although he managed to put some distance between them, he felt that she had somehow captured him.

*****

Diana spun around, her eyes narrowing. Her hands rose to her nipples as she struggled to breathe against an explosion of fluttering wings in her chest. "What the hell was that?" she whispered then turned to her friends and yelled, "Did you guys see that?"

"Bobby Wilson's out with his camera," Mary

cried out.

Diana screamed, took a step toward her friends. Froze. If she ran across the lawn, she'd definitely be the latest hottie on the little runt's website.

Then, again, she could be some animal's dinner. Saying a prayer, she pushed her way through the hemlocks.

Once on the other side, she glanced towards the house and, discovering that the third floor balcony gave Bobby's camera a clear shot over the hemlocks, ran towards the dark cover of the towering pines separating his property from the next. As she ran, she kept glancing over her shoulder at the balcony. She caught sight of a tiny kitten directly in her path just before she hit a tree. Her heart lurched when she realized a tree could not possibly be this warm or wrap its branches around her and hold her prisoner.

Flinging her head back, she opened her mouth to scream then quickly clamped it shut when the towering shadow enveloping her descended. Her mind shut down then exploded with sensation. Warm lips imprisoned hers, coarse material grazed her nipples and thighs, and a hard, hot, unmistakable bulge pressed into her stomach. Logic claimed a man held her; her eyes disagreed.

A man shrouded by shadows, the adult in her that refused to accept her father's tall tales rationalized. A vampire, the child she'd ignored all these years insisted.

Her lungs seized, strangling her scream. Calling upon years of self-defense and kickboxing, she tried to knock his legs out from under him and might have succeeded if there hadn't been a tree in her way. Her heel slammed into it. She yelped into the stranger's mouth.

He grabbed her under the arms and slid her body up higher. Thoughts of escape shattered when his clothes scratched her skin and his erection found a new home in the apex of her legs. Even through his pants, she burned from the heat of his arousal. She inwardly cringed when her body responded. Surely, this stranger felt the moist heat of her desire through his clothes.

Wrapping one arm around her back, he slid his hand down her side and over her hip. Her mind, fearing, anticipating its destination and intent, zeroed in on that hand.

Something inside her shifted when his palm skimmed down her leg, cupped her throbbing heel, and rubbed it with a tenderness she hadn't expected. The pain vanished. Her fevered mind followed the path of his hand back up her leg, inch by inch, until it came to rest on her buttocks.

He drew her closer. Pressed her hips into his.

What she was sure had merely been a means of silencing her evolved into much, much more the moment a soft moan replaced her muffled screams, the moment her hands stopped pushing at his chest and clenched onto his shirt. The moment her body took control of her mind and scattered all rational thought.

Passion overshadowed fear. Her body shuddered then melted into his as he slid his tongue between her lips and licked her teeth as if they were just as enticing as her naked body. He ground the hard ridge of his cock into her and tortured her nubbin until she spread her legs and opened her mouth. Fortress walls no other could scale crumbled as she awaited his invasion.

She wondered if the entire night so far had been nothing more than the beginning of an erotic dream. Shadows didn't feel like this. She didn't act like this. Her stomach fluttered.

It had to be a dream.

One she intended to enjoy as long as it lasted.

She closed her eyes and let the dream unfold.

Cocooned in heat, she burrowed closer, ran her hands over the massive shoulders of the stranger holding her in his arms and weaved her fingers through the long silken strands of his hair before clutching his head to hers. It no longer mattered what was happening or who held her. She'd never felt so needy. Every nerve ending seemed to scream for attention. Her core pulsed in time with her heart, her nether lips contracted and flared in anticipation. Her body hungered for and accepted this stranger who must have been lurking in the dark, watching, waiting to seize what she'd refused all others.

"Diana?"

The fear in Terry's voice sliced through the haze of desire engulfing Diana. She sucked in a breath, filling her lungs with her captor's. The possibility that she was wrong, that this was no dream and she might lose her virginity in the woods with a strange man who, for all she knew, could be a peeping tom or serial killer sent ice through her veins and a scream into the stranger's mouth.

He abruptly broke off the kiss. She expected to feel the ground strike her back, expected him to quickly drop his pants and take what she had worked so hard to preserve. Instead, he tenderly covered her mouth with his fingers.

His face still hid in a shadow darker than she thought possible, but she knew his eyes were intently focused on hers. A sense of calm filled her. She closed her mouth. He pressed his forehead to hers, brushed his lips between her brows so softly she barely felt them, lowered her back to her feet then brushed his fingertips over her eyes. Against her will, her lids lowered. When she raised them, her phantom was gone.

Shaking uncontrollably, she scanned the shadows lurking between the trees and searched for one blacker than normal. A tiny mewl nearly sent her sprinting back through the hemlocks. Clenching the muscles in her legs to fight if necessary, she turned, looked down at the base of the tree that she would have run into if the shadow hadn't blocked her way and watched in awe as a kitten too young to be away from its mother's teat scooted forward on its rear end. If she didn't know any better, she'd swear the ink-black shadow on the ground pushed it toward her.

She peered into the shadow, willed herself to see more but failed to make out anything in the murky blackness. "Who's there?" she asked, her voice cracking.

The kitten stopped moving. The shadow shrank back and joined those between the trees. Part of her grandmother's prediction, the part she'd refused to dwell on all these years, the part that warned her soul mate would be an abomination in her father's eyes, replayed in her mind and sent chills down her spine.

She gasped when the shadow flew straight up into a forty foot tall pine tree. Tilting her head back, she watched in awe when it burst free a few feet from the top, sending a shower of pine needles down upon her before sweeping across the ebony sky.

A rustle in the woods jerked her attention back to the base of the tree.

Another shadow hovered beside it, pulsing like a giant beast drawing in one large draft of air after another before charging.

Never taking her eyes off the shadow, somehow aware that she would not survive this phantom's embrace, she lowered her trembling hands until her fingers grazed fur then grabbed the kitten, spun around, and with a burst of adrenaline-fed speed, ran. Once again blackness engulfed Diana.

*****

"Honestly, Nana, other than knocking myself out, nothing happened last night." Diana listened while her grandmother rambled on about visions and dreams. "Nana...Nana, can I call you later? I've gotta get some ice on this bump...love you, too." She closed her cell phone then sank back against the soft cushions lining her window seat.

"Not a dream," she mumbled to herself then smirked and rolled her eyes. "I think I know the difference between reality and a dream."

Last night, when the moon held domain over the world and its eerie light cast shadows that trembled and swayed, when fanciful dreams converged with childhood beliefs that still lurked within, she'd believed in her dark phantom. But this morning, when dawn shed her radiant light and revealed that a tree was just a tree, and a dream was just a dream, when her brilliance cast the stars from the sky like so many unfulfilled wishes, Diana could not...would not accept that his caress, his kiss, his dark embrace ever existed. To do so would mean that she was just as delusional as her father.

She shuddered, recalling that in her dream, she'd actually believed in her father's creatures of the night. For one terrifying moment.

Leaning her cheek against the warm glass of her window, Diana watched her father drop a handful of pink daisies down the ornamental well he'd bought a year after her mother left. Blowing a kiss after them, he sat on the ground, leaned back against the well, then started to read.

Every morning he sat at her mother's makeshift memorial and read the news, the latest novel, or excerpts from Diana's childhood diaries. No one had been able to convince her father that the woman he'd loved had turned her back on them both.

Running her fingers through the soft fur of the kitten sleeping on her lap, Diana wondered if her mother really was dead, if her spirit hovered beside her father.

She doubted it. She'd spent too many nights and mornings crying for her mother during those first few months, shed too many tears when her mother failed to reappear. No, if her mother was dead, her spirit would have found its way back, even for a moment, to soothe the child she claimed to have loved.

Diana's nails scratched the glass as her hands fisted. She wished she had the nerve to pound on the window and scream down at her father that his daughter was still here, his daughter never left. His daughter could use a little of his love. She blinked away the tears she refused to shed.

When he spoke of her mother, when he insisted only death could keep her away, Diana's heart broke that he hadn't seen what a child barely old enough to read had seen.

Part of her agreed that only death would keep a mother from her child, but part of her remembered the odd emptiness in her mother's eyes when she'd tucked her in that last time. Diana had told everyone who'd entered the house the next day that something was wrong with her mother's eyes, that they'd grown distant a moment before she'd silently strode out the door without turning on Diana's Little Mermaid nightlight. No one understood that her mother would never leave her in the dark.

Her hand instinctively rose to clutch the locket her mother had given her that night. They had talked about her father's vampires, and her mother had laughed softly and promised that vampires only dwelt in the minds of those who never grew up, those who never accepted a nightmare was nothing more than a nightmare.

Touching the tender bump on her forehead, Diana told herself that a shadow was nothing more than a shadow.

She stood up. Could a prediction be nothing more than the ramblings of another damaged mind in her family? Her grandmother had sworn on the phone that Diana's soul mate had found her last night. Other than her phantom lover, no one she might consider even dating had entered her life.

What if she'd missed him?

*****

Three nights after the encounter at the lake, Lucian spent his second night in Cabana's, a small waterfront club in Lake George Village. He missed the tranquility of Mina's Cove and his fellow creatures of the night, missed chatting with them as they strolled down Main Street. There, the scent of a multitude of flowers tickled their heightened sense of smell; there, only the sound of the breeze rustling through the leaves and hushed voices met ears more sensitive than a human's.

Here, the stench of ammonia, sour beer, and a myriad of perfumes and colognes mingled with the smoke billowing in from the crowded deck. Here, music blared, and people yelled to be heard.

He had foolishly thought nothing could be worse than maintaining his shadow form while pitching from side to side in the backseat of Diana's '76 Camaro as she sped around each curve they encountered on the trip here, but a faulty air conditioning system in a club crammed with humans proved him wrong. Every foul odor wafting up from the sweat-covered bodies clung to the oppressive air filling the club and seemed to converge on the corner where he'd spent the last three hours. His stomach roiled.

Normally, he merely closed his mind to an offensive sense, but while stalking Diana he had to keep all of them on alert. The past few nights had proven that the hunter's daughter held some kind of power over his kind. Why else would he find it so hard to maintain control three nights after the effects of Damien's attack had worn off?

Although the room already vibrated in time with the bass, the DJ cranked the music up another notch. Those people more interested in socializing than dancing raised their voices accordingly. Only the melodic sound of Diana's laughter penetrated the din and soothed the pounding ache in Lucian's head. He honed his sense of smell on her scent and wondered how it remained fresh and enticing in this inferno.

His eyes focused on Diana. Her skin glistened as she gyrated in time with the music beside her latest partner. From the moment she'd stepped onto the dance floor, he'd envied the men she blessed with a dance. Recognizing the lust in their eyes, he tore each and every one from her spell. Lost in the music, Diana seemed unconcerned when each partner stopped dancing and strode away.

Lucian smirked. So many stunned faces, so many men wondering how they ended up on the far side of the club dancing with someone else.

His eyes strayed to her hips. For three nights he'd watched them writhe as she brought herself to orgasm in her bed. Temptation sizzled beneath his skin and blurred his vision until Diana's gaze swept over the faces of the men surrounding the dance floor. A young man stumbled from the crowd and joined her.

Lucian tensed when she met the man's heated gaze with a welcoming smile. Diana seduced, teased, and flirted like the woman his mother had described. He sensed the fire coursing through her veins every night, watched her bring herself to orgasm when she finally slid into bed, and caught glimpses of her erotic dreams as she slept. Her constant state of arousal ate away at his control. As far as he was concerned, they should be following and watching Diana's grandmother. A woman with the power to harness such a sensual being could easily weave a spell around one of their vamps.

With nerves raw from fighting his own desires and those of the men around Diana, he watched her enter the dark alcove housing the restrooms. A man twice her size and at least four beers past drunk followed.

A few minutes later, Lucian drew in a deep breath and cursed. Fear now marred her scent. It took only a few seconds to transform into mist and weave through the crowd, but his senses told him even that was too long. He merged his mind with hers so that he could hear what she heard, see what she saw, and feel what she felt. Immediately, he felt the sweat drenching the drunk's shirt seep through Diana's halter and coat her skin, felt her breasts and stomach shrink away. Their minds were so connected that he tasted bile when, no matter how far she turned her head, the drunk's rancid breath managed to creep up her nose.

"Get your hands off me, you asshole!"

The man imprisoned Diana's wrists above her head with his left hand and groped one of her breasts with the other. "Come on, baby. I saw the way you looked at me while you were dancing."

"I'm warning you, back off!" Diana's voice revealed none of the fear that trickled from her mind into Lucian's.

When the man's fingers squeezed and twisted

Diana's nipple until she yelped, Lucian cast caution aside and flung a lanky teen out of his way. He entered the alcove and merged with a shadow just in time to see the man land on the floor. Blood poured from between the man's fingers. Keening like a wounded goat, the man clutched his nose and drew his body into the fetal position. Lucian stared at Diana in awe. If he hadn't seen through her eyes how quickly she'd taken the drunk down, he wouldn't have believed it. The man topped her by at least a foot and had muscles even Lucian found impressive.

"Why'd you give me that look if you weren't interested?" the man yelled from behind his hand. "You crazy bitch!"

"I'm crazy? I'm crazy?" She kicked him soundly in his ass.

Grinning, Lucian leaned against the wall and crossed his arms over his chest. He recalled the kickboxing trophies he'd seen in her room, and the thought of her muscular legs wrapped around his hips sent all his blood straight to the erection he'd been carrying around since that first night by the lake.

His gaze followed taut muscles up her legs to the hem of her skirt, continued on past her exposed stomach, and then came to an abrupt stop.

Diana cupped her left breast with both hands. The pain in her eyes filled him with rage. Her lower lip quivered as she turned her face to the wall.

"All I did was glance around at the club. What am I supposed to do? Close my eyes when I dance?"

Her voice, strangled by the sobs she fought so hard to suppress, nipped at his heart and released the beast that dwelt in them all, that fed his rage and demanded he rip open the man's throat. Shocked that his body shook with a need to avenge the woman he intended to destroy, he dug his nails into his palms and forced the beast back into submission. A rustle of movement caught his eye.

The man rose and swung his fist at Diana's lower back. Lucian blocked the punch and tossed the man out of the alcove before Diana even felt the rush of air from the approaching fist. She spoke, and for a moment he thought she spoke to him, but when he turned around, he found Diana hadn't moved.

"What the hell am I supposed to do? Let some guy maul me just so the bar doesn't get a bad rep? Damn!"

He longed to caress her bruised breast and replace her pain with pleasure, nearly took a step closer to do just that, but a commotion in the club brought him up short.

"The bitch broke my nose!"

Hearing the reply of one of the bouncers as they approached, Lucian positioned himself behind Diana and concealed her in the black shadow he'd maintained since entering the alcove.

The bouncer entered first. "Look, buddy, I don't see anyone. You sure you aren't on something?"

"And broke my own nose? She kicked me in the fucking balls, man. I bet she's hiding in the bathroom."

When he heard Diana's breath hitch, Lucian wondered if she realized her life had once again entered another realm.

*****

They didn't see her. How could they not see

her? Diana opened her eyes. She peeked over her shoulder. A dark shadow like the one in her dreams swept down and captured her mouth. Imprisoned against the wall, unable to move as the kiss stole her breath and all thoughts of screaming, she closed her eyes.

Why not? She'd obviously clonked her head like she had at the lake, obviously passed out. Either that or she was just as crazy as her father.

With a tenderness that belied the strength of the muscles rippling over the chest pressed against her back and the arms wrapped around her waist, lips skimmed over hers, left them with a nip then meandered along her jaw to her neck. Her heart raced. She tilted her head, offering more of her sensitive skin up to her phantom lover. Her legs nearly buckled when sharp teeth grazed her skin and sent ripples of pleasure through her body.

Needing more, she turned around and pressed herself into whatever dwelt in the darkness enveloping her. When she felt the shift that signaled another kiss, she tilted her head back and rose up onto her toes. His hand crept under her shirt and over her wounded breast. While his lips crushed hers and his tongue caressed every sensitive inch of her mouth, his fingers stroked her flesh until the pain from her bruised nipple vanished and a new, more demanding ache took its place. Arching her back, she pressed her breast into his palm.

Her phantom shuddered. Diana reveled in the knowledge that she affected him as strongly as he affected her. When she heard the drunk and the bouncer returning from their search of the restroom, the kiss ended and a finger pressed against her lips. Diana nodded, feeling safe wrapped in this familiar cocoon. Her feet left the floor as a strange tingling sensation skipped over her scalp. Shaking her head, she wrapped her hands around her phantom's neck and tried to ignore the deep, insistent voice in her mind telling her...insisting...

"What'll it be, Diana?"

Diana blinked.

The bartender flung the white washcloth over his shoulder and stared expectantly into her eyes. Glancing up at him, she opened her mouth, shut it, then mutely stared at the twenty dollar bill in her outstretched hand. She remembered checking her hair in the Ladies Room and turning to leave. Then...then...nothing.

She didn't feel drunk. Damn, she only had two beers. Scanning the club, she frowned. Twice her gaze returned to a dark corner directly below a floodlight. Her hand instinctively grabbed hold of her mother's locket.

Someone tapped her shoulder. Grabbing onto the bar for support, she peeked over her shoulder and, finding Terry grinning at her smugly, let out a relieved sigh.

"Got another, I hear." Terry winked.

Diana frowned. "Another what?"

Terry nodded over her shoulder. "Perv."

Leaning to the side, she looked in the direction Terry had nodded. Surrounded by fawning women, a man held an icepack to his nose.

Diana emphatically shook her head. "I did not do that one."

"Di, his blood is on your forehead." He giggled. She reached over and grabbed a napkin from the bar. After dunking a corner in her cosmopolitan, she rubbed Diana's forehead. "See?"

Diana stared at the slight red smudge. Her head spun as she tried to remember the man. After a few moments, her gaze shifted back to the shadowed corner.

"Di?"

"Shh." She squeezed her eyes shut and delved into her mind. "Think damnit. Think."

Bit by bit the events in the alcove unfurled. Heat rushed to her cheeks as she recalled how she'd rubbed herself against the shadow like a cat, how she'd clutched onto it when it had tried to release her, how she'd then followed some internal order to go to the bar and flag down the bartender with the twenty the shadow had pressed into her hand.

Catching the bartender's eye, she asked in a voice that sounded more like a little girl's than her own, "Give me a double of Jack Daniels, please."

When the bartender slid the glass across the bar, she downed it in one gulp then slammed the glass down. The slow burn of the liquor sliding down her throat calmed the hysteria that demanded she run screaming out of the bar.

"Another."

"Another?" Terry grabbed Diana's thigh and spun her around until their knees bumped. "What's up, Di?"

Diana opened her mouth to explain, but what could she say? Even Terry would think she lost it. She retrieved two tens from her purse and tossed them onto the bar.

"Di, you already have a twenty in your hand. Are you alright?"

"This isn't mine." Diana gulped down half of her second drink then clutched the tumbler to her chest and hopped off the barstool. "You hooked up with a hypnotist here the other night, didn't you?"

"Well, I wouldn't exactly say we hooked—"

"I'll be right back."

Pushing her way through the crowd, Diana stopped before the shadowed corner and flung the twenty down. When the twenty disappeared before it hit the floor, she gasped then whispered through lips that barely moved. "Look, thanks for your help, but go play your hypnosis games on someone else, pal. You hear me? Leave. Me. Alone."

Spinning on her heels, she tried to appear unruffled as she walked on rubbery legs to the dance floor and worked her way deep into the security of the writhing crowd. Surrounded by people, far from the eerie shadow, her memory of the events in the alcove seemed ridiculous. No hypnotist was that good. One too many drinks, a bump on the head, and she sees tall, dark, invisible men. Her gaze wandered back to the corner.

"One too many drinks," she snapped, startling the man dancing beside her.

*****

That morning, before he drifted off to sleep, Lucian wondered if the qualities he found so intriguing in Diana could also be proof of her guilt.

Over the past few nights he'd witnessed how the town dealt with Frank Nostrum. Some heaped their pity upon Diana's rigid shoulders while others flung their ridicule at her receding back. And Diana? From what he heard, she knew her father believed he was a vampire hunter, knew the townspeople believed he was crazy.

But did Diana believe in vampires? Did she know her father destroyed them? Had destroyed Marek?

Lucian slid his arm under his head and pondered Diana's innocence.

Could she be the ultimate weapon Frank Nostrum used to ensnare his victims and lure them to their death? She drew men to her like moths to a flame and had the strength and power to take them down before they knew what was coming. The possibility that he may be her next willing victim haunted him but did not cool the blistering lust surging through his veins, did not stop him from seeking her out the moment the sun set.

The remainder of the week passed too swiftly, as far as Lucian was concerned. Diana usually ended each night with a trip to the lake. Voyeurism didn't suit him, went against every moral he possessed and every vow he had taken as a Champion, but he felt compelled to watch.

Every night he ground his teeth against the urge to reveal himself when she floated on her back and offered up her glistening breasts to the stars. Every night his control slipped free when she stepped onto the shore, a thin sheet of water caressing every inch of her supple flesh. How could he possibly contain it when she wiped the moisture from her skin, her hands lingering on the very spots he imagined a hundred times covering with his mouth?

Each and every night he surrendered to the need to touch and whirled around her, inhaling her enticing scent, caressing every precious inch of skin the water had caressed. He believed she felt nothing more than a summer breeze.

On the night the elder's had chosen for Diana's transformation, Lucian ensured her friends would back off from joining her at the lake. He needed these last few hours alone with her.

Taking longer than usual to undress, Diana hesitated with each piece of clothing she dropped on the ground. When her gaze darted across the hemlocks bordering the yard, he darkened the shadow engulfing him. Riddled with guilt over what he intended to do when she returned home, he went over the past week for the tenth time, searching for something, anything that might delay the hunter's sentence and possibly save Diana.

From what he'd seen, Diana didn't believe vampires even existed, much less that her father killed them. Watching her when she was home had revealed nothing. Most nights she and her father ate dinner together, but Frank, peering out the window as if he expected to find someone lurking there, barely spoke. Fearing the hunter may have psychic abilities that ensnare his victims, the elders had banned entering his mind. Lucian had no choice but to watch and listen. He didn't have to delve into Diana's mind. Her loneliness shimmered in her eyes every time she glanced at her father.

Following her when she left her house had only raised more doubts. Too often, her eyes would stray in his direction. Too often, she clutched that locket as if it held some power. But she embraced the night with a fearlessness he doubted could dwell in one who believed in vampires, much less lured them.

Her possible innocence haunted him.

When she finally emerged from the lake and raised her arms up to the stars, he delved into her mind and searched one last time for any knowledge of her father's crimes, for any reason to bring the hunter's sentence to a halt.

Shock, denial, and a strange sense of longing filled him when he uncovered a vision of his hands emerging from a gray mist swirling around her body. Her need, her yearning for his touch was so powerful that he imagined he heard her voice in his mind calling to him, her phantom lover.

Later, driving into Mina's Cove he wished he could tell the vampires strolling down Main Street that he refused to harm the hunter's daughter, that he would kill anyone who tried, but he saw hope in their eyes, hope that tomorrow they would no longer have to fear Frank Nostrum and his pen. They had every right to believe their Champion would protect them, every right to believe Marek's stepbrother would avenge his death.

As he waited at a light, he caught sight of his cousin Tomas and Tomas's friend Diego standing in front of the Town Hall. Tomas waved eagerly. How many times had Marek stood waving on their porch as a child, jumping up and down as he drove up the driveway? Lucian's heart ached; he had no choice. He had to ensure no other vampire lost *his* light in the dark. It was time, way past time for Diana Nostrum to join the creatures of the night.

Chapter Three

"Lucian, you greedy bastard!"

Diego's lust-filled voice boomed in the silent room and grated on Lucian's already frayed nerves. He'd warned the vamp before and twice after entering Diana's bedroom that they would only talk telepathically. *Diego!*

Diego pressed his palm down the length of the hard ridge straining against his jeans. *You've been coming here and watching her every night this week, and you never invited us?*

Lucian clenched his fists when Diego took a step closer to Diana's bed. *I think you should wait outside, Diego. You're making a fool of yourself.*

"Forget it. I'm staying put."

Tomas's nails dug into the footboard. *He can't even remember to keep his stupid mouth shut.*

Come on, Lucian, Diego pleaded, desire shimmering in his eyes as his gaze darted between Lucian and Diana. *We could play with her a little before you do it. You've got her in such a deep sleep, she won't feel a thing, let alone remember.*

"We could," Lucian replied aloud, "Or I could rip your throat out. And believe me, you will remember every second." The sharp stab of his nails growing into his palms failed to penetrate the red haze of anger Diego's cavalier comment spawned. Surprisingly, he found he could no more control his rage than he could the menacing growl strangling his words.

Diego and Tomas hungrily stared at Diana as she

slept beneath a sheet transparent enough to reveal a body that would have inspired Michael Angelo to sculpt a mate for David.

Clues about Diana surrounded them, had bombarded Lucian from the first night he'd followed her home. It amazed him that Diego and Tomas had barely noticed them tonight. They hadn't even glanced at the framed photos of her mother, photos he'd watched her hold to her heart every night. Would they react differently if they'd heard her nightly prayers for the safe return of the woman who'd turned her back on Diana and left her in the care of a man like Frank Nostrum?

Trophies and ribbons for kickboxing were squeezed between toe shoes of various sizes, but he couldn't blame Tomas and Diego for ignoring the extent of Diana's triumphs. They had never watched her practice each skill with a merging of power and grace that had left Lucian in awe, and they didn't know she reveled in her strength but hated the way the muscles in her legs bulged.

And the CDs. Did they understand why she always played sad songs, why tears hovered on her lashes as she sang? He thought he understood.

"Damn."

Lucian turned at Diego's whisper. Diego's hand moved towards Diana's head. Her cheek rested on the edge of the bed, and Lucian, having been in Diego's position every night for the past week, knew just how much the young vamp itched to lift her head and feel the heat of her breath flowing over his loins. He probed Diego's mind. Lewd images of the three of them feasting on Diana's naked body nearly ripped his ever weakening control from his grip. His muscles bunched painfully as he fought to maintain the distance necessary to keep Diego alive. He shared the images with Tomas. *You choose fools for friends, little cousin. If he moves his hand, he'll lose it.*

Tomas visibly paled when Diego's fingertips touched Diana's chin. *Shit, Diego, do you want Lucian to drag you before the elders for rape? Get the hell away from her and let him get this over with.*

Lucian saw Tomas's gaze dart to the alarm clock on the nightstand then to the window and the clear outline of the mountains that just minutes ago had been barely visible against an ebony sky. Although the young vamp's face showed no fear, his hands trembled as he shoved them in the pockets of his jeans.

Diego's fangs receded. He backed away from the bed, his hands raised before him. *Rape? Who said anything about rape? I never said —*

A moan drew their interest back to the bed. Sprawled on her belly, Diana ground her hips into the mattress. Lucian cursed. The sheet delved into the cleft of her buttocks as one of her legs slid out, baring more skin than he felt any red-blooded male, vampire or human, could handle. He refrained from shoving her leg back under the sheet.

Diego licked his lips and drew in a hissing breath. *Come on, Lucian. We wouldn't be her first. She must be at least twenty. Shit, most girls don't make it past eighteen with their cherry.*

She's twenty-five and still pure. Lucian's nostrils flared as he drew her intoxicating scent into his lungs, a scent that never failed to arouse him. But this time the stench of another's arousal followed. Diego stood close enough for his breath to fill her lungs, for his scent to caress hers.

When Diego blinked, Lucian moved. Materializing between the horny vamp and Diana, he leered into Diego's stunned face. "Push me, Diego, and I'll be on you before you even think of running," Lucian warned, his voice laced with menace.

Diego's eyes flared wide before he jerked his head down and stumbled back. His shoulder struck one of the many shelves lining the walls. Two CDs slid off and landed silently on the carpet beside Lucian's black leather boot.

Pick it up, klutz. Tomas looked incredulously at Diego. *Can we remember whose house we're in? You two are having a pissing contest, and her father is probably on his way home.*

Relax, Tomas. He hunts till dawn. We'll be long gone before he gets home. Diego reached down to retrieve the CDs. His hand froze.

Lucian glanced down. Blood dripping from his clenched fist splashed onto one of the CDs. Embracing the pain of his nails grazing bone, Lucian watched Diego rush to Tomas's side and after a quick jab in his ribs, jerk his head towards the blood.

Tomas turned to look just as a fat drop of blood plopped into an already impressive puddle atop Clay Aiken's face. *Ah, Lucian, you're bleeding all over the place. We're not supposed to leave any evi —*

Then I suggest you and your horny friend clean it up. Lucian opened his hands and licked the blood from the deep gashes on his palms then glared at Tomas and smiled. His smile faded when he saw himself reflected in Tomas's mind. With his upper lip stretching high above bloody fangs, he looked exactly like one of the monsters Diana's father believed they all were.

Turning his back on Diego and Tomas' horrified expressions, he stared down at Diana's serene face. He understood their shock. Although he'd always been feared by vampires who broke their laws, none would recognize nor understand the sinister, malevolent creature he'd become since they'd entered Diana's room. He barely knew himself what he'd say or do next.

Tomas sucked in a sharp breath. "What the hell is your problem, Lucian? She's the daughter of the fucking hunter who killed Marek!"

Diego rushed over and dropped to his knees. Within seconds the CD was clean and back on the shelf.

Lucian stared down at Diana. Tonight he would begin a bonding ritual with her. He would force her to take his blood, turn her into his virgin bride, the bride he would never mate with, the bride he would probably never see after tonight.

Over the past week, his eyes had feasted on every inch of her body. Each time his hands had fleetingly experienced the wonder of touching her skin, he'd grown hotter and harder than he thought possible. The deafening roar of her blood rushing through her veins immobilized him with hunger. Would it taste as sweet as he imagined? His erection throbbed within the confines of his jeans. Every muscle clenched as he fought the overpowering need to take her now and relieve the pain he'd endured all week.

"Lucian?" Diego whispered, "Are we—"

"Shh!" Tomas glanced towards the window.

"What now?" Diego whined.

"Listen, damnit!" Tomas' voice shook.

The distant rumble of delivery trucks arriving in the village to restock the restaurants made its way up the mountainside into the silent room warning the three that dawn approached, that the man they all feared would soon return from another hunt.

Lucian continued to gaze down at Diana. Too young to have perfected blocking their thoughts, Tomas and Diego's anxiety filled him with guilt. Tomas, recalling the time he'd accepted a dare and allowed dawn's searing rays to glance across his back, clutched the footboard to stop himself from bolting. Diego, his eyes riveted to the muscles bunching across Lucian's back, held his breath, convinced that any sound might lead to more pain than he thought he could handle.

They both were terrified Diana's father would return and capture them.

The elders had been wrong in sending the two young vamps along. Under normal conditions, even considering entering a human woman's bedroom uninvited would lead to a lengthy sentence. The elders' approval of Diana's transformation had unleashed Diego's disregard for the law that forbade using their powers to molest and had Tomas expecting punishment from above. Tomas and Diego didn't belong here.

None of them belonged here.

Lucian wished Diana had been born to another

man, wished he could gather her in his arms and carry her to safety. Wished he knew why such a thought even entered his mind.

She slept so peacefully, so completely unaware that her life would soon spiral out of her control. She shifted closer to the edge of the mattress, closer to him. Her leg slid out from under the sheet then slipped over the side of the bed. His gaze meandered along the muscles flexing beneath her thigh and calf, wrapped around her slender ankle, slid over the delicate arch of her foot. The tips of her toes languidly stroked the carpet.

"She sleeps on her stomach, maintaining contact with the floor...just like our young," Lucian murmured in awe to his cousin.

"Have you forgotten, Lucian? Our young are taught that trick so they'll always have one foot on the floor if a hunter catches them asleep." Tomas' voice shook with anger. "A hunter like her father."

Lucian raised his eyes. "And I suppose her father taught her the same trick just in case some vampires ever caught her sleeping."

Diego stared at her bared leg and licked his lips. "Not that it's going to do her any good. Nothing could stop you, right Lucian?"

Lucian began to nod, but Diana's nose twitched beneath the curtain of hair covering her face, and he forgot what Diego had asked. Her hair, the color of the rising sun they all dreaded, amber streaked with gold, and his, blacker than the inside of Mina's empty tomb, were glaring reminders of their different worlds.

He wondered how her hair would look kissed by

the sun. Reaching out, he gently lifted a long spiral to his lips. Silk, the finest, flowed through his fingertips. He gathered more hair in his hand to see one last time what lay beneath before the hunger, pain, and madness marred her beauty. Her face would be a study in perfection if not for the tiny crook on the bridge of her nose. He knew she considered it a great fault, had seen her frown at it when brushing her hair, washing her face, or merely passing a mirror and catching site of her own reflection. He longed to brush his lips against it, just once.

Her lips parted, curved up in the softest smile. Her tongue darted out to moisten them. Lucian stilled, certain she'd heard his thoughts, would welcome his touch.

Ah, but would she smile if she knew what he had planned for her? Would she open her arms to him if she knew his embrace would propel her into a never-ending nightmare? Would she be another innocent defiled beneath his hands?

Would he ever survive the guilt?

"I can't do this," he whispered in shock, more to himself than his companions as her hair slipped through his fingers and floated down, shielding her beauty from his eyes. "I can't do this."

Tomas shoved Diego out of his way and grabbed Lucian's arm. "Her father killed your stepbrother. Think of Marek locked in that pen with nothing to shield him from the sun. My God, Lucian, his screams woke us all from our sleep!"

"Her father killed him, Tomas. Not Diana. He should pay for his crimes," Lucian ground out between clenched teeth as he yanked his arm away, "not Diana!"

"He will pay. Her destruction is the ultimate punishment." Tomas repeated the words Olympia had used at the town meeting to incite them all. "We will execute him through her!"

"Then we'll be no better than what her father thinks we are, Tomas. Monsters." Lucian bit off the last word when Diana released a long sigh, bathing his thighs with her warm breath. Every muscle tensed against the immediate wave of desire that washed over him. "This witch hunt is over."

"If you don't do it, Olympia will just find someone else. Don't *you* want to be the one to avenge Marek's death?" Diego asked.

The tendons in Lucian's neck felt as if they'd snap from the battle raging within him. Although he wanted to avenge his stepbrother's death,, his place in their society as a Champion demanded he protect innocent women from out of control vampires.

Was Diana innocent or was she a huntress like her namesake? Whenever he had probed her mind he had encountered hundreds of fortress walls, and no matter how many he managed to breach, he could never uncover the treasure or secret she deemed worthy of such protection. The last wall he had faced brought his digging to a halt. It bore an image of a very young Diana alone in a vast wasteland with her head flung back and her eyes closed tight and her tears flooding the ground at her feet while her trembling lips mouthed the word "Mama" over and over again.

If Diana was innocent, then was he nothing more than an out of control vampire? He had been. A week ago. Before he met Diana. Before he met that abandoned child still calling for her mother.

Diego mentally nudged him. *I wouldn't be surprised if that bastard, Nostrum, used her to draw our males into his pen. Shit, I'd follow her if I thought I could get a piece of that ass.*

Lucian didn't respond, didn't dare tell them he'd wondered the same thing.

After tonight, after one taste of his blood, her eyes would forever burn with an undeniable hunger for him. Every day that hunger would become more and more unbearable until the day the sun rose to find her writhing in her bed, begging him to return and take her, fill her, become one with her.

And when the sun set on that last endless day, only chains would deter her from running into the night in search of the only blood that could soothe the searing pain engulfing her body, from killing any human or vampire in her way as she drank their blood in a never-ending compulsion to appease her hunger for *his* blood.

Of course, he would never answer those calls.

His mother in her infinite ability to find someone's Achilles heel had chosen this punishment for the vampire hunter. Nothing else could wound Frank Nostrum as much as witnessing his only child's descent into madness. No torture could match that which he would heap upon himself when he realized she suffered in his place.

Lucian only now fully understood the extent of that torture. Just imagining the pain Diana would experience, just knowing he would bring her into a horrific nightmare from which she would never escape tore at his heart.

Diana whimpered and rolled onto her back. Lucian lurched forward and, snatching the sheet, covered her before she managed to bare herself to Diego and Tomas. Her hand clutched the sheet between her breasts as if she heard his thoughts.

He shook his head. For one impossible moment, he thought he'd heard her plead for mercy.

Damn it, Lucian, snap out of it!

Lucian bared his fangs at Tomas and followed him as he took a step back. *If I have to do this, Tomas, then I'll do it alone. Get out.* When Tomas did not immediately turn to leave, Lucian took another step forward. *I'm not going to repeat myself.*

Tomas backed towards the window, but Diego, his eyes fixed on the outline of Diana's nipples in the sheet, moved to the foot of the bed. "At least let us check her out. She's naked, man!"

With a flick of his wrist, he tugged at the bottom of the sheet, baring her breasts, stomach, and some of the soft hair covering her mound.

Bastard! A curtain of blood coated Lucian's eyes, casting the room in a scarlet haze. His fangs shot out, longer, deadlier than he'd ever allowed before. The beast dwelling deep within all vampires sprang free of its chains. Detached, he watched his hands grab Diego's arms, heard Tomas' shocked gasp and Diego's scream when his nails tore through skin and muscle as he lifted the vamp over his head.

Tomas bolted to the side just in time to avoid Diego's body as it flew past him and out the window. Blood dripped from Lucian's fangs and two nasty gashes in his lower lip.

What the hell is your problem, Lucian?

Lucian turned away from his cousin's probing gaze as he forced the beast down. *She knows nothing, Tomas, nothing about Marek or her father's hand in his death.*

He wondered if Tomas could sense the doubt that still lurked in his mind. Diana's ability to block him from her thoughts filled him with suspicion. His own inability to think straight whenever he came within a hundred feet of her, whenever he merely envisioned her body, her eyes, her lips, fed that suspicion.

After just one week, he could see himself following her anywhere, even into her father's pen. She *could* be the weapon they'd all wondered about. The irresistible lure. Drawing in a fortifying breath, he reminded himself that if she was the lure and he failed in his duties tonight, the death of the next vampire would be on his head. *Just get the hell out of here, Tomas.*

Tomas moved silently to the window and swung one leg over the ledge. *Don't forget. Olympia said to give her just a drop of your blood. No more. It'll speed things along.* Tomas glanced over his shoulder at Diana. *It's hard to believe that by next week she'll be a Slasher on Fentmore, isn't it, Lucian? That our blood can turn a hot chick like her into one of those creatures?*

Lucian turned away, hiding the bloody tears he could feel sliding down his cheeks. *"It takes no more than the amount of blood in a tear, Tomas."*

*****

Damien paced from the door leading into Tobias' den to the leather sectional. Turning around, he glanced at the clock on the mahogany mantel over the roaring fireplace then paced back to the door. He leaned out into the hall and looked both ways before striding back into the room. "Do you sense anything?"

Tobias dropped his head onto the back of the couch and sighed. "For the hundredth time, no. You're driving me crazy."

They had known each other for centuries; stood beside Caesar, stalked the night with Dracula, and followed their Dark Prince and Mina to the shores of Lake George when Mina's love melted the ice holding Dracula's heart captive and made it possible for them all to live in peace with humans.

Tobias, transformed only months before Damien, outranked him as the second eldest of their kind, the eldest in Mina's Cove during Dracula's absence. Most cowered if Tobias showed the slightest disapproval.

Damien ignored him, glanced at the clock once again, and cursed. All night he had awaited some sign that Lucian had returned. His head throbbed from scanning his stepson's home for his presence.

"Why don't you just go there and wait for him?" Tobias asked.

Damien spun around. "And what? Congratulate him for destroying the life of an innocent woman?"

"Now, Damien, have some faith in Lucian. If Diana is innocent, he'll know and leave her untouched." Tobias rose and, patting Damien's shoulder as he passed, strode to the sideboard.

"I know. I know," Damien muttered.

"And if she's not, he'll do what needs to be

done," Tobias added, holding up a decanter of brandy. "Taste this. It's exquisite."

Damien shook his head. "How can you even wonder if she has anything to do with her father's crimes? My God, Tobias, she's Angelina's granddaughter."

"And Frank is your precious Angelina's son. We all know her blood did not stop him from coming after us."

"That's different and you know it."

Tobias poured some brandy into two snifters and held one out to Damien. "Drink this and relax. You're accomplishing nothing with your infernal pacing except maybe wearing a hole in my carpet."

Damien took the snifter and emptied it in one gulp. He sank down onto the brown leather couch and hung his head.

"Listen, Damien. I know you believe Diana is nothing like her father but think, for a moment. How do we know what that man said to her as she grew up? He's had twenty-five years to mold her into a hunter."

"This is my fault. All of it. I should be the one punished. I broke our most sacred law by bonding with the mother of a human child and using my powers to alleviate her concerns about leaving him."

"You broke two laws, Damien. We do not take someone else's spouse. She had a husband, one she had been quite content with until you entered her life. And the fact that her son has been exacting vengeance upon us all since that day is no one's fault but his. We have to find that weapon." Tobias threw his glass into the fireplace.

Damien placed his on the low mahogany table and raked his hands through his hair. "Why haven't we been able to find it or the pen? It doesn't make sense. We can read minds, even those a mile away, but we have yet to breach his or his daughter's enough to uncover how he manages to capture our vamps."

Tobias' lips thinned. "That, my dear son-in-law, is why I fear Diana might have a hand in our losses."

Damien's head jerked up; his body tensed.

Tobias added, "Both Frank and Diana are quite adept at blocking their thoughts, building impenetrable walls around feelings and knowledge they deem private. How? Why? We are the only ones capable of truly hearing someone's thoughts and uncovering their memories. So what led them to perfect blocking us?"

Damien opened his mouth to reply, to once again find a way to convince Tobias that Diana was innocent but closed it when Lucian's voice entered his mind.

"No!" Tobias swept his arm out. Damien's head flung back as if struck. "Don't answer him, Damien."

"You heard. How can I ignore him when he's begging for guidance?"

"He must do this on his own. Trust me."

Damien couldn't believe his ears. "Why? He's your grandson, for Christ's sake. Why would you turn your...you know how this night will turn out, don't you? You've had one of your dreams."

"Damien, I'm asking you to trust me. I did dream. While I did not discover exactly how this will end, I awoke convinced that it must run its course without any interference."

Damien glared into his friend and leader's eyes. "And what about Olympia? Hasn't she already interfered? Coming up with this insane punishment? I can't believe you agreed to it."

Tobias stared back for a moment then lowered his gaze to his hands. "She's my daughter, Damien. I know I give in too easily to her demands, but my guilt gets the best of me."

He understood his friend's guilt. Transformed by Dracula when Olympia was just a child, Tobias had been forced to watch from the shadows as his daughter grew into a young woman. When Olympia fell ill shortly before her wedding to a young lord, rather than chance losing her completely, he'd transformed her against her will. Damien placed a hand on Tobias' shoulder. "Must we all pay for your guilt?"

Tobias shoved his hand away. "I gave you a woman who loved you, a son who grew to love and admire you."

"You forced me to bond with a woman I felt nothing for! And Lucian was already an adult. He didn't need a father."

"I knew how you grieved when Angelina chose her son over you. I feared that if you had nothing to live for, you would go over the edge and face the dawn." Tobias buried his face in his hands. "It made sense at the time. I gave you my most precious possessions. My daughter and grandson."

"I already had something to live for, Tobias. I had Marek."

"And now you have Lucian. Trust him to make

the right decision for all of us. Trust me that all this was written in the stars long before Diana was even born." Tobias leaned over and lifted the lid of an antique music box. The tinny chime of a minuet filled the room. After a few strains, he pressed down on one of the inlaid ivory butterflies. A slender drawer slid out of the front. Tobias removed a small, yellowed scroll and handed it to Damien.

Damien unrolled the scroll and immediately recognized Mina's handwriting. "Mina wrote this? But when?"

Abject grief filled Tobias' eyes. "Just read it, Damien."

Damien sat beside his friend and held the faded poem under the tiffany lamp on the end table.

When stars burst free from sunlight's glare,
The moon regains its throne in air
The creatures of the night then whisper,
Our future changed when Dracula kissed her
The beast that once would kill for fun,
Gave up his life so she could run

God's Angels touched by love so pure,
Bestowed a gift of life secured
And now his children who once were wild,
In Mina's Cove live meek and mild
And blood still holds a strong attraction,
But only when combined with passion

It is foretold a woman scorned
Shall risk it with a trusting pawn
A rose so pure, a rose so white
Will blind him with its brilliant light

If two do not unite as one,
We all will lose what we have won

Damien raised the paper and breathed in Mina's scent. It seemed an eternity since she and Dracula set out to find more of their kind. He wondered if Tobias had known all these years that his daughter was the woman mentioned in the poem, if he'd given Damien to her in the hope that it would change fate. Guilt kept his eyes from meeting his friend's.

"Forgive me, Tobias. If I'd known—

"You what, Damien? Would have loved my daughter? No one can force someone to love." He gripped Damien's shoulders. "We can protect Lucian, but we must not interfere with his feelings or his decision tonight. Our future rests in his hands."

*****

When the sound of Tomas' feet hitting the ground ensured that he and Diana were finally alone, Lucian turned back to gaze upon the woman he had to destroy, the woman he felt compelled to protect.

How could he protect her? He had already failed, had allowed Diego and Tomas to feast their eyes upon her bare breasts.

He moved to cover her. His hand stilled. The cropped curls covering her mound peeked over the sheet, tempting him to slide his fingers beneath the edge and feel their softness. But his gaze continued lower, past her exposed hip, down the inner thigh of her bared leg. The folds of the sheet drifted between her legs, demanding he give in to the desire pooling in his loins and grasp there.

Diana shifted with a sigh, spreading her legs

farther apart, revealing the crease where her thigh
ended and her softest flesh began. Her scent rose up
and enveloped him. His nostrils flared, but not nearly
as much as his desire, when her hands skimmed
down her stomach and slid beneath the sheet drawing
it lower.

She flicked the sheet aside and skimmed her
fingers over her tender skin. Before his heated gaze,
she spread the moisture from her own arousal.

A low rumble rose from his chest. He bit down,
using the pain of his already torn lip to help him gain
control. It seemed to work until her familiar essence
wrapped itself around him, drawing his head lower
against his will.

He felt powerless, ensnared. Her bare leg slid
across the mattress towards him, brushed against the
painful bulge in his jeans, and inflamed his need even
as it soothed the pain. Her hands seemed to beckon
to him, coaxing him as they crept up then down her
thighs. His eyes burned; yet, he didn't dare blink and
chance missing the moment her fingers sank between
her dewy folds.

Diego's earlier words sliced through his passion.
'We could play with her a little before you do it.
You've got her in such a deep sleep, she'll never
remember.'

But he would. And he would never forgive
himself.

He realized with a start that he had somehow
climbed onto the bed and now knelt between her legs,
that he was bent so far over that his mouth hovered
mere inches from her glistening swollen flesh.

His mother had been right. Diana was her

father's ultimate weapon, the one they'd all been trying to uncover. An enchantress, she could lure them with nothing save the promise of her body. Pain lanced his heart. Fear coiled in the pit of his stomach. He couldn't move, couldn't breath.

His eyes took in the sight before him, and with a weary sigh, he surrendered. If this was a trap, then a night in her arms would be worth greeting the sun in her father's pen.

She moaned as the warm air he'd held trapped in his lungs fell upon her soft, quivering flesh. Closing his eyes and wondering if she moaned for him or some dream lover, he delved into her mind then nearly bolted from the bed when he saw the vision that had enticed her. As if her eyes were open, he gazed through them down along her naked length upon something Diana had never seen and could not possibly dream about.

His face.

But what rocked him, what freed him from the web she'd woven, was her conviction that he and only he would ever gain entrance into her body and that once there, once she'd captured him, she would never let him go.

He started to back away, never expecting her hands to grasp his head, never expecting her to drag it down so quickly and forcefully that his lips met her wet, hot flesh before he could react. He drew in a deep, shocked breath and was lost. Her erratic pulse thrummed beneath his lips, calling to him, sending blood surging to his already engorged cock.

Control, engrained in him from the last time he'd almost drained one of the virgins his mother had brought him, crumbled when Diana's sweet nectar seeped between his lips. Without a moment's hesitation, without a care to the consequences or the approaching dawn and Diana's father, Lucian ran his tongue down from her pulsating nubbin to her sweet entrance.

He covered her with his mouth, delved his tongue between her labia and, encouraged by her ever rising moans, drew the satiny skin between his teeth.

His hands crept up her quivering stomach, skimmed over her ribs, and searched until they found the soft swells that rose up to greet them. Her pebbled nipples pressed into his palms. Cupping her breasts, he marveled at the heat filling his hands.

Her back arched up then fell as her hips rose up to his mouth. He heard her heart thundering in his ears, sensed the tension coiling deep within her core and knew that, while he could never take her virginity as she slept, he could at least bring her to the climax she strove so desperately to attain, one his bite would send spiraling out of control. Yes, before carrying out her father's punishment, he should give her one last moment of ecstasy.

His fangs scraped along her outer lip, slightly piercing it. The droplets of her blood mingled with her juices tasted like the sweetest ambrosia. An alarm went off in his head, warning that soon he'd awake to find himself bound and stripped in her father's pen. No blood could taste this sweet; no normal woman could create such an undeniable hunger. He was doomed.

He had to have more.

When her hips slammed her dripping pussy

against his mouth and her hands fisted in his hair, he sank the tips of his teeth into her skin again, this time into the vein that lay just within her entrance, and nearly roared out loud when her soft cry told him she wanted more, needed so much more.

He drove his teeth deeper then compelled her to stifle her screams from the climax he felt wracking her body as he fed his own voracious hunger.

Her orgasm rocked him. The pain in his groin intensified while her blood warmed his body and soothed the hunger gnawing at the convulsing walls of his veins.

Her hands released their grip on his hair and slid down to the mattress. Lucian squeezed his eyes shut and fought the consuming need to mate. He felt her body relax as her desire ebbed. Now that he only had to deal with his own hunger, he prayed he had enough control to deny it.

His heart slammed against his chest. He couldn't move. Couldn't bring himself to rise and pass his blood to her, to leave and save himself if indeed this was all a trap. He held his breath and waited for her father to appear from the hall, the closet, the window, waited for her to open her eyes and laugh victoriously as her father dragged him off.

Diana let out a satisfied sigh, raised her thigh, and brushed it against his cheek. When he scanned the house and discovered they were still alone, relief poured over him, nearly cooling the fire still raging out of control in his groin. She had somehow enslaved him yet had not handed him over to her father.

Logic demanded he accept this as proof of her

innocence.

He licked the wounds he'd given her then rose from the bed. His gaze fell to the drops of blood marring the pure white sheet between her legs.

"What have I done?" he whispered, wondering if his old addiction to virgin blood and not Diana had overpowered him. He knelt beside the bed and dropped his forehead onto his arm. His hands clenched the sheet. "Diego's right. I have no choice. If I fail, someone else will be sent tomorrow night."

Tears burned his eyes, tears for the woman who had swallowed her own fear to help what she'd thought was a wild animal, for the woman who could never harm any living thing, least of all sweet Marek.

The tears Lucian had managed to restrain every time he'd thought of facing eternity without Marek sprang free to join those for Diana. A deluge of grief overwhelmed him. He pressed his mouth onto the mattress to muffle the wracking sobs he could no longer control.

Fingers tenderly weaved through his hair. *Don't cry, Lucian. I can't bear it.*

His fangs dug into his lip sending a fresh torrent of his own blood into his mouth. Without uttering a word, she had spoken to him. Said his name. Had she delved into his mind? Impossible.

He slowly raised his head, absently swiped the backs of his hands across his chin and cheeks and prayed he would find her eyes open, her lips moving. Her hand slid from his hair, brushed at the bloody tears still streaming down his cheeks, yet her eyes remained closed, her breathing even.

Only one untransformed human could

telepathically speak to him, eavesdrop on his unshielded thoughts. Only his soul mate.

He must have imagined her voice. There was no way God would choose the daughter of a vampire hunter as his soul mate. Unless he wanted him to suffer a fate worst than eternal damnation in hell.

Staring at her face, he watched a tear escape from the corner of her eye, felt his rejection wash over her and clench her heart in a vise. His own heart stuttered.

He rubbed the tense muscles on the back of his neck and recalled how Diana had managed to resurrect the memory of the scene at Cabana's that he'd compelled her to forget, how she'd always seemed to gaze wherever he hid in the shadows. How they'd both so easily lost themselves in a mere kiss.

Could his mother have known that the woman she'd sent him to destroy was his soul mate? His mother, transformed by one of Dracula's spawn, possessed untold physic abilities and often bragged that she knew the identity of a vampire's soul mate as soon as he or she entered the world. Could her need for vengeance be so strong that she would destroy her only son?

He brought the sheet up to cover Diana's breasts.

His soul mate. A goddess who loved to dance naked beneath the moon. A seductress who had raised her hands to the sky and called out for his touch. Had he forced himself upon her tonight or had it been the other way around?

He saw her lips quirk, realized he would have to guard his thoughts around her, realized she had offered herself to him after hearing his thoughts about her destruction. He couldn't help but wonder why she'd trusted he would not harm her. Other than the few moments they'd shared in the woods that first night and their encounter in Cabana's, she had yet to meet him.

How had she known that he could never harm his soul mate, that he would rather face the sun than inflict even the slightest pain? Any vampire, including his mother, would realize that his carrying out Nostrum's punishment would be suicide. His eyes burned. His mother had known when she sent him here that once he gave Diana the scant drop she'd insisted upon he would feel her pain tenfold.

And her hunger? To give a human soul mate the mere drop his mother had insisted on would not bring about the slow, debilitating hunger he'd been led to believe his mother had planned for Diana. No. Because she was his soul mate, that drop would have sliced through her veins and awakened an ancient hunger; one, if denied, that would unleash a torrent of pain too excruciating for a human mind to handle without shutting down completely. But his mind would absorb it all, and his body would be crippled, useless. He doubted he would have had the strength to do anything other than watch Diana suffer and wait for the dawn's rays to enter her room. Neither one of them would have survived.

Why would his mother sacrifice him for Marek? Marek was not her first. Marek had not shared nearly a century by her side. He wasn't even her son.

Shortly after Damien bonded with Olympia, he'd showed up with Marek. Olympia told Lucian the baby was the product of Damien's failed bonding with the human he'd thought was his soul mate. Olympia had only accepted the baby into their family because Damien had threatened to leave if she didn't. Could she have grown to love Marek more than her own son?

He shook his head, clenched his teeth. His mother may be deceitful, selfish, and heartless, but she was still his mother. Even she wouldn't sacrifice her own son.

No, Diana's ability to speak to vampires was a trick, or worse, Frank Nostrum's weapon. The strongest vampire would trust his soul mate and follow her anywhere. He straightened his shoulders. It had to be a trick. God, let it be a trick. His mother loved him.

My poor Lucian. She couldn't have known. Still sleeping, Diana clasped his hand and brought it to rest over her heart. *She loves you. She must.*

He yanked his hand away. *No!*

Diana's body trembled uncontrollably, terror nearly stole her breath away, yet he felt her heart breaking for him, for his torment over losing what he now wondered if he ever truly possessed—his mother's love. Tears blurred his vision, veiled Diana in a crimson haze. *I won't hurt you, Diana. You have my word.*

Dawn lurked behind the mountains, too close to their lofty peaks. Tomorrow night he would find a way for them to meet. And if they were truly soul mates—body, heart and soul—he would find a way to ease her into his dark world and into a community of vampires who would rather face the dawn than embrace Frank Nostrum's daughter as one of their own.

He brushed the back of his fingers along her jaw. She wouldn't remember him, would think him absurd if he told her she'd spoken to him as she slept, but he had plenty of time to bring them back to this moment.

He would take it slow; get her to accept him for what he was before he ever touched her again. A chill ran down his spine. They were not destined to share eternity together just because they were soul mates. Damien's soul mate had refused to give up her family for him.

Now, thanks to his mother, Diana's first memories of him, though buried deep in the recesses of her dream world, would include him coming to destroy her. Hopefully, she would never uncover those memories.

Leaning over, he tenderly brushed his lips over hers. Her mouth molded to his. The sudden desire to mate nearly overpowered him, but logic and the need to look into her eyes when they first made love helped him gain control. Pain from his gashed lower lip sent a jolt of terror into his heart. Blood, his blood, smeared Diana's lips. Before she could taste a drop, he swept his tongue over her lips.

"That was close, goddess," he whispered, smiling down at her.

The futility of courting Frank Nostrum's daughter struck him as his gazed down at her angelic face. His kind would never accept her; she would never accept him. Plus, he still had no idea if she knew of her father's crimes or helped him. No. Soul mates or not, they could never overcome their differences, never trust enough to love.

He could wait until their paths crossed again, when her soul dwelt in one he could trust, one whose father had not killed. It might take a hundred years, a thousand. They may never meet again. Which meant he would never know her touch, never again taste her sweet blood, never again hear her silken voice in his mind.

Diana opened her mouth and drew in a breath as if she was going to speak. He blinked away the crimson tears blinding him then watched in horror as one bloody teardrop landed on her tongue and slid down her throat. *No!*

He flinched as he felt his blood, unable to merge with hers, cutting a path through her veins. Unless he claimed her by filling her with his seed and giving her enough of his blood to carry her through the day, her veins would grow raw from the battle raging within them.

Already her body recognized that his blood was the stronger of the two and craved more. She writhed on the bed. Her silent cries filled his head.

He didn't have to look at the clock to know he had very little time to save her; the skin on his back already shrank away from the heat of dawn's approach. If she really was his soul mate, he couldn't leave until he completed what they'd begun, even if it meant facing the sun unsheltered, even if it meant dooming Diana to eternal darkness without her consent.

Pain twisted his insides, paralyzing him, as he knew it would, as his mother knew it would. Terror engulfed him.

The assault of Diana's agony immobilized him. Lucian fell to his knees.

Chapter Four

Seconds after something sweet slid down her throat, Diana's veins began to ripple, twitch, and burn as if lava, not blood, flowed through them. Strangely detached from the pain, she searched her mind for the cause of the deluge of liquid fire and birthed an image of spiders, scorpions, and an army of red ants. A panicked scream lodged in the back of her throat.

Terror wrapped icy fingers around her pounding heart when her mind envisioned her veins bursting and releasing thousands of the venomous insects into her body. She could feel millions of tiny legs skittering beneath her skin, feel thousands of sharp pincers piercing her raw flesh. Her heart faltered when she imagined them crawling up her throat, injecting their fiery venom as they battled each other in their rush to escape the confines of her body. Her lungs seized.

Breathe.

The moment the command entered her mind, blessed air filled her burning lungs, hope soothed her tortured mind. But then a beast took up residence deep within her ravaged body, tore at her insides, and demanded she sate its hunger. She sank deeper into whatever hellish world she'd dreamed up even as her mind grasped that this was no nightmare. She tossed her head from side to side, refusing to accept such torture could exist in the real world.

Her body craved something, would trade the air she breathed for it. But what? The craving grew unbearable, the inferno in her veins threatened to engulf her, and still she had no idea how to appease this undeniable hunger. Scalding tears filled her eyes, burned a path down her cheeks. She wanted. She needed. What? What?

The beast she imagined clawing at her stomach roared at her ignorance.

As if unknown hands had yanked on her tendons, pulling them until they nearly snapped, her body arched up off the bed, her toes and fingers curled, her jaw locked shut and for one brief moment the pain subsided.

A dream, she silently chanted. This had to be a dream. It started as a dream, didn't it? One moment she was sleeping on a cloud while the chatter of those around her mingled with that of the birds. The memory of the passion that had followed created a flash fire of desire that overwhelmed the conflagration in her veins and melted her tendons enough to drop her back down onto the bed.

Still, the hunger she could neither understand nor identify clawed at her. Balling the sheets in her hands, she struggled to comprehend how such an erotic dream could have evolved into this nightmare.

She recalled the voices that had filtered into her mind, voices discussing plans for vengeance. One drop. One kiss. A mere taste of the sweetest elixir. Abandonment. Her heart shattered. *Oh, God, no! Don't leave me like this!*

Hold on, Diana. For Mina's sake, hold on.

She didn't recognize the voice, but she felt as if she had heard the masculine timbre before, whispering in her mind all week as it whispered now for her to open her eyes. Peering out from beneath her lashes, she turned her head to the side. Her phantom lover stood beside her bed. A fresh wave of tears blurred her vision, tears of hope, relief, and joy. A bright white orb appeared in the window behind him, a shimmering, brilliant, minute dot peeking over the mountains. While the light's warmth bathed her cheeks and soothed some of her pain, her phantom flinched like a man whipped.

All week he had followed her. Even when she had not seen evidence of his presence, she had felt him hovering, watching, protecting. At the lake when the strange mist had swirled around her body, she had known the mist and her phantom were the same and had welcomed his return. During the light of day when her phantom failed to materialize, when logic prevailed and nearly suffocated her with the possibility that, like her father, she had somehow lost sight of the line between reality and fantasy, she told herself that her dreams had somehow been confused with her memories of the night.

Now, she understood and accepted that somehow fantasy had become reality and that, like the wisps of mist rising off the mountainsides surrounding the lake at dawn, her phantom could not last long beneath the heat of the sun's rays. Soon those rays would fill her room, and her phantom lover, her savior, would vanish and leave her to drown in this nightmare that had followed her into the waking world.

Forgive me, Diana. There's so little time.

Little time? He had no time. She knew that as surely as she knew her mind was losing its grip on sanity. Drowning in the lava that now seared her skin as it flowed from her pores, sure that in a second, in a heartbeat her mind would snap, she pressed her elbows into the mattress and lifted her head and shoulders off the bed. Arms of steel wrapped around her waist and cradled her in a soothing embrace. Although his body shuddered from dawn's assault on his back, his lips covered hers with infinite tenderness. Diana sighed into his mouth as she clutched onto his massive shoulders.

Drink. The soft voice once again demanded she obey.

Like a babe at its mother breast, Diana suckled her phantom's lip the moment it slid between hers. Warm honey flowed between her lips, down her throat, and immediately appeased the army of angry insects. She swallowed, instinctively aware that only the elixir responsible for her torturous nightmare could tame the beast threatening to destroy her mind, body, and soul.

Her nerves, no longer raw with pain, tingled as his weight pressed down upon her. An onslaught of butterflies beat back the insects with their wings as she drank until all she could hear were her and her phantom's mingled breaths and the rustle of the sheets beneath her writhing body. Pleasure replaced pain, fear evaporated beneath the heat of passion. Desperate to take in all of him, terrified that if she stopped the beast would revolt, she continued to suckle his lip long after the flow of his elixir stopped.

A kiss meant to sate the beast torturing her body spawned a new hunger.

Her phantom lover's body hardened. His cool skin brushing against hers dulled the lingering sting of her ordeal. His heartbeat reverberating through her body calmed the tumultuous pace of hers while his breath filled her weary lungs. She felt his hands tremble as they glided up over her ribs. Her breasts swelled, anticipating his touch. An exquisite coil of heat tightened in the center of her stomach.

She wanted this, needed this more than air itself. Too many nights dreaming of his touch, too many days denying he existed. He ended the kiss and nipped his way down her neck, over her collarbone and the swell of her breasts, then clamped her aching nipple between his teeth and tortured it with his tongue until she arched her back and silently pled for release.

The heat from his body blanketed her, grew hotter as he lowered himself between her legs. But when Diana felt the hairs on his legs tickle her inner thighs, years of denial insisted she stop him, save herself for her soul mate. Her hips sank into the mattress. *No. Wait.*

You have always belonged to me, Diana. From the moment you were born, you were mine to possess.

As his tongue swept into her mouth, she felt something hard yet as soft as velvet nudge her pulsing nether lips.

Spread you legs wider for me, Diana. Concede what is rightfully mine. The voice in her head demanded she obey.

Unable to deny him anything, Diana slowly spread her legs until she felt his hands grasp her thighs and hold them in place. He nudged in a scant inch, stretching her until she burned.

He felt too wide, too hot. Diana, still reeling

from the excruciating agony she had felt only moments earlier, cringed away in fear. Her hand reached between them and felt a burning shaft bigger and wider than she thought humanly possible. She peeked through her lashes at the impenetrable shadow which was too black, too murky for her to see what dwelt within. She feared that her phantom would invade her body and tear her apart from the inside out. Fear waged war with desire as her hands released their grip on his shoulders and pushed feebly at the mass of muscles rippling across his chest.

He would rip through her maidenhead, split her in two. Her phantom had fooled her into believing he was her savior. The moment he impaled her, she would realize he had been the beast all along.

Yet, even as she shook her head, even as she silently pleaded with him to free her, her hips rose.

How could she open herself to him, offer the virginity she had refused to all others when he was a stranger cloaked in an impossible mass of black mist, a phantom who had come into her room to bring her life to an end? And most terrifying of all, she doubted someone so huge could take her virginity without killing her. She felt him pull away and moaned with relief, even as her body arched up to reconnect.

I'll take away the pain, Diana. You'll only feel pleasure. You have my word. Close your eyes. Trust me.

I can't. I have to save myself for my soul mate. Heat fanned out over her cheeks. In the presence of a being that could not possibly be of this world, her words sounded silly, immature.

Knuckles traced a cool path down her cheeks and along her jaw. *You have been saving yourself for me,*

Diana. For me.

Diana closed her eyes, brought her hands up into the darkness and let her fingers paint the picture of his face. They brushed over a coarse, stubbly jaw, feathered over long, satin lashes, meandered down the straight bridge of a prominent nose, and came to rest on full lips that quirked up in amusement before opening and capturing her fingertips.

She gasped softly when his tongue flicked across the sensitive pads of her fingers and pleasure spiraled down her spine. The instant she relaxed, he slid in deeper, fanning her burning embers, then slid out, leaving her cold. She cried out, wrapped her legs around his hips and tried to draw him back. Returning hotter, deeper, he stilled until she grew accustomed to his size, until her hips rose, then began a languid rhythm, sliding almost completely free before slowly delving back in.

As if the invasion below her waist were not enough, he released her fingers and made his way down her neck, kissing, nibbling, until he reached her breast. Drawing her nipple between his teeth, he tortured the sensitive peek with his tongue, birthing a need that mocked the hunger she had suffered earlier. Muscles she never knew existed coiled tightly until she thought she'd scream from the tension. Her mind focused on their joined bodies, and she realized that, with each thrust, his hips would stop far from meeting hers. She demanded he go deeper, faster, and cried out in frustration when he refused.

Say it, Diana. Say you are mine.

Please, I can't wait any longer.

Mine. He roared into her head. *Say it.*

Yours, only yours.

No one else will ever touch you as I have. Take my blood and seed, Diana Nostrum. Become my soul mate, my eternal mate, my only mate. For all eternity. Mine. You will never offer anyone else what you give to me tonight.

Diana shivered under the wrath that seemed to crash down upon her with each thrust.

He continued holding back until she was nearly mad with need before he drove himself in to the hilt, taking her virginity with a deafening roar that crashed into her mind. His hands slid beneath her and grasped her buttocks, holding her in place as he slammed into her again and again.

Diana shattered. Desire fanned out from her deepest recesses, streaked through her belly and shot down her legs. As she screamed from an orgasm much more powerful than she'd ever been able to bring herself to, he cradled her face against his neck.

Drink, goddess. Accept me. Accept the essence of my life.

As the sweet elixir surged into her mouth, white hot pain pierced her neck then just as quickly evolved into exquisite pleasure. She felt her blood rush up to the spot beneath his mouth. Her body imploded, control shattered. His essence filled her mouth, his seed her womb. Although she knew he felt he was claiming her, possessing her, she realized he would forever belong to her — his blood running through her veins, his soul forever ensnared in her heart.

"Forever," he whispered against her neck.

"Forever," she whispered back, absorbing the shudders still racking his body. She longed to see his face and opened her eyes. How just that her soul mate's eyes mirrored the midnight-blue sky she loved so much. His fingers glanced over her lids, lowering them against her will.

Sleep, goddess.

*****

Heat engulfed Lucian's back. It was far too late to return home, far too late to even attempt leaving Diana's house. He rose, stood beside the bed, and stared down at Diana's blood between her splayed legs. The vein on his neck twitched in rhythm with the one pulsing on hers.

Tenderly drawing the sheet over her body, he bent to rub his knuckles over the pulsating vein. *Remember my touch, Diana. When you feel it again, trust that I will never hurt you.* His knuckles glided over the slight swell of her breast, thumped by one over her erect nipple. *And when I touch you again, do not deny me. You are mine, now, Diana. As I am yours. Mine.*

Sunlight streamed through the window. The skin on the back of his legs sizzled. After yanking on his pants, he grabbed his shoes and sped to the door. Striding soundlessly through the house, he found the entrance to her attic just as he heard the garage door rise.

Transforming into mist, he flowed through the crack between the attic door and the ceiling. Webs clung to his face as he materialized. He moved towards the boxes that bore the thickest layer of dust and searched the darkest part of the massive attic behind them until he found a corner he thought would be safe. As if he could be safe in the house of the most feared vampire hunter since Van Helsing.

*****

Diana pushed her sunglasses higher up on the bridge of her nose and lowered her visor against the sunlight streaming through her windshield. Her eyes burned from straining to see through the glare. Although she knew she should be concentrating on driving, her thoughts kept returning to the smear of blood she'd discovered on her sheets this morning. A small voice, sounding too much like Dr. Ruth, kept insisting only one thing would leave such a mark exactly where...

Of course, she could have scratched herself. She shifted in her seat. There was definitely a little tenderness but no pinching. Scratches pinched, didn't they? Her heart hiccupped when she recalled how heated her dreams had been. A tear slid down her cheek. What had she done? Masturbated and broken her hymen during an erotic dream?

She gripped the steering wheel and told herself to think of something else, something that would not send her to work with red, swollen eyes. Tuning the radio until she heard Gwen Stefani singing about being a rich girl, she forced herself to sing along and tap her nails on the steering wheel.

As usual, traffic crawled through Lake George Village as people haphazardly crossed between the cars. Summer brought a flock of tourists to Lake George. Diana could never understand why the locals complained about the tourists invading their close-knit community or why they counted the days until the tranquility of winter returned.

While she enjoyed horseback riding along snow-covered mountain trails and past iced-over ponds, she welcomed the energy that surged into the village with the first line of cars streaming off the interstate in June.

During summer the sidewalks teemed with activity, and the air filled with the scents of suntan lotion, caramel corn, and meat roasting over charcoal grills. Best of all, the tourists knew nothing about her mother's desertion or her father's obsession with vampires. They never pitied her or watched her for signs that would prove she'd inherited her parents' instability.

Continuing up Route 9, Diana leaned over and tilted the passenger air conditioner vents in her direction. Glancing down at the pink skin on her thighs, she frowned.

She never burned. Well, not this far into July. By the time she pulled into the parking lot of the Hop-a-long Ranch, her hands, arms, and thighs felt and looked as if she'd spent a full day on a Florida beach. Without sun block.

"Howdy, Miss Diana." Stanley Kowalski, known as Old Jake during working hours, lifted his Stetson, swept a long lock of grey hair over his bald spot, and whistled as she stepped out of the car. "Now, what'd you go and do, little lady? Fall asleep in one of them tanning beds?"

"Cut the cowboy act, Stan." Diana pressed her finger down on a rosy thigh. "I don't get it. This is just from driving here."

"Maybe you're coming down with something. Man, that's burnt." He ran his calloused hand down her thigh.

Diana jerked away. "Geez, Stan. Your hand

feels like sandpaper." Following him into the main office, she eyed the brown paper bag on his desk and rubbed her stomach. "Maybe I am getting sick. I'm starving."

Stan sat behind his desk and unwrapped a buttered sesame bagel. Handing her half, he smirked. "You've eaten half my bagel every morning since the day I hired you."

"That's because I never eat breakfast at home. But this morning I raided the fridge and ate enough to last through lunch." Taking a bite, she sat on the edge of the desk and peered at the schedule board on the wall. After she swallowed, she asked in what she hoped was a nonchalant voice, "Any word from Colette Solange?"

"Not yet. If you're planning on running this place when I retire, you're going to need thicker skin." He pointed at the schedule with his bagel. "That child only missed one lesson. Some regulars just up and disappear, Diana. They find a better, closer, or cheaper ranch and are too embarrassed to show their faces here or call to let us know."

"Not them, Stan. Something's wrong. I just know it." She stood up and walked over to the schedule. After staring at it a few minutes, she heard Stan chuckle and turned to find him literally wiping a smile from his face. "Come on, Stan. You know I'm not a nervous Nelly."

Working at the ranch since she graduated from college, she had lost her share of students over the years. At first, she'd assumed she had failed in some way, but Stan had quickly set her straight. She had learned to care about her students while keeping them distant enough to easily bid them farewell when they stopped coming.

When he'd approached her about taking over the ranch, she had regretfully dropped all of her students except Colette's daughter, Luna. For the past two years, the little girl had worked her way into Diana's heart. Like Stan, when Diana measured time in reference to students, she counted lessons and not days. But in Luna's case, Diana felt her absence the entire week. Seven long days.

Every Tuesday, Luna and Colette arrived with their grey Shetland pony shortly after dusk. And every week, Luna, now six, ran with her sleek black hair streaming behind her right into Diana's arms and rattled off every little thing that had happened since they'd last seen each other.

Every week, without fail.

Except last week.

Stan opened the top drawer on his desk and rummaged through it as he spoke. "They'll show tonight and you'll find out it was nothing more than a stomach bug or kiddy party that kept them away. Now, stop your fretting. You'll wrinkle that pretty face and then what will I have to brighten my days? Here." He held out a bottle of aloe lotion. "Rub some of this on. You're making me hot just looking at you."

Although her sunburn had oddly paled by the time they'd finished eating, Stan insisted she spend the day in the office. Still concerned about the blood she'd discovered on her bed that morning and Luna's absence, she agreed. By lunchtime, she had to admit that she'd done something during the night to pop her own cherry.

When an unquenchable thirst joined the insatiable hunger that two hamburgers and a large order of fries hadn't eased, she wondered if they and the blood were somehow related. But a search of the Internet for some disease with all three came up empty. As if worrying about her popped cherry and Luna's absence weren't enough, she'd awoken with a twitch on the side of her neck. By the end of the day, the constant thumping had grown unbearable.

Dusk finally draped its grey cloak over the surrounding mountains. Diana left the cool office she'd virtually hid from the sun in all day and leaned against the post of the covered porch. As the minutes ticked by, she picked at the skin peeling off her leg. She definitely caught something. Sunburn didn't heal or peel this quickly. Still hungry but feeling more energetic than she had all day, she wondered if she'd caught a twenty-four hour bug while she was out with Terry last night.

She let out a relieved breath when the familiar sound of Colette's approaching trailer finally shattered the silence. As soon as the trailer stopped, Luna leapt out and ran into Diana's open arms then wrapped her arms tightly around Diana's waist. Diana glanced at Colette hoping to catch her eye, but Luna's mother quickly looked down and walked to the back of the trailer. When she returned with Luna's pony, Diana opened her mouth to ask what had kept them away last week, but red-rimmed eyes met hers; the words died in her throat.

Her heart sank at the realization that she'd been right and something tragic had caused them to miss last week's lesson. She lifted Luna onto her pony, and softly asked, "Ready?"

Luna shrugged.

Diana wrapped her arm around Luna's tiny waist as they entered the corral and sighed. "I missed you all week, Luna sweets." She waited until they were alone in the corral then asked, "Where've you been?"

A tear rolled down Luna's flushed cheek. "I...I couldn't come," she whispered, her eyes darting to where her mother sat in the waiting area outside the corral.

When Diana lifted Luna from the pony, Colette rushed to the gate. The woman stumbled when the night lights came on with a dull thud. "It's alright, Colette. We're just going to talk first." She cradled Luna in her arms. "Aw, sweets, what's the matter?"

"Ma...ma...my Daddy died." Luna's chin quivered. She pressed her face into the crook of Diana's neck.

Luna's sobs tore into Diana's heart, sent tears streaming down her own cheeks. Marek dead? She had met him only a few times and had immediately liked the gentle giant, had been touched by the way he and Colette doted over Luna.

Memories of her own grief when her mother had vanished from her young life, memories she'd refused to visit all these years, resurfaced. She remembered feeling as if someone had ripped her heart to shreds, and she couldn't bear that Luna had to deal with such agonizing pain.

She sat on the ground and rocked the girl in her arms for the remaining half hour of her lesson, crying with Luna, for Luna and, hearing the soft sobs coming from the waiting area, for Luna's mother, Colette.

Just before their lesson ended, Luna finally calmed down and began to tell Diana everything else that had happened during the past two weeks, ending with the proud announcement that she'd lost one of her front teeth. "See?"

Luna opened her mouth wide and pointed to the gap.

"Luna, no!" Colette cried out, appearing at Diana's side although only a second ago she'd been at least fifteen feet away.

Diana's world shifted.

The precarious line she'd drawn years ago between her reality and her father's vanished, obliterated by a mother's instinct to protect her child. Had Colette remained calm, Diana doubted she would have taken much notice of Luna's incisors. Though a little longer and sharper than most, they were still baby teeth, still small enough to pass as normal. But Colette's were massive and growing. Diana's lungs burned from the air she'd sucked in and couldn't manage to release.

For years her father had battered her with horrifying tales of vampires and had given her "lessons" on how to get away if ever she should find herself in the company of one. Those lessons had obviously become ingrained in her mind, because she found herself immediately searching for a sharp piece of wood. Of course, she'd have to find some way to break free of the paralyzing fear gripping her body.

"Diana, put Luna down this instant. I don't want to hurt you." Colette's malevolent voice and blood red eyes were not nearly as horrifying to Diana as her belief that Diana would in some way harm Luna.

"Oh, God, Colette. I…" Diana swallowed. Colette, beautiful, serene Colette stood before her with fangs and nails that could easily rip a human to pieces. "You can't possibly think I'd hurt Luna."

Colette held out her hand. "Diana knows we're vampires, honey. Let go and run to Mommy."

Vampires.

If the child and mother were vampires, then the father, Marek, must have been one. Diana shuddered. Dear God, she'd shown him and Luna around the stables one night after everyone had left. Luna's father had been a tall, muscular man—no, not a man—a vampire.

She wouldn't have stood a chance if he'd attacked her. A vampire as strong, bloodthirsty, and indestructible as her father had said they were could have killed her in an instant. Indestructible? Marek died. Luna and Colette were definitely not acting as if they were indestructible.

Her gaze darted around the deserted ranch. Were more vampires lurking in the corners the moonlight failed to illuminate? Dark shadows she'd seen every night now appeared ominous. Shapes she'd never considered out of the ordinary now seemed to have arms and legs. Like her phantom lover. Her heart pounded. No. He couldn't be a vampire. He didn't even exist outside her dreams.

She flinched when she felt Luna's face burrow into the crook of her neck. A small hand touched her face. She bit her lower lip.

Luna's hand trembled yet remained, cupping Diana's cheek. "You wouldn't hurt me, would you,

Diana?" With her face still pressed into Diana's neck, Luna's voice was muffled, but her question tore through Diana with as much force as a knife cutting into her heart.

Hurt her? The menacing expression on Colette's face failed to hide the terror in her eyes. Diana doubted she could stop Colette from snatching Luna out of her arms, yet the vampire hovered beside them as if she feared getting too close. Luna and Colette acted as if Diana was the monster.

Shaking her head from side to side, she covered Luna's hand with her own and, turning her face, kissed the small, warm palm. If they were so bloodthirsty, she would already be dead or—God forbid—one of them.

Diana recalled how her father insisted vampires had no emotions to guide them or govern their unquenchable thirst. Then why were the two here so grief stricken?

And her father had never mentioned the fact that they had children, children who obviously were not monsters and didn't consider their fathers one.

Since she could remember, Diana had listened to her father rant and rave, his eyes aglow with glee over his latest victim. She had refused to accept the existence of vampires because to do so would be to accept that he killed them.

"I've already lost my husband, Diana. Don't take my baby." Colette's voice cracked.

A chill ran down Diana's spine. She felt herself tumble back to the night last week when her father had announced he'd caught and destroyed another vampire. How the giant hadn't even put up a fight.

She'd laughed when he'd gone to bed. The man looked as if a strong wind could knock him over. She had always found the idea of him taking down any man, much less a vampire, ludicrous.

"Put her down."

Diana turned and smiled through her tears. "It's okay, Colette."

"Don't hurt her." Her pleading voice contradicted the threat of her bared fangs.

"Colette, I would never do," she stared directly into Colette's eyes, "or say anything to hurt Luna or you. Never."

Luna leaned back and looked at her mother. "Diana loves me, Mommy. Don't you, Diana?"

"More than cotton candy, sweets." Diana kissed Luna's forehead, as a new line appeared between her reality and her father's.

Colette stared back into Diana's eyes a few moments before nodding. "Marek trusted you. Even after he discovered...well, he trusted you."

With a relieved sigh, Diana rested her forehead on the Luna's and closed her eyes. Saw her father dragging Luna into the pen she now believed existed. Reaching into her shirt, she lifted the heart-shaped locket her mother had given her.

"Before my mother left, she gave me this." She unclasped the chain then placed it around Luna's neck and whispered, "She told me this heart was filled with her love for me and vowed it would keep the monsters away."

Luna's eyes widened.

"Do you believe in monsters?" Diana asked.

"Only one." Luna's voice was tinged with anger.

Diana closed her eyes for a moment and swallowed the lump in her throat. "Well, this will keep that one away from you. Do you know why?"

Luna shook her head, her eyes never leaving Diana's.

"Because in here," Diana tapped the silver heart she'd worn since the day her mother vanished, "is my love for you. And if that monster ever sees it, he'll know not to touch my Luna."

"You're not afraid of us, Diana?"

"Should I be?"

"No." Luna rolled her eyes. "Well, sometimes, the males go over the edge and start throwing trees. Then you'd better run."

Diana laughed and gathered the child into her arms.

A short time later, when the lights of their trailer disappeared as they turned out of the parking lot, Diana dropped to her knees. She recalled all the nights her father had come home triumphant after one of his vampire hunts. She'd been about Luna's age the first time she'd heard him discussing his plans for the pen with her mother. So many nights, so many vampires.

Had he lied to her all these years? Or had he never taken the time to discover if vampires were actually as heinous as he had believed they were? How many children had he orphaned? How many widows now slept alone?

She swallowed the lump rising in her throat and gazed up at the stars. Were all vampires like Marek, Colette, and Luna? She scanned the forest surrounding the ranch. Owls hooted, crickets chirped, nightingales sang.   Harmless creatures destined to live their lives between dusk and dawn. She buried her face in her hands. "Oh, Daddy, what have you done?"

The distant sounds of the stable doors slamming shut brought her to her feet.   Never able to hide anything from Stan, Diana knew that if she saw him now she'd only end up blubbering in his arms. Tomorrow, she'd tell him that she simply forgot to sign out. Pulling out her cell phone as she ran to her car, she speed-dialed Terry and made plans to meet her at Cabana's in an hour. She needed a few stiff drinks to numb her aching heart.

*****

"No, way.   You popped your own cherry?" Terry squealed and slammed her palm down onto the table.

Diana cringed and peered through her fingers at the people standing near their booth. "Why don't you get a frigging megaphone? I think the people on the dance floor didn't hear you."

Terry giggled, "I'm sorry. It's just so funny."

Diana leaned across the table and scooped another handful of pretzels from the bowl. "Funny? I must be the only woman in this bar who saved herself for marriage and you think it's funny that I lost my cherry to *myself*?"

"Di, you couldn't have." Terry leaned back and shook her head. "It's impossible."

"There was blood on my sheets this morning, Terry. And no, it's not my period." Diana tilted her head back and drank the last of her beer. "God, I'm so thirsty."

"Blood, huh?" Terry frowned. "Did you check for scratches?"

Diana raised her brows. "No, Terry. I just immediately jumped to the conclusion that it was from losing my virginity. Of course I checked for scratches!"

"So you went at it in your sleep and popped your cherry." Terry whistled. "Man, Di, you must have had some horny dream."

"You have no idea." She glanced at the empty beer bottles on her side of the table. "I'm getting another. Want one?"

"That's four. Don't you think you've had enough?"

Diana bit down on her lower lip to stem the fresh tide of tears she could feel burning her eyes. She'd lost so much today. Her virginity hardly seemed important compared to the realization that vampires, creatures with long, sharp teeth dwelt in a world she'd believed held nothing more frightening than a handful of criminals. And, even though he rarely gave her much attention, she mourned the loss of the father she hadn't believed could hurt a fly. "I think I'm going to need a hell of a lot more than four tonight, Ter."

"Just because you popped your cherry? You're still a virgin, silly. Just not physically." Glancing at the beer bottles, Terry sighed. "Di, you can't even handle one beer, much less four. Why are you letting this get to you?"

Diana groaned. She wished she could tell Terry about her father, but it was just too humiliating. And she could just imagine how Terry would handle the news that Diana now agreed with his theory that vampires roamed the streets of Lake George. Instead she raised her head and, blinking back her tears, said, "I wanted the love of my life to be the one who popped it, Terry. I wanted him to feel it and know, without a doubt, that he was my first."

I did.

Diana froze. "Did you hear that?"

"Hear what?"

Someone chuckled behind her. She glanced over her shoulder and glared at the group of young men grinning down at her. "Get lost, jerks."

Looking at her as if she were crazy, they turned their backs on her.

"Thanks a lot! I just made eye contact with one of those hunks. Geez, don't cry. Look, when your grandmother told you that line about a true soul mate lurking in your future but only if you kept your virginity intact, you should have seen it for what it was. Some old lady tricking her granddaughter into keeping her legs closed until marriage!"

"You didn't see the way her eyes welled up when she said a child from a quick fling could destroy my chance of spending eternity in the arms of my one true love. Like she knew."

Terry still smirked. "Typical grandmother trick."

Diana shook her head. "She had my father at fifteen. Maybe when she was older she met her soul mate but it was too late." Diana wagged her finger in front of her friend's face. "And you know as well as I do that she's psychic. She's been right about everything she's seen in my future and past for twenty-five years." She flung herself back against the hard wood of the booth and raised her hand to clutch the locket, then remembered she no longer wore it. "Oh, God, you don't think those tears were because she knew I'd screw up, do you?"

"Yeah, right. You're gonna get pregnant from fingering yourself." Terry let out a bark of laughter. "I've been doing it since I was thirteen." She held her arms wide and frowned down at her belly. "Oh my God! I must be sterile! Either way, there's no such thing as a soul mate. God, I'd hate to imagine—"

Diana stared at Terry. Her friend's mouth moved, yet only the pounding of a heart rang in her ears. She focused on the rhythm, felt her own heart speed up to keep pace with it. Every beat seemed to call to her. "I gotta go...uh...get a beer," she mumbled, unwilling to even attempt to explain this phenomenon to Terry.

"Di, wait. You've had enough."

"I have to...Shit!" She scratched at the insistent twitch on her neck. "I have to go to the bar."

Her chest felt as if a hundred butterflies struggled from within to break free. She stared at the crowded bar then turned to Terry. "My grandmother always said I'd know when my soul mate was near by the way my heart beat."

"Romantic mush," Terry muttered, shaking her head.

The room swayed as if she sat on a boat floating on the undulating swells of the ocean. Holding onto the table until it stopped, she took a deep breath to quell a sudden wave of nausea. "I really think he's here."

"At the bar? Fine, get me a beer while you're

there." Terry smirked, "And listen, Di, if your soul mate has a cute brother, have *him* bring my beer."

Diana slid out of the booth then stood up. The room tilted. For the first time, she welcomed the warning that she'd gone beyond her limit. She wanted to get drunk, to block out every thing that had happened tonight, to forget that her father—

"You don't look so good, Diana. Maybe I should just drive you home."

Come to me.

Chapter Five

Lucian arrived at Cabana's much later than he'd planned. He'd wasted precious time explaining the turn of events to the elders and requesting more time. The meeting had gone so well, and he'd found Diana's scent so easily that when he'd zeroed in on the ranch, he'd felt confident that she had nothing to do with Marek's death. But as he'd soared over the ranch, a sight met his eyes that nearly sent him crashing to the ground and shattered his confidence that destiny had finally sent someone to fill the endless, lonely hours of his life. He'd hovered high above the scene, telling himself that his eyes had deceived him, that the trailer just looked like Marek's, that the child wrapped in Diana's arms merely resembled Luna, and that the woman standing beside Frank Nostrum's daughter and Marek's daughter couldn't possibly be Colette. But their voices rose up to his ears and he could no longer deny the truth. Diana Nostrum knew Marek's wife and daughter.

As the trailer had pulled out onto Route 9, he'd probed Colette's memories. His heart missed a beat and a roar of denial lodged in his throat when he uncovered a recent memory of Marek standing beside Diana as she lifted Luna onto a grey pony. To make matters worse, when he'd tried talking to Colette, she insisted that Diana's grief over Marek's death was proof of her innocence.

Tears? Tears proved nothing. He wondered how many other vampires knew Diana, how many relatives of her father's victims had memories that included time spent wrapped in Diana's arms, time trapped in the spell she had so easily cast over him during the past week. How many had met her? Trusted her? Her guilt weighed heavy on his mind, and he doubted he'd ever trust her.

He had returned to Mina's Cove and dipped into the minds of every vampire, searching for any memory that included Diana, but none of the vampires strolling hand in hand down Main Street, shopping in the all-night boutiques, or eating at the all-night restaurants had ever encountered her. A slight shift and he searched the minds of the vampires sitting along the shore of the town beach, swimming in the lake, and picnicking in the park but found no memory that included the hunter's daughter.

Lucian transformed into mist and whisked past the bouncer and smokers milling around the entrance. After materializing in a dark corner, he made his way to the central bar. Immediately Diana's scent overpowered those filling the club and called to him like no other woman or vampire's ever had before. Following the trail of her scent, he found her standing beside a booth.

He entered her friend Terry's mind and through her watched Diana's every move, heard Diana's every word. Now, watching Diana through Terry's eyes, he wondered if his soul mate had tricked him last night, if she had used some inner power to speak to him. He snatched the bartender's attention from a group of women at the other end of the bar. A minute later, he held a cold bottle of beer up to his lips.

Diana's voice, a whisper that crackled with fear and the question she asked Terry caught his attention and filled him with dread.

"And that? Did you hear that?" Diana gazed towards the doors leading to the deck overlooking the lake.

"What?"

"I could swear someone spoke to me again. Right in my ear...this time from o-outside."

Lucian lowered the bottle and forced down the beer trapped in his mouth.

Terry slid out of the booth "Yeah right. I can barely hear you over the music but you hear someone calling from the deck? That's it." She wrapped her arm around Diana's shoulder. "I'm taking you home."

He stood up, his eyes darting from one face to another as he searched for the vampire calling Diana.

"Home? But I can't. I...there! He just said it again! He wants me to come to him."

The bottle in Lucian's hand shattered. Maintaining contact with Terry's mind he watched Diana glance around. Her hand rose to the spot on her neck where he'd taken her blood; his fangs responded, surprising him with the speed and length of their growth. He closed his eyes, willing his wayward teeth to recede. How could he still react this way after knowing that she knew Marek, that she might have helped catch him?

And who the hell was calling her? Luring her outside? *Show yourself,* he mentally roared.

Nostrum's daughter looks like hell, Lucian. Diego's voice slithered into Lucian's mind.

Lucian searched the club. Since when had the young vamp learned to shield himself from other vamps, from older, stronger vamps? *What brings you to Cabana's, Diego? Did my mother send her boy toy out to watch me?*

Can't find me, can you?

Come out of whatever hole you're hiding in and face me like a grown vamp.

Diego appeared behind the man standing next to Lucian and, bringing his mouth up to the man's ear, whispered, "Go piss in the front seat of that sissy-ass corvette you have parked outside." When the man nodded and left, Diego shifted closer to Lucian. *What brings you here, old timer? If I remember correctly, you were ordered to stay far away from Nostrum's daughter after you passed on your blood.*

The elders want me to keep an eye on her. Lucian stared into the vamp's eyes. *Just in case she decides to rip open some poor vamp's neck.*

Diego blanched. *Olympia said the bitch would be out of control from the hunger by now. That she'd do anything for a taste of any vampire's blood.*

My mother doesn't know everything, Diego.

Your mother knows more than even the elders when it comes to Diana Nostrum. Even if she didn't, she'd use her powers —

Grow up, Diego. My mother is not the most powerful vamp in Mina's Cove. The sooner you realize that, the sooner you'll get your balls back.

She said I could play with the bitch tonight. She told you to stay away. Diego lifted his upper lip just enough to expose the tips of his fangs. *If I were you, I'd be more concerned about pissing off your mother then keeping an eye on some damn bitch. Olympia may not be as powerful as Tobias, but I'll bet my balls that she's more powerful than you. She carries the blood of Dracula in her veins. And now, so do I.*

Lucian mentally wrapped his fingers around Diego's neck and squeezed until the vamp's eyes bulged. *I didn't have to lose my balls or become one of my mother's slaves to get a taste of Dracula's blood, you fool. I was born with it running through my veins. And — if you still doubt who is stronger — Dracula and Mina both held me to their necks whenever my so-called mother decided a night on the town was more important than feeding her baby. Just because I don't flaunt my powers, doesn't mean they aren't there. Got it, boy toy?* He released his mental hold on Diego and watched the vamp grab onto the bar for support and drag in one long breath after another. With nothing more than a glance, Lucian shifted the entire crowd around the bar until a wide path opened to Cabana's entrance. *Leave. And don't ever follow me or go near Diana Nostrum again.*

When Diego didn't turn to leave, Lucian emitted a low growl. *Better yet, let me help.*

Diego vanished. Lucian smirked, picturing Diego's face when he materialized in the middle of Albany's garbage dump.

Glancing back towards Diana, his grin faltered when he realized that the voice she had mentioned hearing was Diego's. The vamp had tried to lure her outside. Lucian didn't have to enter her mind to discover how Diego's call had affected Diana.

Her eyes still darted around the bar, her chest rose and fell too quickly as far as he was concerned, and her skin paled before his eyes. Coupled with her anxiety, her hunger for his blood during the course of the day had taken a heavy toll on her body and mind. If he left, if she went another night and day without his blood, the hunger would grow unbearable. She'd go insane and rip out the throats of humans and vampires alike trying to sate a hunger only his blood could appease. Another day, another night, and fangs would replace every tooth in her sweet mouth. He'd be bound to abandon his soul mate on Fentmore Island where the Slashers would smell his blood and probably rip her to shreds.

Sighing, he admitted that he still needed more proof of Diana's guilt before casting her into that hellhole. He'd find out tonight, one way or another, if she'd helped her father kill Marek. Then he'd either feed her hunger or leave her to suffer for her sins.

Shifting his gaze to Terry, he stripped her mind of any concern regarding Diana then compelled her to go home after telling Diana that she had a headache, one he produced a moment before the words left her mouth.

Come to me, he sent the seductive command that she'd understand and not be able to deny. He let out a relieved breath when she took a step in his direction.

*****

As Diana pushed her way through the crowd of people surrounding Cabana's central bar, the cacophony of butterflies in her chest grew more and more frenzied. Any one of the men she brushed against could be the man her grandmother had foretold would bring everlasting love into her life. No one, not even Terry, understood just how desperately she needed love in her life.

But for all she knew, half the strangers here preferred blood to the beers and cosmopolitans in their hands and were only waiting for the right moment to sink their teeth into her neck. How many closed-mouth smiles hid fangs? How many eyes could hypnotize her and draw her into a deadly embrace?

Recalling Luna's whispered words when she'd hugged her goodbye at the ranch, Diana shuddered. 'Don't be afraid, Diana. All the Slashers live on Fentmore Island.'

Slashers. Just the name brought up visions of long, sharp fangs ripping into flesh. She couldn't move, couldn't breath as she recalled the many nights she'd sat unprotected on the porch in defiance of what she'd considered her father's ridiculous belief in vampires. She might have believed him if her mother hadn't insisted vampires didn't exist.

Why couldn't she breathe? The bodies around her seemed to block all the air from reaching her burning lungs.

A strong hand emerged and clamped around her left arm. Her gaze dropped to the long fingers wrapped around her arm.

Oh, God, she knew that hand, had seen it at the lake erupting from the swirling mist that had always left her yearning for its touch.

Her phantom lover.

Or vampire?

Swallowing a scream, she forced herself to look away from her phantom's hand. Her gaze slid past the black hair sprinkling the taut muscles along his forearm, past the biceps bulging out from a short, black sleeve, past the raven-black hair that fell in soft waves to his shoulders. When she finally saw his face—the stubble coating his chiseled jaw, chin, and cheeks and surrounding full, soft lips parted in a crooked smile—whatever breath she'd managed to drag into her lungs whooshed out with a wheezing scream.

She'd kissed those lips, felt them take possession of her mouth, glide along her jaw and down her neck. Oh God, every nerve in her body tingled from the memory even as her body started to tremble with fear.

Tearing her gaze from his mouth, she peered up into the same midnight-blue eyes that had taken her breath away in her dream last night. The pain she'd felt in that dream, the horrible burning in her veins returned with a vengeance. Diana drew in a sharp breath and felt her legs buckle just as darkness obliterated the face of her phantom lover.

*****

"Damn." Lucian slid his arms around Diana and caught her limp body against his chest. He willed her heart rate to slow down then lifted her into his arms and carried her down the dark hallway and out the emergency exit. When he reached a spot where no one could see, he leapt into the air. Her hunger merged with his and singed him with its intensity. He soared higher, veiled them in darkness, and slit open his lower lip with his fangs.

Her lips parted on a whimper as if she unconsciously knew that a drop of his blood hovered inches from her mouth. His body hardened with need, his fangs ached from the hunger coursing through his veins, and every muscle strained to bring his mouth to hers.

One kiss and he doubted he could maintain the distance he needed to uncover her guilt. One kiss and she might once again wrap him in a cocoon of desire. Logic demanded he simply let his blood drip down into her open mouth. The first drop of his blood landed on her lips; her tongue swept it into her mouth. Moonlight kissed her cheeks, nose, and the crescents of her lashes. She looked so innocent, so pure with her hair flowing over his arm and her tongue glancing over her moist lips, searching for more of his blood, more of his life's essence.

Another drop.

He slowed the progression of its descent, watched it splatter on her tongue. With an anguished roar of defeat, Lucian slid his torn lip between her silken ones. Diana immediately started to suckle.

The air around them crackled from the desire he refused to appease. His blood surged up to his mouth, pulsed behind the cut as his very soul demanded he feed his mate. He thought he had complete control until Diana's tongue slid over his wound and caressed his fangs, until her lips shifted and bestowed the kiss he'd struggled to avoid. The power of her lips merging with his, of her moans vibrating through his body sent him soaring up through the clouds. Crushing her soft yielding body to his, nicking the inside of her lip with one of his fangs, he turned their kiss into a feast of ecstasy. Her pure, sweet blood, now carrying the faint taste of his own, flowed into his mouth and down his throat while his continued to sate her hunger. The scent of her body weeping for his as passion replaced hunger drove him mad with desire.

When he could take no more, and he felt the imminent return of her consciousness, he closed the tiny cut in her mouth and started to descend to the town park overlooking the lake. The air lifted her hair, wrapped it around his face. A silken caress that almost sent him back into the clouds for one more kiss. One more taste. Her eyes fluttered opened just as he alit on a bench. Cradling her on his lap, he waited until he felt her awareness fully return.

"Think you can stand?"

"Stand?" Diana frowned then glanced around at the trees surrounding them. "How...how..." She stared into his eyes. A bright crimson blush spread across her cheeks. "Did I faint?" she asked rubbing her temples.

"Looked that way to me." He grinned when her tongue darted out to lick a drop of his blood from her upper lip.

"I never faint."

Diana shifted to stand but he drew her back against his chest. "Maybe you should rest a minute."

"I..." She swayed and rested her palms on his chest to steady herself.

Lucian felt her heart pound and her lungs seize as surely as if they were his own. Her eyes swept over his face, widened with fear each time they met his.

"Breathe," he whispered, afraid she might faint again.

Diana whimpered; her eyes shimmered. "I know you. Your eyes. Your voice. We've met before."

He shook his head. "I'd never forget meeting you."

"I'm sure...I saw...I...f-felt..." She closed her eyes and brought her hands up to feel his face.

He grasped her hands and gently removed them from his face before she could feel her way towards discovering that he was indeed her phantom. "Not a good idea."

She jumped to her feet. After a fleeting glance toward his lap, she peered at his mouth and backed away.

"How did I get here? Who are you?" Her voice cracked. "How long have I been out?" Her hands rose to her neck; her fingers trembled as they grazed the skin covering her veins. "Someone called me...and... And..."

"Calm down."

"Calm down? Calm down?" She raked her fingers through her hair, snagged one on a curl, and yanked it free. Her eyes widened as she glanced past him to the park beyond. "How the hell did you get me here?"

"I carried you."

"Five blocks?"

Nodding, he rubbed the back of his neck and cracked his shoulders in a way he thought would convince her. He understood her fears, but he had no time for them. The scant blood they'd shared was barely enough to hold her over till dawn. He had yet to unveil her guilt or innocence, but he had to feed her more so she could survive another day without his blood. "I won't hurt you. I just thought you could use some fresh air."

When he stood, she tilted her head back and frowned up at him as if he were crazy. "You didn't have to take me all the way to the park for fresh air."

"About fifty people were smoking outside Cabana's." Lucian closed the gap separating them. She drew up her shoulders and tensed, but she didn't step back. He smiled, impressed. "And, considering that I had no idea how long I'd have to hold you, I thought a bench was a good idea."

Diana's lips thinned. "I am not heavy."

Laughing at the anger and indignation lacing her words, Lucian shook his head. He drank in the sight of her. The woman stood there in a mini skirt and miniscule halter that he doubted most women could squeeze into.

"Sweetheart, you are far from heavy." He knew his desire shone in his eyes, saw her darken and widen when she noticed. "Look, you fainted in a bar filled with men who would just love to get their hands on an unconscious woman with half your looks. I don't take advantage of drunk," he changed his choice of words when her eyes narrowed and her brows nearly met, "or unconscious women. Let's just say you're lucky you landed in the right arms. Okay?"

Diana bit her lip for a few moments then nodded although her eyes still held suspicion. "Okay. Guess I was lucky."

"Guess we both were." He grinned and breathed in the scent of her body responding to his. His body hardened as her eyes swept over it beneath her lashes. Reminding himself that she may have led Marek to his death, that he had to win her trust if he expected to uncover the truth, he held out his hand and asked, "Feel up to a walk?"

Diana hesitated a moment before sliding her hand in his. The moment their skin touched, Lucian felt a jolt of pleasure ripple up his arm. When he wrapped his fingers around her hand, the feeling surged through the rest of his body. The night would not last forever, and he had much to learn from Diana Nostrum before he gave in to the desire and hunger slicing into his every thought.

A man singing a sultry rendition of Enrique Inglesis' song *"Can I Have This Kiss Forever"* broke the silence surrounding them.

"It must be midnight." Diana looked around. "Midnight Music in the Park is starting."

"I'd say you owe me at least a dance." Lucian stepped in front of her and grinned down into her startled face. "One dance and one kiss?"

Diana's eyes still held uncertainty, but she nodded and rested her free hand on his bicep. It tensed under the heat of her touch. Every muscle tensed in anticipation of more.

An owl high in the maple tree casting them in a shadow hooted woefully. People strolled past, some working their way to the outdoor theater, some enjoying each other's company on this warm, clear night. Lucian darkened the shadow surrounding them, wanting more privacy than the tree bestowed. Diana's fears nibbled at his conscience, but her arousal destroyed his determination to keep his mind on weaning information from her. They swayed to the music, keeping a scant inch of air separating their bodies.

"I don't even know your name." Diana's gaze shifted away from his mouth to his eyes. As he opened his mouth to answer, she cursed under her breath and slid her hand from his. She dug her nails into the spot where he'd taken her blood last night. "Damn!"

When he raised his hand and moved it towards her neck, her eyes widened. He slid his knuckles down the side of her throat. Her vein leapt at his touch then stilled.

Diana sighed and smiled. "That's been driving me mad all day."

Filled with guilt by her offhanded referral to the madness that he knew could overtake her if he failed to sate her hunger, he took her hand in his then drew her body into a tight embrace. Bringing his mouth to her ear, he whispered, "I'd say this means I get two kisses." He brushed his lips over the whorl of her ear.

"I'd say you have to do more than soothe a twitch for a kiss."

"Like what?" Enjoying himself, he smiled and sent a vision of straight, fang-free teeth into her mind.

"I don't even know you."

"Yes, you do. I'm the man who saved you from kissing Cabana's floor."

Laughing, Diana relaxed and leaned closer. Her hair flowed over the hand he slid up her back and sent the sweet fragrance of jasmine drifting up to fill his lungs.

"Lucian," he murmured in her ear before pulling away to gaze into her dazed eyes.

"Hmm?" Diana blinked.

"My name."

"Oh." Her lips quirked up in a lopsided grin. "Mine's Diana."

"Diana. How fitting. The name of a goddess."
Lucian watched her eyes twinkle. "She frolicked in
the forest nude, didn't she?" He shifted, bringing his
mouth very close to hers. "And bathed in the lake."

Diana stared up into his eyes. "Nude. She was
quite vain, you know. She felt she was too beautiful
to allow any mere mortal to look at her body."

"Alas, poor Actaeon. If he were not a mere
mortal, do you think she would have turned him into
a stag or opened her arms and allowed him to feast
his eyes upon her body?"

"Oh, goddess's are very picky." Diana grinned.
"It probably would depend on his looks more than his
mortality."

"Really? And do I have what it takes to win over
a goddess?" Lucian hooked Diana's chin with his
finger and tilted her face up. His hands itched to
explore every curve of her body. It took all the
control he had to keep his fangs from exploding into
view.

"Are you a mere mortal?" Diana's grin failed to
reach her eyes.

He maintained his composure, although a bevy
of alarms went off in his head. "That depends on
what you consider a mere mortal."

When she opened her mouth to respond, he
drew her closer and stole the words from her mouth
in a crushing, yet tender kiss. The ground shifted
beneath his feet, the voice of the singer and hushed
conversations filtering from throughout the park
dissolved, and his resolve to uncover the truth about
Diana Nostrum receded into darkest depths of his
mind. Pricking his lip with his fang, he tempted her

senses with a taste of his blood.

Shrouded in the shadow he'd enveloped them in, he merged with her mind and absorbed her every reaction to their kiss, to his blood.

Her hunger overpowered the last remnants of her fears. She strained against the confines of their clothes to get closer and moaned when his blood slid into her mouth. She wondered about the sweet taste of his kisses, compared the feel of him to that of the phantom she convinced herself was really just a product of some dreams or premonitions. Her body strummed with a desire that could only be matched by his.

Growling, Lucian deepened the kiss until he thought he'd drown in their combined passion. He tore his mouth from hers, but remained merged with her mind. Had she bewitched him, again?

Her thoughts filtered into his mind. She'd never been so forward. Her logical side warned she'd gone over her beer limit, reacting more to the excessive amount of alcohol she'd downed than to Lucian. Ah, but her romantic side shoved logic aside and insisted her body ached with need because she'd finally found her way into the arms of the man she'd waited for all these years. She wondered if he too felt as if he'd found that special someone.

Kiss me again, Lucian. Her voice slid into his mind, sweeter than any angel's song. He realized his error when, just before his lips touched hers, he saw, reflected in her eyes, two tiny points peeking out from beneath his upper lip. Tiny, but big enough to yank her out of the fog of desire she'd been so lost in.

Diana backed away, recreating some distance

between their bodies. Her nails dug into his flesh.

Everything in Lucian demanded he decimate her misgivings with another kiss and feed her hunger until she had no will left to refuse him. Common sense demanded he resist.

Her teeth snagged her lower lip and pierced the sensitive skin. A tiny bead of blood emerged then burst.

"You owe another," he murmured and brushed his knuckles down her cheek. "Will you deny me?"

Diana's lower lip slid free as she shook her head. Before she could change her mind, he took possession of her lips, silencing any fears that might drive her away, gently compelling her to accept that she'd only imagined seeing his fangs, that the teeth she now slid her tongue over were flat and smooth. Swamped by her emotions and her body's reaction, he struggled for control, but that control quickly turned to ash beneath the fire that erupted in her core. He slid his thigh between her legs to fan the flames then grabbed her hips and drew her up the length of his thigh and pressed his erection into her soft, warm stomach. His tongue teased her lips until she opened them and offered herself up to his invasion.

Her legs buckled; her arms tightened around his neck. *I do know you. I know this kiss.* She pulled back.

Her voice and the fear in her eyes brought him to his senses. "You know, goddess, I believe we have met."

Diana's eyes widened before narrowing with suspicion. "When?"

"Sadly, only in my dreams." He lifted a spiral of her hair and twisted it around his finger.

Smirking, she muttered, "That's such a lame line."

"I have dreamt of you" He held her gaze. Letting her hair uncurl from around his finger, he watched it glide down and land on the slight swell of her breasts. "I recognize your kiss."

Lucian squarely met her probing gaze. He hated lying to her, but he had no choice. No matter her guilt or innocence, he had to gain her trust. "Just last night, I dreamt of this kiss."

She leaned closer. Her heart beat fiercely against his chest. "Last night?"

"Did you dream last night?" He grinned and brought his lips back to hers. Her desire, her inability to deny it shocked her. He could see it in her eyes, in the slight tensing of her back. Part of him regretted enthralling her last night and implanting the command that she give in to her desires when they touched. Part of him wished he could determine if her hunger stemmed from her transformation or from a natural attraction to him. Either way, only her fears had the power to subdue her. Fears he had to calm if he planned on completing their bonding. Suspicion still lurked in his mind, but the idea of spending an eternity of nights tasting, touching, possessing Diana kept hope alive that he'd succeed in proving her innocence.

During the walk back to Cabana's, Diana carried on a one-sided conversation in her mind. Lucian grimly noted that if she'd actually been talking, she would have passed out by now from lack of air.

She begged him not to think she always hooked up with men she'd just met, explained that she rarely kissed anyone like this until a second date, and rattled on and on about her phantom. She talked about their time at the lake and in the alcove at Cabana's as if she truly believed he'd been there. Then she shocked him by listing all the other times over the past week when she'd either sensed his presence or caught site of a shadow and was sure it was him. She talked so much to him with her mind that he almost believed she knew he could hear.

As they crossed the parking lot, she winced and clutched her stomach. Lucian realized that she needed much more of his blood than he'd thought and much sooner than he'd anticipated.

*****

As soon as Diana reached her car, she unhooked her micro purse from the loop of her skirt and took out her keys. Her stomach muscles cramped. She leaned on the car for support. Cold sweat broke out on her forehead. How many beers had she drunk?

Over the top of her car she noticed that all the people smoking outside Cabana's suddenly stamped out their cigarettes and quickly reentered the club. Even the bouncer went in and closed the door behind him. "Isn't that strange. Everyone—

She felt Lucian grab her shoulders and roughly swing her around to face him.

"What—?" Her question dissolved when Lucian's mouth covered her own.

Cinnamon mixed with that unbelievably sweet taste unique to his kisses filled her mouth. Her legs trembled when his hand cupped her buttocks and drove her hips into his.

With a deep, guttural moan, Diana grasped onto

his shoulders and rose up onto her toes, bringing that solid shaft of heat where she wanted it most. The hand supporting her back bathed her with liquid fire as it slid up, firmly pressing her breasts to his chest, then cradled her head and shifted it so he could delve his tongue even deeper. Moan after agonizing moan rose from her throat as she savored his taste and alternated between sucking on his tongue and lower lip, something she'd never done while kissing other men, something she couldn't stop doing with Lucian. Her muscles relaxed; the pain ebbed.

She felt the hand on her buttocks glide lower, felt the tips of his fingers draw the hem of her short skirt up then brush along the tender crease where her thigh ended and the cheek of her rear end began. Tearing her mouth away, she murmured against his lips, "Someone—"

"Trust me, no one will come out."

He obliterated her concern over the eeriness of the lot emptying out with another bone-melting kiss. She swept her tongue into his mouth, found what felt like a gash on his tongue and wrapped around it the same way a baby would wrap her tongue around the nipple of her bottle. Suckling his tongue, unable to stop herself, Diana drove her hips firmly into his as her head swirled with a multitude of decadent images that seemed so real, so familiar: Lucian crouched behind a bush, breathing in her scent as she stood naked before him; Lucian growing more and more aroused as she seductively danced in the moonlight; Lucian holding her naked body beneath the towering pines, crushing her against the wall in Cabana's alcove. Another, from her dream last night, swept before her closed eyes with more clarity than even she had dreamt: Lucian raising her hips and bringing his head down between her legs because...because...

Because she'd wanted him to.

She felt as if she were in a familiar embrace, as if they'd shared all of her visions and more. Her confusion over the images began to draw her out of the wave of desire enveloping her but then his fingers dug into the crease below her buttocks. Every nerve seemed to converge between her legs as she felt the delicate lace of her lace thong slide over then between her quivering nether lips.

His kiss grew more demanding, as if he knew what he'd done, as if he knew how very much she wanted and needed his fingers to follow that thin strip of lace and push it deeper into her heat.

Take me now, Lucian, she silently begged, wishing she had the nerve to voice her desires. A growl rumbled through his body into hers, sounding more animal than human. A painful, rending growl so like the one she'd heard by the lake. The one that had not been part of a vision. The one that had sent her friends running for cover.

He suddenly tore his mouth from hers. The rhythm of his ragged breathing matched hers. She realized by the shocked expression on his face that he too had been taken by surprise by their lust for each other, that he too could not believe how quickly their kiss snapped all logic and control from their grasps.

Stop searching for reasons to run. Stop thinking of your phantom. A man holds you in his arms. Only a man. Her subconscious thoughts whispered into her mind, calming her fears, insisting she listen. Lucian's eyes glowed in the moonlight as they peered with amazing intensity into hers. She blinked, trying to recapture thoughts that only a moment ago seemed so important.

Still clasped in his iron embrace, Diana cringed when her gaze fell to his mouth and beheld a smear of blood on his lower lip. "Oh...I think I-I bit you."

Lucian touched the blood on his lip then glanced at the crimson smudge on his fingertip. His pupils dilated when he gazed down at her mouth. "There's blood on your lips." He slid the pad of his finger over her lips then held up his finger. "Your blood or mine? Or both?" Holding her gaze, he licked some off then slid his finger between her lips.

Without thinking, Diana ran her tongue over the pad of his finger.

Their gazes locked. Diana felt his finger slide free.

His hands cupped her face as his eyes narrowed. "Goddess or not, you've enchanted me, Diana."

Diana closed her eyes as his hands brushed down her face. Lucian's voice came to her as if from across a vast ocean.

Open your eyes, my mate, see me for what I am, accept me, and never fear me.

Her lids felt so heavy, too heavy to fully rise. Through her lashes, she saw his mouth open as his hands tilted her head to the side. Liquid fire saturated her thong, slid down her inner thighs as she felt her blood surge up to the spot on her neck that throbbed and pulsed with renewed vengeance.

A sense of calm swept over her. When he opened his mouth and revealed two razor sharp fangs, her stomach clenched with need. She wanted this, needed it more than her next breath.

Lucian's head descended swiftly. She tensed, expecting him to bury those fangs deep into her neck, expecting the pain to break the spell he'd cast over her. His lips skimmed over her vein, until she silently begged him to take her now. Pain, white hot pain stole her breath away but when she would have screamed, pleasure replaced the pain and a million stars burst to life beneath his mouth. Too soon, he raised his head, ripped open his shirt and, holding up what looked more claw than nail, sliced open a gash above his heart.

The minute shred of her mind that she still retained control over knew she should scream, fight, or at least find the sight of his blood flowing from the gash repulsive. She licked her lips and gazed up into those magical eyes that reminded her so much of the night sky.

"Take my heart, goddess. Take my life's essence and make it your own." Lucian buried his hands in her hair and gently urged her forward. The moment her mouth touched his skin and she tasted his blood, she felt her feet leave the ground. His throaty moans filled her ears, his heart beat in time with hers, and sweet ambrosia filled her mouth.

A kiss. No more than a kiss.

Diana opened her eyes. The pain she'd felt a minute ago had vanished. Lucian held her face in his hands as he brushed his lips over hers before pulling away and smiling down at her with shimmering eyes.

"That was some kiss," she murmured, feeling drowsy. She lowered her eyes and stared at his shirt.

For some reason, she'd expected it to be torn. Running her palms over the hard muscles covering his chest, she fought the urge to rub against him like a cat. "I-I'm really tired. I'd better get home."

He hooked her chin and tilted her face up. "I want to see you again." Glancing at the sky, he smirked and added, "Tonight."

Diana nodded as he brushed his lips across the bridge of her nose then, still holding her gaze, took the keys from her hand. "And I think I'd better drive you home. Just in case you feel faint again."

Diana glanced around the parking lot. "But what about your car? How will you get home?"

"Don't worry. I'll call a friend."

She didn't question him when he parked quite a distance from her house. Somehow, she doubted she'd ever question anything he did. They spent the rest of the night in the car and talked, uncovering more and more about each other. She learned how seriously he took his job as a cop, how much he loved and admired his stepfather, and how work and family kept him busy most of the day. She talked about how close she and Terry were, how much she loved her grandmother, and avoided any mention of her father or Luna.

Shortly before dawn, after a very passionate kiss, a Cadillac Escalade pulled up. Lucian introduced the young man as his cousin Tomas. The man appeared shy and avoided meeting her gaze as he mumbled a quick hello then slid into the passenger seat. She expected another kiss before he left, but Lucian merely winked over the roof of the car.

She watched them drive away until she could no

longer see the red glow of the car's lights. Vulnerable to the night creatures that she now knew existed, she could not shake the feeling that one watched as she fumbled with her house key, one filled with hatred, one more evil than even her father could imagine.

Chapter Six

"Damn, it's hot today." Diana smoothed out a corner of her towel then shimmied to flatten out a lump of sand that kept pressing into her stomach.

"You're kidding. I don't think it even hit eighty yet." Terry glanced at her watch and moaned. "I swear, if I didn't have to work, there's nothing I rather do than sun all day."

Diana rubbed her cheek over her towel and grinned. "I can think of a few things."

Terry snorted. "Oh, I get it. You popped your cherry so now you're...burning!"

"Burning doesn't begin to describe—Ah! That's cold." Glaring over her shoulder, Diana watched Terry coat her back with sun block. The chill lingered, soothing the sweltering heat enveloping her body. "Where did you have that? In your cooler?"

Terry nodded. "Feels great, doesn't it? Girlfriend, you two-timing your beach buddy? I've never seen you this red."

"I'm really burning? We just got here." Diana hissed when Terry squeezed a line of lotion down each of her legs. "That feels so good."

"So, tell me about last night." Terry smoothed the lotion over Diana's legs as she spoke. "I still can't believe I left you in Cabana's."

"One minute you're trying to drag me out of there and the next you're gone." Diana reached into the cooler and felt around for a water bottle. After a few sips, she squirted her face. "That must have been one killer headache."

"Fast and furious. But by the time I got home, it was gone." Terry wiped her hands on Diana's towel. "So, I hear you got yourself a real hunk after I left."

"I don't have him, yet."

"That's not what I heard." Terry said in a singsong voice. "Tina told Linda who, of course, told me that when you were walking up to the guy, his eyes nearly burned a hole in anyone who blocked his view. According to her, that man wanted to sca-rew you, honey."

The woman sitting on a sand chair not two feet away raised her head from the book she'd been reading. Her gaze darted to the little boy eating a sandwich beside her than back to Diana.

Diana dropped her forehead down to the towel. "Terry, would you please talk a little lower?"

"You're blistering! Diana Nostrum, you must be hot to trot!" Terry laughed. "Get it? You're so horny, you're blistering? So where'd you two run off to? The nearest motel?"

Rising and snatching up her towel and beach bag, Diana stomped up the hill toward the picnic area separating the beach from the cabins her father rented. Terry caught up, shoving her towel into her beach bag.

Diana spun around and glared at her. "Terry, if you don't learn to keep your voice down, I swear our friendship will die a sudden death!"

"Yeah, yeah. You've been saying that since we were eleven and I said, a little too loud for your sensitive ears, that I thought it was cool that you got your first period. Big deal."

Diana scanned the picnic tables scattered beneath

the trees until she found one that ensured some privacy. As soon as she dropped down onto the cool bench, she retrieved their sandwiches from the cooler Terry plopped onto the table. "Big deal? Terry, I went into the cafeteria not five minutes later, and everyone started chanting that a woman was in the house. And what about Tommy Millwood? Thanks to you, my entire Bio class knew I was going to let him feel me up before he did."

Terry held her hands up. "Okay, on that one, you're right. I did screw things up a little."

"A little? He had a camera rolling and a group of Peeping Toms in training at the window of his den."

"Hey, look at it this way. Thanks to me, you found out he was a perv." Terry took the sandwich Diana handed her. As she unwrapped it, she chuckled. "You have to admit, it was pretty funny." When Diana scowled, she rolled her eyes. "All right, I'll keep my voice down. So tell me about this guy."

Diana leaned towards Terry. "I'm planning on jumping his bones the first chance I get." Diana ignored Terry's incredulous expression and picked the tomatoes from her ham sandwich. "Didn't you tell them I didn't want tomatoes?"

Nodding her head, Terry continued to frown. "Just because you popped your cherry?"

Diana shook her head as she chewed. Taking her time, she unscrewed her water. "No. It's just that I'm convinced he's the one."

"Because of the butterflies you felt before you met him?" Terry shoved her shoulder into Diana's. "You're whacked."

Taking another bite of her sandwich then tossing a crumb to a squirrel, Diana slowly chewed and pondered her decision.

She couldn't be certain Lucian was her soul mate, but he sure turned her on. And the trepidation that had always helped her keep her dates at a distance fled the moment he'd kissed her. She'd never felt so depraved, so undeniably alive. Nerve endings burst to life; muscles never before exercised, never called into service, clenched with unimagined strength, and a hunger she'd never experienced unfurled, overwhelmed, and consumed her. "I feel so...so powerless with him."

Her heart tumbled with fear and excitement just from imagining what would happen tonight. She nearly choked on her sandwich when Terry bumped her shoulder again.

"You had no willpower? You can't be serious."

Tossing another crumb to the patiently waiting squirrel before swallowing the last of her sandwich and balling up the square of foil, Diana glanced around to make sure no one was around in case Terry blurted out something embarrassing. Leaning close to her friend's ear, she continued in a hushed voice. "He's so damned hot, Terry. And I'm so tired of waiting."

"Okay, so he turns you on and you've got the go ahead from Nana Lina, but do you like him? I mean, you have to at least like him the first time."

"We talked for hours last night, and I loved every minute of it." Gnawing on her lip, she added, "Part of me is terrified that he is the one Nana Lina made me wait for."

"Why?"

"She said that my father would consider him an abomination. You know what that means."

"No offense, Di, but your father's nuts." Terry snorted then bit into her sandwich.

"Still, I could have sworn I saw fangs—"

"What?" Terry finished chewing then took a long drink of her water before continuing. "You're not saying you think he's a vampire, are you?"

Diana turned away from the laughter in Terry's eyes. "I know it sounds crazy, but—"

"Think, Di. If vampires existed, why on earth would they hang around here?" She waved her hands around. A piece of lettuce flew off her sandwich.

Picking at a sliver of wood sticking up from the picnic table, Diana mumbled, "Well...they sure looked pointy."

"We've lived here all our lives, we know practically everyone, and we've never once met one or heard of any bodies turning up at the morgue with holes in their neck. Have we?"

Thinking of Luna, Diana forced herself to shake her head. "Let's just imagine there are vampires, Terry. Let's just imagine we found one. What would you do?"

"Oh, let me think." Terry squinted then slapped herself on the side of her head. "That's right. We have our very own vampire hunter living right under your roof. I guess we'd call him and every damn man with two strong arms and a stake who lives within a hundred miles of us."

"But—"

"But nothing. They *don't* exist, Diana, so snap out of it and answer my question. Do you like him or not?"

Diana swallowed the lump in her throat. "Yeah, I like him...I like him, a lot."

"Then go for it." Terry stood and stretched. "I hate to say it, but I have to get back to the office. Your Dad is driving me crazy with his new schedule of events."

"Wait. I'll go with you. I don't have a student till three, and I need to speak to my Dad." Diana tossed the ball of foil in a nearby garbage pail then followed Terry up the steep hill to the lodge that held the main office, laundry room, game room and small apartment her father used on the nights he worked too late to warrant driving home.

When they stepped into the office, Terry sped past her and rushed to the bathroom to change back into her shorts and shirt. Diana sat at the antique desk her mother had bought when they first opened Frank's Lakeside Cabins and picked up the walkie-talkie.

"Dad? You there, Dad?" She released the talk button.

"Ten four, Little D."

Diana grinned and shook her head. No matter how hard she tried, she couldn't get him to stop using CB lingo on the walkie-talkie. "I was just wondering if you'll be staying here tonight after the campfire."

"That's a ten four, Little D. The Monday Campfire Jamboree will hopefully go well into the night. Then I'll have to be available to go searching for the drunks who wander into the woods."

Sitting on the edge of the desk, Diana twirled a pen between her fingers. "Oh."

The pen slipped through her fingers and dropped onto the desk. Drunks. She wondered if Jamboree nights had always been just an excuse to hunt something more elusive than a drunk. She suddenly remembered Luna's tear-stained face...Marek's gentle nature. "Terry's staying over."

Terry emerged from the bathroom.

Diana hopped off the desk and moved to the side so Terry could get to her chair.

"You know how Terry likes to strut around in her underwear so beep before coming in if you come home early." When Terry opened her mouth to deny the lie, Diana shot her a warning glare. "I gotta go, Dad."

"That's a ten four. Don't let her invite any strangers in. I swear, someday that girl is going to invite some vampire into my home, and you know—"

"I know, Dad. They can't come in a house unless invited. Terry knows, too."

"Well, you just remind her. If she has a new boyfriend, I don't want him in my house until she sees him during the day. Same goes for you. No inviting in. They can't come in unless—"

"I know, Dad. I'll see you tomorrow."

"Over and out, Little D."

"I'm sleeping over?" Terry winked.

"Very funny. But if I have my way, someone will."

"You go, girl!"

Later, when Diana arrived at the house she and her father shared, she found a long white box propped beneath the mailbox. Lifting the lid, she gasped. Three dozen long-stemmed, red roses lay nestled in a bounty of baby's breath. She slid the small card from the envelope. A smile spread across her face.

She flipped open her cell phone and called Terry.

"Frank's Lakeside Ca—"

"Roses, Terry. Three dozen."

"No way. What's the card say?"

Diana drew in a deep breath. "Are you sitting?" Without waiting for a reply, she read, "The goddess Diana could threaten to turn me into a stag and still I'd refuse to stop gazing upon your beauty. Here's a rose for each time I thought of you today. I'll call at 8:30. Lucian."

"That's heavy. I'm not sure I like the goddess crap, but shit, I'd forgive anything if a guy gave me three dozen roses."

"Long stem, Terry." Diana ran her fingers over the card. "Tonight, I wear the pink thong."

"And that cute little tank top with your Mudd low, *low* risers." Terry's laughter was cut off by the beep of another call. "I gotta go, Di. Call me tomorrow with all the details."

When the moose/cuckoo clock in the dining room mooed at nine, Diana peeked out the window then jumped when she saw Lucian climbing the steps of her porch. He cradled a long white box, exactly like the one sent earlier, under one arm as he tried to balance a pile of DVDs with his other hand. Wearing denims and a pristine white button-down shirt, he looked even sexier than she remembered.

The doorbell pealed. She pressed her hand

against her chest and glanced down at the low rise jeans and white, cropped tank top she'd decided to wear. She regretted not choosing something newer or more feminine for their first date. She'd opted to stay in for a casual night of pizza and TV, but now, taking in the drab living room and meager furnishings and smelling the ever-present scent of garlic, she wished she'd taken him up on dinner at the Lakeside Inn.

Her heart pounded and the wretched butterflies battered her ribs. To make matters worse, the odd twitch in her neck returned with a vengeance.

*****

The greeting Lucian had practiced all the way to Diana's house fled from his mind the moment the door opened. He heard her silent plea that he not find her less desirable than the previous night and not regret his decision to waste another with her.

Less desirable?

If anything she looked too good for night three of the bonding ritual. This night tested a couple's determination to bond. Those bonding were only allowed to exchange teasingly scant amounts of blood to carry them over to night four. And as far as sex, sinking himself into Diana was not an option. Normally, the couple helped each other maintain control. Tonight's success rested entirely on his shoulders. Judging by the way his body sprang to attention at the sight of Diana, he had a long night ahead of him.

Her jeans hugged her hips so low that he expected to see some evidence of the soft curls he had run his fingers through on the first night of their bonding. Her belly button quivered when his gaze rose to it. He tore his eyes away and continued up over the slight ripple of each rib. Her tank top, cut off right below her breasts, had a neckline so low it revealed the lace edging of her bra. Watching the swells of her breasts rise and fall gave him an instant erection. His fangs throbbed, his mouth went dry, and his knowledge of the English language or any other he'd encountered in the past eighty years dwindled to a simple "Hi."

He shoved the box of roses toward her. He'd planned on dazzling her with a short romantic monolog but watched mutely as she clutched the box to her chest, pushing the swells of her breasts even higher. Her heart pounded in his ears. His heart beat picked up speed and surpassed hers. Gritting his teeth, he brought his heart and body under control.

When he raised his eyes to her face, he shifted and croaked, "Your hair."

Diana frowned, brought her hand up to her head, and shyly grinned. "Oh, yeah, I had it blown straight at my friend Cindy's shop."

"Oh." He cringed at his loss of words.

Reaching out, he weaved his fingers through the long silky tress draped over her shoulder. When his knuckles thumped over her erect nipple, she drew in a sharp breath and nearly dropped the box of roses. On the night he'd taken her virginity, he'd compelled her to trust him and give in to her desire at his touch. Oh, she desired him. The air surrounding her body shimmered from her rising temperature, and her scent revealed that her body had already begun to prepare for his invasion. He wished he could free her mind and discover how she'd react without his influence,

but he couldn't take a chance that her insecurities and
fears might hinder the progression of the final nights
of the bonding ritual.

"Well, it's hard to tame all those curls. They
tend to get a little wild." Diana raised a trembling
hand to her hair.

"I like wild." He cleared his throat as he drew
the fingers of both his hands through her hair until
they slid free and grazed her buttocks. "My fingers
glide right to the end."

"And that's bad?" she asked in a husky voice.

When he didn't answer immediately, her smile
faltered.

"Bad?" He looked into her eyes, lost himself in
their depths for a moment then shrugged, and
grinned. "I like it when they get trapped in all those
curls."

"Oh." Diana blinked. "So you prefer my curls?"

"Prefer? I guess so, but—"

Lucian jumped back as the door slammed shut in
his face. "Diana! I didn't mean you don't look just as
beautiful with it straight. Diana?"

He stared at the door, expecting it to swing open,
expecting her to laugh and tell him she'd only been
kidding. But the door remained closed. He knocked,
rang the bell, then knocked again and still she ignored
him. Finally, he banged his forehead on the door and
almost fell through when the door swung open.
Diana reappeared with her hair dripping wet.

"Now, where were we? Oh yeah, you like it
when your fingers get trapped in my curls." She
planted her hands on her hips and grinned.

"You didn't have to do that." He felt like an

awkward teen on his first date.

Water dripped onto the front of her shirt, creating little windows that revealed the lace design of her bra and dark round nipples beneath it. The longer strands of hair that rested on her skin below the edge of her tank sent rivulets of water down her flat stomach and into the band of her jeans.

"You're getting all wet." His voice cracked. His damn voice cracked.

"So I am." Her eyes twinkled. "Coming in?"

Her choice of words, her wet shirt, and the sudden rise of her nipples immobilized him. All the powers he possessed couldn't stop his body from turning to granite. Needing more time to regain control, he smiled into her eyes and said, "You haven't invited me, yet."

Diana blinked; frowned. "Do I have to?" *Please say no. Please, please, say no.*

Her silent plea accomplished what his powers could not. The erection he'd imagined bursting through his zipper died a sudden death. He gently touched her mind, heard her run through her father's warnings about inviting anyone she'd only seen at night into their home. The ridiculous notion that vampires couldn't enter a house unless invited never ceased to amaze him.

He stepped back. Could she already know what he was? Did her father? "A gentleman never enters a lady's home without a proper invitation."

"Maybe I don't want someone who only enters after a proper invitation." She stared intently into his eyes. "Maybe I don't want a gentleman."

Lucian felt his erection spring back to life. He

stepped over the threshold and leered down at her. "I can be anything you desire."

Diana's face lit up as he took another step in. She turned and, swaying her hips provocatively, led him into the kitchen. "I'm making a salad. The pizza's already here."

Watching those hips, heeding their call, he was surprised to discover he'd crossed the entire living room and entered the kitchen without moving his feet. He could only imagine how Diana would have reacted if she turned around and seen his feet floating above the floor.

Once again in control, he leaned against the chipped white Formica counter beside the sink and watched her rinse the lettuce. When she moved closer and began to rotate the handle on the salad spinner, her hips slightly bucked into the counter again and again, faster and faster. Forcing down the need to grab those hips and turn them toward the painful erection straining against his jeans, he grabbed one of the tomatoes on the windowsill over the sink, rinsed it, then cut it into small perfect wedges. "You have any onions?"

"No, but I have mushrooms."

"Even better."

She opened the refrigerator. The cool air met her wet shirt and bra. Lucian was amazed by his connection to her. He felt the chill go through her as she bent over and grabbed the package of mushrooms and when she turned around and she found Lucian standing directly behind her, he felt the sudden leap in her arousal.

Their gazes met, held.

The sound of a cow mooing broke the spell. "You own a cow?"

Diana frowned. "A cow? Oh, no, that's the moose in our cuckoo clock." She rolled her eyes. "Don't ask."

Taking the package of mushrooms from her hand, he tossed it onto the counter than grabbed her hips. His thumbs slid under the waistband of her jeans as he glanced down at the peaks pushing against her nearly transparent tank top. "Do you have any idea what that wet shirt is doing to me?"

Hooking her fingers into the loops of his jeans she beamed. "I was hoping you'd like it. Damn!" She winced then scratched furiously at her neck.

Lucian understood how she felt. His own vein pulsed in anticipation of her teeth sinking into his neck each time they touched, each time he merely thought about touching her. "What's wrong? The twitch bothering you again?" He dipped his head and brushed his lips over the throbbing vein. "Where, here?" he murmured against her neck. "You scratched yourself." One fang slid into the tiny scratch and opened it enough to release her blood.

Diana winced. "I did?" She glanced down at her short nails.

Gently drawing her flesh into his mouth, Lucian nearly moaned out loud as her sweet taste flowed over his tongue and down his throat.

The room tilted. He gingerly sucked on her neck, soothing the twitch until the thumping under his lips all but vanished. He merged their minds and felt Diana focus on the flutter of pleasure that took its place to slide over her breasts and down her stomach.

She tilted her head to one side. *Oh, yes.*

Lucian stilled. Would he ever grow used to her voice flowing into his mind? When her fingers sank into the front of his jeans, and she pulled his hips closer to hers, his cock jumped, strained to rise up and touch the tips of her fingers.

Grinding his teeth, he regained control and took his time licking the cut. When he was sure that no more blood would escape, he reluctantly pulled away. He raised his head and turned away. Licking her blood from his lips, he grabbed the mushrooms. "I'll rinse these."

What the hell just happened? Diana's dazed voice slipped into his mind as she crossed the kitchen to stand beside him.

Out of the corner of his eye he watched her empty an entire box of croutons into the salad bowl.

Leaning over, he murmured in her ear, "Yup, I do know how to kiss neck." He lifted a crouton from the mound covering the lettuce and popped it into his mouth.

Diana bumped him with her hip. "I wouldn't be so smug, wise guy. You're tossing the mushrooms caps in the garbage and the stem bottoms in the salad."

*****

Later, sitting on the deck overlooking the small pond in her yard, Diana watched Lucian sink his teeth into his fourth slice of pizza. She couldn't stop herself from inwardly tacking his hunger onto the list of reasons why he couldn't possibly be a vampire. Ordering the pizza with extra, extra garlic had done nothing but given her a good dose of guilt and a sore throat. He'd obviously needed no invitation into her home; although, if she wanted to be a stickler, she'd invited him the moment she opened the door.

Shadows cast by the citronella torches surrounding them slashed across his face and sharpened the outline of the muscles flexing along his jaw as he chewed. A nightingale sang a melancholy song from a nearby maple tree. A light breeze threatened to extinguish the votives covering the table. Slivers of moonlight floated across the pond, merging with each other for brief moments before going their separate ways.

Other than kissing her neck, Lucian had been a perfect gentleman. Too perfect for her taste. Reaching down into the cooler beside the table for another soda, she wondered how she could loosen things up a little.

"Smells like it might rain," he said, waving a moth away from the candle.

Diana nodded and continued to rummage through the ice for a diet coke. Her hand wrapped around the can then froze. Biting her lip, she jiggled the can. Letting out a long sigh, she brought the can to the table, aimed it in his direction, and lifted the tab.

Soda shot out, drowning the votives, the pizza, and Lucian. Diana gasped in shock. She'd expected a slight spray. "Oh, I'm so—" A bark of laughter escaped. "I'm so sorry!"

Soda dripped from Lucian's chin as he stared at his drenched shirt. A low growl rumbled from his side of the table. She leapt up from her chair. When Lucian raised his head then blinked as a drop fell from his eyebrow into his eye, she clamped a hand over her mouth to stifle the giggles tickling her throat.

"You don't look sorry." He rose slowly from his chair to reveal just how much soda had landed in his lap.

She pressed both hands over her mouth, but the giggles burst free.

"No. You don't look a bit sorry." Lucian started to inch his way around the table towards the cooler.

"You wouldn't!" Diana took a step back. She nearly bolted when he leaned over the cooler and once again growled, sounding uncannily like a tiger. "Lucian, don't you dare! Drop that can. Lucian!"

Diana's eyes widened when he straightened and shook a can of Sprite in each hand.

"No. I wouldn't say you look the least bit sorry." He shook the cans more vigorously as he stared at her exposed stomach.

With a flick of his thumbs a thin stream of ice cold soda shot out from each can directly at her bare skin. Shrieking, Diana ran down the steps. His impeccable aim had her screaming all the way down to the slope leading to the pond.

Lucian grasped her hips with hands still cold from the cans. She sucked in a sharp breath then, with a swipe of her foot, knocked his feet out from under him and burst free. She could hear his startled laughter and grinned as she turned back towards the house. Sure that she had enough of a lead to get away, she yelped in surprise when his arms snaking around her waist halted her progress. This time, when she unsettled him, he held on tight and took her down with him. They rolled across dew covered grass then down the muddy slope into the shallow water at the pond's bank.

A strand of muddy hair clung to Diana's lips. Her hands were useless trapped between their stomachs. She tried blowing the hair away but only succeeded in giving it a chance to slide deeper into her mouth.

"You've got a killer leg there, goddess," he said, grinning. "I—"

Diana shoved against his chest with all her might and sent him tumbling further into the pond.

"Oh, now you're going to be really sorry!" He swiped dripping hair from his eyes.

He stood in the knee-deep water chuckling. Diana giggled at the sight before clambering up the slippery slope. She lost her footing and slid on her belly back down to the water's edge. Realizing she'd landed at his feet, she rolled onto her back as he approached and swung her leg at his ankles then gasped when he easily avoided contact.

The twinkle in his eyes clashed with the predatory stance he took just before he rushed her. Diana dug in her heels and tried to shove herself back up the slope, but only succeeded in digging herself deeper into the mud.

Her short tank top rested above her breasts, exposing her lace-clad breasts. Lucian's eyes seemed to devour the sight, and Diana couldn't help but moan in response.

Her moans turned to a squeal of glee when she felt his arms glide beneath her back and knees and lift her from the ground. "Lucian," she pled, giggling, when he slung her over his shoulder and started to carry her back to the house, "put me down!"

Lucian's laughter filled her ears as he carried her into the house and up the long flight of stairs to the second floor. Halting on the landing, he asked, "Which way to a full length mirror?"

"What? Why would—Hey!" she twisted her head and giggled from the tender smack he'd just delivered to her bottom. "Okay, it's at the end of the hall."

Once inside her room, she pointed him to the bathroom where he carefully set her on her feet in front of the mirror before turning on the light.

"Oh, no." Diana's hands flew to her face. Mud and grass covered her. Pulling down her shirt, she turned away from the mirror and found Lucian still chuckling as he leaned against the sink. "I wouldn't look so smug. You don't look so hot yourself."

"Men like being dirty. Haven't you heard?" He glanced meaningfully down towards her hips. "You've got a clump of grass stuck in your jeans. You know, it's amazing how many tiny, creatures live in the mud around ponds."

"Ew. My father uses that pond to breed bait." Unzipping her jeans, Diana turned her back on him and frantically tried to scoop out as much mud as possible.

"Bait?"

She glanced over her shoulder, shocked by his serious tone. Lucian's eyes caught the light and glowed, sending a chill down her spine.

"What kind of bait?" he asked, his voice cold.

"Bait worms. For fishing." She looked at her reflection. Her shoulders slumped. Some sexy vixen.

Seeing the reflection of Lucian standing behind her, she tacked his reflection onto her list of...

A glob of mud slid down her stomach.

She'd had such high hopes for the evening. While she loved the sound of his deep laughter reverberating in her bathroom as he plucked mud covered grass from her hair, her cheeks burned. "I look like shit."

"You could never look anything but beautiful. Even with this long, fat worm trapped in your hair."

"Very funny," she muttered. Something splashed into the toilet behind her. "Please tell me that wasn't a long, fat worm." She squeezed her eyes shut.

"Okay, it wasn't a long, fat worm."

Diana glanced over her shoulder than spun around and jumped back when she caught him lifting another worm from her hair.

Within seconds she stood fully dressed in the shower as hot water washed over her. When a worm dropped to the bottom of the tub, she screamed, leapt back, lost her balance. Screamed again.

Lucian appeared beside her and wrapping his arms around her waist, brought her descent to a halt. "Okay, just relax, Diana. They don't bite."

"Oh yes they do. Just get them out. Please." Seeing her reflection, she rued the day she installed the mirrors over the tiles surrounding the tub. While most of the mud streamed from her hair, the hot water pouring over her face melted her mascara. It blackened her face from her eyes to her jaw. Alice Cooper in the flesh. "I'm so embarrassed. Some first date."

Lucian turned her to face him and hooked her chin with his finger. "I have never, and I mean never, had so much fun." He brought his lips to hers for a brief, tender kiss then slid her tank top over her head. "Don't look anywhere but at me. Okay?"

Something slid from her bra as he removed it and landed with a tiny plop at her feet. Whimpering, she wished she'd bothered to put on shoes and curled her toes to avoid touching whatever slithered past on its way to the drain. "Was that another worm?"

"Trust me, Diana, you don't want to know."

"There's more. I can feel them," she whispered.

"You don't have to whisper. I don't think they understand English."

"I'd laugh if I wasn't so disgusted."

Her eyes widened as the force of the shower uncovered one in Lucian's hair. Raising a trembling hand, she plucked it out and dropped it to the water rising at their feet. Tiny, slimy bodies bumped against her ankles. She tried to ignore it but when the water reached her calves, she shuddered.

"The drain's clogged," she said in a small voice she barely recognized as her own and turned to steal a glance down at the drain. Before she could see anything, Lucian caught her cheek in the palm of his hand and forced her to return her gaze to his.

"No, it's not," he stated in a hushed voice.

"But I can—" The water whooshed down the drain.

She bit her lip and lifted her hand to retrieve another squirming worm from his hair.

His fingers wrapped around her wrist and brought her hand back down to her side. "Don't worry about me."

"But—"

"I'm fine. Close your eyes, Diana," he softly ordered.

She did and felt his hands push her jeans and the thong she had so hoped would entice him over her hips and down her legs. He took her hands and placed them on his shoulders then lifted first one foot and then the other to remove her pants completely. She heard her clothes smack onto the tile floor outside the tub.

Still keeping her eyes closed she whined, "This isn't how I envisioned the first time you saw me naked."

"Hmmm. Tell me more."

Her nerves tingled as his clothes brushed across her skin when he straightened. "Well, you dressed and me not might give you a clue," she murmured, amazed that her voice sounded so husky.

"I like the way you think. Turn around. I'll wash your hair." He grasped her hips and nudged her to move.

Turning, Diana peeked through her lashes at their reflection in the mirrors. She couldn't have drawn a more decadent picture of the two of them if she tried. Suds flowed from her hair over her breasts, slid down her belly, and gathered on the cropped curls covering her mound. Lucian, fully clothed, stood behind her, his eyes filled with lust as he gazed at the reflection of her body.

For years she easily held men off, making them wait weeks before they could so much as touch her breasts over her shirt, months before they could lay their eyes upon her naked body. By the time she'd run out of various types of foreplay to satisfy theirs and her needs, her body had been screaming for release. But her mind, her very soul, had had no problem taking control and maintaining her virginity.

Not so tonight. She prayed Lucian was her soul mate. If not, if she'd picked the wrong man at Cabana's, her grandmother was going to be very disappointed. She looked at the mirror beside her. Heat pooled between her legs at the sight of the bulge in his jeans.

When she saw him slide his hand between the buttons of his shirt and pull out a long writhing worm, she started to turn around. "This isn't fair. You must be dying to get out of your clothes."

"I will," he said, turning her back around and pushing her head under the hot spray of water.

He finished rinsing her hair then looked at her face in the mirror. She smiled and, holding out a loofa already covered with shower gel, raised her trembling hand over her shoulder and held her breath.

"Tell me you've never done this before," he demanded.

"Only in my fantasies."

"Then watch closely. Someday, I promise, you'll do the same for me."

His hand drew the loofa over her shoulder, down her arms, back and legs. Diana followed his progression with her eyes, bit her lip, and held her breath until the rough sponge skimmed over her ribs. An ache that shocked her with its intensity filled her breasts as the loofa slid higher. Her eyelids fluttered as it swirled around a taut peak then slid down into the narrow valley between her breasts and rose up to torture the other peak. When the loofa grazed over her stomach, the twitch in her neck returned. Heat radiated all the way down her legs. She let out a soft cry and closed her eyes when Lucian sent the loofa lower and delved between her trembling thighs.

"Watch," he demanded, his voice deeper than before, vibrating through her body and echoing in her mind.

Her eyes flew open. Her knees nearly buckled. She leaned back, not caring what lay beneath his clothes other than the amazing heat that always seemed to rise from his body. His arm encircled her waist and pinned her against him as his other hand moved lower, rubbing the loofa over her throbbing nether lips again and again. No matter how many times she had imagined this as she'd washed and done to herself exactly what he did now, her body had never grown so enflamed. Never had her knees given out, never had she bucked uncontrollably. She watched him lower his mouth to her neck and the vein that seemed to jump from one electric jolt after another. When he drew it in, the scratch there pinched for just a second before all hell broke loose in her body. Fire surged through her veins, a vast void convulsed deep within her. Her clit strummed, her labia flared then clenched. She let out a soft cry and flung her head back onto his shoulder. His mouth covered hers with a possessive kiss that took her breath away.

The now familiar taste of cinnamon mixed with that exquisite sweet honey filled her mouth. She cried into his mouth as her orgasm intensified and engulfed her.   Drawing his tongue in deeper, she sucked greedily as her body convulsed completely out of her control.

When he raised his mouth from hers, she let out a whimper, reached up to grasp his head and drag it back down.

"You have to get out now, Diana." He clenched his teeth. "Now."

Her eyes flew open. "Lucian—"

"Please, Diana. I've already brought us further than I should."

"But—"

"Diana, go!"

Diana turned and stared into his eyes. Reaching up she kissed him, slid her tongue between his lips.

Lucian pulled away. "Out!"

After wrapping herself in a robe, Diana went to her father's room and retrieved his robe. She returned to the bathroom and, resisting the urge to peek, hung it on the hook behind the door. Grabbing Lucian's clothes, she turned to leave.

A long, deep groan stopped her. She chastised herself as she glanced through the gap in the shower curtain. When she saw his hands clutch the knob and spin it as far toward cold as it would go, she grinned. Leaning forward, she drank in the sight of his muscles flexing over his broad back and firm buttocks. His hair clung to his broad shoulders. Water raced down his spine, his thighs, calves. She clenched her hands in the clothes to stop herself from reaching out and sliding her fingers down his slick skin. Standing there, with his hands flattened against the mirrored wall, he looked too perfect, too beautiful to be real. She reached out for one touch, just to prove that this night had not been just another dream.

"You're not helping, Diana." Lucian tipped his face up and arched his back.

Diana flicked a glance at the mirror in front of him and felt the floor drop beneath her feet. Telling herself she'd seen more than was there, that the water swirling down the mirror had distorted his size, she swallowed the lump in her throat and swiftly left him alone.

When he entered the living room a short time later, she had two steaming mugs of coffee ready and the image of his cock imprinted permanently onto her mind.

Lucian joined her on the couch. After taking a mug he draped his arm around her shoulders and drew her against his chest. "What you do to me, woman, could wipe out an army."

Diana smiled. "Cold shower help?"

He kissed the top of her head. "I didn't think it would."

Snuggling closer, Diana brought her lips to his Adams apple.

Sleep.

*****

The doorbell rang. Thinking her father had returned, Diana sat up and gasped when she realized that somehow she had ended up in her bed. Alone.

Sunlight stabbed at her eyes but didn't blind her to the dozens of roses filling her bedroom. Vases of every shape and style covered her dresser, desk, and shelves. More were scattered over her floor.

A card propped against a vase on her nightstand caught her eye. She smiled as she read it aloud. "Tonight."

The doorbell rang again. Grabbing her robe, Diana ran to her window. The twins, Mary and Cind, stood on the path leading to her porch. Cindy dabbed her eyes with a tissue as Mary glanced up. When Diana waved, Mary's mouth dropped. Instead of waving back, she grabbed Cindy's arm and practically dragged her to their car. Diana frowned as she watched the car screech away from the curb and speed down the street. "What the hell was that all about?"

All concern about Mary and Cindy's behavior fled when she turned around.

"No," she whispered.

She moved from vase to vase, shaking her head in amazement.

Lucian had removed every thorn.

Chapter Seven

When Lucian's teeth clamped down on one of her pebbled nipples, Diana whimpered from the sudden stab of pain even as she thrust her breast up and silently begged for more. He complied, biting down, piercing the sensitive skin. Suddenly, a painfully bright light obliterated her view of the top of his head. She blinked until her eyes adjusted then glanced down. "No!"

A loop from the lace edging of her sheet, not Lucian's teeth, held her nipple captive. After slipping off the lace, she squinted into the glaring rays streaming in through her window and cursed the sunlight for intruding upon her dream.

Glancing at her clock, she groaned. She'd climbed back into bed only an hour ago. She rolled over, covered her face with her pillow, and tried to slip back into her dream, but the heat of the sun beat on her back, snatching her away from Lucian's waiting arms.

A gentle breeze flowed through the open window and cooled the sweat covering her body. She wrapped the sheet around her and ran to close the window. Her hand hovered on the window sash. Birds chirped excitedly, heralding the dawn. A light rain must have fallen sometime during the night; the scent of dew-covered grass and damp soil mingled with the aroma of coffee and bacon coming from her neighbor's kitchen. But the roses filling her room cast the sweetest scent. Lifting one, she ran her fingers up the smooth stem.

Glancing down at the front lawn, she frowned. Only Mary and Cindy's odd behavior marred the beauty the morning.

Their early, obscenely early, visit would have been enough to shock her, but what really stumped her was the way Mary had grabbed Cindy and pulled her away. Just before she'd dozed off and entered her delicious dream, Diana had figured the visit had something to do with Cindy crying, but that didn't explain the twins' obvious shock at seeing her wave from her bedroom window, and it didn't explain why they would flee as if the devil himself had appeared. Or why neither answered their cell phone when she tried to call a few minutes later.

Shrugging, Diana slid another rose from one of the vases on her floor and held the crimson blooms up to her lips as she crossed the room. The petals felt like satin, like Lucian's lips had felt each time they had brushed over hers last night.

Sitting on the window seat facing her backyard, she stared at the pond and pictured her and Lucian swimming in the sun-dappled water, lying naked on the grass, making love beneath the heat of the sun. Her skin tingled. The reflection she'd seen in the shower flashed before her eyes. Lucian standing behind her, his mouth on her neck.

Her stomach lurched. She bit her lip and shook her head. She *saw* his reflection. Even if she hadn't, she'd lived twenty-five years before discovering a vampire. It would probably be twenty-five more before she encountered another. Her gaze swept over the blood-red roses filling her room.

Every thorn. Hundreds, maybe thousands.

It would take hours.

The stems clenched in her hand bent.

"Stop it, Diana Nostrum," she muttered, staring down at the ruined flowers. "If your soul mate was a vampire, Nana would have told you."

Her hand trembled. While Nana had never used the word vampire, she had implied that Diana's soul mate would not be accepted as Frank Nostrum's son-in-law. Cradling the bloom, Diana whispered, "Dad hated all my boyfriends."

Other long forgotten conversations with her grandmother came back to her. One where her grandmother had warned her that it wouldn't be easy to accept her soul mate for what he was, to accept the life he led.

"No. Lucian is a man. Nothing but a man!" She stood and, letting the sheet fall from her body, strode to her closet to get dressed for work.

By mid-morning Diana clutched her pounding head and prayed the Advil would start working soon. It amazed her that her lack of sleep had left her so sensitive to the blinding sunlight. Donning sunglasses stopped her eyes from tearing, but did little to alleviate her headache. By noon, her strange hunger returned with a vengeance. Two hamburgers and a double order of fries sated it for all of one hour.

Realizing she'd never get rid of whatever bug she'd caught without sleep, she talked Stan into giving up his office for a couple of hours and took a quick nap. Still, by late afternoon, she could barely find the energy to walk.

The side of her necked pulsed and fluttered, nearly driving her mad. She scratched at it, welcomed one of Stan's painfully rough massages, gently rubbed her knuckles over it like Lucian had, and scratched it some more, but nothing helped. By the time she clocked out, she had blood crusted beneath her fingernails. The twitch remained.

As she crossed the parking lot, her cell phone rang. Seeing Nana Lina's number in the display, she flipped the cell phone open and sat on the hood of her car.

"I had another vision," Nana Lina said before Diana could even say 'Hi'.

"About me?" Diana touched her neck. She could feel her vein pulsing beneath her fingers.

"It was so strange, Diana. You were Medusa, well, you had snakes in your hair."

"Snakes?"

"I'm not sure. It was all misty. And I kept seeing a loofa."

Heat flared over Diana's cheeks. Her heart skipped a beat. Nana Lina's ability to capture bits of the past never failed to amaze her. Or embarrass her. "How odd."

"And I saw your soul mate, Diana. You met him, didn't you?"

"I think so." Diana chewed on her lower lip. "We're supposed to see each other tonight. I...well..."

"What's wrong?"

"Nothing." Diana moved her cell phone to the other ear and glanced around the parking lot of the ranch.

"Diana. You know I can always tell when something's troubling you."

"Well," she flopped back onto the hood and

stared at the purple swirls rising up into the sky as the sun set. "It's not something you normally talk about with your grandmother."

"You can talk to me about anything, Diana. You know that." After a moment's silence, she added, "Even sex."

"Yeah, well, I..." Recalling just how good Lucian's soapy hands had felt as they slid over her skin, she nearly groaned. "God, Nana, I...I..."

"You've been waiting, and?"

"And waiting, and waiting." She rolled onto her stomach. The hood, still hot from hours beneath the sun, warmed her nipples through her shirt. Her neck pulsed; her stomach growled. A group of ranch hands passed on their way to the only other cars in the lot. Diana waved then cupped the phone to her mouth and whispered, "Okay, okay. I want to, I really do. So much it hurts. But what if he's not the one? What if I'm wrong and I...you know...and it turns out that I'm wrong?"

"Wait, are you saying you didn't yet?"

"I just met him." She thought she heard her grandmother mumble something about losing her touch and frowned. "You can't know everything, Nana Lina. Nana?" After what seemed like a very long stretch of silence, Diana glanced at her phone to make sure she hadn't lost the connection. "Nana Lina?"

"Shh."

Rising up to her knees, Diana held her breath. She could almost see her grandmother closing her eyes, inwardly reaching for her sixth sense.

"All in black?" Her grandmother asked in a

hushed voice.

"Not last night. But the night before, when I met him, he had on black."

"I see a tattoo."

Diana slumped down onto her heels. "Not that I saw. Look, maybe your vision is off..."

"Some bird. A raven, I think. Did you see him naked?"

Pleasure swirled between her legs as she once again saw the shower spray Lucian's back, saw the water pour over his firm buttocks. "No, I just saw his back."

"Well, he has one. You just haven't seen that part of him yet. Did he kiss you?"

"Oh, yeah." She blushed at how husky her voice sounded.

"You've been kissed by quite a few men over the years, honey."

"What's that got to do with it?" she asked, oddly annoyed that they should be compared to the unbelievable kisses she'd shared with Lucian.

"Well, was his better, special?"

"Special? I'd say his blew the others away."

"And now, after all these years, you're considering giving this man your virginity after — what? — one date?" her grandmother asked, her voice rising with anger.

Diana moaned. "God, Nana, I don't know what's come over me. If he hadn't kicked me out of the — well, I would have last night."

"Look, you don't need a psychic, Diana. You've always said you had no problem stopping men when they went too far. But with this man, it only takes a few kisses and you're out of control. He's your soul mate."

She leapt off the hood and started pacing around her car. "Well, it was more than—" She suddenly noticed the sun had finished its descent. A knot formed in her stomach. Darkness enveloped the parking lot. She glanced up at the lone light pole. "Come on. Light, damnit."

A second later the sensor kicked in and the light buzzed to life. "Nana?"

"Are you alone?"

The sudden question brought her pacing to a halt and raised the hairs on the back of her neck. "Yes, why."

"Where are you?"

"At the ranch. Next to my car." Her voice boomed in her ears although she barely spoke above a whisper.

Diana glanced around the empty parking lot. The shadows between the lofty pines abutting it encroached on the scant circle of light from the weak bulb. "I have to go."

"Listen, Diana. I'm going to tell you one more thing then I want you in your car and out of there."

"What? What?" Slowly turning, she searched the dark depths for some sign of danger. Someone was out there. She felt eyes watching her every move. Her lungs seized.

"When the time comes, remember everything I ever told you about your soul mate. Everything, Diana. And then, if what I told you makes sense with what you see, try to hold on to the fact that he *is* your soul mate. Try to accept—"

A sudden gust of wind kicked up sand and pebbles from the makeshift lot and hurled them in her direction. Diana ran around the car, one arm flung over her face. The mini-sandstorm seemed to follow her, pelting her back as she flung open the door. "Accept what?"

"What he is."

"What are you saying, Nana?" A shudder tripped down Diana's spine. Part of her wanted to scream at Nana Lina and stop her from saying the words she'd said so many times before. Another part needed to hear it, needed to hear that soft voice remind her that love mattered more than anything else.

"Get in the damn car, Diana!"

Diana flung herself into the driver's seat, slammed the door, pressed the lock button, and stared wide-eyed at the sand hitting her windshield. "You're scaring me, Nana."

"Just remember this, Diana. When soul mates reunite, their bodies recognize each other immediately and long to become one. But sex isn't all that matters. Only if they stay together—accepting and trusting each other—can soul mates' hearts become one. Diana, if you open your heart and soul to him and accept him and the life he leads, you could experience a love most people only dream about."

A gust of wind rocked the car. "I gotta go." Not waiting for a reply, she flung her cell phone onto the passenger seat and, expecting to see a fang-toothed maniac, peeked into the rearview mirror.

*****

Olympia stepped out from behind a tree and

watched Diana's car speed out of the parking lot. Swatting away the dirt the tires had kicked up, she snarled, "Diego!"

Diego poked his head up from the bush he'd been hiding behind. "Is she gone?"

"Of course, she's gone, you fool. Do you think I'd be standing here if she wasn't?"

Standing in the moonlight, her sleek black hair draped around her shoulders like a cape, her low-cut shirt revealing the edges of her aureoles, and her fangs dripping with blood from the rabbit that had dared to cross her path, Olympia knew she could not look more enticing or terrifying. She watched Diego draw in a fortifying breath before he stepped into the parking lot.

"Tell me, Diego, do you think it's healthy to lie to me?"

"Lie?" His eyes darted from the quivering rabbit lying on the ground to Olympia's fangs. Glancing over his shoulder, he took a step back.

"You said he did it. You swore!" She crossed her arms under her breasts and watched the sweat bead on his forehead.

"He did!" Diego stared at the receding brake lights of Diana's car and raked his hands through his hair. "I swear he did."

"You saw him do it?"

"Well, not exactly." He took another step back. "But I know he did. She started moaning and whimpering. I couldn't even get into her mind. The pain was so overwhelming it blocked out everything else."

Olympia grabbed Diego's face in both hands and

bestowed a kiss she ended with a vicious bite. Blood filled her mouth when her fangs sliced through the tender flesh. Glaring down at him as he clutched his torn lip and dropped to his knees, she pointed down the road and asked, "Did that look like a woman in pain? Did she look like she was dying of hunger? Like she was *insane*?"

Diego licked his tattered lip. "God, Olympia. I'm telling the truth. She was hurting so much it made me sick."

"Sick? Over a human?" Olympia wondered if she'd misjudged Diego. He had been doing special favors for her ever since he'd entered puberty and she'd introduced him to pleasures only a female vamp with centuries of experience could provide. He'd become so addicted to her body and blood, so easy to manipulate with promises of more, that she'd even been able to convince him to try and bond with his high school sweetheart. Convincing him the next day that little, innocent Maria had cheated on him had been easy. Diego had grown to trust Olympia. He'd immediately brought the bonding to a halt then abandoned poor Maria, mad from her uncompleted transformation, on Fentmore Island. "Maybe Diana's transformation brought up the memory of Maria. Maybe that made you too sick to notice Lucian failed!"

"Maria didn't react to my blood till the next day. And even then, she wasn't in pain."

Olympia glared at him. "What about Lucian? Did you read him?"

"It was even worse for him. I got hit with a wave of pain so, so—" His eyes flew open. "One drop. Oh no, you didn't."

Realizing her error, Olympia tried to change the subject. She ran her hands over her breasts and licked her lips. "Come here, Diego, and give me what I want."

Shaking his head, Diego backed away. "You told him he was to give no more than a drop of his blood. You insisted I stop him if he tried to give her more. I wondered about that."

"Now, Diego, you're letting your imagination run away with you."

"It doesn't matter how much blood a vampire passes to a human that first time. How much shouldn't have mattered to turn Diana into a Slasher. What matters is that he not return, that he never feed her growing hunger for his blood. That's how they grow mad. Waiting and waiting to feed that hunger. That's how they turn into Slashers. Not right away and not from the pain!"

"Listen to you!" Olympia laughed, stalking him as he backed into a tree. "I've watched scores of humans turn into Slashers. They—"

"I know more than you ever will how our blood poisons humans. After I brought Maria to Fentmore, I found out everything I could about our blood so I would *never* create another Slasher. It doesn't hurt like that." Crimson tears filled his eyes. "Except if the human is a soul mate. That's why we have to be especially careful with them. If too little blood is offered to a human soul mate the first time, the pain is unbearable. That's why Maria didn't feel as much pain as Diana. She wasn't my soul mate. She only turned into one of those monsters because you made me stop feeding her."

Olympia's lip curled up, revealing one, long fang. "I never—"

Diego shook his head and bared his fangs then cut her off with a deafening roar. "What have you done? Is Lucian just another pawn in one of your sick games?"

"No." Olympia turned her back on Diego and stared down the road. How she wished she could just break the necks of Diana and her grandmother. But she'd never win back Damien if he knew she had a hand in their deaths. "So they're soul mates. A minor glitch."

"Minor glitch? Minor glitch? It's a minor glitch that your son suffered even more than she did? That her pain became his, only worse. If he finds out—oh god—if he finds out he harmed his soul mate, that he turned his soul mate into a Slasher, he'll go over the edge, Olympia. I know he will. He'll face the dawn."

"He'll survive. Which is more than I can say for that she-devil." Her nostrils flared. She drew in a deep breath. Diana's scent still lingered in the air. It didn't make sense. She could smell Lucian's blood mingled with Diana's. "The fool must have given her too much."

"How could you do this to your own son?" Diego stared at her, his eyes filled with condemnation.

"I did this for Mina's Cove."

Diego continued to stare at her in the way that too many of her kind did whenever they questioned her love for her son.

She loved Lucian. Why did everyone always

doubt that? Everyone, even her own father always brought up some minor mistake she made raising him or her lack of affection towards him during his boring existence. Did a mother have to kiss her child every year just to prove she loved him? So what if she left him to fend for himself when he was scarcely old enough to walk. She'd locked the door, didn't she? And so what if Dracula and his perfect mate had to feed Lucian when he was a baby. She had a right to go out and feed. And why does everyone have to dwell on the scars he carries from the one morning she didn't have time to grab him when she'd sought shelter from the dawn. Tobias heard his screams, didn't he? He got him inside on time.

Damnit, she loved her son. "Anyway, Lucian will never find out that Diana is his soul mate."

"If he doesn't continue to feed her and complete the bonding, he'll realize it when she goes mad. He'll feel her torment. *He'll* go mad!" Diego closed his eyes and drew in a ragged breath. "He has to go to her and give her more of his blood. He has to bond with her. Yes, yes, and if they mate it will sooth her. He has to bond with her."

Mist swirled around Diego's feet as he ran with preternatural speed.

Realizing he'd dematerialize unless she broke his concentration, Olympia hurled a mental shriek that would slice through his mind. When he stumbled, she let out a relieved sigh. "Get back here, Diego."

Furious that he continued to transform, enraged that he dared ignore her, she pooled her anger into a massive ball and hurled it directly at his legs.

The sound of bones cracking soothed her anger.

Somewhat.

She'd managed to convince the elders that Diana's descent into hell was Frank Nostrum's punishment, but Frank had little to do with her reason for picking Diana. Someone else loved Diana even more than her father. Someone else considered her the only bright spot in her otherwise dark existence. Diego would not interfere with Lina Nostrum's punishment for stealing Damien's heart.

She strode over to Diego's writhing body. "Listen, you worthless piece of shit. When this is all over, Lucian will be fine." Squatting down, she kissed his furrowed brow and, releasing a breast from her shirt, slid her nipple over his lips. "I know you want Diana. I saw how hard your cock got when you told me how she looked in bed. Before I take her to Fentmore, I'll let you play with her. Okay, baby? I'll let you suck her little tits. I'll even let you rut between her legs like the animal I know you are."

While he suckled, she scraped her nail up the zipper on his jeans. He stared up at her with those doe colored eyes the young female vamps found so appealing and silently begged for her blood. She smoothed back his dark brown hair from his brow and rubbed her knuckles over his square jaw. This young vamp others considered so handsome was not her type at all except in one very important way. He allowed his dick to rule his head, something she'd discovered years ago, something she used to her advantage again and again. Piercing the skin of her breast with her nail, she watched his pupils dilate as he watched a drop of blood emerge.

"But Lucian," he murmured, running his tongue

up the side of her breast and capturing the drop. He moaned as the blood she'd addicted him to stirred a hunger she knew he couldn't refuse.

"I was given free rein by Tobias in carrying out Nostrum's punishment."

She pushed his head away from her chest. Shoving her breast back into her shirt, she grabbed Diego under his arms and, ignoring his screams of pain, flung him over her shoulder. "Let's go. When we get home, you can show me all the wicked things you're going to do to little Miss Diana."

"What about Lucian, Olympia?"

"Don't worry about Lucian. I'll take care of everything. If he's is not strong enough to carry out a simple sentence for the sake of our kind without going over the edge, it's certainly not my fault."

"He won't stay away from her when he finds out." Diego cried out when she dug her nails into his thighs. When he continued, his voice trembled. "His guilt will get the best of him if he's experiencing her pain and hunger. Knowing him, I bet he gave in and fed her that night."

"You are so ignorant, Diego. Why do you think their being soul mates was so perfect? I know my son. He would have given in to his guilt with her first whimper even if they weren't soul mates. This way he was too busy dealing with his own pain to worry about hers." She frowned then shook her head. "No, he would never have been able to give her more, once the pain hit him. Pain has a way of sapping one's power, doesn't it?"

She took to the sky. Diego needed a lesson. One he'd never forget. As she neared the northern inlets of the lake and Mina's Cove, she noticed a rocky slope leading down to the shore. Diego's thoughts of finding a way to tell Lucian filled her head. Each time she'd shove more of Diego's body over her shoulder, his fear of tumbling to the ground and down that slope entered her mind. Each time he tried and failed to gather enough power to ensure his survival if she happened to drop him, her fangs throbbed and her thoughts grew more sinister. His nails pierced the soft flesh of her thighs as he struggled to hold on.

And still, the fool's thoughts centered on warning Lucian.

"You really should work on shielding your mind, Diego. I know you're planning on telling Lucian that I knew Diana was his soul mate."

"No, no I wouldn't. I swear, I—"

Tired of hearing his whining voice, she paralyzed his larynx then opened her hands. Diego's knees slammed into her chest as he struggled to remain on her shoulder. Olympia slid her fingers around his ankles and flung his legs over.

She hovered beneath a cloud and took in the show. Not looking to kill the young vamp, she aimed his flailing body towards a tree then grinned when it broke his fall. Still, his descent down the slope was a site to behold. Watching, she winced when his face bounced off the trunk of a lofty pine, bit her lip when his already battered legs slammed into another. The force of the impact sent him spinning through the air.

She frowned. His body picked up an amazing amount of momentum when it again hit the ground. As he tumbled another ten feet towards the lake, she swept down from the sky and caught his ankle in both hands a moment before his head would have hit a huge boulder protruding from the ground. Digging in her heels, she brought his body to a sudden halt.

She flipped over his limp body and drew in a sharp breath. Diego's cheekbones were either shattered or hiding beneath the raw, blood-soaked flesh swelling before her eyes. One glance at his legs confirmed her little trick had accomplished much more than she'd intended. His left one, bent at an impossible angle, bled profusely from a gaping hole beneath his knee where the ragged end of a bone jutted out.

She considered leaving him. At the rate he was bleeding, the rate their kind bled, he'd be dead before dawn and the sun would erase any evidence of her crime.

But the extent of her handsome vamp's injuries intrigued her. It would take the remainder of the night and the entire day for him to recover. His body healing itself would surely be a spectacle worth losing sleep over.

As she lifted him and resumed their flight to her house, Olympia licked at one of the gaping wounds marring his face. Burrowing her tongue as deep as possible, she spread her saliva along torn muscles and tendons.

When they arrived at her house, she laid Diego on the couch and licked every gash from his accident. His eyes fluttered open. He curled his lips, maybe hoping to scare her by baring his fangs, but the fool's face was so swollen his mouth merely formed a lopsided grin. One of his precious fangs was chipped, and the other, nothing but a ragged stump. She watched him run his tongue over them and discover their shortcomings for himself.

When he squeezed his eyes closed and turned his head away, Olympia released a weary sigh. "You really left me no choice, Diego. Planning to tell Lucian about Diana. Now this is going to hurt but do try to be a man about it."

She grasped one of his legs and, twisting it back and forth, tried to realign the bone. His screams ricocheted through her head.

The air crackled with the power Diego's body drew in to heal itself. Olympia added some of her own to speed up the process. She never tired of watching their kind mend. Tonight, she'd torture her young slave. Tomorrow night, after she properly paid her twin puppets for warning her about Diana's condition, she'd deal with Lucian and Diana.

*****

Resting her cheek on Lucian's shoulder, Diana smoothed out the blanket they'd laid on the ground and watched Lucian bite off a chunk of meat from the bone of the rib he held in barbeque sauce covered fingers. "You're a mess."

Lucian glanced down at the pile of crumpled, soiled napkins on the ground beside his paper dish. "I'm out of napkins."

"Here." She tossed some of hers in his lap. Gazing at the couples and families scattered around the bonfire, she smirked. "Looks like everyone's running out of napkins."

He eyed the ribs on her dish. "Aren't you eating those?"

Although her hunger had disappeared after

Lucian's passionate greeting when he'd picked her up for their date, Diana scowled. "Touch them and die."

His smile vanished; he leaned over. Closing her eyes, she shivered when his tongue slid over her chin. She parted her lips as he approached her mouth, but he veered away and licked her cheek. She opened her eyes to find Lucian wiping his mouth with a napkin.

"Best barbeque sauce I ever tasted. Oh, I missed a spot." He leaned over then licked and nibbled at her lips until she clenched her thighs together and slid her tongue into his mouth.

"Now can I eat your ribs?" he asked, nodding toward the one he'd already stolen from her plate.

Diana giggled and shoved him away. "Tease!"

"Having fun?"

"I haven't been on one of these midnight trail rides since I was a teen." She let out an exaggerated sigh. "Very popular date with the boys in my school. Stealing off into the woods for a kiss. Those were the days."

Lucian tossed the rib onto the dish and swept her into his arms. "I'm just going to have to wipe those memories right out of your mind."

"Oh, really? And how do you propose to do that?" Giggling as he carried her towards the line of trees on the edge of the clearing, she wrapped her arms around his neck.

In reply, Lucian began to nibble along her jaw. "I have my ways."

When they returned to the clearing, Diana tried to remember what had led them into the woods, but Lucian's kisses had been so mind-boggling she couldn't seem to remember much of anything accept his delicious lips.

*****

Later, as they made their way down the mountain, Lucian glanced over and watched Diana skillfully steer her horse with nothing but her knees. Her hands rested lightly on the saddle horn, the reins loosely draped over her thighs. She glanced over and, upon catching his perusal, smiled softly.

Every few seconds, Diana would lean over and talk to her horse in a lilting, hushed voice. Lucian watched in wonder when the horse would tilt its head closer to her mouth as if intently listening to every word.

They made their way around a bend. A wave of anger swept over his shoulders, raising the hairs on his neck and setting his senses on alert. He reached over and grabbed the reins of Diana's horse, drawing it closer to his.

He scanned the surrounding forest, searching for whoever watched, whoever dared intrude on his time with Diana.

Diana nudged her horse even closer to his and leaned over just as a rock flew out from a cluster of bushes on her right and struck her horse's flank. With an ear shattering whinny, the horse reared, tossed Diana from its back, then bolted down the trail.

Lucian reached her side a second after she hit the ground. He slid his hands beneath her and lifted her into his arms, all the while torn between his need to care for her and his desire to find whoever had thrown the rock. The anger he'd sensed moments earlier told him that this was no accident. "Are you alright?"

"I'm fine, Lucian. Someone threw a rock at my horse. I saw it right before it hit, but I didn't have time..." She wrapped her arms around his neck and rested her forehead on his cheek.

"You should see a doctor."

"Relax, big guy. I'm all right."

He glared into the shadows. "If I ever find out who did it—"

"It was probably just some teens fooling around."

He sent a silent threat into the shadows. "You could have broken your neck."

"I'm fine."

He lifted her onto his horse then easily leapt up behind her. Wrapping his arms around her waist, he let her warmth calm his pounding heart. When he'd seen her tumbling over her horse's back, terror had immobilized him. He tightened his hold, and rubbed his cheek against her satin curls.

Diana brought her hand up and caressed his cheek.

He kissed her temple. His reaction, his fear over losing her rattled him, left him oddly bereft.

She shifted, tilted her face, and offered the lips he'd grown to crave as much as her blood. When he only stared into her eyes, she nibbled, licked, and tortured his mouth. The passion of their kiss calmed his fear and anger. She tasted so sweet. Swinging her leg over, she shimmied until her hip pressed into his crotch.

He raised his lips a hairsbreadth away from hers and whispered, "Diana."

His hand slid out of her hair, over her shoulder,

down until it halted right above her breast. She rose up and arched her back. He loved the way she responded to his touch, the way she gave herself up to him. When his hand moved down her arm, she closed her eyes.

Touch me.

Hearing her soft plea, unable to deny her anything, he tugged her shirt from her shorts as he nibbled on her lips. "Tell me what you want, Diana," he asked, his voice so low he wondered if she heard it. "Tell me."

"I want...I want..." she stammered, blushing profusely, "I want you to touch me."

He grazed the skin of her stomach then cupped her breast over her shirt. Smiling against her lips, he asked, "Like this."

"No," she breathed.

"Unbutton your shirt for me, Diana," he demanded more gruffly than he'd intended.

Diana didn't seem to mind. If anything, her eyes darkened with desire as she raised trembling hands to her shirt. She hesitated, glanced in the direction of the others in their group. Lucian brought his horse to a halt.

"We're alone, goddess. Now bare those beautiful breasts to me." He held her gaze as he thumped her nipple with his knuckles.

She started to unbutton her shirt. Every button that slid free sent a surge of blood to his groin, amplifying his pain. Keeping his fangs in check had never been as hard as when she spread the sides and revealed her lace-clad breasts. A deft flick at the clasp, and her bra opened. Lucian slid his finger under one lace cup and peeled it away then proceeded to do the same to the other.

"God, Diana, your beautiful." He wanted to bare his fangs and roar with victory that she had been born for him, that no other could rival his mate.

He loved the way her breath hitched when his fingertips brushed over her breast as he explored every inch with the faintest touch. They tripped over her hard nipple, slid below and lifted her breast. She arched her back, all the encouragement he needed. Her cry when his mouth took possession and drew her nipple deep into its heat startled the horse into taking a few nervous steps. Lucian mentally calmed the beast as he delved into her mind and absorbed her reactions.

He knew when she felt his erection grow even harder, felt its heat burn into her hip. He knew the moment a void opened deep in her core and demanded he fill it. His teeth grazed her skin, bit down gently around her bud. Completely merged with her mind, he felt the tendrils of heat spiraling down to her swollen pussy. Wherever his body, his mouth, his hands touched her, her skin sizzled. Feeling her body's reaction and his at the same time heightened his desire and inflamed him more than he'd thought possible.

Weaving one hand through his hair, she held his head to her breast, while her other hand slid between them and tentatively touched the bulge in his jeans, traced the length of his cock.

Lucian groaned and lost the battle to control his fangs. She whimpered, a little fearfully he thought, when he grew larger beneath her hands.

Unwilling to frighten her for any reason, he released her nipple and trailed kisses up to her neck. He licked the vein that now throbbed in time with her heartbeat. She pressed her bare breasts into his shirt.

Take me, Lucian. Please, I want...I want...I need you. Take all of me. Make me yours. Please, Lucian, please. When he heard her thoughts, when she spoke to him in a way she thought he couldn't hear, once again he nearly rent the night with a roar that would surely have sent her screaming for help. He kissed the tiny cut on her neck that remained from their sojourn into the woods earlier. Slipping the tip of his fang into it, he absorbed the maelstrom of sensations that swept through her body as he tenderly drew her blood into his mouth. He shifted her until she straddled his lap. He wouldn't take her here, but he would please her. Grasping her hips as he supped on her neck, he ground her heat into his.

Lucian covered her mouth and muffled her screams when she climaxed with a violence that almost knocked them both out of the saddle.

When she came to her senses, he planted tiny kisses along her jaw as he re-clasped her bra and buttoned her shirt. Without a word he shifted her back into position, took up the reins, and nudged the horse into an easy trot down the path. They made their way around a bend and came upon her horse. Blood dripped from a scratch on his flank.

Lucian's heart felt like it exploded and ripped free of his chest. Someone was trying to kill Diana.

She leaned back against his chest.

He kissed the top of her head, breathed in the scent of jasmine and her arousal. Every muscle twitched to soar into the sky, find whoever had attacked his mate, and tear their throat out. Trapped by her ignorance of his powers, he drew her even closer into the protection of his embrace.

"Will I see you tomorrow?" Diana asked, tilting her face up to kiss his neck.

Would his absence save her? Leave her vulnerable? Was she safe during the day?

He heard a twig snap on his right and, jerking the reins to the left, shielded Diana with his body.

"Would you relax? You're acting like someone's out to get us."

He tore his eyes from the dark shadows and looked down into the shimmering dawn that always dwelt in Diana's eyes. Grasping her to him, he sent a silent plea to Mina, asking, begging her to offer a prayer to her angels for him. For Diana.

The feeling that someone watched their every move stayed with him the rest of the night.

Soaring over Diana's house, guarding her as she slept through the last few hours before dawn, he scanned the area for any mental or physical clue but came up empty. Few vampires could shield themselves from him. Only one could leave no clues of her presence.

Chapter Eight

Nearly a week after she'd met Lucian, Diana tilted her head back over the inner tube and gazed up at the multitude of stars blanketing the sable sky. The fingers of one of her hands skimmed the surface of the cool water while those of her other rested in Lucian's warm palm. The river shimmered, reflecting the sparkling lights above. Fireflies twinkled along the shore like faeries dancing in celebration of another hot summer night.

"Star light, star bright, first star I see tonight, wish I may, wish I might get the wish I wish tonight."

"That's three, Goddess. I thought you could only wish on the first star you saw." Lucian hooked his leg with hers.

"I made an agreement with the man on the moon when I was thirteen." She giggled. "He gives me two extra wishes for every, well, for every night I dance for him. I figure I have a few hundred wishes coming to me."

"You're blushing."

"I am not." She splashed some cool water on her burning cheeks.

"You're definitely blushing. I can see it."

Diana stared at his face then frowned. "No you can't. It's too dark, even with the moonlight."

Lucian rolled over onto his stomach, then reached out and hooked his arm around her tube before it could float away. "So tell me about this dance. It must be pretty special to warrant a wish."

"It's just a dance." She wondered how he'd react

if he knew she danced naked for wishes. When she shrugged, he laughed.

"What's so funny?"

"I just thought of the kind of dance I'd grant wishes for." He tugged on the edge of her tube, spinning her until her head was even with his. She hung her head back and stared up into eyes that never failed to entrance her.

"If I were the moon," he said, rising up on his elbows, "I'd want you naked while you danced, then I could touch every inch of your skin and bath you in my light."

He cradled her head in his hands and leaned down. Brushing her lips with his as he spoke, he added, "And when the sun rose and sent me back into hiding, I'd suffer every second of the day, knowing its rays now caressed my goddess."

Diana rose up and closed the minute gap between their mouths. No one had ever spoken to her like this. Like she was truly a goddess, an endearment he used in place of her name more and more often. Their lips met, tenderly embraced. The passion that coiled in her body whenever she so much as thought of him, unfurled. She raised her arms, wrapped them around his neck, and moaned until his lips parted and his tongue gave her what she craved. Over the past week, she'd grown addicted to his kisses, spent their time apart counting the minutes until he wrapped her in his arms and crushed her trembling lips with that miraculous mouth.

How could his kisses taste so sweet, gratify a need that bordered on pain? She nibbled at his lower lip then moaned when he slid it into her mouth. A rumble rose from his chest, sent her heart pounding when she sucked it in deeper. Every muscle clenched. She suddenly heard the animals, birds, and insects surrounding them, smelled the pine trees, wild flowers, and earth along the bank rushing past as the current picked up speed and seemed to hurl them down river.

His hands left her face, skimmed down her neck, over her shoulders, then cupped her breasts in a way she could only describe as possessive. She thought she heard him saying her name, chanting it reverently, knew it had to be her imagination since his lips never left hers. Liquid heat slid between her nether lips, so hot she expected it to sizzle as it slid into the cool water.

Silently she begged, pleaded and implored him to rip off the bathing suit that had suddenly become too coarse against her sensitized skin and make love to her out here beneath the gaze of her beloved moon.

Lucian wrenched free of her grasp, slid off his tube, and disappeared below the water.

Diana cursed and clenched her fists. Still moving with the current, she waited for him to surface. As long seconds passed with no sign of him, her nails dug into her palms. "Lucian!"

He shot up out of the water at least thirty feet away and let out a roar that sent the birds in the surrounding trees shooting into the sky. Although his roar and the sight of his black tee-shirt clinging to his chest enflamed her desire to the point where she too considered submerging into the river to extinguish the inferno engulfing her body, her stomach lurched. He sounded a little too much like a wild animal.

She watched him disappear beneath the surface and fought to contain the panic closing her throat. A second later, faster than anyone she knew could have swam such a distance, he shot out of the water a foot away from his tube.

"Will I ever see this dance?" he asked, as he swiftly caught up with his tube.

Still unsettled from his roar and the speed of his return, she closed her eyes. "Maybe, if you stay around long enough, I'll show you."

Lucian settled back into the tube. "Oh, I'm not going anywhere."

He sounded so sure. She wished she could feel the same way, should since her grandmother held no doubts that the man floating down the river beside her was indeed her soul mate. But ever since she discovered the truth about Luna and Colette, Diana found herself wondering about everyone she met. Especially those she only saw after the sun set.

She had yet to see Lucian during the day. His excuses always made sense but her doubts grew with each passing day. "I never knew they had midnight tubing. It's amazing how many things you've introduced me to. Midnight horse trails, all night fairs. Restaurants that serve six course dinners in the wee hours of the morning."

Holding her hand under the water, Lucian tugged and brought her tube closer to his. "You just have to know where to go. Are you enjoying this?"

"I'm loving it." Something soft bumped against her but. "It's a little scary, though, when you can't see what's under the water." She rolled onto her stomach, rested her cheek on the tube, and glanced over her arm at Lucian. He flung his head back, dunking his hair into the water then turned. His eyes met hers.

She drew in a sharp breath at the desire burning in his gaze. He always wanted her. Never hid his desire.

Never went further than foreplay. She yelped when something slid under her stomach.

"You have nothing to fear, Diana. I'm here."

He didn't say it in a boastful way or like a man flexing his muscles; he said it as calmly as if he were commenting on the weather.

"You know, there's bears up in them there hills," she mumbled with an exaggerated twang, "and they's mighty big."

"Not big enough to get past me." He rolled over, wrapped his arm across her back and brought her tube closer. "If you're really scared, we could always bring our tubes to that pond at your house."

Diana laughed at the lecherous look he cast her way. "Is this an elaborate plan to get me naked in the shower again?"

"I have a photographic memory." His voice grew deeper with every word. "I merely have to look at you to remember every detail of that night."

Heat enveloped her wherever his burning gaze alit; her legs, buttocks, back. She rolled onto her back needing to feel it travel over her breasts, down her bare stomach to the spot where the river rose up to cool the fire between her legs.

"Anyway, that bikini really doesn't leave much to the imagination. You're shivering. I told you to keep your cloths on."

Diana humphed.   "I'm shivering because I thought you drowned."

*****

Lucian glanced at the scratch on her neck. He'd sipped her blood each night over the past week, only enough to satisfy his hunger during the daylight hours and relieve the throbbing that seemed to annoy her more and more. If he continued, she would notice that the scratch never fully healed. He reached out and brushed his knuckles over it. "You've been at this again. That twitch is still bothering you?"

"It's not so bad. Well, most of the time."

He wondered how long it would take before she noticed that his presence aggravated her twitch until his mouth gently sucking on the open sore appeased her body's need to merge completely with his. No one had ever tampered with the timing of the bonding ritual. He and Diana were only a week into the first stage: one night merging their bodies and blood followed by a month of denial. He needed three more weeks.

As soon as he'd discovered that Diana was his soul mate, he'd gone to Tobias, requested, and received approval to pass minor amounts of blood to appease her. Luckily, for him, his elder had a knack for being vague. Lucian found a loophole and used it to rationalize sating his own hunger. Tobias, more likely than not, meant feeding the hunger that could destroy Diana's mind and body. While the pulsing vein in her neck annoyed her, it wouldn't harm her body or mind. But Tobias had only said to appease her, and sucking on her neck certainly seemed to do just that.

Lucian! His mother's enraged voice sliced through his thoughts.

Ignoring her, he pulled Diana's tube closer, lifted her out and, dragging her under the water, drowned himself in her kiss. His mother could wait. There were too many hours left to enjoy with Diana before dawn broke over the mountains. When he felt her hands slip into his pants and cup him, he decided he'd spend every second of every night with this goddess before giving her up to the damned sun.

As the weeks passed, his mother's voice summoning him became more and more insistent and rattled his thoughts.

*****

"I've been calling you for weeks. How dare you ignore me? I can't believe I had to resort to using this human gadget to speak to my own son."

Lucian gripped the phone. "You know I've been busy. I have to watch Diana constantly during the night hours, just in case she's helping her father."

"You've been out with that slut every night for a month and you still haven't decided what to do?"

Lucian winced and held the phone away from his ear. The distance prevented Olympia's angry voice from piercing his ears but did not stop her rage from slamming into his head. "I'm supposed to find Nostrum's weapon, aren't I?" he coolly asked.

"Yes, but you were only given a week. Let me send Diego. He's itching to get his hands on her."

"Send him and I'll return him to you with a broken neck. I have the elders' approval to take as long as I need, Mother. If you go behind my back or do anything to hinder me from uncovering more information, I swear, I will personally bring you before the elders for usurping their orders."

He strode into his kitchen and glanced out the window. Tonight Diana had plans that didn't include him, plans she'd refused to discuss. Jealousy had kept him awake all day. By the time the sun's last ray shining over the mountain ridge above his home had blinked out, he was already dressed and heading out the door. The thought of someone else kissing her lips, touching her body enraged him.

But what he couldn't handle, what nearly sent him over the edge was imagining someone else feeling her body quiver as she laughed at his jokes, someone else listening to her wish upon a star or speak to the moon as if it were her dearest friend, someone else wiping the tears she shed from some scene in a movie.

Someone else watching her eyes darken with desire.

The emptiness and despair that overwhelmed him when he so much as thought of never again sharing those times with her, shook him. The moment the UV sensors on his roof had chimed, he'd bolted out his door, slamming it so hard behind him the hinges had cracked. The sound of the phone ringing and the possibility that she'd changed her mind had sent him running back into the house like some lovesick fool.

When he'd heard his mother's voice, a new, more terrifying fear took root. Without him, Diana would be helpless against Olympia or any vampire she sent her way. All month Diana had survived accidents that could have turned deadly. "One more attempt on her life, mother, and you'll have to face me."

"Now, Lucian," his mother's voice took on the tone of a doting parent, "you know I would never do that."

He went to the front door, opened it, and stared out into the darkness, probing for some clue of Diana's whereabouts.

"You have to watch out for that witch, Lucian. Mark my words, she's the weapon! You're all the proof I need."

His mother's voice drew him away just as he imagined he caught Diana's scent on a breeze. He frowned at how strong it seemed, as if she were just over the ridge separating his home from Marek's.

"Me? What the hell are you talking about?" He raked his hand through his hair. He had to get off this phone. It no longer mattered where Diana had gone tonight, he had to find her. He hadn't tasted her blood the last few nights, his guilt over manipulating Tobias' words getting the best of him. His hunger drove him mad. Nothing soothed it except Diana kissing him, Diana wrapping him in her warmth, Diana relieving some of the pressure by feeding off the gash he opened in his mouth just before bringing it down to meet hers.

Just last night, he'd even chanced leaving before dusk to find her. Luckily, the sun's rays were too weak to do any harm. Drawing in a deep breath, he shook his head. Could she be so close? It didn't matter. Wherever she was, he'd soon find her. Nothing mattered but seeing her, feeling her. "I'm fine."

"Are you? Are you sure you're not delaying the punishment because she's worked her wicked spells on you? Are you sure she doesn't already have you so twisted that you'll follow her anywhere?"

Lucian's heart stilled. Anywhere?

His nostrils flared as another gentler breeze surrounded him with her scent. Slamming the door behind him, he set out to follow that scent *anywhere* it led until he found his mate.

*****

"Are the torches for me?" Diana asked Colette as she picked up the salad bowl from the picnic table.

Colette stopped clearing the table and gazed at the torches encircling the yard. Her eyes shone. "I always light them. Marek bought them. He bought the tree lights, too."

Diana gazed at the multitude of tiny white lights sparkling in the Weeping Cherry trees lining a wide path to the lake. "They're beautiful. Did Marek have a problem with his night vision?"

"Night vision?" Colette shot a worried look across the yard at her daughter.

Luna skimmed her feet along the ground, abruptly halting her swing, and stared intently into her mother's eyes. After a moment she shook her head. Another moment passed. Luna brought her finger up to her chest and drew an X.

Watching the scene between mother and child, Diana wondered if they somehow spoke to each other.

Colette turned her attention back to clearing the table, her brows furrowed, her hands shaking.

It had taken a month of weekly lessons for Diana

to convince Colette that she meant them no harm, that she would never reveal their secret. Each week, Colette had peered into the shadows and gripped the gate surrounding the corral. By the end of the lesson her knuckles would be white and a glistening sheen of sweat coated her skin.

Last night her fear had escalated when a group of ranch hands suddenly emerged from the saloon and started to run toward the corral, yelling. "We got two live ones!" "Whoa, Diana, don't let em go before we rope em in!"

Diana knew exactly what they were talking about, had even begun to laugh, but Colette's strangled cry cut her laughter short. "It's alright, Colette, calm down. They're only talking about tomorrow's charity fair." Fangs had slipped out between Colette's lips. Diana, praying the men were to far to notice, hissed, "Colette, please!"

She'd passed Luna over the gate to her mother then spun around and smiled brightly at the approaching men. "Hi, guys."

"Don't you let them go, Di. We gotta get them to buy some of these tickets." Jacob, the oldest hand on the ranch, waved a book of raffle tickets in the air. "Wouldn't want the tot to miss all the fun tomorrow."

"I already bought some for them." She glanced over her shoulder. "But I don't think Luna's going to be able to make it. I was just ending her lesson early because she feels like she has a fever."

Jacob leaned to the side and peered around Diana. "She don't look sick."

Diana cringed. The stench of rotten teeth and stale alcohol sent bile rising up her throat. "I'd step back, Jacob. Luna just said she felt nauseous."

Jacob leapt back a step. "Well, git her outta here! I don't want her vomitin all over the place!"

Luna screamed.

Diana spun around. Her eyes flew open in shock. A bee had managed to entangle itself in a lock of Luna's hair. Without a moment's hesitation, Diana lifted the hair away from Luna's chest and plucked the bee out.

Accepting the ensuing invitation hadn't been easy. She couldn't bear the thought of missing one moment with Lucian, much less one night. And just the previous night, she'd started an argument, demanding he find some time during the day for her.

She needed that more than he knew. A few hours during the day. A few hours in the sun.

Lucian hadn't taken the news that she had plans which didn't include him very well. And when she refused to tell him where she intended to spend their first night apart, he'd stalked off, cutting the night short.

And now, with one stupid question about Marek's night vision, she'd blown a perfect night. She followed Colette's rigid back into the kitchen.

She put the salad bowl in the sink, aware that Colette stood beside the table, a stack of dirty dishes still in her hands.

"How do you know about our night vision?"

"Doesn't everyone?" Diana pumped dish detergent onto a sponge.

"No, Diana. Most people don't know we exist. Most people would never believe in us even if a little girl showed them her fangs. Most people would figure she had fake ones and laugh it off. But you didn't. You knew they were real. Because you're not like most people, are you?"

"You bared your fangs, Colette. Remember?" Diana straightened from the hard edge of anger in Colette's voice. She couldn't bring herself to turn around.

Colette slammed the pile of dishes on the counter. "I'm talking about your father."

Diana gripped the edge of the counter. "My father? What do you know about my father?" Her voice cracked.

Colette leaned over and turned off the water with one fervent twist of the handles. "The question, Diana, is what do you know about your father and his pen? Where is it? Where's my husband's ashes?"

Diana slowly turned. She stared at Colette. Even though her tears blurred the woman's face, she saw the return of the mistrust, the fear. "I..." She blinked, felt her tears spill onto her cheeks, watched Colette's crimson ones spill onto hers. Diana swallowed the false denial. "I'm so sorry, Colette. I never believed it. How could I? He's my father!"

She took a tentative step forward.

Colette, a feared creature of the night, someone who could probably rip her to shreds without breaking a sweat, scurried back and swung a chair between them.

"Don't come any closer!"

Diana watched her scan the shadows of the room as if she expected someone to suddenly appear. "Oh, God, Colette, you can't think I'd —"

The screen door swung open.

"Wanna see my dolls, Di—"

"No!" Colette lunged toward Luna, knocking Diana across the room as if she were nothing more than a pesky fly. She grabbed Luna, spun her around, and shoved her towards the door. "Run, Luna!"

Diana slumped against the wall, the pain in the back of her head nothing compared to the knife twisting in her heart. "My mother lied to me. She lied to me then left me with him."

She stared blindly at her lap and let loose the grief she'd contained since she'd first discovered her father's insane tales were true and her mother's promises were false. And what of Lucian? Why would he only see her at night? Was he a vampire? Probably not. Which meant she could never trust him with her knowledge of Colette and Luna. She lifted her eyes.

Her heart felt like it cracked. Colette cradled Luna against her side, protecting her. As a mother would. As her mother should have. "I believed my mother. Even when I was old enough to know that my father was too normal to have delusions. I kept telling myself that my mother would never lie to me. But she did, didn't she? She even lied when she told me she loved me. My God, she left me, a little girl, with a man who killed vampires. A man who left me alone every night to hunt them!"

Diana angrily swiped away her tears. "You wouldn't do that, Colette. You'd protect Luna. You'd worry that the creatures your husband sought might go after your daughter for revenge."

When Luna moved to step away from her mother and toward Diana, Colette tightened her hold.

"So you had nothing to do with Marek's death?"

"Oh, God, no. I liked Marek. He was always so kind. If I had any idea what my father planned, if I believed his tales, I would have done something to stop him. You have to believe me." She watched Luna clutch the locket she'd given her and recalled what her mother had said when she'd given it to her. She'd told her the locket would keep the monsters away than had added, "Not that you'll need it. The monsters are more afraid of your father than you could ever be of them. They wouldn't dare touch Frank Nostrum's little girl."

She had raised fearful eyes to her mother and asked, "So there really are monsters, Mommy?"

Her mother had leaned over and kissed her. Diana remembered wondering why her mother was crying. "Sometimes people like your father can only see monsters because they can't get past the legends and the fangs, Diana. Sometimes the monsters are no different from you or me."

"Oh my God, she knew." Diana shook her head at Colette and Luna. "She wasn't telling me vampires didn't exist. She was telling me they weren't monsters. But I couldn't believe that. I never wanted to believe it, because if I did, then I had to accept that my father was no better than a murderer. H-he killed s-so many. I heard about every one. Even poor, sweet Marek. I'd just pat him on the back and tell him he was doing a great job. Oh, God, it's all my fault, isn't it. If I'd done something to stop him, Marek—" She clapped her hand over her mouth. Her stifled scream filled the kitchen. When she felt Luna's tiny hands grasp her cheeks, her scream evolved into a wail she couldn't seem to control.

Until the screen door once again flew open and slammed against the wall. Diana drew in a sharp breath.

Lucian stood in the doorway, his eyes darting back and forth, his hands clenched around a gun.

Diana jumped up and, after pushing Luna back into her mother's arms, stood in front of them. "What are you doing here?" Her voice shook.

She cared for Lucian more than any man she'd ever known, felt in her heart that they were soul mates, but couldn't live with the death of another vampire on her conscience. Colette and Luna, caught up in the escalating emotions of the evening, had twice revealed their fangs. "You can't just barge into someone's house swinging a gun around!"

"What?" Lucian raked a hand through his hair. "I'm a goddamned Champion! I hear a scream, I barge in. It's my damn job!"

The three females flinched when he slammed the door shut, his eyes still scanning the room.

"A Champion? What the hell is a Champion?" Diana narrowed her eyes and put her hands on her hips. "Why are you here?"

"I just told you, I heard a scream."

"No. Why are you even close enough to hear anything that's going on in this house?" She swiped at a wisp of hair that clung to her wet cheek. "Are you following me?"

"What?" Lucian took a step closer.

Diana puffed out her chest and reached behind her to gather Colette and Luna behind her back. "I told you I had plans tonight." Her voice shook with anger. "You're not one of those overbearing jealous nuts who follows their girlfriends around, are you?"

"Nut? Did you just call me a nut?" He shoved the gun in the back of his jeans.

Diana crossed her arms over her chest. "If you're following me, then, yes, I'm calling you a nut!"

"I am not the one screaming my head off as if someone's killing me for," he bellowed, waving his hands around the kitchen, "no apparent reason!"

"You're avoiding the question, wise guy. What are you even doing here?"

"I live nearby. Since I had no plans tonight," he said, raising one eyebrow, "I figured I'd take a walk along the lake. Now, will you please tell me what the hell happened?" Lucian traced a finger down her wet cheek, then reached over and tucked a stray curl behind her ear. "You've obviously been crying and that wasn't some randy raccoon I heard screaming."

His voice, filled with concern, and the touch of his fingers gliding down her cheek nearly undid her. Nearly. She longed to throw herself into his arms and pour her heart out but doubted Lucian would believe her father hunted vampires. And what if she told him the woman and little girl cowering behind her were real night creatures, that she would do anything to protect them? That she was screaming because her failure to stop her father had led to the death of a vampire she'd considered a gentle giant?

Oh, yeah. Lucian would understand. He'd understand as he called the men in white to come and take her away.

Of course, she had to consider the possibility that he might believe her. Then what? Would he call her father and enlist his aid in capturing Colette and Luna? Knowing the Lucian she'd grown to care about, she doubted it, but she couldn't take the chance.

"Well?" He leaned to the side then scowled when she shifted to block his view of Colette and Luna.

"I saw a, um, mouse."

Lucian's brows drew together. "You saw a mouse? Diana, you work at a ranch. You must see them all the time."

She flung her hands behind her back, held one of her fingers out, and mumbled. "It bit me."

"You screamed like that because a little mouse bit you?"

"It hurt!"

"Really? I'd better take a look at it then." His eyes narrowed.

She frantically wriggled her index finger, hoping Luna would see it and know what to do. "I'm fine."

"Let me see it, Diana. That is, if there is anything to see." He leaned his hip against the counter and crossed his arms.

"Are you calling me a liar? I'm telling you a mouse *bit* my finger." She felt Luna grasp her finger and gritted her teeth. The pain, though piercing enough to bring tears to her eyes, didn't last long. She brought her hand out and waved her finger in front of his face. "See?"

Lucian's pupils dilated. "You expect me to believe a mouse did this?"

Colette stepped out from behind Diana and looked at her finger. "Luna, go to your room!"

"But, Mommy!"

"It's really not that bad." Diana turned her bloody finger around.

"Not a word, young lady. To your room, now."

The gash across the pad of her finger spewed blood. Luna's fang had gone completely through, piercing the nail. Diana mutely watched as Lucian cursed and brought her finger to his mouth. Her stomach flipped as he licked both sides before grabbing a dishtowel draped over a chair and wrapping it around her hand. His tongue darted out and licked her blood from his lips.

"Lu—" Colette looked at Diana, Lucian, then back at Diana.

Then back at Lucian.

Just as she had when Luna and her mother had stared into each others eyes outside, Diana noted subtle changes in Colette and Lucian's expressions. As if they were having a discussion. A private, silent conversation. Her heart sank. Her eyes burned.

As they continued to ignore her, she searched for some way out, some way to avoid meeting his eyes.

"Diana, are you alright? You look so pale?" Colette's soft voice met her ears just as Diana's vision cleared enough to make out the names scrawled beneath a childish drawing on the refrigerator of two, tall stick figures.

"Diana?" Lucian took hold of her hand.

Tearing her eyes away from the drawing, Diana forced herself to look at the man who filled her every thought, every dream.

"Must have been a big mouse." She mumbled, wondering how wise it was to bleed so close to vampires. Her eyes widened when her blood seeped through the towel and started to drip onto the floor. "I don't feel so good."

*****

Scooping Diana up into his arms just as her legs gave out, Lucian watched her eyes flutter then close. "Why was she lying to me, Colette?"

Colette shook her head. "I think she was protecting us."

"From who?"

Colette simply stared at him.

"Me?" He shifted Diana so that her head rested on his shoulder. The vein in his neck nearly burst free from the skin separating it from her lips. Diana groaned. He carried her into the living room and laid her down on the couch. "That's ridiculous. Why would she think I'd hurt you or Luna?"

Colette lowered her eyes. "Because she knows."

Ice cold fingers wrapped around his heart. "So, she was protecting you from me." Although the idea that Diana thought he would sink his teeth into a helpless woman and child made him sick, he had to admire her bravery. He gazed down. She looked so pale. So frail. "Faints at the sight of blood, yet she stands up to a vampire to protect her friends."

Colette began to nod then jerked her head up. She swatted his slumped shoulders. "You big oaf. As far as Diana was concerned, she was only standing up to a man."

"But you just said she knows."

"About me and Luna. Not you."

Lucian felt the fingers around his heart release their grip, slip away. "That's why she screamed? She realized you were vampires?"

"No, no. She's known about us for a while."

"Before Marek?" The fingers returned, this time squeezing so hard he thought his heart would stop beating. "Then Olympia was right. She must have led her father to him."

"She found out after Marek died. Open you eyes, Lucian. She made it quite obvious tonight that she would never help her father."

He longed to believe that, but the safety of his niece and sister-in-law weighed heavy on his shoulders. "You shouldn't have invited her here. What if you're wrong? What if this was all an elaborate act?"

"We trust her." Colette brought her chin up. "As a matter of fact, we're all going into town to watch the fireworks." She glanced down. "Well, as soon as she comes to."

Lucian examined Diana's finger. His blood already mingling with hers and his saliva had worked its magic. The gaping wound had already sealed into a mere scratch.

Over the past three weeks his hunger had gnawed at him, weakening his willpower more each day until he thought he'd go mad. Blood surged through his veins, pooled in his eyes. Seeing Diana through a red haze terrified him. His fangs shot out. His nostrils flared; the smell of her blood permeated the room. He closed his eyes, clenched his fists, flung his head back and roared until his fangs receded with his hunger.

Drawing in a shaky breath, he glared at Colette's shocked face. "First we're going to get this covered and wake Diana. Then I'll go with you into town, just in case you're wrong."

"You still don't trust her. What does she have to do?"

"More than what could have been a very good act."

"Men are such fools." Colette shook her head as she went to get a band-aid. When she returned, she handed it to him and rumpled his head. "Well, not Marek. He trusted me the moment we met."

"Marek trusted everyone, Colette. That's the problem." He wrapped the bandage around Diana's finger.

"What was with the gun, Lucian?"

"I wasn't sure what the hell was going on in here. I felt her distress before I heard her scream and, well, I couldn't come in baring my fangs."

"I thought she was going to wrestle it out of your hand." Colette laughed softly. "When she accused you of stalking her, I thought I'd die."

"The little spitfire called me a nut." He ran his finger over Diana's lower lip. "I think I'm in big trouble here, Colette."

"Can I still go see the fireworks?"

Colette and Lucian turned. Luna peered out from the hall leading to her room. She glanced at Diana's prone body. Her chin scrunched up. "Did I kill, Diana?"

"What?" Lucian frowned.

Luna ran across the room, wrapped her arms around her mother's waist. "It wasn't my fault. She pulled her hand away before I let go."

"You bit her?" Lucian's eyes narrowed. "What

the hell is going on? Will someone tell me why she screamed?"

"No." Colette lifted her chin. "If Diana wants you to know, she'll tell you."

"Luna, you'll tell Uncle Lucian why Diana was crying, won't you?"

Luna glanced up at her mother then looked at him and shook her head.

He stalked them across the room, taking one long step forward for every two they took backwards.

Colette bared her fangs when they bumped against the wall. "Back off, Lucian. You're scaring Luna."

He gritted his teeth. "I will when you explain to me why my niece bit Diana."

"She told me to!" Luna held up her finger and wiggled it. "She wiggled her finger in front of my mouth right after she said a mouse bit her."

Diana moaned. Lucian leaned down and whispered into Luna's ear. "You'll tell me why Diana screamed, won't you, Luna Moona."

"No." When he continued to stare into her eyes, Luna gasped. "Stop it. Daddy said it's really, really rude to sneak a peak into someone's head."

"Lucian, you didn't!" Colette lifted Luna into her arms. "I can't believe this is you."

"Well, what do you expect, Colette? I have to protect you and Luna. I—"

"And Diana," Luna said, twisting around in her mother's arms. She pointed a finger at him and wagged it in front of his face. "You have to protect her for me, Uncle Lucian."

Lucian hooked Luna's chin. "I do?"

"She gave me the locket her mommy gave her. It protected her from monsters, but she gave it to me. Then I got scared cause now she has nothing to keep her safe. So I'm giving her you."

"Me?"

"Grandpa said I could. He said you would take care of her for me. He pinky promised!"

Lucian cleared his throat. "Grandpa Tobias?"

When Luna nodded, he lifted the locket.

How many times had he seen Diana reach for something on her chest, seen her sigh when her hand came away empty? He slid his nail into the side of the heart and opened it. The tiny picture of a young woman kissing the cheek of a baby sent a lump to his throat.

"Still don't trust her, Lucian? She gave that to Luna the day she found out what we were." Colette whispered. "That very day. I bet that was her most precious possession."

He snapped the two sides of the heart back together, felt it slide through his fingers. Luna's small hand wrapped around it, clutching it as he imagined Diana had a thousand times since her mother had given it to her. "Don't worry, Luna. I won't let anything happen to Diana."

"Promise, Uncle Lucian? Cross your heart and hope to fry?"

"Cross my heart and hope to fry. And no calling me Uncle tonight." After Luna nodded solemnly, Lucian returned to the couch.

"Diana." He leaned over and brushed his lips over hers. His heart swelled. "Come on, Goddess, open your eyes."

He never expected her to bolt upright just as he leaned down to once again whisper in her ear.

Chapter Nine

Strolling beside Diana, Colette licked the ice cream dripping down the side of her cone. "You two look hysterical."

"Thanks a lot," Diana and Lucian said in unison.

Lucian glanced at Diana. She hadn't said much since coming to back at Colette's. He hadn't been able to get close enough to talk to her privately. For some insane reason, Colette and Luna acted like they had to protect her from him.

"I think Lucian's bump looks funnier than Diana's, don't you, Mommy?" Luna popped a piece of caramelized corn in her mouth. "His is all red and lumpy."

Colette giggled. "Oh, Luna, I think you're making him blush!"

Lucian came to such an abrupt halt that Colette, Luna, and Diana continued on a few more feet before realizing he was no longer with them. When they turned, he crossed his arms and glared at their surprised faces.

"I believe I'm red from anger, ladies. I've been the brunt of your jokes about my bump for the entire ride here, during the fireworks, and that ridiculous tour through Alien Attack." He reached up and tenderly touched the lump above his brow.

"I think it's cute." Diana walked up. Her fingers slid around his neck and pulled his head down.

He closed his eyes, needing her kiss. Just before she awoke at Colette's and slammed her forehead into his, he'd come to a frightening realization. Sometime during the last month, he had fallen in love with Diana Nostrum. Sometime during the last month, she became his life's essence.

Her lips pressed gently onto the bump. Not what he'd wanted, but he felt his anger at the three females dissolve.

He opened his eyes. They stared at his forehead then burst out laughing. He spread his hands out. "It's just a bump, for Chrissakes!"

Tourists ambling up and down the sidewalk turned to peer at him. Some giggled; some merely shook their heads and moved on. Diana, Luna, and Colette clung to each other as their laughter grew more and more out of control. Tears rolled down Colette's face.

Lucian's heart ached. For the first time since his stepbrother's death, Colette was having fun—smiling, laughing, crying tears that had nothing to do with grief.

He watched Diana whisper something into Colette's ear, wondered what she could have suggested to make his sister-in-law emphatically shake her head. His mouth dropped when Colette stifled a hiccup, ran up, and kissed his bump. He watched Diana's eyes grow wide.

"What?" Lucian frowned, grasping just what the love of his life and his sister-in-law had done.

He strolled over to the Frankenstein in front of the House of Wax. "Hey, Frank," Lucian grinned into the green face. He winked at the vampire beneath the costume. "Do you find anything funny about my bump?"

Frankenstein shook his head then doubled over

and slapped his leg.

Luna squealed. "You got lips. Pink and red lips on your bump."

"Traitor!" Diana yelled, wrapping her arms around the little girl before she could run away. "Now, you must be tickled until you pee pee in your panties."

"No, don't." Luna gleefully wriggled free and clutched her crotch. "I've been holding it in all night."

"Oh, Luna." Colette grasped her hand and quickly led her across the street.

While Colette took Luna into the public restroom, Diana and Lucian waited on a nearby bench. Lucian stretched his legs out in front of him and crossed them at the ankle. Diana lifted his arm, draped it over her shoulder and snuggled against his side. Her warm breath flowed over his neck as she peered up at him. By now her finger had healed completely, but her blood remained on the bandage, and when she brought her hand up to his cheek, the hunger he'd denied much longer then he should have, reared its ugly head.

The stench from the bathroom mingled with the odors rising from the dumpsters behind the nearby restaurants and bars. The incessant chatter of the people milling in the nightclubs, restaurants, and attractions coupled with the pounding bass of the various radios, bands and DJ booths assaulted his ears. The simplest breeze pelted his skin like a thousand grains of sand. His hunger devoured him, weakened his power to control the overload of sensations surrounding him. His stomach roiled. He drew in a deep breath and held it until his lungs burned.

Diana's hand grabbed the front of his shirt. "Stop that. You're scaring me."

Her voice accomplished what he with all his powers and strength could not; calmed the beast that would have driven him to sink his teeth into her flesh. He brought his forehead down to hers. "By holding my breath?"

"You held it too long." She tilted her head up until the tips of their noses touched.

Lucian chuckled. "Scared I'll pass out? Bump my head?"

Diana blushed and rested her cheek on his chest. "You have lipstick on your forehead."

He kissed the top of her head. "I know."

"I thought so. Thanks."

"For what?" He shifted so he could see her face.

Diana's eye welled. "For bringing a little light into their lives."

He chucked her under the chin. *She'd* set their dark world aglow. They spent their entire existence avoiding the sun's dreaded rays, yet they basked in the warmth of the light that seemed to follow Diana wherever she went. "You did that, Goddess. Not me."

She leaned over and kissed his neck then took a tissue from her purse and tenderly wiped away the lipstick.

He recalled his mother's warning that if he fell under Diana's spell, she'd introduce him to the sun and a pain he could never imagine. Well, he'd definitely fallen under her spell, and she had become his sunshine, his light in the dark. And the mere thought of losing her when he revealed what he was, what he'd done that night in her bedroom pained him more than if someone thrust a red-hot poker into his heart.

He had no doubt that sometime in the near future, he would lose Diana.

What could he possibly offer her to convince her to accept eternal darkness by his side? A life devoid of sunshine? Children doomed to spend their days abed, keeping one foot on the floor even as they slept in case some misguided fool tried to plunge a stake through their hearts? Teens who were virtual slaves of their community until they could control the erratic behavior of their adult fangs?

His eyes burned. Diana loved the stars peeking through the ebony blanket covering the night sky, the pools of moonlight floating across lake, the fireflies arising from the grass and bushes, calling them the fairies of the night.

But she also loved the heat of the sun on her bare flesh, how bright the colors of flowers looked in the middle of the day, and recounted with glee each and every time she caught sight of a hummingbird hovering over a bloom as it drank the sweet nectar.

Because of his carelessness she soon would have to bid farewell to the sun and enter a life where one year of darkness would only age her one day. She could spend the endless nights by his side as his mate or alone. Either way, now that she'd tasted his blood, there was no turning back. Diana either completed the bonding ritual with him or joined the Slashers on Fentmore Island. Even if she accepted him, even if she grew to love him enough to want to be his mate, he had no doubt that once she discovered what had transpired the night he, Diego, and Tomas had entered her bedroom, once she grasped why they had been there, she would want nothing more to do with him.

"What's wrong, Lucian?"

He gazed down at her concerned face. "Hmmm?"

"You look like you just lost your best friend." Diana pressed her body into his side.

"You've captured me, you know.   And I'm terrified by the thought of you setting me free."   He shrugged, embarrassed that he'd spoken aloud the fears he'd only just discovered. "Let's walk by the lake while we wait."

*****

When they reached the lake, Diana stared up into his face. Her hand trembled as she slid it up his chest. She'd wondered about his absence during the day long before tonight.

She'd seen the way his eyes had dilated exactly like Colette and Luna's when he'd seen her finger, the way his tongue had wrapped around it and drawn her blood into his mouth for a second before he'd removed it.   And she'd seen the drawing with Lucian's name.   They'd all assumed she'd fainted from the sight of the blood, but Diana knew the growing evidence pointing toward the possibility that Lucian might be a vampire had been too much for her to handle.

When she awoke to find him gazing down at her, his heart in his eyes, she made a decision she hoped she wouldn't regret. She knew, vampire or not, she couldn't just turn her back on him. Not because her grandmother considered him her soul mate or because her body recognized him as such.

Lucian had worked his way into her heart. If she was right, if he was indeed a vampire, then she had to give him the opportunity to reveal himself, had to convince him that he could trust her with his secret. What choice did she have?

Somehow, Lucian had become the very air she breathed.

She longed for his touch more now than ever before. Flattening her palm on his chest she felt his heartbeat flow into her, merge with her own, and set it on fire. How could she walk away without ever knowing what it felt like to make love to the one man who could awaken her body with a mere glance? She had to take this further, had to let the bud of love lodged in her heart bloom before she made any decision.

Colette and Luna emerged from the bathroom and joined them. Colette looked at Diana and Lucian then turned to Luna. "I think it's time we went home."

"But I wanted more caramel corn and cotton candy." Luna crossed her arms and stuck out a perfect pout.

Diana yawned. "Sorry, sweetie, but I'm pooped."

Later, when she and Lucian returned to the car after they had made sure that Colette and Luna were safely in their house, Diana turned to Lucian and calmly asked, "Can vampires go out during the day if it's cloudy?"

Lucian, in the midst of backing out of the driveway, nearly slammed into the white picket fence he'd helped Marek put up only last year. "Vampires?"

Diana brought her hand to his cheek. He was so beautiful it took her breath away. "Yes, Lucian, vampires. I know you know about Colette and Luna."

"Well," he hesitated, threw the car into park then shifted to face her. "If there are scattered clouds, no. But there are times when the clouds are dense and completely blanket the sky. On those days...I'm told...vampires can come out."

She smiled. "Tomorrow, you're calling in sick and taking me on a picnic."

Lucian's jaw dropped. "Excuse me?"

"It's supposed to rain. I love picnics in the rain. Take me home, Lucian."

"You're awfully bossy, all of a sudden."

"You want bossy? Okay. Tomorrow, we're going to have a picnic in the rain. Then, I'll go home. At exactly, hmmm, eight, you're going to pick me up and take me to your house."

"My house?" Lucian pulled up to the curb in front of Diana's house.

"Yes, so you'd better clean up the place."

He smirked. "You got that right. Anything else, boss?"

Diana slid over and brought her lips to his ear. "You're going to make love to me, Lucian." She pressed her breasts into his arm, felt his muscles harden. "I've been waiting a whole month for you to make a move, now I'm taking charge. And, Lucian?"

He opened his mouth, then simply nodded.

She slid her hand down over his stomach, over the waistband of his jeans then cupped the hard ridge rising up alongside the zipper. "You're really big and, hmmm, how can I put this? You'll be my first, which means I'll be real tight."

"You're killing me, you know that?"

"Well, I just figured that once you felt how very tight I am, you might feel the need to be extra gentle."

"I will."

"But you won't."

His eyes dilated. "I won't?" he asked, his voice huskier than she'd ever heard it.

"Don't go wild on me," she whispered, then ran her tongue along his lower lip, "but, don't be too gentle either."

"I won't hurt you."

"I know. Now, kiss me goodnight."

Lucian drew her onto his lap.

Diana moaned. Linking her arms around his neck, she brought her lips to his. She felt his fingers dig into her hips as his mouth crushed hers. His tongue slid past her lips and took possession of her senses. Enflamed, she ground herself onto his cock and greedily sucked his tongue deeper into her mouth.

Suddenly she was standing on the sidewalk on wobbly legs watching Lucian close the car door. "Lucian? How..."

He smiled, his lips drawn between his teeth. "Rain, huh? What time do you want me to pick you up for the picnic?"

*****

The weatherman erred, and Diana found she was neither surprised nor frightened when Lucian called to say he couldn't see her until dusk. She spent the day wondering if she was right or if her revelation that vampires really did exist had clouded her judgment where he was concerned.

Plenty of people were too busy to socialize during the day. She should be grateful that he took his job so seriously. And how many mothers suck the blood from their children's cut fingers? Plenty. And he'd said he lived near Colette and Luna. That would explain his name on Luna's picture. Plenty of kids called neighbors and friends of the family uncle. Plenty.

She spent her day waiting for sunset, waiting for Lucian, and convincing herself she had jumped to a ridiculous conclusion.

The day dragged on. Just when she thought she would smash all the clocks in her house, it was time to get ready. After pouring herself a glass of wine, she slid into a lavender scented bath. Candles rested on every available surface. She ran the fat soapy loofa up her leg and grinned. Her body trembled with need. With her heart more involved than it would have been a month ago, she longed to offer him what she'd worked so hard to keep over the years. She only hoped he'd believe he was her first after he entered her and found nothing barring his way.

An hour past dusk, she sat clutching the phone and staring bleakly at her reflection in the mirror above her vanity. Her make-up couldn't be more perfect. The sun dress she'd bought that afternoon flattered her figure.   Two thin straps tied at her shoulders were the only things holding it up, and she'd imagined in the store how it would feel sliding over her bare breasts when Lucian untied them, imagined his eyes when he beheld her sheer pink thong. High heeled shoes with a satin ribbon that tied around her ankle created the picture of innocence and sensuality she'd been striving for.

But Lucian never came.

The doorbell rang, but it was her father.

The phone rang, but it was Terry asking her to go to the movies.

A car pulled up, but it was her neighbor's date.

And now it was ten and she was all dressed up with nowhere to go.

The phone rang again. "Please, God, let it be him," she prayed as she picked up the receiver. She kept her voice calm. "Hello?"

"Oh, Diana. Thank God you're home."

Diana gripped the phone.   "What's wrong, Stan?"

"It's Midnight. He got out again and I can't get him to come in."

Diana's chin dropped down to her chest. "Don't worry, Stan. I'll be right over."

"I'm sorry, Diana."

"That's okay.   I have nothing else to do." Grabbing her coat, she cursed herself for bringing up vampires to Lucian. He probably marked her off as a nut and had gone out with someone else.

Lucian glanced at his watch and cursed. The sun had set later than usual, then, just as he was about to leave, Diego had arrived and insisted on speaking with him. After divulging that Olympia knew Diana and Lucian were soul mates from the beginning, Diego begged Lucian to help him find somewhere safe from Olympia's wrath. Unable to ignore the terror in Diego's eyes and saddened by way his scarred cheekbones had marred his looks, Lucian had wasted another hour setting him up in Albany.

When he finally approached Diana's house, the site of her father sitting on the steps of the porch forced him to park further down the street. He crept up to their house, his eyes focused on Frank Nostrum. The man leaned back, puffing on a cigar as he talked on the phone.

Rage consumed Lucian. He hid behind a tree. Listened.

"Sure, Diana's got it all under control. Hey, if anyone can coax him in, Diana can. When she talks the talk, they'll follow her anywhere. Stan, relax. The dumb animals can't resist her."

Lucian felt his lungs seize. He slumped against the trunk, gazed up through the leaves at the stars, the gift he'd planned on surprising her with if she chose him tonight.

"My mother says it's her inner voice that speaks to them. They trust her. Yeah, he'll come in. Rain tomorrow? Nah, the sky's clear. Either way, he'll be in the pen long before dawn."

Lucian pushed himself away from the tree with trembling hands. Turning, he ran faster than he had ever run—not from the web Diana had supposedly spun to entrap him, not from a weapon more dangerous than any his kind had imagined—he ran from the truth, refusing to accept that the woman he'd fallen in love with and the woman the vampire hunter described were the same.

At first he drove around aimlessly, wondering how he could ever return to the life he led before Diana. Eventually, he found himself standing in Colette's backyard while Luna held a tea party with her dolls on the lawn.

"Luna. Uncle Lucian wants to ask you something."

Luna glanced up, a tea cup of water poised at her lips.

Lucian cleared his throat. He swallowed the lump lodged there since he left Diana's house. "Has Diana ever spoken to you, well, like we do? Just with her mind?"

"What a silly question." Luna giggled and sipped at her tea. "Wanna join my tea party?"

"Luna, answer Uncle Lucian." Colette reached out to grasp Lucian's hand. "He's serious."

Luna rolled onto her back and burst into a new fit of giggles.

Colette sat on a bench and covered her mouth, trying to hide her own laughter.

"Laugh all you want, but I just heard her father say she could lure them into the pen because she talks the talk," he muttered, plopping down onto the bench. He flung his head back and gazed up at the moon. "Talks the talk. Damnit, Colette, you know what that means."

"Yes, I do. The men at the ranch told me the horses follow her back into the pen every time they escape because she talks the talk. The horses trust her."   Colette smiled down at Luna.   "She's a horse whisperer. Right, Luna?"

"Yup.   Diana said she always gets called by Stan—you know, Mommy, Old Jake—well, he calls her whenever a horse gets out. Cause she talks the talk." Luna glanced down at her locket. "The horses know she'll help them."

Lucian recalled how on the Midnight Trail Diana had continually whispered in her horse's ear, how it had tilted its head as if intently listening. Running his hands through his hair, he shook his head and grinned. "I'm such a fool."

Colette patted his knee. "We're all fools when we fall in love, Lucian. We constantly worry that our heart will be broken. Try to trust her. Especially tonight."

He planted a huge kiss on each of their cheeks before rushing out to his car. The ritual would begin much later than he'd hoped, but it would begin. He only hoped he'd be able to stop grinning by the time he saw Diana.

And hurry, Lucian, Colette called as he drove away. *Damien and the elders are already waiting at the ritual grounds.*

Hating that the elders would bear witness to their bonding, Lucian slammed his palm on the steering wheel and wished he were human.

He found her a half hour later. He had no idea how he would seduce her if his late arrival had set up a wall of mistrust around her heart, but he had to succeed.

*****

"Cheer up, Di. He was probably some married

guy looking for a quickie." Terry draped her arm
over Diana's slumped shoulders and steered her into
the mall. "Let's go check out the hot new manager at
the Multiplex."

"No. Something must have happened. He
would have at least called. Maybe I should check at
the hospital."

Come to me.

Diana glanced over her shoulder and watched
the glass doors they had just walked through slowly
close. Her heart lurched. No one had come in behind
them.

Come to me.

She turned her head and stared the other way
toward the doors to the east parking lot. The familiar
cacophony of butterflies that always warned of
Lucian's arrival took up residence in her chest. She
started to walk toward the doors, her steps speeding
up as the heat coiling tightly between her legs grew
more and more intense.

"Di? Where are you going? Di!" Terry grabbed
her arm.

Diana glared at her and yanked her arm away.
"Let go."

Terry gasped. "Great, you broke a nail. I just
had them done, too."

"Oh, God, I'm so sorry, Terry." Her eyes darted
between her friend and the dark exit.

"Shit, Di. What's gotten into you? You know the
east lot is virtually empty at night. You do not want
to go out there."

"Didn't you hear him? Lucian. I have to go,
Terry," she whispered, "Don't tell anyone I left. He's

waiting for me.

"I didn't hear anything." Terry's eyes focused on the darkness beyond the glass. "Look, I don't like this, not one bit. You sure that's him?"

Diana could barely hear over the pounding of her heart. "I have to go to him, Terry. I'm so hot for him I can barely wait."

"You mean you're finally going to do it? With this Lucian guy?" Terry stared at her a moment then held up her hand. "No, don't tell me. If this turns into an all-nighter, the less I know, the less I can tell."

"Promise me, Terry, if anybody asks, I spent the night at your apartment. Better yet, leave your phone off the hook."

*****

Lucian watched Diana turn away from her friend. Before taking a step in his direction, she wrung her hands. Her pounding heart resounded in his head. Lines of worry furrowed her brow. And still, she came to him.

His soul mate, the most beautiful creature he'd ever seen, strode toward him in a wisp of a dress that clung to her every curve. Closing his eyes, he saw her without that dress, saw her dancing in the moonlight for wishes, for stars. He longed to kiss her full lips, skim his teeth along her slender neck.

Last night, he had nearly lost control each time her lips rose to his, each time she had moaned and pressed her softness against his cock.

Peering through the glass, he could see her steps falter than stop. She raised her wrist and glanced at her watch. He'd wasted too much time already, had no time to deal with her anger, and reluctantly used his power to pluck it from her mind. Merging their minds, he compelled her to join him.

When Diana came through the doors, he stepped out of the shadows and silently called to her.

She turned and smiled. As he took a step closer, the light from inside the mall lit his face. Her hand trembled as it rose to her neck. She glanced back at the doors.

"I...last night..." Eyes filled with fear met his.

Don't fear me, Diana. I will never hurt you. Never.

She tilted her head. "Did you say something?"

He didn't answer, merely held out his hand. Diana stared at it. "Where are we going?"

Lucian smiled. He knew exactly what she expected from this night. What she'd expected every night. What he, up till now, had withheld.

He doubted she'd come with him if he told her where he intended to take her; doubted, after the incident with the worms, that unless she were overpowered by her passion she'd willingly lie naked with him upon the sacred ground.

But tonight he couldn't take her, couldn't compel her to leave with him. Tonight she had to come willingly. They could not leave until she placed her hand in his.

She crossed her arms under her breasts and glared at him. "You don't bother to call and let me know that you're going to be late and now I'm supposed to just go off with you? Maybe I was wrong about you. Maybe I don't know you as well as I thought I did."

His eyes fell to her chest and the small bumps from her erect nipples. He had to have her tonight, couldn't waste anymore time. Reluctantly, he blocked every thought in her mind except the desire he could smell racing through her veins. The more aroused he became, the more the blood she'd taken in boiled in response, inciting her to once again merge the two.

She fought back with a mental shove that nearly succeeded in releasing her from his hold. He grinned, proud that she did not give in so easily. But the night was short and, unfortunately, he did not have the time to give her what he knew she needed, time to be sure that he should be her first.

I will win you know. He grinned smugly.

Diana's eyes opened wide. Her hand rose to grasp the locket that now hung from Luna's neck.

He took a step closer.

Stop right there, buster!

He obeyed with a bow.

"You heard me," she whispered, awe filling her voice. Her cheeks flushed. "You've heard me all along."

He chuckled and ran his knuckles down both sides of her neck, down over the swells of her heaving breasts. He stopped just short of touching her nipples. "Our souls were once one, Goddess. We do not need words to know what the other desires."

He felt Diana's valiant battle for control, but her mind welcomed his touch, her body craved it. "You know? About us being soul mates?"

"Don't you?"

They stared into each others eyes.

Submerged in her mind, Lucian was shocked by the extent of her arousal. All of her nerve endings converged beneath his hands, waiting for them to continue. Her nipples throbbed painfully as they tightened. Her clit pulsed, her inner muscles tensed, and her body wept.

A cloud passed over the moon, casting them in darkness. A cool breeze lifted the wisps of her curls. Diana shivered. Without a thought, he warmed the air surrounding them.

"One night," she murmured and reached out until her fingers left the cocoon of warmth, "by the lake. The air around me grew warm. And other nights...a warm breeze..." Her fingers trembled as she raised her hands to his face. "You?"

Unable to speak, fearing her reaction, he nodded, inched his knuckles lower, closer to where she longed to feel their touch.

"The breeze," she breathed, and glanced down at his hands resting on her breasts.

Still unable to voice his confession, he whispered into her mind. *Your breeze, Goddess. Your phantom.* Merging their memories of that first week, he watched her expression soften then flush. *And tonight...your lover.*

Blinking, Diana whimpered, "I'm dreaming aren't I? You're...I...I can't handle this."

"Say the word and I'll leave and never bother you again, Diana. Or take my hand, take me."

He thumped his knuckles, one by one, over her sensitive nipples. She swayed then grabbed his hand.

Before she could change her mind, before her hand could slide free and change the course of the night, Lucian moved. He brought his mouth down upon hers. Opening up a small nick on the inside of the corner of his mouth, he gathered a few droplets of blood onto his tongue. When her lips opened beneath his assault, his tongue and life's essence delved in.

Still kissing her, he lifted her into his arms and took to the sky. Soaring over the treetops, he headed to the clearing where the elders waited.

Look up at the stars, Diana. Make a thousand wishes, my goddess, and I'll grant each and every one.

She tore her mouth from his. Instead of looking up at the sky, she gazed into his eyes. Blessed him with another glimpse of the dawn that dwelt in hers. Doubts and fears he'd harbored since meeting her turned to ash beneath the radiance of her gaze.

Wind lifted her hair as they descended. This time, shielded by the silken curtain of her hair, she brought her lips to his. Heedless of the late hour, of the elders waiting below, Lucian slowed their descent and lost himself in their kiss.

When their feet touched the blanket of grass in the clearing, he ended the kiss.

Backing away, he started to unbutton his jeans.

Looking dazed, she silently watched him remove his clothes. Still merged, he saw himself through her eyes, followed the path of her gaze. She took in the muscles on his arms and legs. Her eyes widened as they focused on the curls at the base of his cock. Her tongue darted out to moisten her lips. His cock jerked, grew longer then he thought it ever had. Blinking, she sent her gaze back up the length of his torso.

"Your tattoo." She gasped. A smile swept across her face, lit her eyes.

Touching the black raven tattooed across his chest, he grinned. "I take it you like tattoos?"

"My grandmother said my soul mate would have one. A raven, just like yours." Reaching out she ran her fingers over the tattoo. Over his heart.

The feel of her fingers burning a path across his skin never failed to amaze him. Tonight he would feel her searing touch over his entire body. Hissing from her fingertips grazing over his nipple, he stepped back. "Tonight, I please you."

Compelling her to remain where she was, he walked to the edge of the clearing and sat with his back against a tree. As he bent one leg, he nonchalantly rested his arm on his knee.

Proving that his blood strengthened her, as he knew it would, she followed. Lucian burned with desire as he watched her approach. When only a few feet separated them, he remembered that they were not alone. That the elders surrounded them as witnesses. They would remain until his union with Diana was consummated, until she offered her body and blood up to him.

"Undress for me, Diana. Let the greedy creatures of the night dwell upon your beauty. Show them that you are giving yourself to me of your own free will."

Diana peered into the shadows surrounding them. She jumped back when an owl hooted from a nearby tree. After a few agonizing moments, she met his gaze and untied the straps holding up her dress. As the dress slithered down her body, the collective gasp of the elders set his blood boiling. Still holding his gaze, she untied the sides of her thong. Completely exposed, her eyes once again darted to the shadows.

"You're beautiful, Diana. Any goddess would envy you."

"I'm afraid I'll wake up and realize this was just another dream."

Taking her hands, he pulled her down onto his lap, turning her so his body shielded hers from the elders. He wanted to spread her legs and taste her sweet juices mixed with the essence of her life as he had that night in her bedroom, but he refused to expose her to the elders anymore than was necessary.

Sliding his hand down her belly to her silken curls, he spared a moment enjoying the pleasure of their touch upon his skin before delving further down. He caressed her swollen lips, spreading her moisture over them while his tongue imitated his movements on her mouth. When a warm drop landed on his thigh, he gave her what she had been silently begging for and plunged his fingers into her moist heat. Her guttural moan sent a jolt of exquisite pain to his already engorged cock.

Diana spread her legs wider and wider, covered his hand with both of hers and pushed his fingers deeper. With a growl, Lucian took possession of her mouth and merged their minds. Her cries filled his head. The slick muscles surrounding his fingers convulsed as she shattered in his arms.

Standing, supping on lips he dreamt of every day, he carried her to the center of the clearing. He laid her upon the damp ground, compelled her to feel the touch of satin. Opening her eyes when his lips released hers, she reached out.

And screamed.

Through her eyes, Lucian saw himself kneeling

between her legs, his blood red eyes fixed on her terrified face. His fangs, so damned long from wanting her, so damned sharp. His heart shattered when she continued to scream and scrambled back. Tears filled her eyes.

"Diana, please..." Lucian inched closer, realizing too late that moving forward on his hands and knees made him look even more animalistic, more dangerous.

"Oh, no, no, no." She squeezed her eyes shut. "Oh, Lucian, no." She hugged her knees and began to rock back and forth.

Consumed with grief over her loss, he rent the night with a roar that ripped free of his throat, seemed to shred the flesh. The pain was nothing compared to the pain of her rejection.

With a yelp, Diana covered her ears.

An argument amongst the elders filtered into Lucian's mind a moment before he felt them open his mind and heart to Diana. Shocked by their intrusion, he watched her face as his emotions crashed down upon her head. She winced when she felt the pain of her rejection. Exposed to his torment over his existence as a night creature, she buried her face in her knees.

"Do you want me to take you home?"

When she shook her head, he silently thanked the elders. "If it meant winning your heart, I'd sell my soul to be a normal man."

"A normal man with no soul?" Raising her head, she peered out from her lashes. Her lips turned up into a sad smile. "Not very appealing."

Smiling back, he bared his fangs. "This is

better?"

Diana laughed on a stray sob. "I don't seem to have a choice."

"Yes, you do, Diana. You can leave."

She held out her hand. "No... I can't."

He crept up to her, lowered his head and rested his cheek in her warm palm.

"Will you drink my blood, Lucian?" Her voice quivered.

He closed his eyes. "Exchanging blood is inseparable from our passion."

"Is one bite enough to change someone into a vampire?"

Lucian stilled. Lifting his head, he steeled himself for her reaction to the fact that it was too late, that she'd already started to change. "Diana, I—"

"Will it hurt?"

Closing the gap between them, he ran the pad of his thumb over her trembling lips. "When you scream, Diana, it will be from infinite pleasure. Not pain. You have my word."

Her gaze flicked between his teeth and eyes. She brought the tip of her finger up to touch one of his fangs. The point pierced her skin.

"It doesn't hurt," she murmured, staring at the drop of blood rising on her fingertip.

While holding his gaze, she ran the tip of her tongue over the small hole, entrancing him.

She reached up, wrapped her arms around his neck, and brought him with her as she laid back down. "I want you, Lucian. Man or vampire."

His heart felt as if it would burst free. Resting his forehead upon hers, he drew in a shaky breath. "I feared..." He brushed the tip of his tongue over her lips, rose up to gaze into her eyes. "Never have I been so afraid."

Her eyes filled with horror as he bit down on his lower lip. His blood splattered her breasts. She mentally cried out to him that she didn't understand. Her cry changed to one of rapture when he thrust his cock into her. He stilled, reveled in the feel of her body's embrace.

When she wriggled her hips, he withdrew then entered her deeper and deeper until he was buried to the hilt in her moist heat. Cupping her face in his hands, he gazed at the gift she gave him with every glance. "My gift for you, Diana." A curtain of cascading stars arose from the ground, surrounding them in a shimmering cocoon. "For my goddess," he whispered, "a million stars to grant her every wish."

"Oh, Lucian." Diana blinked as tears filled her eyes.

Raising his hips, he groaned from the caress of her body on his cock. Plunging back into that slick heat, he brought his mouth to hers and kissed her tenderly. His blood flowed over her tongue, down her throat.

That sweet, sweet taste...blood!

He felt her stomach lurch, her mind rebel. Shifting the kiss, he slid his lower lip between hers and rejoiced when she only hesitated a moment before taking what little blood he was allowed to offer tonight.

His rhythm had been slow, torturous, but swiftly picked up momentum when her nails dug into his hips. He slammed into her, caught himself, and tried to be gentler.   Diana moaned into his mouth and raised her hips.

Faster, Lucian. Harder. Faster.

Lucian smiled against her lips.   *Your every wish, goddess.*

Take me. Her mind cried out to his.

He drove himself into her again and again, sending her higher and higher, until her body started to tremble beneath his.   He swept the hair from her neck.

Yes, oh, yes, Lucian. Take me. Take all of me.

Lucian tore his mouth from hers and brought it to the spot on her neck that had pulsed incessantly for weeks.

The sound of her blood flowing in her veins roared in his ears.   He sucked the quivering flesh between his teeth, teased, nibbled, and licked until her head fell back. "You belong to me, Diana. Only me."

She cried out when his fangs sank deep into her flesh and brought her hands up to push his head away. But when he sucked deeply, when her blood surged through her veins and rose up eagerly to fill his mouth, she clutched his head to her neck, sinking his fangs deeper, silently begging him to suck harder.

Lucian drove his burning cock in and out of her convulsing body. He shuddered and growled like a wild beast against her throat. Her blood flowed into him as his seed filled her womb. When she thrust the sensations coursing through her body as she climaxed into his mind, Lucian felt his own soar even higher.

Every star surrounding them exploded and blanketed them with flaming sparks. Unimaginable pleasure streaked through her body into his, pooled where they were joined.

Her screams sent birds soaring into the air, squirrels, raccoons and chipmunks scurrying through the forest. She shattered over and over again, taking him with her as he spilled more and more of his seed and drank more and more of her blood.

Filling her with his seed while taking in her life's essence consumed him. The hunger he'd denied for weeks mushroomed.

He forgot about the night, the elders, the ritual.

There was only Diana. Diana surrounding him, Diana filling him, Diana screaming from the power of their union.

She'd chosen him, offered up her life to him. He couldn't get enough of her.

Am I dying?

Diana's inner voice was so weak, Lucian almost didn't hear it.

He tore his mouth from her neck, his gaze frantically darting down to the woman he'd vowed to protect. A scant droplet of blood escaped from each of the two gaping holes over her jugular and trailed down her neck.

Her hands slid from his head and dropped lifelessly onto the grass, her head hung over his arm.

"No," he whispered, disbelief and terror nearly immobilizing him. He withdrew his arm from behind her neck. Diana slumped to the ground, her breathing shallow, her eyes fluttering.

Did I take too much? He cried out to those watching as his heart nearly imploded. The curtain of stars he'd created for her dissolved. "Answer me," he sobbed. *Answer me!*

No. Tobias replied in a soothing voice that slid into his mind. *She must learn that she needs you to survive. You have taken her to death's door but stopped before she could enter. Tomorrow night you will feed her hunger, and she will do the same to you.*

A nightingale trilled from a nearby tree. Lucian recalled how terrified she'd been of the worms that had slithered from the muddy grass into her hair and clothes at her pond and gathered her into his arms to keep her away from the ground. His heart thundered in his ears. Blood dripped from the wounds on her throat, covered her lips, her breasts. He licked her until her skin bore no sign. Sitting with her on his lap, he tenderly dressed her.

Her skin was too pale, her breathing too shallow as far as he was concerned. She had no idea when she asked if one bite would transform her that he'd sealed her fate long ago without her knowledge or approval, and it broke his heart that he'd betrayed her trust tonight. He leaned over and brought his lips to her ear. "I would rather face the dawn than hurt you, Diana. If I could, I would take back that first night, even if it meant losing you. Forgive me, Di—ah!"

Rage slammed into his head, pummeled him as surely as if someone's fists battered his brain. The power of Olympia's attack grew stronger with each passing second, warning that she approached.

Damien, can Olympia stop us from bonding? He yelled out to the one elder who would know.

He probed the darkness with his mind and could almost hear Damien's sigh of resignation.

Another elder answered, anger lacing every

word. *She would be banished. Once a bonding ritual has reached this point, it is against our laws to interfere.*

Another laughed bitterly. *Since when has Olympia followed our laws?*

Lucian gritted his teeth and slammed his own rage back at his mother. He rose to his feet, Diana clutched in his arms. Her eyes fluttered open for an instant before she leaned her head against his chest and brought her lips to his skin before once again passing out. He examined the wounds on her throat and was relieved to see they were already closing.

Damien stepped out from the shadows. *Take her to her home, Lucian. She'll be safe there.*

His heart dropped at the thought of returning her to her house and the control of a man more dangerous than the Slashers on the Isle of Fentmore. But her father and the Slashers were meek compared to Olympia. The threat of banishment would not stop her and now that the bonding ritual had reached this night, now that Diana's hunger would grow to unbearable proportions as she transformed, their bonding had to continue on to completion. For her sake.

He silently thanked the elders as he felt their combined powers wash over Diana as they bestowed her with enough strength to carry her through the day.

His grandfather appeared beside him. "With our help, your mate will be fine. She must be under her roof and you under yours."

Tobias was right. The ritual forbade any contact between him and Diana until tomorrow night. Her father and the sun would protect her until then.

Chapter Ten

The next morning, a bright, white flash exploded behind Diana's lids. Crying out from the pain, she shielded her eyes and peeked through her lashes. Sunlight streamed through her window. Rolling over, she dragged herself to the far side of the bed and turned her back to the glaring rays.

She heard her kitten mewling and peeked over the edge of the mattress. Squinting, she reached down and ran her fingers through the soft fur. Recalling Lucian's claim that he was her phantom, she smiled. "So, the big bad vampire has a soft spot for kittens."

Her room seemed brighter than usual, the white and yellow gingham her mother had insisted on covering the windows and bed with practically blinding her. She had hated them, but after her mother had vanished from her life, found them comforting to see them the moment she awoke.

Not today. Today they captured the sunlight and hurled it back at her with a vengeance. And her head! It felt like a road crew was using jackhammers on her skull. Clutching her forehead with one hand as she shielded her eyes with the other, she sat up.

"Advil," she muttered to herself. "At least three."

The short walk to her bathroom took forever. Each step sent a jolt of pain into every muscle; each peek to check her progress allowed the light to stab at her eyes. She stood before the mirror and stared in shock at her pale reflection as she probed her memory of the previous evening.

A smile slowly appeared as, bit by bit, images flashed before her eyes.

Her alarm went off. Music filled her room, but Diana only heard the sound of Lucian's roar when he'd taken her virginity. Although his lips had been on hers, she could have sworn he told her he was her first and last and wondered why he had been so confident when her maidenhead had not been present.

Oh, but that roar. It had sent a multitude of electric shocks hurtling through her body.

Just thinking about it had her quivering with passion, and she knew if she so much as touched herself where he'd filled her, she would tumble into an orgasm.

With a shake of her head, she mumbled, "I'll wait. Let it brew all day." Lifting her eyes to the mirror, she smirked, "And then *I'll* be the animal."

The sound of her cell phone ringing set her heart pounding. Lucian? As soon as the thought entered her mind, logic stepped in. Even before she'd known her lover spent his days asleep, she'd never expected a call until evening.

With a groan, she glanced at the bathroom door. Her cell phone, unfortunately, was on her nightstand. Reaching out to grasp the wall, her dresser, then the footboard of her bed, she slowly made her way through the room. By the time she reached her cell phone, she'd missed the call and was already receiving another. She glanced at the display. Both calls were from her grandmother.

She flicked the phone open and smiled when her

grandmother spoke before she'd even gotten the phone to her ear. "Diana?"

"Tell me what happened to me last night," she demanded, entering into their usual game.

"I know, I know. That's why I need you to come over. We have a lot to discuss, and I have so much to explain."

"I have students—"

"You have to come over, Diana. I had a vision last night. You're in danger."

Diana shook her head in denial even as a chill ran down her spine. "Lucian would never hurt me."

"I don't think it's him. I...you must come over."

Diana's mouth went dry. She'd never heard her grandmother sound so frightened. "But today I get to lead an advanced trail group up Pikes Peak. On Midnight. I've been waiting all year—"

She brought her hand to her chest. "Is that it? Will he smell Lucian's blood and throw me?"

"No, no. The horses are used to it by now."

"What?" Diana plopped down onto the bed.

"Listen, you go to work. You have a way with animals. But come here right after, you hear me? Before sunset."

*****

Diana arrived at her grandmother's house much earlier than she'd originally planned. Her grandmother opened the door before she could knock and embraced her, clucking the way she had when Diana had run to her for comfort after her mother had vanished.

"My poor, poor baby. Midnight wouldn't let you ride him?"

"The horses were fine. It was me." She rubbed her temples. "I have this wicked headache."

Nana Lina wrapped her arm around Diana's and drew her into the dark living room. As usual, every shade was pulled down, and a fire glowed brightly in the fireplace. Diana would have thought her grandmother had set the scene for her, if not for the fact that her home always looked this way.

Her grandmother switched on the lamp beside the couch. The soft, golden light set her gray hair aglow. Fine lines sprang from the corners of her green eyes and curved around the outer edges of her mouth, yet she still looked much younger than her sixty-four years. "Nana, you're not…"

Her grandmother laughed. "Oh, no. Not quite, my dear."

"Not quite?" Frowning, Diana sat down on the plush couch before the raging fireplace. Even with its heat battering her, she wrapped her sweater around her and shivered. "But the lights, or should I say lack of. And what about you always having a fire lit and the heat up, even on the hottest days?"

"Let's talk about you, Diana. Last night was your first of the final stage of the bonding ritual. Do—

"Bonding ritual? No, we just—"

Her grandmother sat beside her and grasped her hands. "Last night was part of a bonding ritual. To them, it's very sacred. It's a ritual of commitment. You to him, him to you."

Diana let her grandmother's words sink in. The chill that had plagued her all day wrapped around her heart. "I didn't know."

"He didn't tell you? How could he not tell you?"

"I don't know." Picturing the curtain of stars surrounding them the moment he entered her, she sighed. "Let's face it, Nana, if I didn't want to commit to him, I wouldn't have...well, you know. But a bonding. I'm not sure I like the sound of that."

"Let me explain how the ritual works, dear. It lasts two months. During that time, there's four nights where you mate. The first night of the ritual, you only taste each other's blood as you mate. Then for a month, you must not mate or exchange blood. But in the case of human soul mates, the hunger is too strong so the elders allow some blood exchange. Then on the first night of the second month, that would be last night for you, he —"

Diana shook her head. "You're losing your touch, Nana. Last night was the first night we...um...you know, mated." She swallowed, not liking the animalistic sound of the word or the way her grandmother shook her head.

"No, dear. You're too pale for it to be the first night. Last night must have been second time you mated. But I'll leave that little explanation up to him."

Recalling her dreams, Diana opened her mouth to ask if they were real but her grandmother shook her head before she could utter a word.

"Let him explain. And don't beg, or I'll kick you out right now. As I said, last night was the first night of the second month and final stage of the ritual."

Drawing in a sharp breath, Diana glared at her grandmother. "My dream... Oh, God. The blood on my bed." She couldn't believe Lucian had deceived her all this time. She wanted to scream, to cry her eyes out. "But until last night we haven't shared any blood. This is so sick."

"Think Diana. You must have."

After a few minutes, Diana closed her eyes and let out a ragged breath. Her hand rose to her neck.

"I think he's been drinking my blood since the night we met. And then, the night before last, well I got a nasty cut on my finger and Lucian, well, he licked it. I thought I felt him suck on it but as soon as the thought entered my mind, he released my finger." Diana peeled the bandage from her finger. She thrust her finger under the lamp. "What the hell? I know I cut it!"

"His saliva sped up the healing process."

Diana closed her eyes. Tears burned as they welled behind her lids. "Oh, God. He's been carrying on this ritual behind my back!"

"Diana, he's your soul mate."

"What the hell does that have to do with it? Does that make it alright for him to trick me?" Drawing the sweater tighter around her chest, she bent over as a painful stab of hunger pierced her stomach. "Go on, Nana. You might as well tell me about this ritual I've been tricked into."

"Last night he had to drain you. They believe that his love will stop him just before you die."

Diana recalled the terror she'd seen in Lucian's eyes when she'd opened her eyes and found him cradling her in his arms. "Lucian wasn't so sure," she said sarcastically.

"I guess it's natural to panic. Tonight, you will

have to do the same to him."

"Drink all his blood?"

"Almost all of it."

Blanching, Diana shook her head.   "Oh, I couldn't."

Nana Lina grasped her chin and stared into her eyes. "Diana, you love him."

"It's only been a month."

"Yet, you do."

Diana hung her head and stared at her hands. "To a certain extent, yes, but definitely not enough to trust myself to drink almost all his blood without either throwing up or killing him. And definitely not enough to become a damn vampire." Her head shot up. "Am I already one? Oh, no, did he turn me into a vampire?"

"No, not completely. You're soul mates, Diana. That's all that matters." Her grandmother frowned. "For some reason he somehow started the bonding ritual without your knowledge. Trust him. I saw him not only as your soul mate but also as your protector. And I know your heart will guide you tonight."

"How will I know when to stop? I'm not a vampire. I have no idea how to tell the difference between most of his blood and all of it." She closed her eyes. A wave of nausea swept over her. She remembered how Lucian had bitten down onto his lip, how his blood had covered her breasts. "I'm gonna puke."

"You'll do fine."

"No, Nana, I'm gonna puke, now."

Nana Lina rushed from the room and returned a moment later with a waste basket. She shoved it into

Diana's hands just in time.

As soon as her hands closed around the rim, Diana started throwing up all the food she'd ingested over the course of the day to appease the gnawing hunger that had hit her on her way to work and had yet to abate.

"Diana," she smiled, handing her a wet wash rag. "I know you'll do fine. I've never been wrong before, have I?"

"You've known about the vampires. Am I the only one who didn't believe in them?" After she swiped the cloth across her mouth, Diana folded it and pressed the clean side to her cheeks. Although she still felt the chill deep in her bones, the wet cloth cooled her burning skin. She dropped her head onto the back of the couch and closed her eyes. "I just want to cry. I want...I want to break something. I want..." Shoving her knuckles against her eyes, she sobbed, "He's been lying all along."

Why hadn't Lucian told her all this? How could he begin this strange ritual without asking her if she even wanted to bond with him?

And what the hell did it mean to be bonded?

"Are you still weak from last night?" Nana Lina lifted her hand and pressed two fingers to her wrist.

Yanking her hand free, Diana scowled. "God, Nana, I'm not dead." She took off her shoes and tucked her feet under her legs then sent her grandmother a smile of gratitude when she draped a thick throw over her lap. "You couldn't have given me a better hint about him being a vampire, Nana. But I always told myself that Dad was a little loony in that department. Believing in them and telling me he destroyed them."

"Dia—"

"But he did, didn't he?" Diana swatted at the wave of fresh tears that flowed down her cheeks. "He killed a little girl's father. Did you know that?"

"Let's talk about you, dear. Last night, when you gave yourself to—"

"Lucian." She groaned. "At least that's the name he gave me."

"As I was saying, when you gave yourself to Lucian after seeing that he was a vampire, you offered your life to him. He, in turn had a decision to make."

"Oh? Poor guy. Had to decide to screw or not to screw?"

"No, Diana. He had to decide whether to accept it—your life—and you as his bonded mate, to refuse and leave, or to end it if he chose."

"Back up! Did you just say he could have killed me?" Diana jumped up on her knees. "It would have been nice if someone had informed me about that!"

"Diana, we'll never finish before dusk if you don't stop interrupting."

"He never said I could die. He never even said it was a damned, what did you call it, bonding ritual? I trusted him." Diana started to tremble.

"In your heart, you knew exactly what you were doing."

"No! I thought I was deciding whether or not to screw. Not turn into a vampire. I'm so cold." Her eyes widened and filled with a fresh wave of tears. "And I'm so hungry, Nana. What has he done to me?"

Leaning over, her grandmother lifted a panel on

the massive coffee table and revealed a hidden compartment.

"Hey, I never knew that was there!" Diana leaned over, nearly toppling off the couch.

"Diana, listen. You're acting this way—"

Standing up and pacing before the fire, Diana laughed nervously. "I'm just a little tired. And completely freaked out. What with finding out a vampire's been drinking my blood and I," she squeezed her eyes shut, recalling how sweet his kisses were, how she'd suckled his lip, "I've been drinking his. Oh, God. I have vampire blood in my veins."

"Sit down. Now, Diana." She held out her hand, revealing a round wafer. "Take this."

Diana glanced down at the pink wafer. "A Necco? I never liked those things." She began to turn away and gasped when her grandmother firmly pushed her back down onto the couch.

"It's not candy, Diana. It's...it's medicine. Now, take it."

Within moments of biting down on the hard disk she felt calmer, the edginess she'd felt all afternoon abated, and the hunger, while still there, no longer hurt. Her chills slowly ebbed.

She turned wide eyes on her grandmother. "How is it you know all about their rituals? How did you know I'd need one of those?"

"Because I've been through it." Her grandmother sighed. "Sometimes you lose, Diana. Sometimes love doesn't conquer all. You find your soul mate, but it's too late. You have a husband, a child. Sometimes you think you can lay down with a man and walk away unscathed. But you don't."

Tears welled in Diana's eyes. "You got pregnant and had to get married. That's why you were always so adamant that I stay a virgin. But you must have gone through the ritual if you knew how I'd need that wafer."

Nana Lina rose and walked over to the fireplace, gathering the thick sweater she always wore across her chest. "We nearly completed it. We spent our month in each other's arms, fighting our desires, our hunger. It was torture, but our love was so strong." She swiped at a tear, and whispered, "We nearly made it to the final night. It's magical, Diana."

Diana couldn't imagine being wrapped in Lucian's arms and not giving in to her desires. It seemed the moment he so much as touched her, she had no control over her body.

She should be angry, should want nothing more of him and his secrets. But she knew that the moment she saw him, her passion would overpower all else. And seeing the look on her grandmother's face as she recalled her final night, Diana could barely stop herself from running out in search of Lucian. "Tell me about it, Nana."

"Well, I've already told you what will happen tonight. But there's one more. You make love, equally exchanging passion for passion, blood for blood. You each completely drain each other at the same time until your blood has completely merged and become one. And then, just a few hours before dawn, you go before the oldest elder and declare yourselves bonded mates. I hear they all turn out to celebrate."

Her voice broke, tearing at Diana's heart even

though the words bonded mates trapped the air in her lungs. She rose and, walking up to stand behind her grandmother, wrapped her arms around her. She rested her chin on her grandmother's shoulder.

"What happened, Nana? I can tell by the way you described it that you experienced the last night."

"No, I didn't. Your father was just nine years old. He saw us that last night. By the lake. We thought we were alone. When I'd left the house, Frank had been fast asleep and I felt secure since he never had been one to awake during the night."

Diana nodded. "Once Dad's out for the night, war could break out right in front of the house, and he wouldn't know about it until the next day."

"Well, something or someone woke him that night."

"Maybe Grandpa?"

"Your grandfather, bless his soul, knew I had fallen in love. Accepted it. He would have stopped Frank if he'd seen him leaving the house. Anyway, Damien and I were discussing our declaration and how I must let the elders know that I accepted him as a vampire and wished to bind myself to him for eternity. Frank ran up and started pelting Damien with rocks, calling him a monster and begging me not to leave him. What could I do?"

Her grandmother turned, wiping tears from her face. "How could I leave my child? I thought Damien and I could see each other in secret until Frank grew up, but their most revered elder discovered that I already had a husband and child. They are one of the few of their kind able to bear children and consider it a crime to take a human mother from her offspring. As punishment, Damien was forced to bond with another." Her voice broke on a sob.

It struck Diana that wherever her grandmother's tears had streamed down her face, the fine lines that told her age vanished. She raised her hand and touched the crow's feet on the outer corners of Nana's eyes. "Your wrinkles aren't real, are they?"

"My life is longer than it should be because his blood runs through my veins."

"Oh, Nana." She knew she would do anything to experience the love that shone in her grandmother's eyes when she spoke of Damien. Even continue this bonding ritual with Lucian. Just the thought of losing Lucian, of never seeing him again broke her heart. "I'm so scared. What if I take too much blood and lose Lucian? How will I go on? What would become of me?"

"They believe humans go mad from uncompleted bondings, become what they call Slashers."

Shuddering, Diana slid her arms around her grandmother. The scent of fresh baked bread and Dove soap soothed her. "Slashers. I've heard about them."

"They're bloodthirsty creatures capable of draining a vampire in seconds. If they can't find vampire blood, they drain each other and humans."

"If they're killing humans, why isn't it all over the news?"

"Because the vampires have been protecting themselves and us. By law, any human who tastes a vampire's blood and doesn't complete the ritual must be brought to Fentmore, a secret island, and abandoned there."

Diana shook her head. "But you didn't—"

"Oh, for weeks I imagined every shadow, every noise was Damien coming to take me there."

"So they're wrong about humans going mad?"

"Most do. In a way, we all do, Diana. We're never warm, and a hunger we can never appease consumes us. Your grandfather, bless his soul, invested all our money and eventually found a scientist who claimed to have found a cure for vampirism."

"A cure?"

"Well, not like he claimed. But it does help." Nana Lina walked over to the table and lifted another wafer then popped it into her mouth. "These help maintain my sanity, satisfy the hunger, and control the need to do something, anything, to get what I'd lost. But they do nothing for my heart. Sometimes I think that's what drives us mad, not the bloodlust."

Diana sat with her grandmother on the couch and leaned her head on her shoulder. "What became of Damien?"

"I never saw him again. I call to him, but he never answers." She sighed. "I think he's afraid to open his mind to me, afraid he'll discover I'm mad and be forced, by law, to bring me to Fentmore."

"That's why Dad hates them and hunts them down?" Even knowing how many he claimed to have destroyed, her heart still broke for the young boy her father once was. "Because he thought one had almost taken you from him?"

Drawing in a shaky breath, Nana Lina kissed the

top of Diana's head. "I feel responsible for every one he's killed. But, Diana, he's gone over the line this time, and I fear you'll pay for his crimes."

*****

"He'll pay for this!" Olympia shrieked, tearing her raven hair from her head. "Betrayed by my own son!" She flung back her head and let out a bloodcurdling scream, but it did little to relieve her rage.

Tomas pressed his back against the wall. "Aunt Olympia, wait until he can explain before you freak out."

"What could he say? What could he say?" She threw an ancient bowl at the plasma television on the wall above Tomas.

Before the shattering glass had a chance to land on his head, the coward sped to the other side of the den.

Olympia flung the couch between them across the room with one hand. "He's bonding with her. I can feel it. Will that family ever stop tormenting me?"

Tomas merely nodded, her spittle dripping down his cheeks. He let out a ragged breath when she spun around.

She turned her wrath on Damien. Sitting on the only furniture she hadn't upturned, he looked just as handsome as the day she'd first seen him walking beside her father and Dracula. Her heart ached. "And you. How could you allow him to bond with the daughter of the man responsible for Marek's death? You swore he was only trying to find out how her father overpowered his victims. You swore he didn't even know she was his soul mate."

Damien merely shrugged his shoulders. "I lied. You had no right to plot the demise of your own son's soul mate. Stop dwelling on Marek and embrace the son of your loins and his chosen mate."

She glanced at an overturned end table and sent it hurtling toward his face.

Damien scowled. The table veered away from him and slammed into a wall. He was upon her immediately, claws and fangs ready for battle. Pinning her to the wall, he brought his face close to hers.

She inwardly cursed her body when it reacted the way it always did in his presence. One look from him, one touch, and she melted. But he never gave her the look she craved, never touched the way she needed. "Damien..."

"Do not tempt me, Olympia." His voice shook. "I could rip you to shreds, and young Tomas, here, would be my witness that you dared assault your mate and elder!"

"I could just see you and the elders watching my son and that spawn of the devil mating." Glaring at him, she pushed him away. "How could you stand by and let this happen? Why protect Lucian? He's not even yours," she hissed.

"As Marek was not yours. You might have convinced everyone else at that meeting that you mourn for Marek and only want vengeance for his death, but I know it's jealousy that drives you. You want to destroy anyone related to Angelina."

"You dare say her name in my house?"

"You know as well as I that she's mad. What more do you hope to accomplish by going after her granddaughter?"

Olympia knew Angelina had not gone mad. Unlike Damien, she had wanted to see Angelina writhing in agony and calling out incessantly for his return. She'd waited a week after their ritual had been brought to a halt. Nothing could have shocked her more than finding Damien's human whore functioning as if she didn't carry vampire blood in her veins, as if the hunger wasn't gnawing at her insides.

Damien had believed her when she had told him that his lover was already beyond help. And when she vowed to keep Angelina's madness a secret for him only if he promised never to seek her out, he'd stayed away from the whore all these years.

"Lucian has the right to bond with someone he could love. Someone who loves him," Damien's voice was weary. "At least she will never spread her legs for every male that reaches maturity."

"I wouldn't have had to if you'd satisfied me!" Olympia sank down to her knees as Damien and Tomas left. She glanced at the portrait of her son and stepson on the wall over the fireplace.

Marek had been a necessary sacrifice, Lucian an unavoidable victim. But she would miss their company. At least with them around, she had always known someone loved her.

Angelina would pay for saddling her with a mate whose heart she'd stolen. Somehow she would take Angelina's granddaughter from her and leave her with no one but the son who had kept her from bonding with Damien.

Just as she now hated Lucian for putting an end to her plans, she felt Angelina must surely hate Frank.

"You'll pay for this, Lucian. From this day on, I have no son." She hugged her knees to her chest. "And all because of that damn family. Oh, but they will pay. Now, they all will pay."

*****

Lucian stood in the hallway, listening to his mother rant. Although Olympia had never been an overtly loving mother, his heart broke at her words. She'd disowned him. And if that wasn't enough, he would now have to spend every waking moment protecting Diana from her.

Leaving the house he'd grown up in, he stared up at the stars. He'd already wasted too much time. Tonight he and Diana would mate again. Diana would drain him, bring him right up to death's door, and hopefully stop before he died. Then he would be so weak, he'd have no choice but to trust her to protect him from her father through the rest of the night and the next day.

But who would protect Diana?

As if he'd heard his thought, Damien appeared.

"I'm coming with you tonight. I have a place where you'll be safe from Olympia and Frank. They'll never find you."

Lucian felt his fangs stir in anticipation of being with Diana again. "And if Olympia does? If she finds us while I'm too weak to help Diana?"

"Then she will have to get past me." Damien winked. "Now, let's go get your chosen one."

Chapter Eleven

Standing on the secluded beach as instructed in the message Lucian had left on her voicemail, Diana glanced at her watch again. So much had happened in such a short amount of time, but she'd been prepared for this night by her grandmother. For years.

All the warnings about saving her virginity for her soul mate. For Lucian. She felt her ire rise again that he had somehow taken her virginity as she'd dreamt of him, had even entered her into a bonding ritual without her consent. Remembering her grandmother's pleas to trust the reasons behind his actions, she forced her anger down.

Her grandmother had spent the entire afternoon convincing her that Lucian and she were destined to be together. That if they failed to complete the bonding, all vampires would become as vicious as Slashers. She'd refused to divulge why, but told Diana that Lucian had no choice but to begin the ritual without her knowledge.

Somewhat pacified about being thrust into this ritual without her approval, Diana vowed that when the time was right Lucian had better explain why he felt the need to take her virginity while she slept.

And now, according to her grandmother, Lucian would give himself to her. She'd continue the ritual, but when it was time to go before the elders, she had better feel more than lust for Lucian, visions or no visions. She was never going to close her eyes to her own doubts or suspicions again. Life was too precious to chance making a wrong move.

Two shadows emerged from the woods, and she knew immediately that one was Lucian. Grabbing the backpack her grandmother had packed and insisted she take, she stood and tried to appear calm.

Lucian glanced at the bulging backpack and raised his brows. "Planning on being gone long?"

She smirked. "Well, if tonight you choose me, I figure I'll be gone at least until tomorrow night. There's no way I'm leaving you alone after taking that much..." She swallowed, unable to say the word.

"You know about tonight? But how?"

She held out her hand to him. "From what my very wise, very loving Nana Lina tells me, tonight you place your life in my hands. Tonight, I rule."

He swept her into his arms. "So, tonight, I am the slave, and you're the master?"

Brushing her lips over his, she nodded. "So she says. And then, you have a lot of explaining to do, buster."

"You can't be talking about Angelina."

They both looked at Damien.

A tall, muscular man with long brown hair stood behind Lucian. He stared at Diana, his hands clenched at his sides. When Diana calmly nodded, he adamantly shook his head. "But how could she tell you anything? She's not well. She's...she's..."

"Fine, last time I saw her, which was less than an hour ago." Diana said, moving out of Lucian's arms. "You know Nana Lina?"

Lucian wrapped his arm around her waist and drew her back against his chest. "Damien, what is all this about? How do you know Diana's grandmother?"

"Damien? You're Nana's vampire?" Pulling away from Lucian's grasp, she strode up to the trembling vampire. "And just where have you been hiding all these years? Huh?"

Diana glanced at Damien's fists quivering at his side.

"She's really fine?" Damien stepped up to her and gazed into her eyes. When she nodded, his shoulders sagged. "I didn't know. I didn't know."

Cupping Diana's face between his hands, Damien smiled. "You look so much like my Angel."

"Can someone fill me in here?" Lucian demanded.

"Diana's grandmother is my soul mate, Lucian. But sometimes soul mates meet at the wrong time." He ran the pad of his thumb over Diana's cheek. "Angelina was married and had a child she couldn't leave. When we failed to go before the elders, they ignored my pleas to allow me to wait for Angelina's freedom and chose your mother as my mate."

Diana turned tear-filled eyes to Lucian. "She still loves him."

Damien's fangs shot out with a speed that shocked Diana. She jerked out of his hands and inched closer to Lucian.

"I was told she went mad. What could I do?"

"Oh, I don't know. Gone to see for yourself?" Diana crossed her arms under her breasts and, scowling, leaned back against Lucian chest.

"He didn't dare, Diana." Lucian explained in a hushed voice. "If a vampire does not complete the bonding ritual with a human then sees with his own eyes that the human has gone mad, by law, he has to bring the human to the Isle of Fentmore."

"I couldn't do that." Damien grabbed Diana's shoulders. "The Slashers, they're mad from needing vampire blood...their chosen vampire's blood. Because they cannot have it, they drain any vampire they can trap. They even kill each other simply because they smell the vampire blood they each carry. Angelina and I went all the way to the last night. Her blood is more vampire than human. They would have torn her to pieces."

"But she didn't go mad." Diana felt like stamping her foot. "God, do all men think women can't handle losing them? Or is it just you vampires?"

"My, God. Olympia has been lying to me all these years." Damien raised his eyes to Lucian. "That's what was behind her sending you to Diana's that night. Not revenge for your stepbrother's death. She thought losing Diana would push Angelina over the edge."

"Damien, enough." Lucian yelled.

"Revenge?" The backpack fell from Diana's hand.

"We have to go. Now." Lucian caught the backpack before it hit the ground.

Diana tried to breathe; found she couldn't draw in any air. Revenge? "Lucian, we met because you..." She turned to Lucian. His eyes darted away. "Lucian?"

Damien, stared intently at Diana. "It doesn't make sense. Why wait all these years to get back at Angelina? Unless she's been trying and...I have to know what else she's done."

Diana felt a bolt of white fire slam into her head. She stumbled back, grasping her head, then wailed when the heat intensified. Her childhood flashed before her eyes. Memories she'd long forgotten. Those she wished she could forget came to life with heartbreaking clarity. Her knees buckled beneath her.

She relived the stillbirth of her brother, the tragic accident that took her baby sister from their lives, and the fire that took her grandfather's life. The morning she awoke to find her mother had vanished replayed, resurrecting the pain she'd managed to get through then. Pain she doubted she'd survive again.

And with every painful memory, Diana saw herself and her grandmother clinging to each other for support.

Unable to take any more, she wrapped her arms around the back of her head and screamed.

*****

"Enough, Damien!" Lucian yelled, immediately blocking Damien from Diana's mind.

"Don't you see, Lucian? Olympia discovered that Diana is Angelina's lifeline."

Lucian focused intently on Diana as she huddled on the ground, wiping from her mind what had just occurred, removing the memory of Damien's slip. When he finally relaxed, releasing a long, weary breath, he met Damien's gaze. *You will never do that again. Do you hear me, Damien? Never.*

Lucian, what have you done to her?

Raising red-rimmed eyes, Diana glanced around as if she didn't know where she was. She took hold of Lucian's outstretched hand. When he pulled her up to her feet, she swayed. "Lucian, what..."

Lucian swept her into his arms. "No more talk about the past. The night is too short, and we have more important things to do." *Damien, show us where we'll spend the night.*

"But Lucian, I have to ask you something important," Diana mumbled, then moaned and clasped her head. "Why can't I remember?" She blinked. A tear rolled down her cheek. Holding Lucian's gaze, she brought up her hands and touched her cheeks. "Was I crying?"

Seeing her chest rise and fall as she grew more and more agitated, hearing her heart rate rise to an alarming rate, Lucian immediately regretted what he'd done.

"Wait. Wait, I—" she gasped then clutching her chest, started to wheeze loudly.

"Lu—"

Her mouth closed.

Hating that he had to enthrall her, Lucian slowed her heart down until it beat in time with his then set her mind at ease. *Nothing matters except us, Diana. Nothing.*

Lucian shook his head, his eyes on Damien. "Damien, we have to leave."

Damien continued to stare at the spot where Diana had waited for them.

"Damien, the night grows late and the longer we wait the more likely it is that Olympia will find us." Lucian moved to stand beside his stepfather. "You want to go to Diana's grandmother."

Damien raised his eyes and nodded. "I've waited this long, I guess I can wait another night. You know, if you'd gone through with Olympia's plan, Angelina would probably have given up."

"What are you talking about? What plan? Lucian, what—"

"Diana, not now. Please, just trust me." Lucian glared over her head at Damien.

He brushed his fingers against the side of her breast. Merged with her, he felt a flash of heat beneath them fan out to encompass her entire body before converging between her legs. She writhed in his arms and brought her lips to the vein pulsing along his neck.

Damien apparently had not missed the fear and confusion that had flared in Diana's mind before her eyes had glazed over with passion. And he knew exactly what her moans as she nibbled on Lucian's neck revealed. *You can't do this to her, Lucian. She should know everything before we proceed. There should be no secrets between bonded mates.*

Lucian turned his back on Damien. *Once we're fully bonded, I'll tell her everything.*

Damien came to stand before him. *You should tell her first. It's not right to continue the ritual with this secret.*

Lucian cradled Diana's head against his chest. *What if she refuses to bond? I can feel her muscles already cramping from the hunger. What if she's not as strong as her grandmother? I can't take that chance, Damien. I won't.*

With a sigh, Damien nodded. He walked up to bank, hesitated a moment, then became a blur as he soared over the lake. Lucian tightened his grip on Diana and followed. She licked his neck where his pulsed throbbed.

"Diana, stop it. We have to get to a safe place," he ground out between clenched teeth.

With a sigh, she rested her head on his chest. "You're afraid. I can feel it. You don't think I'll stop in time."

"I fear for your safety, not mine. There's someone who would destroy what we have."

"This Olympia you were talking about?"

"Yes."

After leading them up a mountainside for what seemed like an eternity, Damien glanced over his shoulder and nodded toward a small cottage nestled in a grove of towering pines. *Take her into the cottage. I'll stand guard outside, but at dawn I'll have to join you inside. Then we will both be in her care.*

Lucian carried Diana into the front garden and stopped. Still wary of a possible trap, he inspected their surroundings with his eyes and mind. Confident that they were the only vampires in the vicinity, he brought Diana into the dark interior of the cottage.

Her eyes still appeared dazed. His heart sank, recalling the way they had lit up upon his arrival at the lake. He searched for a way to bring them back to life.

Something scurried across the floor and squeaked at his feet. Lucian glanced at the tiny creature and grinned. "Just what I need."

When Diana turned to him, he bared his fangs.

"Don't you dare." Diana leapt from his arms and pushed against his chest.

"But I'm starving."

He watched her feel along the wall for the

switch. The sight of those long fingers gliding over the smooth surface sent a bevy of electric jolts to his groin. When light filled the small room, a scrawny mouse froze in front of the stone fireplace. Lucian captured its gaze and ordered it to come to him. The mouse obeyed.

Diana ran up to the mouse. "Shoo! Shoo! Go on, get out."

The mouse ignored her and continued its journey.

"Run. Lucian, you let him go. My God, is this what you do? Go after poor defenseless mice?"

"Only when I have no immediate blood supply on hand." He waggled his brows. "Ah, but why would I need such a measly snack when a meal stands before me?"

Diana giggled. "You rat, I believed you."

Tossing her backpack onto the floor, he grabbed her around the waist and ground his erection into her stomach. With a flick of his eyes, he sent the mouse scurrying out the door. Diana squealed with delight when he nipped at her ear.

"A comfortable chair would be nice." Damien called from outside.

"Don't move." Lucian kissed the bridge of Diana's nose. Lifting a chaise, he rushed out to find out what Damien really wanted.

*****

Diana watched from the doorway as he and Damien stood toe-to-toe arguing. When he finally strode away from Damien, he shocked her by giving a small shrub a vicious kick.

"Is everything okay?" she asked when he

returned.

"Oh, Damien's still freaking out about your grandmother."

"It's so sad."

Taking her face in his hands, he kissed her until she melted against his hard chest.

"Look into my eyes," he commanded in a voice that would put Bella Lugosi to shame.

Wriggling free, Diana held up her hands. "Stop right there, Dracula. Tonight you follow my commands, remember? I'm in charge."

She felt the blood lust he had been joking about surge through his veins. His pupils dilated as he slid his fingers under her T-shirt. Diana held his gaze. Felt him grow entranced by her eyes.

"I can feel your emotions." She held her palm over his heart. "Feel your body's reactions at the same time that I'm feeling my own."

"It's part of the ritual, Diana. We're merged. Unfortunately, you'll hear most of my thoughts, too."

"This should be interesting." She grinned up at his concerned expression. "Now, undress me. Slowly."

Lucian blinked.

"I thought I said slowly."

Diana stood before him, her hands on her hips, the tattered remnants of her clothes scattered around her. A red thong, its straps torn from the delicate lace triangle, slid from his fingers. Running his hand through his hair, he growled. "God, woman, you're turning me into an animal."

"Not just any animal, Lucian. My animal, to do with what I please." Diana slowly licked her lips, amazed how his eyes seemed to glow from some internal fire.

Lucian took a step closer then halted when Diana held up her hand.

"Whoa, tiger. Stay right there." She sashayed over to a huge bed tucked into an alcove. A multitude of burgundy satin pillows were scattered across a matching comforter. Her nether lips throbbed as decadent images flashed before her eyes and her power over tonight's outcome filled her with a host of possibilities.

She primly sat on the edge of the bed and put her hands on the knees of her closed legs then glanced up. His eyes shimmered with desire and unfathomable hunger, his clothes strained against flexing muscles. And his mouth, his beautiful mouth; slightly parted lips revealed the glistening tips of razor-sharp fangs. They seemed to grow as she stared in awe.

If anyone had told her a mere week ago that such a sight would have her trembling with longing, she would have called them mad.

Something still bothered her, but whenever she so much as spared it a moment's thought, her body's ever demanding hunger for Lucian roared to life.

Taking a deep breath, she cleared her throat. "Now, you undress. And this time, no matter what happens, you will make it last. Do you hear me, Lucian? I mean sloooowwww."

"That voice." His heart slammed against his ribs. "If I didn't know better, I would swear I'm standing before a dominatrix." He grinned, confident that he would be in control in no time. "No, problem."

"Wrong, wise guy. I'm in control all night."

Diana decided she could get used to hearing Lucian's every thought.

He reached up to unbutton his shirt. As the first button slid free, Diana spread her legs a mere inch.

Lucian's grin faltered. Unable to tear his eyes away from her knees and the miniscule shadow between, he slowly released another button.

Her legs opened another inch.

His smile disappeared.

Another button.

Another inch.

His hands sped to tear open the next button.

And froze when her legs slammed shut. Fire surged through his veins. "You're killing me."

She opened her legs to where they'd been. "Liar. You love it. Now, remember, the way to win this is game is to move slowly."

Another button, another inch. With a slight toss of his head flames filled the flagstone fireplace across the room and cast a golden light between her legs.

"Cheater," Diana mumbled, her voice catching when her gaze moved to the bulge in his jeans.

Lucian licked his lips and freed another. By the time he'd removed his pants and stood before her completely naked, Diana's legs were spread wide, revealing just how much she had enjoyed her little game.

Across his body, muscles flexed as he awaited her next command. Her breathing grew ragged. She licked her suddenly dry lips. His erection grew. She marveled that she had taken in its entire length the night before.

"Come here," she ordered in a hoarse voice and

pointed to the spot between her feet.

Lucian drew in a sharp breath then slowly moved to stand before her.

"Kneel."

Holding her gaze, he knelt between her legs.

She ran her finger over his lips. "Tell me what you want, Lucian."

His nostrils flared as her essence enveloped him in a heady embrace. "I want you, Diana. Only you."

She brought her hands back to her knees. "Then prove it."

Lucian placed his hands over hers and spread her legs even farther apart. He moved between them and slowly dipped his head, his eyes fixed on her face. When her eyes closed in anticipation, he changed direction and grazed his teeth over a pert nipple.

Diana would have fallen back onto the bed from the jolt that shot through her breast if his arm hadn't suddenly encircled her back and held her in place. He set to suckling her breast, his fangs tormenting her sensitive peak. Desire spiraled down and pooled between her legs.

His abs ground into her, torturing her nubbin.

"Not fair," she whimpered, "I'm supposed to be in charge."

When he pierced her skin just above her nipple, she writhed from the pleasure/pain of his suckling. Just when she thought she couldn't take anymore, that she'd tumble into an orgasm, he released her. She fell back with a cry then sighed as the cool satin pillows embraced her damp skin. She held her breath and whimpered as she waited for his touch. Endless seconds passed with nothing but his warm breath answering her silent pleas.

She knew without opening her eyes that he was staring at her quivering moist flesh and spread her legs wider. She heard him draw in a hissing breath. When he let out a deep rumbling growl she trembled with uncontrollable need. An unbearable ache throbbed where she awaited the touch of his lips, and she begged him to hurry. Still he hesitated. With a guttural cry, she reached down to bury her hands in his silken hair and draw his head to her.

His mouth finally took burning possession, his teeth tormenting her outer lips, his tongue flicking along her inner heat. Her muscles clenched painfully, wanting more, demanding release. Every nerve ending seemed to converge beneath his mouth and follow the path of his teeth to her most sensitive spot. Her hips bucked when they made contact.

Lucian roared into her depths.

Diana's screams shattered the silent night.

The door to the cottage burst open.

Diana could barely focus on the figure charging into the middle of the room. Even as her heart lurched, her hands refused to let go of Lucian's head.

Lucian snarled against the molten flesh beneath his lips. *Leave us!*

Damien took in the scene and halted. "I heard her scream and..." He spun around and left, slamming the door behind him.

Damien already forgotten, Lucian drove his tongue deep into Diana's heat again and again, feasting upon her juices. He stopped to torment her bud, swirling his tongue around it, sucking it until she begged for mercy. His fangs grew even longer, piercing the soft flesh beside her throbbing nubbin.

Diana gasped from the slight prick of pain then groaned with pleasure as he drew her flesh into his hot moist mouth and sucked voraciously at her sensitive clit. She screamed again as every clenched muscle burst free, every nerve sent one fireball after another to her core. A vast void opened deep with her, demanding to be filled.

Gasping for air, she vaguely felt Lucian release her, rise then push her further back onto the bed. Her eyes fluttered open. A lump formed in her throat. Tenderness mingled with untold passion filled his eyes.

"Take me, Diana. Make me yours," he whispered, as the head of his throbbing cock nudged its way in.

Looking into his eyes, Diana grabbed his hips and brought them forward with so much force she felt the air rush out of her lungs.

Her hunger grew tenfold. Her mind revolted when she finally grasped exactly what she hungered for. A long guttural moan of denial rose from her.

She wanted this, wanted him, but his massive size and the idea of just how much blood she'd have to drink to drain him appalled her. Her stomach clenched at the thought even as her hunger seized control.

Lucian's hands tortured her breasts as his mouth bore down on hers.

*****

After enjoying the feel of her lips brushing across

his for a few moments, Lucian offered her his lower lip and, after a fearfully long wait, almost came when he felt her newborn fangs pierce it. He let her have her way for awhile, enjoying the sensations her suckling sent through his body. But tonight she had to take much more than his lip could offer.

He closed his eyes, struggling with the wave of doubts that threatened to tear him from her arms. Because of his own manipulations, Diana's actions tonight were led totally by her body's needs, while her emotions and thoughts had been weakened to the point where they would be useless when she needed them most, when he needed them most to survive. Because of his own manipulations, every time she doubted or tried to grasp the strands still linked to the memories he'd taken from her mind, her desire took hold.

He grimly resolved he had no choice. He had to release his hold before they went any further.

But when he pulled away and saw his blood dripping from her fangs, saw the undeniable hunger burning in her eyes, his own passion overpowered his logic. He released a roar of triumph that this goddess had accepted him, then clutched the back of her head and brought her mouth to his neck, all the while slamming his cock deeper into her heat.

Diana tentatively brushed her teeth against his coarse skin.

As soon as the first drop of blood entered her mouth, their minds merged, became one. The hunger obliterated all but Diana's need to feed. The harder she sucked at the tiny scratches, the faster he thrust himself into her. When he suddenly buried himself to the hilt and his white hot seed poured into her, the blood trickling into her mouth grew sweeter, hotter, and she experienced a hunger so powerful that she was lost to its demands.

She opened her mouth and bit down on the throbbing vein just as the stab of his teeth piercing her neck sent her spiraling into a vortex of passion. Suckling harder and harder, drawing in more and more, she imploded into a mass of writhing ecstasy.

Deep in the recesses of her mind, she knew Lucian had only taken a small amount from her, knew she had to be careful of how much she took from him, but she couldn't seem to stop. They were one being and she couldn't bear the thought of tearing their souls apart.

"Diana," Lucian, aware that she had lost control, moaned against her throat, "enough." He couldn't pull away even though he felt himself growing dangerously weak. Tonight he had no choice but to offer her his life and trust that she would not bleed him completely even though he knew that only passion and her faith in her grandmother's visions had led her this far. If he died, he had no one to blame but himself.

Diana continued to suckle, a ravenous babe at its mother's breast, unwilling to stop until she'd taken in every sweet drop.

Her small frame writhed beneath his weight. He tried to rise and alleviate it to some extent but after only a hairsbreadth separated them, his arms began to tremble. Never had he felt so weak. The sound of her suckling grew faint. He had to release her mind.

If he died tonight, he'd never have the chance to

ask her forgiveness. He could no longer deny that his own selfish need to possess her, to have someone beside him for the endless nights ahead, had led him to withhold why he'd begun their bonding ritual. Each time he'd given her more of his blood, he'd insured that her hunger for him would grow.

And if he was totally honest, this night could have been postponed. He could have relieved her hunger just as he had during the month of abstinence and given her a chance to love him.

Only his fear that she might never agree to join him in eternal darkness had driven him to proceed. And now he wanted nothing more than to free her and discover if she'd choose on her own to stay by his side. He opened his mouth to speak.

*****

Lucian's massive chest crashed down upon Diana's, knocking the air from her lungs.

With a shriek, she tore her mouth away from his neck and tried to lift his head. "Lucian?"

He lay sprawled over her, his head resting on her shoulder, his weight pinning her to the bed. One glance at the vein she'd been feeding on so voraciously revealed the absence of the strong pulse she'd felt only seconds earlier.

"Oh, God, Lucian! What have I done?" Tears streamed down her cheeks.

She pushed at his chest with all her strength and watched in horror as he flopped to the side. Leaning over, she pressed her ear to his chest and let out a gut wrenching wail. "Damien!"

The door once again crashed open. Damien charged into the room and placed himself between the bed and any possible threat.

"What?" His eyes darted around the room. "What?" He was exasperated, shielding his eyes from another embarrassing scene.

"Oh, God. Help me."

He lowered his hand.

Diana, her body set aglow by the fire, sat in the middle of the bed and rocked as she cradled Lucian's head against her breasts.

"Diana, what's wrong?"

"I took too much, Damien," she sobbed, "I've killed him."

Damien smirked. "He's fine."

Diana shook her head. "No, I can barely hear his heartbeat." Opening Lucian's mouth, she slashed open her wrist with one of his fangs.

"No!" Damien grabbed Diana's wrist and clamped his hand over the gaping wound. Blood spurted through his fingers. He pressed his fingers into the gash.

Diana screamed and tried to pull free. "I have to give him back his blood." She tried again to wrench her hand free. "Damien, let go of me!"

Dragging her off the bed, Damien brought her into the bathroom, grabbed the first aid kit and within seconds had her wrist stitched up. The floor and his clothes were covered with her blood. He turned to her and laughed at her shocked face. "I'm an elder, Diana. One of my jobs is to quietly, usually unknowingly, attend bondings specifically for situations like this. You'd be surprised how many times I have to stitch up some part of the females' bodies. You all, humans and vampires alike, think

e heat of the approaching dawn,
inds. Glancing down at the blood
, he decided to spare Lucian the
 He quickly washed them and
r the fireplace. Grabbing a throw
l wrapping it around himself, he
.

come on, time to get up."
d then snuggled deeper into the
ms. "Go away, Daddy."
r ran down Damien's spine even
nk had no idea where they were.
ark about their whereabouts and
d by the sunlight as they, they
hat harm would it do to let her

the bed, he lay down on the other
losed his eyes.
f gears filled the room. The three
heard nothing. Sunlight began to
racks in the blinds. Solid shutters
he windows, completely shutting
ays.
n faster. Slowly the bed lowered
ad opened beneath it. When it had
t, another bed slid out from wall to
alcove.
s returned, if the sensors detected
ound the cottage, the bed carrying
urn.

*****

She glanced around, disoriented

you've gone too far."

"But he looks..." She ran to the bed, unmindful of her nakedness.

"He's fine. This is a test of your love, Diana. And a sign of his faith. He trusted you to stop as soon as he passed out and you did."

"But I've never told him I love him. I'm not even sure I do."

"But you're here." Damien rested his hand on her shoulder. "Why are you here if you don't love him?"

"My grandmother...she saw us." She ran her fingers down Lucian's cheek. Her heart clenched at how cold his skin felt. "He's my soul mate. What else could I do? My God, I could have killed him, couldn't I?"

"No, Diana. It would have never gone that far. We don't leave our loved one's lives in the hands of another so easily. I knew you stopped as soon as I lost touch with him. I felt every drop you took." He draped a blanket around her shoulders.

"Yes, but—"

"He's fine. We can lose quite a bit of blood after the point of unconsciousness, so don't worry. Actually, you stopped sooner than I thought you would." Her tears continued as she lay down beside Lucian and draped most of the blanket and her body over his.

"Promise me he'll be alright, Damien. I couldn't bear it if I lost him." She laid her head on his chest. "I just couldn't bear it."

"I promise. But you have to promise not to give him any of your blood. Do you hear me? Not a drop.

Tonight and tomorrow you must possess his life's essence, and he must know what it is to hunger for you. This way you are both truly pledging to live only for each other."

Diana ran her fingers through the damp hair covering Lucian's chest. How had she come to this? She barely knew Lucian, yet she had just pledged her life to him.

She realized with a start, that when she'd opened her own vein to save him, she'd neither considered nor cared if she died in the process. All that had mattered was saving Lucian.

And when she'd thought she'd killed him, the terror that had gripped her had nothing to do with the fact that she might have killed someone and everything to do with the fact that she couldn't imagine losing him, couldn't bear the thought of facing one day without seeing his smile.

"I promise. Not a drop." Diana stared down at her soul mate's face and felt her heart swell. "You know, up till now, it's been mostly me trusting my grandmother's prophecy."

"And, now?" Damien asked.

She leaned over and kissed Lucian's lids. "Now, I know he holds my heart. I love him, Damien. So much, it scares me."

"Never fear love, Diana. It's God's most precious gift."

*****

Damien sat on the floor beside the bed, watching the two lovers until Diana drifted off to sleep. Her mouth parted and revealed two small fangs.

"Ladies and gentlemen, we have a newborn in

the house
remember
Angelina's

If not
lifetime of
had put an
he had kil
Angelina h

"Ah,
eyes, "how

A han
to see Diar
would wait
she underst

"So yo
Lifting
dripped fro
already has.

Diana
and, with a

Damier
anything, e
glanced at
entangled a
them safe d
their trust. N

If he l
Lucian woul

Losing I
and that Dan

Lucian n
his son all th
her with his l

For Angelina.
When he felt
Damien drew the b
covering his clothe
sight, and strippe
then hung them ne
from the couch an
went to wake Dian

"Diana. Dian
Diana stretch
crook of Lucian's a

A shiver of fe
though he knew F
With him in the
Olympia as trapp
should be safe.
sleep a little longer

Climbing ont
side of Lucian and

The whirring
sleeping on the be
seep through the
slammed against
out the dangerous

The gears sp
into the hole that
dropped fifteen fe
take its place in th

When darkn
no motion in or a
the three would r

Diana awoke

you've gone too far."

"But he looks..." She ran to the bed, unmindful of her nakedness.

"He's fine. This is a test of your love, Diana. And a sign of his faith. He trusted you to stop as soon as he passed out and you did."

"But I've never told him I love him. I'm not even sure I do."

"But you're here." Damien rested his hand on her shoulder. "Why are you here if you don't love him?"

"My grandmother...she saw us." She ran her fingers down Lucian's cheek. Her heart clenched at how cold his skin felt. "He's my soul mate. What else could I do? My God, I could have killed him, couldn't I?"

"No, Diana. It would have never gone that far. We don't leave our loved one's lives in the hands of another so easily. I knew you stopped as soon as I lost touch with him. I felt every drop you took." He draped a blanket around her shoulders.

"Yes, but—"

"He's fine. We can lose quite a bit of blood after the point of unconsciousness, so don't worry. Actually, you stopped sooner than I thought you would." Her tears continued as she lay down beside Lucian and draped most of the blanket and her body over his.

"Promise me he'll be alright, Damien. I couldn't bear it if I lost him." She laid her head on his chest. "I just couldn't bear it."

"I promise. But you have to promise not to give him any of your blood. Do you hear me? Not a drop.

Tonight and tomorrow you must possess his life's essence, and he must know what it is to hunger for you. This way you are both truly pledging to live only for each other."

Diana ran her fingers through the damp hair covering Lucian's chest. How had she come to this? She barely knew Lucian, yet she had just pledged her life to him.

She realized with a start, that when she'd opened her own vein to save him, she'd neither considered nor cared if she died in the process. All that had mattered was saving Lucian.

And when she'd thought she'd killed him, the terror that had gripped her had nothing to do with the fact that she might have killed someone and everything to do with the fact that she couldn't imagine losing him, couldn't bear the thought of facing one day without seeing his smile.

"I promise. Not a drop." Diana stared down at her soul mate's face and felt her heart swell. "You know, up till now, it's been mostly me trusting my grandmother's prophecy."

"And, now?" Damien asked.

She leaned over and kissed Lucian's lids. "Now, I know he holds my heart. I love him, Damien. So much, it scares me."

"Never fear love, Diana. It's God's most precious gift."

*****

Damien sat on the floor beside the bed, watching the two lovers until Diana drifted off to sleep. Her mouth parted and revealed two small fangs.

"Ladies and gentlemen, we have a newborn in

the house," he whispered with a smile. He could remember feeling the same sense of awe upon seeing Angelina's new fangs.

If not for Frank Nostrum, he would have had a lifetime of memories with her. As a young boy, he had put an end to their bonding and now, as a man, he had killed the fruit of their love. Thank God, Angelina had no idea what her son had done.

"Ah, Angelina," he whispered and closed his eyes, "how I long to see you again."

A hand gently grabbed his shoulder. He turned to see Diana groggily gazing at him. "She said she would wait an eternity for you to return. She told me she understood why you stayed away."

"So you think she might forgive me?"

Lifting her hand, she caught a crimson tear as it dripped from his jaw. "She already has, Damien. She already has."

Diana rubbed her cheek against Lucian's chest and, with a sigh, dozed off.

Damien longed to see Angelina. He would risk anything, even banishment to be with her. He glanced at the two young lovers, their limbs entangled as they slept, secure that he would keep them safe during the night. He would never betray their trust. Not even for Angelina.

If he left, Olympia could attack Diana, and Lucian would not have the strength to stop her.

Losing Diana would drive Lucian over the edge, and that Damien wouldn't risk.

Lucian might not be a son of his loins, but he was his son all the same. And Diana? He would protect her with his life.

For Angelina.

When he felt the heat of the approaching dawn, Damien drew the blinds. Glancing down at the blood covering his clothes, he decided to spare Lucian the sight, and stripped. He quickly washed them and then hung them near the fireplace. Grabbing a throw from the couch and wrapping it around himself, he went to wake Diana.

"Diana. Diana, come on, time to get up."

Diana stretched then snuggled deeper into the crook of Lucian's arms. "Go away, Daddy."

A shiver of fear ran down Damien's spine even though he knew Frank had no idea where they were. With him in the dark about their whereabouts and Olympia as trapped by the sunlight as they, they should be safe. What harm would it do to let her sleep a little longer?

Climbing onto the bed, he lay down on the other side of Lucian and closed his eyes.

The whirring of gears filled the room. The three sleeping on the bed heard nothing. Sunlight began to seep through the cracks in the blinds. Solid shutters slammed against the windows, completely shutting out the dangerous rays.

The gears spun faster. Slowly the bed lowered into the hole that had opened beneath it. When it had dropped fifteen feet, another bed slid out from wall to take its place in the alcove.

When darkness returned, if the sensors detected no motion in or around the cottage, the bed carrying the three would return.

*****

Diana awoke. She glanced around, disoriented

by her surroundings. Cherry mahogany walls held dozens of sconces that lit a room much bigger than the cottage she deduced, after seeing the cables rising on either side of the bed, was above them. She had no idea how they'd come to be here, but Lucian and Damien were with her and even though they slept, she felt comforted by their presence.

A glance at Lucian's undulating chest told her all she needed to know.

No longer tired, wondering how late she'd actually slept, she knew that today she would have to protect the two sharing the bed. She had no idea from what, had no idea how she could even hope to fight off whoever had led them to seek out this place, but she knew she would die trying.

She sat up and searched the room for her backpack. Groaning, she remembered Lucian dropped it by the front door.

"Great. No clothes, no toothpaste, or toothbrush." After a failed attempt at running her hands through her tangled hair, she swore under her breath. "No brush."

At least the room was comfortably warm and the furniture plush and inviting. She crept out of bed. One corner of the room looked like a small library. Running her fingers along the shelves holding dozens of books, she couldn't help but smile.

Lining the shelves were books by the same authors that filled the bookcases in her grandmother's den. She wondered if her grandmother had spent the day after her bonding ritual here.

Damien must have known this place was safe because he had used it for himself. The cottage and this room had played a part in their bonding. She felt a rush of warmth at the thought of the love her grandmother felt for the handsome man sprawled on his stomach with one arm protectively draped over Lucian's chest.

She grinned at the thought of Lucian thinking he lay in her embrace as he slept.

With a chuckle she strode over to an ornate chest. On top was a large book encased with leather. Embossed in gold, the title sent a chill down her spine.   "The Laws of the Clan of Mina," she murmured.

Lifting the heavy book, she curled up on an overstuffed chair that faced the bed. The day would feel like an eternity with no way to tell the time and nothing to do but read and wait.

Her stomach growled. She glanced around at the various pieces of furniture, somehow confident that Damien had food stashed somewhere for her, that he'd made certain this would be the haven they needed.

They were safe, she was sure of it. Safe from whomever Lucian felt wanted to put an end to their bonding.

After she'd found a small refrigerator tucked beneath a table and finished the sandwich and coke within it, she returned to the couch and opened the book. A stark white envelope was wedged between pages yellowed with age. Damien's name, written in a sweeping script she instantly recognized as her grandmother's, was scrawled across the front.

Diana stared at the envelope for a long time before deciding that her grandmother would understand her need to read the enclosed letter. Unfolding the page, she immediately smelled her grandmother's favorite perfume. A lump formed in her throat before she began to read. Here and there, tiny round areas of faded ink revealed where each of her grandmother's tears had fallen. Taking a deep breath, she leaned back and began to read. . .

My darling,

How can I explain why I sent you away? Will you ever forgive me for not pledging my love for you before the elders? Did you look into my son's eyes? Did you see the pain I saw? Pain I caused?

You are my love, my life.

But Frank is my son, and he was my love and my life long before we met. Please understand why I chose him.

I will never forget our time together. You were so patient with me as you explained how loving you would change my life. I would have gladly given up ever feeling the warmth of the sun for you and would have done anything to keep you by my side for eternity. Anything, except hurt my child.

I'll never forget the look in your eyes when I took Frank's hand and not yours.

Last night, I hungered for you so much that I had to hold a pillow to my face to silence my cries. And every minute apart seems more unbearable.

Come to me, Damien. We may not be able to spend eternity together, but couldn't we at least see each other from time to time? My life is nothing without you.

Please, my love, come back to me. Let me love you.

I'll always be your
Angel of the Night

"Oh, Nana." Diana softly cried.

Running her fingertips over the extensive wrinkles in the paper, she envisioned Damien crumpling it up in anger, than carefully smoothing it out, refolding it exactly as her grandmother had, and saving it in his book. How many times had he taken it out to revisit his loss? How could he ignore what he must have considered the signs of her grandmother's impending madness?

Her heart broke for the man who had so gallantly charged into the cottage to protect them last night. His soft snores mingled with Lucian's. Uncurling her legs, she rose and put the book back where she'd found it. A shiver ran down her spine.

Suddenly, her heart began to pound erratically. Something was wrong, terribly wrong. She could feel it.

Chapter Twelve

"Where is she?" Frank Nostrum bellowed from the landing of Angelina's stairs.

"Frank, if you'll just relax—"

Bounding down the stairs, he collided with her at the bottom. When she tumbled to the floor, he moved to offer her a hand. She reached up. Her heart sank when he shoved his hand into the front pocket of his trousers.

He glared down at her. "Terry called sick with guilt because she let Diana leave the mall with a man you said was her soul mate. Now, where the hell is my daughter?"

Angelina stared up at the man her son had become. While his body was built to perfection, his soul had shrunk, leaving him heartless in his need to destroy any he deemed undeserving the right to share his world.

He grabbed her arm and yanked her up from the floor than shoved her into the dark living room. "God, you disgust me. Living like the vampire you wish you were."

He pushed her down onto the couch than strode over to the picture window facing her and flung open the heavy drapes.

"Frank, no." Sunlight poured into the room, blinding her, thrusting shards of pain into her eyes. She buried her face in her hands and whimpered as the heat, more unbearable than she'd ever imagined it would be, scorched her exposed skin. She reached for the few wafers scattered across the end table, hoping she wasn't too late to stop the sun from doing too much damage, but Frank unveiled another window, sending a beam of sunlight across the table. She flinched away empty handed.

"You are not a vampire. When will you get that through—?"

His face twisted with horror when he turned to face her. She knew what he saw. Saw it through his eyes. The skin on her hands and neck grew red. "My God, mother, what has that demon done to you? Have you been seeing him all these years?"

"No, Frank. Please close the drapes." She sobbed into her hands as she dropped to the floor and crawled blindly to a spot safe from dawn's scalding rays. "Have mercy on me. I'm your mother."

"My mother?" His face filled with hatred. "Have mercy? You were willing to leave me for that monster. How dare you ask for mercy?"

"But I didn't, Frank. I didn't leave you." She crouched behind an ottoman, fear nearly immobilizing her. He took pleasure in killing vampires. If he felt she was one, he wouldn't hesitate to do the same, would probably enjoy every minute of it. She had tried so hard over the years to get him to forgive her, to show him that she truly loved him.

Frank squatted down in front of her and pried her hands from her face. "Terry said the man ran off into the woods with Diana in his arms. Ran faster than anyone she had ever seen. And she spoke to Diana last night. Want to know what she said, mother? Diana told her she had to go with this man because you told her he was her soul mate. She mentioned a bonding. We both know what that means, don't we mother?"

Angelina glared into her son's cold grey eyes. "You have no idea what it means to bond with anyone."

He grabbed her shoulders and dragged her to the window. Ignoring her screams, he brought his face up to hers. "Diana told me she was spending the night here. What did you do, mother? Offer my daughter up as a sacrifice to your demon lover?"

In her struggle to escape the searing rays, Angelina knocked her wig off.

Frank let out a low moan and stared in horror at the grey wig lying at their feet. "You were twenty-four. A wife. A mother. How could you believe a vampire was capable of love? You sold your soul to a creature that wanted nothing but your blood."

Angelina broke free and ran to a dark corner. Frank tossed the wig into the fire then turned and peered intently at her face. With a curse he strode over, yanking his shirt from his waistband. He spit onto it.

"Frank, no!"

Ignoring her, he scrubbed mercilessly at her tender skin. Glancing down at the black smudges marring the stark white cloth, he shook his head then raised incredulous eyes to her. "You've fooled us all these years." A sob caught in his throat. "I always thought you looked younger than you should, but the grey hair and the wrinkles." His chin quivered as he turned and glanced at the walls on either side of her. "The wrinkles."

To her horror, every portrait she had painted over the years was wrenched from the wall and sent, one by one, to join her wig in the fire.

"I should have known," he spat out, wiping at his eyes with the palms of his hands, "Dad always said you were the best at painting old people. I used to stare at those damn paintings, convinced I could bury my fingers in the deep wrinkles you were so, so good at."

Angelina watched him stride to the front door. When he turned, she cringed, expecting another outburst. Instead, he spoke so softly, she barely heard him

"You'd better pray I find my daughter before it's too late for her, too."

The door slammed shut. Trapped in the corner, Angelina watched the sunlight inch closer and closer. She whimpered when it glanced over the toes of her shoes. When it touched the exposed skin on her ankles, she yelped and charged through the fiery rays to the stairs.

Sitting on the edge of her tub later that afternoon, she winced as she dabbed ointment over the blisters covering her cheeks. They would heal quickly. Since her time with Damien, she rarely got sick and always healed within twenty-four hours, but the smallest cut produced excruciating pain.

She'd always known that Damien's blood running through her veins had permanently changed her. She puttered around the house every night then usually slept most of the day. Cosmetics and lies about face-lifts and chemical peels covered the fact that her body barely aged over the past forty years. And although she ate, her hunger for Damien never ceased.

Closing her eyes, she popped a wafer into her mouth and said a silent prayer of thanks to her deceased husband. He had accepted that vampires existed, that they were not the demons of lore, that her heart would always belong to one, yet had still taken tender care of her. He had opened an all night diner and left her in charge, understanding her need to sleep during the day. Using her job as an excuse, he had taken her place during the day so Frank would never question her absence. If not for her husband, she would have gone mad and lost everything she had sought to gain by leaving Damien. And when he had died, Diana's love held her together.

The shrill ringing of the phone nearly sent her tumbling into the tub. Wincing as she rose, she hurried into her bedroom and snatched up the handset before the answering machine came on.

"Hello?"

"I just wanted to see if you changed your mind."

A shiver of fear ran down her spine at the sound of her son's cold voice. "Changed my mind?"

"Don't be coy, mother. Tell me where she is."

"I don't know, Frank. I told you—"

"Tell me, Goddamnit. I've looked everywhere." He sobbed, tearing at her heart. "She's all I have left."

She almost felt sorry for him, but the pain of her burned skin reminded her just how cruel he could be, how he might hurt Diana if he knew that she too had the blood of a vampire running through her veins. "I swear, Frank. She never told me where she went." She sat on the bed and wearily closed her eyes.

"What about this man? I know she told you about him. It can't be your lover. I killed him."

She clutched the phone, still refusing to believe she'd lost Damien. "Frank, please calm down."

"Calm down? Calm down? My daughter is probably spreading her legs for some monster as we speak."

Glancing at the clock, Angelina chose not to point out that, with the sun perched directly overhead such a thing was highly unlikely. She took a deep breath and began to lie to her only child. "No, Frank. You're wrong about this man. Diana met him at the ranch in broad daylight. He couldn't possibly be what you think."

"Say it, mother. A vampire. And why should I believe you?" His voice grew even shriller, his words more intelligible by his sobs. "What happened? Did some other vampire come along and promise to return your lover to life if you gave them Diana? It won't work, you know. Once they die from the sun, they stay dead, mother. You gave up your granddaughter for nothing. Nothing."

"Frank." The phone shook in her hand. "Now you listen and listen well. I gave up that vampire for you. You. Why can't you remember that? I chose you, damnit. Your daughter might live under your roof, but she's still a twenty-five year old woman with the right to stay out overnight without worrying that her father is scouring the town looking for her."

"But—"

"No buts, Frank. Let her grow up. She met a man and decided to spend a night with him. Period. Now if you have a problem with that, than I'd advise you to keep it to yourself otherwise she might decide living at home isn't all that great after all." She took a deep breath and tried to calm her racing heart.

"Swear she's not with a vampire." His voice finally sounded normal.

"You have my word." Tears burned her eyes.

"Well, at least I know it's not your vampire. I personally nailed him to the post and didn't leave until his screams stopped. I know you don't believe me, but I've never forgotten his face. Those eyes haunted my dreams, mother. The vampire I killed was yours."

"No." She bit down on her knuckles. It couldn't be Damien. She'd know if he'd died. She'd know.

"I wish you could have heard his screams. He begged me to spare him and cried for his mother."

She shook her head, refusing to admit she'd heard those screams, felt the need to answer those cries, could almost hear them even now. But she'd been hearing a child cry for its mother ever since she lost the baby that was hers and Damien's.

"Goodbye, Frank," she mumbled and, without waiting for his reply, hung up the phone.

The afternoon hours lagged. Knowing instinctively when the sun had finished its descent, she rose to open the blinds. As soon as she raised the first an overpowering sense of foreboding rushed over her. She released the cord and rushed from window to window checking all the locks. Glass shattered somewhere downstairs.

She ran to lock her bedroom door. Her eyes darted about the room as she frantically tried to remember her visions. Dark, bleak, frightening visions. She'd thought they foretold danger for only Diana. Now, feeling the evil emanating from whom or whatever had entered her house, the same evil she'd sensed in her visions about Diana, she realized their fates were intertwined.

Angelina flung her sweater to the closet floor then grabbed the oversized, woolen one her husband had insisted she always keep fully stocked with enough wafers to last a month. He had placed one such sweater in every closet in the house. He hadn't foreseen this night, had only included her wafers on the necessary medications list he'd written the day after the attack on the World Trade Center.

She caught sight of an old pocket book. Deciding to take as many wafers as possible she grabbed the bag, then reached up to the shelf and retrieved one of the boxes of wafers stacked there. Trying not to scream when the sound of an approaching helicopter filled the room at the same time another crash resounded from below, she emptied the contents of the box into the bag.

She draped the strap over her shoulder. The weight of the wafers dragged it down. The straps dug into her flesh. Taking off the bag, she slung it over her head then slid one arm through the opening. Within moments she had the sweater on and buttoned over it. She turned to leave the closet just as her bedroom door burst open.

If she weren't so terrified, she would have laughed when she saw the woman standing in the doorway surrounded by the splintered remains of the molding. Barely five foot six with soft curves in all the right places; she didn't appear strong enough to remain upright in a strong wind much less break down a door. Oh, but her beauty could stop any man's heart. Thick black hair tumbling down over full breasts and narrow hips, fawn colored eyes so pale they were nearly gold took Angelina's breath away.

Angelina's eyes darted to the dark hallway behind the woman, expecting to see someone more capable of breaking down her door.

A snarl drew her attention back to the beauty. She immediately realized how wrong she'd been. Fangs dripping with saliva protruded from a cavernous mouth. All beauty vanished as the woman's face twisted with rage.

Angelina clutched the bag to her stomach. Her heart pounded so fiercely she was sure it would explode.

"Why aren't you insane? You should be a fucking maniac by now. Why aren't you a Slasher?" the woman yelled, spraying the floor with spittle.

Angelina stepped back from the hatred coating each word. "I have no idea," she lied then began to repeat her answer over and over in her mind in case the vampire before her probed for the truth.

After a moment, the woman laughed. "It doesn't matter. I think you are. I've decided you're a danger to us."

"Who are you?" Angelina asked, hoping to stall just in case she had somehow breached the wall Damien had erected between their minds.

"Who am I? Who am I?" Olympia's eyes grew increasingly wider then suddenly returned to normal. "Oh, that's right. You wouldn't know. You haven't seen or spoken with my bonded mate for how long? Forty years?"

Shaking her head, Angelina once again saw the beauty of the vampire before her. Her heart fractured. "You're Damien's bonded mate?"

The vampire slowly crossed the room and extended her hand. "That's right. I didn't introduce myself. I'm Olympia, Damien's mate, lover, and the mother of his two, well, one son." When Angelina ignored her outstretched hand, Olympia leered and bared her fangs. "And you're the naïve human who spread her legs for him and gave up her blood to appease his hunger after a few meaningless words. We laughed about it every time we made love."

"You lie."

"Really? If he loved you, why did he turn his back and never return? Why did he bond with me?" Olympia pouted. "Oh, you poor thing. You thought he loved you, didn't you? I keep telling him that he should stop his little game with humans."

Every fiber of Angelina's heart told her Olympia was lying. She had to be. This all couldn't have been some sick game. "Then why are you here? If I'm just someone Damien took advantage of, why are you here?" Angelina spat back before thinking. "I'll tell you why. Because he did love me."

Olympia moved so quickly, Angelina lost sight of the vampire. Her back slammed into the dresser. Before she could catch her breath and react to the pain shooting up her spine, she felt Olympia's hands clamp around her neck.

"I could kill you, right now. Do you know that? One flick of my wrists and your precious neck would snap. But death would is too good for you. You should suffer. Suffer the way you and your granddaughter have made me suffer."

Angelina's lungs burned; her fingers clawed at the hands growing ever tighter around her neck. Staring into eyes filled with pain, her heart broke for Olympia.

Olympia brought her face up to Angelina's. "You stole my mate. And now, your whore of a granddaughter has seduced my son into betraying me."

Olympia sliced open Angelina's cheek with one fang then dragged her tongue across it. Spitting the blood onto the floor, she released Angelina's neck and wiped her arm across her mouth. "Your blood is foul. It contaminates every body it flows through. I can never be happy, Damien can never be happy with me as long as you and your spawn walk this earth."

Angelina's heart slammed against her ribs. Damien was alive.

Olympia's fist flew towards her face.

When Angelina came to, it took her only a moment to realize she hung suspended from a helicopter. A rope tied around her waist was all that prevented her from tumbling to the ground below. Suddenly, she plummeted some twenty feet then came to an abrupt halt. Her shocked screams turned to cries of pain as the rope wedged between her ribs. Grasping onto the rope, she craned her neck and gazed up at a black helicopter. Leaning out of the opening, Olympia gleefully waved a huge ax.

"We've been waiting for you to wake up. Your new friends are growing very impatient." She pointed the ax down.

The loud whirring of the helicopter failed to

drown out Olympia's words. Angelina's heart missed a beat before she dared to glance down. A crowd of snarling creatures leapt at her dangling feet. Her eyes widened at the dagger-like teeth filling their mouths. Her hands flew to her bulging pockets.

The Isle of Fentmore. Forty years ago, Damien had warned her that she would end up here if she refused to complete the bonding. He'd nearly cried as he explained how and why she'd go mad and how their laws demanded they send any Slasher they discovered to the Isle of Fentmore. Every time her unanswered call to him had her doubting his love, she reminded herself of his vow that he would never return and chance finding her in such a state, would never be the one bound to abandon her on Fentmore.

She dropped another foot then came to a bone jarring halt. Her scream rent the air when a mouth closed around her ankle. Teeth ripped through her flesh as her attacker dropped back down to the ground. Before another could do more damage, she reached into her pocket and tossed a handful of wafers to the crowd. The Slashers dove for them, surprising her with their apparent familiarity with them. The ones directly below her began to amble away, already feeling the calming effects. She took another handful and tossed it farther away.

"Why are they leaving?" Olympia screeched, peering down. "Bring this thing lower. I want to see where they're going."

"No way, Olympia. I can't chance going any lower than this," the pilot yelled over his shoulder. "If the scent of her vampire blood is strong enough, they'll come back."

Olympia slammed the ax against the side of the doorway when more Slashers drifted away. "Something is luring them away from her."

She leaned out and caught sight of Angelina's arm as it swung out again and again. The crowd grew less and less dense. Letting out a roar of anger, Olympia cut into her own arm with the ax. "If she's covered with pure vampire blood, they'll come back."

She dropped the ax to the floor, and was reaching out with her good arm to hold onto the door when a gust of wind rocked the helicopter. Olympia screamed, lurched back and forth.

Below, Angelina alternated between tossing out wafers and untying the knot at her waist. The longer she hung here with her ankle dripping blood, the more Slashers she would have to deal with. The rope gave just as she heard a scream from above. She landed in the outstretched arms of a Slasher. From the look on its face, she knew it had devoured some wafers and let out a sigh of relief. She jumped from its arms and took off, scattering wafers to clear a path. The sound of the helicopter as it left filled her with both dread and relief.

*****

Lucian knew without opening his eyes that Diana still laid cradled in his arms, could feel her leg draped across his hips, her warm breath fanning his face. His soul mate.

He grinned. His very wild soul mate.

Images of the previous night flashed in his mind. Diana had been insatiable. Groaning from the throbbing ache in his groin, he moved along the path of her breath and brought his lips to hers.

He never expected her to giggle in response and pulled away to ask her what she found so funny.

Giggles from a distance?

His eyes shot open.

Damien, his face no farther than an inch away, winked. "Love you too, son." With a smirk, he rubbed his thigh against Lucian's erection. "Glad to see me?"

"Shit." Lucian leapt out of the bed and spun around. Diana, giggling uncontrollably, lay sprawled across the couch.

"I knew it," she said, wiping tears from her eyes. "I've been watching you two and waiting to see what would happen when you woke up."

Damien's booming laughter filled the room.

"Very funny." Lucian grimaced in disgust and swiped his arm across his mouth. His eyes flew open. He ran to a small wastebasket next to the bed and began spitting into it. "God, Damien, I had my tongue in your mouth."

Damien's grin vanished, and then he too began to spit over the side of the bed.

Diana squealed in pain as another fit of laughter took hold.

Glancing up, a hint of glee lingering in his eyes, Damien smirked. "I wouldn't laugh, Lady Godiva."

Lucian's head swung around as Diana screamed. Her legs, spread wide and revealing way, way too much to Damien, quickly clamped shut. Her breasts, no longer jiggling from her laughter, disappeared behind her hands. She vanished beneath the cushions of the couch. Lucian's eyes flashed with jealousy as he turned and looked at Damien's groin. Relief poured over him like a fine, cooling rain. Damien's cock remained unaffected. "Diana, why the hell are you hanging around here naked?"

Peeking out from under the cushions, she scowled. "I would have put on clothes if you two had bothered to bring my backpack down with us."

The two men smirked.

She smirked right back. "Oh, but I'll never tell who's bigger!"

Lucian and Damien both glanced down at themselves and then at each other.

"Well, I would be if—" Damien began.

"Yeah, keep telling yourself that, old man." Lucian straightened his back and proudly jutted out his hips.

"Boy, Lucian, you must have really enjoyed that kiss." Diana winked at Damien.

Lucian ignored her and glared at Damien. "Where the hell are your clothes?"

"Ah, I had a little accident and had to wash them." He grinned and looked away from Lucian's troubled gaze. "It was nothing, Lucian. I tripped outside."

"Actually, I prefer being naked." Diana was still covered by the cushions. She smiled back at Damien.

But Damien no longer smiled.

*****

Damien stared at a spot behind Diana, yet when she turned to look, she saw only the bookshelves. "Damien?"

Lucian grabbed Damien's arm. "Damien, what's wrong? What do you see?"

"Diana, quick get on the bed." Damien ordered,

virtually dragging Lucian into the middle of the mattress.

Diana sprang to life, no longer concerned about her lack of clothing. The urgency in Damien's voice reminded her of the foreboding she'd had earlier about her grandmother. As the bed began to rise, she turned to him and dared to ask, "It's Nana, isn't it. You feel it too?"

"She's in trouble. She's calling me." He closed his eyes. "Oh, God, she's terrified."

"Where is she, Damien? Can you see where she is?" Lucian asked, wrapping his arms around a now terrified Diana.

"I can't tell. But—Ah." he clutched his stomach. "Oh, God, the pain."

Diana buried her face into the crook of Lucian's neck. "Tell me it's not her pain he's feeling, Lucian. Tell me it's not Nana."

But Lucian only tightened his grasp on her shivering body.

Within moments after the bed reemerged in the dark interior of the cottage, the three were dressed and bolting into the night. Lucian swept Diana into his arms and once again followed Damien's lead.

When they finally reached Angelina's house, Damien fell to his knees in the middle of the lawn and let out a gut-wrenching roar.

Diana, realizing they were too late, screamed and tore at Lucian's iron hold on her. "Let me go! Let me go to her!" she sobbed. "She needs me!"

"She's not here, Diana." Lucian turned so she could see Damien. "Look at him. If she were here, dead or alive, he'd already be at her side."

"She'd be better off dead," Damien muttered, his shoulders hunched in defeat. "This is my fault. Even though I knew from the beginning that she would never leave her son, I still pursued her. I thought if we bonded, if she felt the hunger, she'd have no choice. When that failed I blocked her out all these years and told myself I did it to keep her safe. But I was a coward. I was too afraid to see or hear any sign of her pain, to face what I'd done to her. And now it's too late."

Diana knelt beside Damien. "Too late? Damien, where is she?"

The anguish in the eyes that rose to meet hers sent terror into her heart.

"The Isle of Fentmore." Damien's voice was hushed as if just saying it would propel them to the dreaded place.

"Well, at least she's well enough to send you her location." Lucian patted Diana's shoulder. "We'll just go and get her out of there."

Damien shook his head. "Not Angelina. Olympia's sending out word to all of the elders that she found a Slasher and brought her to Fentmore."

Diana turned to Lucian. "Olympia?"

He turned his back on her. "My mother."

"Your mother brought my grandmother to that island? Why?"

Damien's head shot up. "Tomas?"

"Who's Tomas?" Diana asked, her stomach suddenly queasy.

Damien turned to Lucian, his face stricken. "He's got Tomas."

Staring up at the sky, Lucian closed his eyes.

Blood dripped from his clenched fists.

"Lucian?" Diana's voice quivered. Somehow, she knew exactly who had this Tomas.

When Lucian turned to her, his eyes were filled with rage, his voice menacing. "This is all your father's fault. He stopped Damien and Angelina's bonding ritual. He killed my stepbrother. And now he has my cousin."

Diana backed away. For the first time, she truly feared Lucian. Moonlight glinted off fangs, longer than she'd ever seen. "Your stepbrother..."

The memory of her father standing in the kitchen, ranting like a madman that he'd finally killed the vampire he'd spent years hunting collided with the one of Luna sobbing for her murdered father. Diana glanced at Damien and gasped at his resemblance to Marek. Why hadn't she noticed it earlier?

Daring to meet Lucian's gaze, she asked, "Marek was your stepbrother?"

Suddenly she was on her back. Lucian's weight crushed her into the dew covered grass. "You knew?" he asked, his eyes filled with blood. His nails pierced the tender flesh on her shoulders. "You knew all this time that your father killed Marek?"

"Lucian, you're hurting me," she cried.

"But I searched your mind. I found nothing!"

"She's like her grandmother, Lucian. Her mind is stronger than most. And just as you hid the thing that shamed you most about Olympia, she hid what she could not face about her father." Damien looked up. "Get off of her."

Diana's heart shattered when Lucian continued

to pin her to the ground, his eyes still filled with hatred.

He brought his face close to hers and stared intently into her eyes. "Marek died screaming in agony. All these years, you knew what your father did, didn't you? You knew and did nothing. Now, because of you, he has my cousin."

"What could I do, Lucian? He's my father," she sobbed, the pain of his nails grazing against the bones in her shoulders nothing to that of her heart breaking. "He's my father!"

Damien leapt on Lucian's back. "It's not her fault, Lucian."

"If I'd done what I was supposed to, Tomas wouldn't be in that pen." He brought his face down to hers and snarled. "Mother was right all along about you. You tricked me. This was all part of your father's plan. You blinded me, tricked me into believing you were my soul mate so he could take Tomas."

"No, Lucian, you can't believe that." His face blurred in a crimson haze. Blinking away the tears searing her eyes, she lowered her voice. "I love you, Lucian. I gave up my humanity for you. We've bonded."

His pupils seemed to dilate when a drop of his blood landed on her quivering lower lip and her tongue immediately darted out to capture it.

"Not quite, Diana. Not quite." With a roar, he flung Damien from his back.

Diana felt his weight lift. Saw nothing but a blur of grey mist shoot up into the sky. Pushing herself up on her elbows, she searched the yard for Lucian.

He'd vanished.

Clutching his arm in pain, Damien sat slumped against the steps of her grandmother's house. She jumped up and spun around. "Where is he? Damien, where's Lucian?"

"Gone."

"B-but what about our bonding? If we don't complete it..." She ran and knelt before Damien. "Damien, if he doesn't return, what will become of me? How will I survive without him?"

"You'll go mad, my dear."

Diana turned around to see who had spoken. A petite, dark-haired beauty stood in the driveway, her eyes twinkling with glee.

Damien sprang to his feet and shoved Diana behind him. "What have you done with Angelina?"

"Oh, let me see," Olympia tapped her index finger against her fangs. "Angelina? Oh, yes. Well, you know she was quite mad—nearly drained me—so I had no choice but to bring her to Fentmore. Poor thing. They surrounded her the minute I dropped her into their midst. And now I have another Slasher to deliver."

Damien leapt at her, his teeth bared, his fangs dagger sharp. "I'll kill you!"

Olympia vanished and reappeared behind Diana. "Ah, ah, ah."

Feeling the sharp edge of Olympia's nail prick the skin over her jugular, Diana held up her palm. "No, Damien."

He froze. Diana forced herself to smile. "It's alright, Damien. Lucian will find me."

"Lucian?" Olympia let out a bark of laughter.

"He's the one who called me to come and bring you to Fentmore."

Recalling the look in Lucian's eyes before he'd vanished and his condemning last words, Diana could not find any reason not to believe Olympia. Her throat closed. A sharp, piercing pain ripped into her heart.

"Now, how should I handle this one, Damien?" Olympia turned Diana to face her.

No longer afraid, Diana met her gaze. If anything, she welcomed death either at Olympia's hands or the Slashers on Fentmore. An eternity of darkness loomed before her. An eternity without Lucian.

Olympia tsked. "Oh, dear. It seems my beloved son has finally obeyed his mother and drove the poor child over the edge."

"Leave her alone, Olympia. You can't hurt her anymore than Lucian has." Damien shook his head. "You'll only be giving her what she wants if you kill her."

Hooking Diana's chin with her finger, Olympia snickered. "My, my, such empty eyes. What, no tears for my son?"

"Olympia, please, leave the girl alone." Damien inched closer.

"No, Damien. She's mine. My reward for all the years I've wasted loving you while you loved that whore. My reward for hearing you call her name out in your sleep." She hoisted Diana over her shoulder. "One step and I kill her right now. One step."

"Where are you taking her?"

"Can't you see? She's mad."

Diana wished she were mad. Her grandmother gone. Her father probably dying at the hands of Lucian or some other vampire. She could have dealt with anything if Lucian had stayed by her side. Anything. Closing her eyes as Olympia took to the sky, Diana hoped the trip to Fentmore would be a swift one. Hoped the Slashers would end the nightmare that was now her life.

*****

For two hours, Angelina walked amongst the crumbling two-story buildings lining the streets of the small town. No lights shone from their broken windows; no lights shone anywhere. But the moon was full and her enhanced senses revealed the condition of her new home.

The streets were strewn with trash and covered with dried pools of blood. The smell of decay and urine assaulted her, forcing her to stop again and again to retch. Every now and then she'd reach a dead end marked by a towering wall and was blessed with an occasional whiff of fresh air that flowed over it. She grew more and more convinced that if she could just find a way to the other side of that wall, she'd be free.

Every time she'd begin to feel safe, more Slashers would arrive. Some would pass her, fresh blood dripping down their chins. Others would pounce on the wafers she'd toss as soon as they bared their teeth. And some were too busy feeding on each other to pay her much mind.

Her ankle continued to leave a trail of blood in her wake and surprisingly only a few Slashers stalked her. She hadn't been with Damien for forty years and could only conclude that the scent of her blood overpowered his. Too many grabbed each other in her presence for her to think otherwise.

How the Slashers survived was beyond her. She'd passed a small group rummaging through a basket of fruit and surmised that for some reason the vampires fed them regularly. The bodies lying about, their throats ripped open, revealed that the fruit did not fully appease their craving for vampire blood. The splintered ends of bones protruding from the gashes explained why the normal teeth of the Slashers were now jagged and razor sharp.

The opening to another alley caught her eye. She could detect no motion within it and decided it would be a safe place to bring Diana when she arrived. The vision she'd had weeks ago of Diana in a helicopter with a dangerous force no longer baffled her.

When she heard the helicopter return, her heart broke. Diana would be terrified. She ran through the streets toward the sound. Slashers ran in front, behind, and beside her, led by the scent of the fresh vampire blood running through Diana's veins. Angelina's hands already held the wafers she planned on using to lure them away before her granddaughter ever touched the ground. For what seemed like the hundredth time, she called for Damien.

She turned a corner and froze. The crowd below the helicopter, though still quite small compared to the one that had greeted her, were attacking each other as they frantically tried to be the first to reach Diana. Their nostrils flared. Their roars rent the night.

And Diana?

Angelina had expected to hear her screaming in terror, to see her frantically trying to climb up the rope.

Diana's arms hung at her sides as she stared down at the teeth snapping at the air inches from her descending feet.   A tremulous smile, her only reaction.

Chapter Thirteen

Damien took a deep breath and rang the doorbell of the small Cape Cod. When the door opened he grabbed hold of Frank Nostrum's neck and lifted him until their faces were level. "Don't move. Don't talk. Don't even breathe. Just listen."

Frank shook his head in denial. "You're dead. I watched you die!"

"Poor Frank, you saw me in Marek but you failed to see yourself." Damien spat into his face.

"Myself? What the hell are you talking about?" Clawing at Damien's hands, Frank shook his head. "Oh, God, it wasn't you. The eyes were the same, but the mouth... the mouth was not as full."

"And what about his nose, Frank? Ever seen that crooked bridge before? In the mirror? On your daughter's nose? Ever notice how your ears look too small for your head, too, Frank?"

Frank glared back. "What are you saying? That he wasn't a vampire? I saw his fangs."

"Oh, he was a vampire, Frank. He was my son." Damien fought the urge to snap Frank's neck, to release the grief and rage choking off his words. "Mine and your mo—"

"No." Frank struggled to get free. "You're crazy."

"Am I Frank? Did your brother cry for his mother, Frank? Your mother?" Damien nearly smiled at the horror filling Frank's eyes, but his heart still ached for the child he heard years ago beg his mother not to leave. The child who'd faced a monster to keep his mother.

"I have no brother! That baby died right after he was born. I went to his funeral," Frank cried, his voice sounding like a small child.

Damien probed his mind and felt his anger shift. Frank had held Marek for what he'd thought was the first and only hour of his life, had fallen in love with him the instant their eyes met, had cursed God for taking his brother so swiftly. "He lived, Frank. He was the vampire you mistook for me."

"I did not kill my brother. I didn't." Frank stared at him with imploring eyes. "I wouldn't."

"We took him after he was born to protect him from monsters like you." Damien dropped the sobbing man to the floor.

"My mother would have never given him up. You didn't see her when she held him. She would never—" Frank's head dropped to his chest. "If she knew he was yours, why would she give him up and not me?"

"She never knew. We have doctors, vampires committed to *protect* life, vampires who inform our orphanages as soon as one of our own is born to an unbonded human female."

"No. It can't be." Frank stared up at Damien.

"I knew, as soon as I laid eyes on him, that he was my own. Mine and your mother's. I took him into my home and prayed you would never lay eyes on him. How did you find him, Frank? How the hell did you get your hands on Marek?"

Frank closed his eyes. Tears seeped from beneath his lashes. "He came to me. He showed up at my door one night and asked if we could talk. I should have known it wasn't you. After all these years, to just walk up to my door? I told him we had to go someplace more private, that I knew a place where no one would hear us. My God, he walked right into the pen. I should have known something wasn't right."

"He walked into the pen?" Damien rubbed the tension from the back of his neck and tried to make sense of the scene Frank painted.

"He hesitated. But then he mumbled something about trusting me, about needing to tell me something, and followed me in."

Damien slumped down next to his enemy, his anger overwhelmed by his grief. Marek trusted everyone, was said to have the purest heart of their kind. But to walk into a pen they all feared? To even approach Frank Nostrum? "Did you listen to him, Frank? Did you ever bother to find out why he'd come?"

Frank leapt up. "How could I not listen? The whole time he raved like a lunatic. He said he was my brother, he said his name was Marek, but I thought you were trying to trick me. And what if he was my brother? He was still no better than an animal. A sick, dangerous animal that needed to be destroyed for the safety of mankind!"

Damien sighed. "Diana's in trouble."

Frank froze. "Diana? What have you done with my daughter?"

"Not me, Frank. We too have lunatics who believe they're saving their own race by destroying another. But then, again, like the lunatic I'm talking about, you've always been more driven by jealousy, haven't you, Frank?" He reached up and nearly tore the man's arm off. "Sit!"

"Diana's with my mother." Frank stated but his voice caught.

"That's right, Frank. She is. They have your mother, too."

"I just saw her." Frank shifted away, eyeing Damien warily.

"They're gone, Frank. God, will you just listen. I need your help. Someone's taken them to the Isle of Fentmo—"

"No." Frank once again leapt up. "But they're not like the Slashers. God, Diana has never even met a goddamn vampire, much less bonded..."

"You know about Slashers?"

"One of the vampires we caught thought he'd be spared if he gave away a few secrets." Frank cast his eyes down. "My mother swore Diana hadn't met any vampires," he mumbled then glanced up. "Are you telling me my mother lied to me?"

"I'm sure she only wanted to protect Diana from you." Damien rose, snatched a set of keys from a small glass table, took hold of Frank's arm, and pulled him towards the door.

"Where are we going?" Frank tugged back. His heels slid across the floor.

"First we're going to release Tomas." Damien dragged Frank to the car, ignoring the nauseating smell of the man's fear. "Get in and drive."

Frank quickly opened the car door and slid across the passenger seat to the driver's side. Damien joined him before he could even think of opening the other door. His hands shook so much that he couldn't get the key in the ignition. He screamed when Damien's hand shot out and grabbed his wrist. With Damien's help his hand steadied and the engine roared to life.

As they backed out of the driveway, Damien took hold of his arm. "Just remember, Frank. Don't try anything. I'm your only chance at saving your mother and daughter. Do you hear me? Your only chance. Now let's go get Tomas."

"Who the hell is Tomas?"

"Don't be coy. I know you have him in your pen." His anger drove his nails deep into Frank's arms.

"Ow! What are you talking about? I didn't put anyone in the pen."

"Don't play me for a fool. I see him. He's just a babe, for Christ's sake," Damien said through clenched teeth. The man amazed him.

"A baby? What do you think I am? I've never taken babies." Frank's arms shook so fiercely, the car swerved.

"Not a baby. A babe, just twenty-five, just entering his eternal years. And don't tell me you didn't put him there, he's calling for my help as we speak."

Frank drove through the village than continued north on Route 9. "I swear you, I mean Marek, was the last vampire I put in the pen."

Damien stared at Frank, could see the confusion etched across his face. "I know he's in there. I can still hear him calling for help. If you didn't put him there, then who did?"

"How the hell should I know?"

Damien watched the cars whiz by. "Frank, did Marek ever mention how he found out you were brothers?"

"That's why I didn't believe him. He said his mother sent him to me." He let out a short, bitter laugh. "My mother would never hand a vampire over to me, much less her own son. She hates me." He clenched his hands around the steering wheel. "She never forgave me for taking her away from you."

"You fool. She loved you more than me. That's why she stayed. How could you be so blind?" Damien shook his head. "I guess I shouldn't talk. I believed Olympia, Marek's stepmother, had grown to love him. She fooled us all. She must have sent him to you. This was all part of her plan and now she's sacrificing Tomas, Diana, and Lucian just to get back at me and Angelina."

"Who the hell is Olympia and what has she done to Diana?"

"Nothing yet, I hope. If she hurts one hair on Diana or Angelina's head..." The handle on the passenger door snapped off in Damien's hand. "We'll get Tomas to help us. If only I could break through the wall Lucian's put up in his mind, I could recruit his help, too."

Frank turned and drove up a steep unfinished road. After only a few minutes, he veered off the road and entered the woods.

Damien held onto the back of the seat as the SUV bounced and seemed to head straight for a tree. At the last moment, Frank swerved around it and came out on a path so narrow the branches of the trees and bushes lining it brushed against the vehicle. The path grew so steep, he was sure they would flip over and tumble down the mountainside. He would have thought Frank planned to do just that in an attempt to get away if the man hadn't been flicking on his blinker before every sudden turn.

"I don't think you have to worry about getting a ticket here, Frank," he muttered, shaking his head and grinning when Frank cast him a completely baffled expression. "Never mind. Just step on it."

He immediately regretted his words. His head slammed into the roof as they sped up.

When they finally stopped before an outcropping of massive boulders, Damien scanned their surroundings and immediately concluded they were alone and very near Tomas.

Frank turned to gaze intently at Damien. "Why are you helping my daughter? What do you care if she and my mother die?"

"I could never purposely harm a human, Frank. Even you. It's against our laws."

"Laws?"

Damien let out a long sigh. "Yes, laws. We're not monsters who spend our nights looking for blood. We have families, schools, jobs, and laws just like you. Anyway, Diana is the grandchild of my soul mate. I love her as if she were my own granddaughter."

He slid across the seat and followed Frank out the driver's door. "When your mother refused to complete the bonding ritual, I was so heartbroken, I wanted to drag her away and force her to stay with me. And when I didn't, I was sure she'd gone mad, like the Slashers."

Frank looked at Damien. "So you thought you left me with a mad woman for a mother."

Damien nodded. "I felt her madness was my fault. It only made sense that you'd grow up hating us. The hardest thing I've ever done was protect you, Frank. You killed my family and friends but you were still Angelina's child and in a way, mine. Too many times, I argued with elders that even though you'd captured and murdered our kind, we could not, by law, kill you. We can only kill in self defense. And so, they waited for one of those you captured to do just that."

Frank swallowed. "I always thought you just wanted my mother for—"

"Her blood? Oh, Frank, you have no idea what we're all about. Now, let's get Tomas and go save your daughter."

They walked along a narrow path until a huge metal gate covered with ivy blocked them from continuing further. Frank sorted through his keys and with a shaky breath opened the padlock.

Damien followed him through the opening, still wary enough to keep his hand wrapped around the back of the man's neck.

Towering cement walls topped with a multitude of five foot treacherous spikes surrounded a massive clearing. Not a tree or bush sprang from the level ground. In the middle, a crucifix shot up some twenty feet. Tomas, his naked body covered in sweat, hung with his hands and feet nailed to the wood.

Upon seeing them, he broke down and began to cry. "Damien! I knew you'd come. I knew it."

Damien instantly took in the direction the youth

faced. The rising sun would come from his side, extending the time it took for its burning rays to kill him. "My God, Frank, what kind of monster are you?"

"He didn't do this, Damien. Olympia did. She's crazy." Tomas sobbed. "Oh, God, get me down. These nails are killing me."

Damien climbed up to the pole and tore the nails from Tomas' hands and feet. Screams of agony sent a flock of birds into the dark sky. Gently cradling Tomas in his arms, he carried him out of the pen. Blood poured from the gaping holes. "Take off your shirt," he yelled to Frank.

Frank ran up to them and tore off his shirt. "I didn't do this, Damien. You have to believe me."

Damien shredded the shirt. Wadding the pieces up, he shoved them into the open wounds. Tomas let loose a heartbreaking wail then passed out.

They had only a few hours before dawn, not enough time to get to the Isle. Gathering the boy in his arms, he raced back to the car. By the time he reached it, blood was already dripping from the saturated cloth. "If I don't get him stitched up soon, he'll die."

Frank grabbed his arm. "I have a kit in the trunk. I've nearly lost a few of my men while..." He clamped his mouth shut and ran around to open the trunk.

A large black box filled the trunk. What appeared to be an innocent flashlight lay across the top. Frank shoved another light to the back and unlocked the box. Opening it, he tossed the contents aside then let out a sigh of relief and held out a suture packet.

Damien's hands blurred as they moved over the wounds. A few minutes later, Tomas' wounds were sealed.

Tomas' eyes opened to mere slits. "I was so scared. She said we were going to burn the pen down and catch the hunter. The next thing I knew, she had my hands nailed and—" His eyes flew open. "She found out about Lucian and Diana. When I lied and told her they didn't bond, she went berserk. She mentioned Fentmore."

"It's alright, Tomas. I'll take care of everything." Damien lifted Tomas up into his arms and turned to Frank. His gaze fell to the man's outstretched hand. Two small white capsules rested upon his palm.

"They're pain killers," Frank said.

Damien eyed the capsules suspiciously.

"Take them." Frank drew in a shaky breath. "I never could stand to hear them scream. I always slipped them a couple of these. Then if they didn't take effect by sunrise, I left."

Frank's shame poured into Damien mind. With a quick nod, he took the pills and convinced Tomas to swallow them. "Thanks. Now, take us to Angelina's. We'll figure out what to do next while Tomas sleeps through the day."

Lucian! Damien called his stepson again and again.

*****

The other children in Luna's class ignored Ms. Tindela's pleas to return to their seats. Luna felt those crowded around the bank of windows press closer as they peered into the night, hoping to be the first one to pinpoint where in the surrounding forest the vampire would emerge.   Another anguished roar, much closer than the first, had them nearly hanging out the windows.

"Children, get down."   Ms. Tindela began tugging at their wriggling legs. "You'll fall and break your necks."

"There goes another one," Caitlin, Luna's dearest friend, squealed with delight.

They all watched as a young pine soared over the treetops.

"We have a lot to learn before dawn, children. Tomorrow night —"

"I see him," Luna yelled, jumping up and down. "See? He's lifting another one."

Another sapling soared over the treetops, landing with enough force to bury its roots in its new location.

"Oh, my," Ms. Tindela gasped.

Moonlight shone on the face and bare chest of the vampire Luna had known all her life. Muscles bulged from his neck as he let out an ear splitting roar that sent some of the children scurrying under their desks.

Fallon let out a long whistle. "Boy is he ever over the edge!"

Luna tugged at Ms. Tindela's skirt. She peered up, her eyes filling with tears. "But that's my Uncle Lucian. You told us only teens in pooh-betty went over the edge."

Ms. Tindela ran her trembling hands over Luna's head. "Usually. It takes an awful lot to push a full grown male over. Children, please come away from the window. He's dangerous."

"He's coming this way," Fallon yelled, obviously no longer in awe of the charging vampire. "Run!"

Twenty first grade vampires charged. Desks flew across the room, tossed out of their way with mere flicks of their wrists. Luna heard screams and the sound of crashing desks coming from the other classrooms facing the woods. By the time the entire school sat huddled in the hallway, a line of elders had entered the schoolyard. Glad she'd stayed in the classroom, Luna opened the window and watched.

The elders cautiously approached Lucian, ducking as one when a tree soared towards their heads. In the state he was in, with his senses overloaded by his emotions, Lucian seemed to have no idea that they were even there.

*****

Every time Lucian thought of Diana and her deception, his heart shattered anew. He wanted to hurt her as much as she'd hurt him. Needed her to pay for Tomas' certain death, for tricking him into betraying his own kind while blindly falling victim to her wiles.

But more than anything, he needed her to convince him he was wrong.

Tonight was their third of the final stage. They should be together so that their love could appease their hunger until the final night. They should be together!

And tomorrow night should have been one spent baring their souls with completely open hearts and minds as they made love and fed upon each other until their bodies and blood merged to become one.

Would she have hidden the truth about her knowledge of her father even then?

"Diana!" he roared, feeling the muscles in his throat tear, the pain nothing compared to the pain crushing his soul.

He still loved her. The impact of just how much nearly suffocated him.

And now dawn hovered below the horizon and it was too late. Too late to change the course he'd taken and return to complete their bonding.

Today, Diana's hunger for him will consume her. As his for her will disrupt his sleep until night falls. If he hadn't deserted her, she could have held on, bolstered by her faith that when he returned at dusk, her undeniable hunger would be appeased.

Now, because of him, she would have no hope. She would allow the hunger to creep into her mind and destroy it.

He wrapped his arms around the young tree before him. Unmindful of the bark shredding his already raw flesh, he yanked it from the ground and flung it high into the air. He probed the night, searching for her and again felt nothing. It didn't make sense. His blood ran through her veins. Her emotions should be tangible enough to touch, even if they were hatred for him, even if she tried to hide them from herself. But he felt nothing! As if she had managed to cut him from her life.

He spun around, his eyes searching for something, anything to destroy. He snarled viciously at the line of elders standing before him. "Leave me."

"Calm down, child," his grandfather demanded.

"Child? I've suffered in this wretched existence

for nearly a century." He groaned, falling to his knees. "I want it to end."

"Lucian, you must listen to us. There is so much you don't understand."

"I understand that you forced Damien to spend eternity with someone he didn't love. Is that your answer for me? Do you have someone already lined up?"

"Lucian, let's discuss this inside. Dawn is only moments away." His grandfather held his hand out.

Lucian raised his eyes, not caring that the elders would see his tears. "Why didn't you warn me? You must have known. Why did you let it go this far?"

His grandfather's hand fell to his side. "You know we're not allowed to reveal what we know. And once you entered the bonding ritual, we could not interfere. The ritual is based on trust, Lucian, not just passion and love. That's why you couldn't find the truth about her father when you probed her mind. Your blood, the moment it entered her veins, altered your powers over her."

Lucian shook his head, his guilt bringing a bitter taste to his mouth. "No. I was able to lead her into the first night of the final stage. I blocked out her doubts."

"Only because deep down she wanted them blocked. If she had wanted to accept the knowledge that you may have gone to her to hurt her, she would have, no matter what you did."

The other elders began to mumble to themselves and shift nervously closer to the school.

"Come, Lucian. Let fate take its course."

"Leave me," Lucian demanded, his voice hoarse

from the lump lodged in his throat.

"We can't force you to take shelter, Lucian. You know that," his grandfather said.

Eternity stretched out before Lucian, dark, empty. A nightmare without Diana. "Then I suggest you leave."

Chapter Fourteen

Angelina and Diana cowered in the corner of a dark alley and warily eyed the sidewalk. Terrified that the next group of Slashers would be too ravenous to accept the wafers if they caught a whiff of Diana's blood, Angelina flung a handful as far away from them as she could.

Diana touched the tips of her fangs. "They're still there." Her voice cracked.

Angelina looked at the blood seeping from Diana's wounds. "Your fangs are the least of your problems, Diana. How are you feeling?"

"Hungry. Tired." She drew her knees to her chest. "And I'm so cold." She reached into her backpack and retrieved a wafer.

"You just had one." Angelina clasped her wrist in a viselike grip. "Drop it, now."

"But it hurts, Nana Lina. It hurts so much," she cried as she dropped the wafer into the backpack. "How could he leave me?"

Angelina watched as her granddaughter's eyes once again overflowed with crimson tears. A torrent of tears was better than the way her eyes had looked when she'd first been lowered from the helicopter.

She had stared vacantly at the ravenous pack that immediately surrounded her the moment she fell to the ground.

When the first one bit down on her wrist, she hadn't even flinched. Then as more joined in, feasting upon her exposed arms and neck, she'd merely closed her eyes, the tendons bulging on her neck the only sign that she felt every ragged tooth ripping into her flesh.

It had taken almost half of the wafers Angelina had stashed in her bag to draw them away from her willing granddaughter and the fresh vampire blood coursing through her veins.

And now, too weak from her blood loss to leave the alley they'd taken refuge in, Diana could only sit and battle her hunger. One moment she'd give in to her anguish over Lucian's desertion then, mumbling incoherently about him and her mother deserting her, trying to throw herself into the hungry jaws of the Slashers. The next moment, she'd curse them both and try to steal their only weapon as her eyes darted to Angelina's neck.

Angelina moved the backpack as far away from Diana as she could. "You're stronger than this, Diana. Just hold on a little longer. Someone will find us."

"Nana, I can't take it. Oh, God, I'm going to be like them, aren't I?" she cried. "This was his plan all along, you know. Olympia told me. This was his plan from the very beginning."

Angelina cringed watching the tears fill the open scratches trailing down Diana's cheeks. Her granddaughter had clawed at her face the last time she'd brought up Olympia's revelation. "You mustn't believe her, Diana."

"No, it's true. He came to me while I was sleeping, took my virginity, and gave me his blood before I even knew he existed. Just so I'd go mad. That's the only reason why he started bonding with me. Not because he loved me. Not even because he was my soul mate. He wanted me to go mad all along!"

"Diana, please."

"I thought he loved me." Diana started to giggle. "I thought my mother loved me, too. Silly me. Silly, silly, me. I can't hold on to my mother or my soul mate." Her voice grew shrill. "Do you think when I become one of these creatures, I'll finally find someone who'll want me?"

"I won't let that happen to you, do you hear me, Diana? I'll never let that happen."

"You can't stop it. You can't!" Diana hugged her knees to her chest and began to rock. "It's not just the unbearable hunger for blood that drives them mad, Nana. It's because they gave their chosen vampires their love then watched them devour it and toss the remains back in their faces!"

"Diana, calm down. You'll survive, just as I did." Angelina tossed another handful of wafers at a small group of Slashers and shuddered as they pounced on the promise of temporary sanity. They clawed and snapped at each other like a pack of wild dogs. Within moments after swallowing the wafers, they calmed down and left. She turned to hand some to Diana and froze.

Diana's upper lip curled up as she gazed at her own wrists. "Don't you see, Nana? You survived because you left him. Damien didn't rip your heart to pieces. Damien didn't leave you. Oh, God, I can't take it anymore."

Diana shoved herself to her feet. Her legs buckled, sending her crashing face first onto the trash covered ground. She whimpered when her grandmother grasped her shoulders and tried to lift her from the filth. "Just leave me here. I don't want to live without him. I'm so tired." She rested her cheek on her hands. "I'm so very tired."

"Diana Nostrum, you get up this instant. Lucian's not worth this. No man is worth losing the will to live. Diana, please." She shoved until her granddaughter rolled over.

Diana's eyes rolled back, revealing only white. Angelina leaned over and grabbed her wrist. Barely feeling a pulse, she feared Diana wouldn't make it off Fentmore Island alive. Baring her fangs, she tore at her own wrist and held it to her granddaughter's mouth.

Blood poured over Diana's lips and, for a second, she weakly sucked at the oozing wound. But when she blinked than gazed up at the wall towering above them, she turned her head away. "Please, Nana, just let me die. We will anyway when we run out of wafers. It hurts so much when they bite."

"Don't you dare give up on me. Don't you leave me here alone." Angelina sobbed. "Now, drink, drink for me, Diana."

Diana released a long breath. "Only for you, Nana. Maybe, if by some miracle we get out of this hellhole, you and Damien could—"

"You the lady with the wafers?"

Angelina glanced up. A man at least six foot four with muscles that would put Arnold Schwarzenegger to shame stood not two feet away. He let out a long breath when she nodded.

"Come with me, then." He turned and walked towards the wall.

"Wait. My granddaughter's too weak to walk."

Angelina cried, terrified that the giant would leave. She picked up Diana's backpack and hugged it to her chest. "I won't leave her."

The man returned and looked down at Diana. "If you ask me, you're wasting your time."

Angelina backed up.   A group of Slashers hovered on the sidewalk at the opening of the alley. "I'll give every last wafer to them."

"Okay, okay." He swept Diana into his arms as if she weighed no more than a baby. His eyes flicked over the dozens of wounds covering her. "How'd she get away?" he asked as they ducked into a doorway she hadn't noticed earlier in the wall.

"I threw them some wafers. I don't know how they even knew what they were but they quickly forgot about Diana and dove for them." Angelina puffed, trying to keep up with the man's breakneck pace as they made their way down a long, dark tunnel. "I knew you would come, but I was still scared."

He stopped and spun around. "You knew?"

She leaned against the wall, relieved for a chance to catch her breath. "I'm psychic. I saw Diana here. That's why I stashed so many wafers in her backpack. And I knew a giant...I mean tall man would help us if we had them. I don't usually see visions with myself in them so I wasn't sure if it was real."

He frowned, then grinned and shook his head. "I guess after seeing the creatures on this island, I could believe anything. Here, let me carry that."

Angelina's jaw dropped when he deftly shifted Diana into the crook of one massive arm, but when he reached out for the backpack, she pursed her lips and took a step back.

"Look, lady—"

"Angelina."

"Yeah, look Angelina. If I wanted to steal those from you and—"

"Diana."

"Well, you'd both be lying in that alley. Dead." He held out his hand.

Angelina hesitated a moment more before relinquishing the backpack.

"Man, how many of those things did you bring?" he muttered, flinging the strap over his shoulder and resuming their journey.

Angelina swiped at the damp hair clinging to her forehead. "Every one I own. There's about four hundred. I packed some of them in Diana's backpack the other night. The rest I grabbed just before I was taken."

He stopped at what looked like a dead end. Bringing his face up to the wall, he mumbled something then stood back. The wall slid to the right, revealing a young boy.

"Dad's back," the boy yelled over his shoulder.

A slender woman, no more than twenty years old, ran through the door and wrapped the man and Diana in her arms. "Thank God, you're back. We were so worried."

Angelina entered the room then quickly realized it wasn't a room at all. Thirty foot walls surrounded a small town. Towering pines lined cobblestone streets. The tops of swing sets were visible behind some of the white picket fences that surrounded dozens of flagstone cottages.

A squat man wearing a black suit and tattered top hat ran up to them. Removing his hat, he bowed then after running his fingers through the few strands of hair covering the top of his head, plopped the hat back on.

"Welcome! Welcome! I'm Mayor Cutter. I see you've met John and his family." He glanced at Diana's limp body cradled against John's chest and frowned. "They didn't tell me she was in such bad shape." He withdrew a wooden whistle from his breast pocket and blew.

A group of young men carrying a wooden stretcher suddenly appeared at the end of the road and ran up to them. Angelina watched as John adamantly refused to put Diana down.

"I'll carry her to Doc Jenkins." He took off, the woman and boy running to keep up with his long strides.

But when Angelina moved to follow them, the Mayor blocked her path and clucked.

"Now, now. She'll be just fine. Doc Jenkins always keeps fresh blood on hand for Night-timers. Our lookouts have been watching you ever since you arrived." He slid her hand into the crook of his arm. "We would have come sooner, but it took you so long to find your way into the alley. And when you finally did, John was working in the fields on the other side of the island. No one else is brave enough to enter the city at night."

"I really should go with my granddaughter," Angelina firmly stated, pulling her hand away.

"If you insist, we'll both go." He linked his arm in hers and led her across a small square. "I'm dying to hear all about the outside world."

Angelina blinked when a woman pushing an odd stroller smiled, baring small fangs. "How many live here?"

"Oh, well, that depends on whom — or should I say, what — you're asking about. Over the years, we've grown to a total of three hundred inhabitants. Fifty Survivors, one hundred Night-timers, and one hundred and fifty Fentmorians — you know, those born here. And we haven't lost one to the Slashers since we finished the wall, twenty years ago!"

Angelina shook her head. "How many are normal?"

"Normal? We have the quote normal unquote people, like yours truly, who never even believed vampires existed until we arrived here. We're the Survivors. Our plane crashed here over thirty years ago during a blizzard. There weren't that many Slashers then. First one I saw nearly took my head off!" He chuckled, tugging down the collar of his coat to reveal a mass of bulging scar tissue as he led her down a street lined with one-story buildings.

Wooden, hand painted signs were nailed above each door. Angelina noted they had a grocer, barber, blacksmith, and tailor. One long building had an equally long sign with the words "CLARA'S KITCHEN" surrounded by artfully painted flowers. The last building on the block bore a huge red cross.

Angelina winced when her sore ankle twisted in a crevice in the street. The Mayor wrapped his arm around her waist and nearly toppled her as he strove to help.

"We were ninety Survivors, then. We crashed in

the hills and realized, before we ever set foot in the city, that the place was crawling with blood sucking maniacs. But they're sensitive to the sun. Oh, they don't incinerate like in the movies. But they do burn, so they stay indoors. Well, we spent our days during those first years here building a wall around the city and our nights hiding out in the hills. You had to see the Slashers, then. Coming out at night, staring at that wall like it had magically appeared." He chuckled again and opened the door to the doctor's house. "Ah, here we are!"

Angelina shielded her eyes from the bright lights filling the room. "You have electricity?"

"Oh, we have it all. We were on our way to Malhali, a small Caribbean island our company purchased, expecting to take advantage of the wave of tourists searching for a less modernized Hawaii. Our plane had doctors, scientists, carpenters, and electricians and was stocked with enough supplies and building equipment for a year." He arched his brows. "And of course, yours truly, politician extraordinaire, was hoping to help organize their government. Unfortunately, we crashed not long after we took off."

"If you had carpenters and building supplies, why didn't you build a boat?" Angelina asked, waiting for her eyes to adjust to the lights.

"Oh, we did. We tried again and again. Our boats would be at sea for hours, sometimes days, then we'd spot land." Closing the door, he snorted. "We'd find ourselves landing on this island. We lost quite a few since we'd land on the shore of the city."

"We tapped into the power of the river that first

year," an elderly man drawing blood from a patient lying in a bed added.

Angelina's heart lurched when she realized the patient was Diana.

"What are you doing? She's already lost too much blood." She ran across the room, prepared to personally yank the syringe from his hand.

A hefty nurse blocked her way and gently grasped her shoulders. "We can't give her a transfusion until Doc Jenkins knows her type. Why don't you take a seat?"

She led Angelina to a wooden chair on the opposite side of the bed.

"How far into the bonding," the doctor asked, withdrawing the syringe from Diana's arm. He handed the vial of blood to the nurse. "Katie, get this to the lab."

"Tonight would have been their last." Angelina leaned over and clasped Diana's cold hand in hers, recalling how often Damien had helped her deal with the excruciating hunger she felt before their last night. How many times had he answered her pleas for his blood, for his touch?

Doc Jenkins shook his head. "That's going to make this one hard to match. Their blood's almost completely merged, unique. Hopefully, one of our Night-timers, one whose original blood type matched hers, bonded with a vampire related to the one she bonded with. Sometimes that works."

"Then test my blood. I might match." Angelina stood.

"I figured as much. Wearing a sweater in eighty degree weather pretty much gave it away. And John said you called her your granddaughter," he tossed the syringe in a wooden pail. "Judging by the fact that you look more like her sister, I'd say your ritual took place when you were about her age."

"I nearly made it to the last night." Angelina watched as he tied a rope around her arm.

"Well, we don't get many sane ones that far into the bonding." He whistled. "Whenever someone gets lowered into the city, we wait and watch. Not all come in completely mad. We rescue them and try to make their lives a little more comfortable."

The nurse grinned, baring small fangs. "And for that, we're eternally grateful."

"Katie, here was one of our first. We get more and more every year." He glanced up at Angelina then over at Diana. "Don't get many your age, lately. It's the teenage vampires that drop the most off. You know, they always think they've found the love of their life until the next one comes along."

She nodded, remembering how at sixteen she'd been sure Frank's father was her true love.

"All done." He pressed a small ball of cloth over the tiny hole and handed the sample of her blood to the nurse. "Every now and then, we get one in with those wafers. You came just in time. Our scientists have almost figured out how to make them, but our supply is running frighteningly low. They help our Night-timers."

Angelina nodded. "The temperature here helps too, I bet."

He nodded, taking in her sweater. "During the summer months, at least. You wouldn't happen to know where we are, would you?"

Shaking her head, Angelina explained. "I was unconscious, but judging by how quickly the helicopter left me than returned with my granddaughter, this island can't be too far from New York."

"We figured that much. We weren't in the air too long before the crash."

The doctor began to stitch up Diana's wounds. "One good thing about her going so far, she won't have any scars to remind her of her arrival. Poor thing, she must have been terrified."

A lump choked off Angelina's reply.

A half hour passed. The more labored Diana's breathing became the more Angelina prayed. Just as she thought she'd scream from the tension cramping her muscles, the nurse arrived and handed a slip of paper to the doctor. He glanced down as Katie spoke close to his ear. Seeing their grim expressions, Angelina drew her chair closer to the bed and grasped Diana's hand.

"I'm sorry. You're not a match." Doc Jenkins ran his hand through his hair. "I always feel so helpless when this happens. We'll just have to wait and see if she can hold out long enough for us to test all our Night-timers."

The night drew to an end and no matter how hard she tried to stay awake, Angelina soon fell into a deep sleep with her head resting on the bed beside Diana's hand.

She dreamt of Damien and Frank. They sat huddled over a map while another man she instinctively knew wasn't Lucian slept on a nearby couch. Her couch.

Damien, help us, she tried to yell.

Although her words sounded like nothing more than a groan, Damien raised his head and looked directly at her. He winked.

Hold on, Angelina. We're coming.

She tried to get closer, to touch him, but no matter how fast she ran, the distance between them remained.

Get Lucian, Damien. Bring Lucian to Diana. She needs him, she cried, her sobs strangling her words.

She watched in horror as Damien closed his eyes and turned back to the map.

She'll die if he doesn't come. She needs his blood! Her words sounded like nothing more than babbling to her ears but once again, she knew he understood.

Damien just shook his head. The room faded and for a moment she hung suspended in darkness. Gradually, she could make out a cluster of pine trees. Her eyes adjusted. Something moved in the clearing between the forest and a small brick building.

"No," she wailed, realizing the enraged vampire tossing a tree like it weighed no more than a toothpick into the air had to be Lucian. Blood covered his bare chest and arms and saturated his pants. *Lucian! Lucian!*

But he didn't hear her. She watched in horror as he held his arms up toward the amber sky above the horizon. Angelina realized he awaited the rising sun, knew he had no intention of taking shelter. Drawing closer, she saw the anguish on his face and reached out to touch him. Her hand passed through him. No matter how hard she tried to get his attention, he saw nothing, heard nothing.

"Don't cry, Nana. I'm not afraid to die."

Angelina lifted her head. "Oh, Diana!" she cried, "You have to call Lucian."

Diana's lips trembled. "He won't come. You didn't see his eyes. He hates me."

"He's hurt, Diana. He thought you'd tricked him. Give him a chance. Call him." She sat on the edge of the bed and cupped her granddaughter's face in her hands. "He loves you."

"No, he hates me."

"You listen to me, young lady. You're dying. The Slashers took too much blood and your body isn't accepting mine or any from the supply here. Call him."

"I can't. He has to come back to me on his own. I won't beg him to!"

Angelina scowled down into Diana's once vibrant green eyes. "If you love him, you'll call. He's dying from the guilt. I saw him, Diana. He needs to know you still love him. That you forgive him."

"You can feel that? He wants me to forgive him?" Hope lit her eyes.

"Open your heart to him. Close your eyes and see him with nothing more than your love, then you'll see what I did." Angelina brushed a wayward curl from Diana's forehead. "Go to him, Diana. Scream out his name with everything you've got."

*****

Diana closed her eyes and tore down the walls she'd erected to protect herself from Lucian's hatred.

His anguish slammed into her heart before she saw him kneeling on the ground while a sliver of the sun peeked over the horizon. A group of men glanced at the coming dawn then, turning from Lucian, rushed towards a building.

Get up, Lucian! Get away from the sun! She screamed with her mind; found that it like her body had barely enough energy to keep her connection to Lucian. The vision started to fade.

He lifted his head, glanced at the horizon. To her horror, instead of bolting for shelter, he tilted his head up higher and closed his eyes.

Her eyes flew open. "He's killing himself!"

"Don't stop, Diana. Tell him you love him. Tell him you're dying. He'll find shelter if he thinks he could save you."

Diana fought off the fatigue and squeezed her eyes shut. *I love you, Lucian. I'll always love you.*

She felt the heat of the sun burning his skin. *No! You have to come back for me!*

Sobbing, she used her own impending death to seduce him away from the dawn. *I'm dying, Lucian. If you ever truly loved me, let me see you one more time. There's nothing to forgive. Nothing. Oh, God, Lucian, get up!*

Lucian's back flinched as the first ray struck his shoulder.

Get up, you idiot! She watched as he raised his head, felt her heart swell when a grin spread across his face. With a bolt of speed that took her breath away, he charged into the building.

I'm coming, Diana.

She feared he thought she had meant that her hunger for him was killing her. *Hurry, Lucian. The Slashers took too much blood.*

*****

The rays of the sun seared Lucian's back as he sprinted the last twenty feet to the school. By the time the metal doors closed behind him, smoke rose from his back. The smell of burning flesh and the razor sharp sting from the multitude of slashes covering his body nearly sent him to his knees.

Only Diana's last words and the weakness he detected now that she had once again opened her heart up to his kept him from passing out.

He had to get to her before she died.

Nearly a hundred children sat huddled against the walls lining the dark hallway of the school, their quiet sobs and the comforting words of the teachers the only sounds meeting his ears. He opened his mouth to demand an explanation of why the children remained in school during the day then closed it with a groan. Their terrified eyes as they stared at him told him all he needed to know.

The teachers hadn't dared send the children out of the school with him out there. The windows of the school had metal shutters for emergencies such as this, but that didn't alleviate his guilt that these children were separated from their parents during a time when they should be home, safely tucked into their beds.

"I'm sorry," he mumbled

Luna pulled away from Ms. Tindela's grasp and timidly approached. "You okay, now, Uncle Lucian?" She tilted her head back and frowned up at him.

"Yeah, I'm okay now." Squatting, he winced. Seeing the concern on her face, he grinned. "How's my favorite girl?"

She pinched her nose between her fingers. "You

smell awful!"

He laughed at the sounds of disgust and fake retching that erupted from the children as one by one they gathered around him. Their eyes widened as they gazed at the damage a few moments in the sun had wrought. He doubted any of these children would accept a dare to face the sun even for a few seconds.

"You must be the strongest vampire ever," Fallon yelled from the back of the mass of bobbing heads.

"And the craziest," another added.

Lucian chuckled. "Love can do that sometimes."

Luna pouted. "I thought I was your favorite girl."

"You are, Luna Moona. You're my favorite little girl, but Diana is my favorite big girl."

Luna's eyes lit up. "Diana? My Diana?" She grasped the locket. "She gave me her heart," she announce proudly to her friends. "It's special. She put all her love in it so the monster that got Daddy would know she loved me and leave me alone."

Lucian's guilt washed over him anew like waves crashing upon the shore during a winter storm.

Luna's face beamed. "She said she'd always come if I got scared and called her. I did one day, when mommy was sleeping. Diana said that she'd kill the monster before she let it hurt me or my mommy."

"A girl can't kill a monster." Fallon scoffed then yelped as he received a swift punch in his arm from Luna. She turned around and faced the children. "Diana can, can't she Uncle Lucian? She can kick even better than that Chinese guy in the movies. She showed me once. Her leg swung over her head and broke a big branch right off a tree!"

Lucian chuckled.

Luna turned to glare at him.

He swallowed and wagged his finger. "Luna, what have we said about telling fibs?"

She stomped her foot. "It is not a fib. She broke a branch off a tree with just her foot. Mommy saw it, too."

Lucian recalled how Diana had kicked his feet out from under him when they were in her yard and all the trophies lining the shelves in her room, the figures atop them always with a leg flung out. "So she was going to kick this monster to death?"

"Yup. She's the best kicker in New York."

Lucian drew in a hissing breath as a small finger from the group gathered behind him poked the raw flesh on his back.

Rising, he gazed over the children's heads to the group of elders standing at the end of the hall. "I have to go. Now."

They nodded. His grandfather took out a cell phone. After mumbling a few words, he snapped it shut. "My helicopter is refueling. You'll be protected from the sun in it. I'm sorry, Lucian. It seems, your mother took two women to the Isle of Fentmore earlier this evening in the other one and hasn't returned."

Lucian swallowed his rage. He had to stay in control, for Diana's sake.

His grandfather let out a long weary sigh. "Olympia thinks that she is above our laws just because she is my daughter. She disrupted your bonding and must be punished."

"Banishment?" Luna asked, her voice sounding oddly relieved. "You're going to banish Grandma?"

Lucian took the little girl's hand. "It's the law, Luna. We can't keep producing Slashers. They're too dangerous to us. That's why anyone who purposely hinders the completion of a bonding ritual of a couple must face banishment. They're risking everyone's life. Do you understand?"

Tears welled up in her eyes. "She hurt my Daddy."

Lucian shook his head. "A bad man hurt your Daddy. Not Grandma."

She dropped her head. "She did. I heard her."

Lucian glanced up at the elders. They seemed as confused as he and slowly made their way through the children.

"What did you hear, Luna," Desmond, the youngest of the elders asked, placing his hand on Luna's shoulder.

"She told Daddy that the hunter was his brother. That he'd never hurt Daddy because they shared the same blood. She told him to go to the hunter and trust him." Luna's chin quivered. "Daddy was scared but Grandma swore she knew the man wouldn't hurt him. She said she'd follow and told him that he should do what the man said."

Lucian's fists clenched. He glared at his grandfather. "Has she no heart? She sacrifices her sons like we mean no more to her than the vermin she crushes beneath her feet!"

"I hate to admit it, but we are all pawns in my

daughter's eyes. She used my guilt against me when she convinced me to bind Damien to her, even though he begged me to keep him free until his chosen could join him." He dropped his head.

"But to kill her own son?" Lucian struggled to remain calm. He knew his grandfather's grief matched his own.

"Marek was adopted, Lucian, you know that."

"She raised him from infancy as her own. She must have loved him." He'd never forget the day his stepfather had brought the baby into their house. He'd felt a bond with him unlike any he'd had before or since.

Until Diana.

He glanced up at his grandfather. "I always thought Marek looked like Damien, but I assumed one of his parents was another vampire. He was Damien's and Angelina's son, wasn't he?"

When his grandfather sadly nodded, Lucian snarled. "Damien always treated me like his real son and my mother repaid him by sending his only son to his death. Banishment isn't good enough."

"No, it isn't. Now that we know about her crime, we must take action." Desmond demanded.

His grandfather turned, his shoulders slumped, and walked down the hall. "So be it."

The sound of an approaching helicopter drew everyone's attention away from the departing elders.

Chapter Fifteen

Doc Jenkins stood beside Diana's bed holding her wrist between his fingers. Shaking his head, he tenderly tucked her hand under the sheets. "I'm afraid she won't last through the day."

"She has to. Lucian can't come until sunset." Angelina grasped his arm. "There must be something we can do to keep her alive until he arrives. Why won't feeding help? Why can't I let her feed from me?"

He continued to shake his head, and patted her trembling hand. "It won't do any good. She needs a transfusion to replenish the massive amount of blood she's lost. Feeding from you would only satisfy the craving."

"But it might give her enough energy to hold on until Lucian comes. We have to at least try." She battled the massive lump in her throat, the searing sting of tears in her eyes. "Please, let me at least try."

"Angelina, even if Lucian walked through that door this instant, I doubt she'd make it."

Angelina lost her battle to remain strong and slumped into the chair, her wracking sobs tearing at her chest. "This is all my fault. If I'd kept her away from them like her father had wanted, she'd be home right now. Not in this Godforsaken place."

Katie, the nurse who'd remained beside Angelina all morning, squatted beside her chair and wrapped her arm over her shoulders.

The sound of a helicopter hovering overhead drew everyone but Angelina and Katie to the

window.   Angelina covered her eyes when they
shoved the drapes aside, allowing the bright rays of
the midday sun to wash over the room. Diana didn't
even flinch as a beam slashed across her face.

"Three in two days. If they keep this up we'll be
overrun by Slashers."   Katie muttered, rising and
drawing a curtain halfway around Diana's bed.

"They're dropping a box in the square!"   Doc
Jenkins shouted.

"A box?" Katie peeked around the curtain.

"It looks like a coffin," one of the orderlies
uttered in a hushed voice.

"Why would they be dropping a coffin on our
side of the wall?" Katie's voice trembled. Her hands
clenched the curtain. "What if it's a vampire? What if
the one that brought you here heard we're helping
you?"

"Does that woman never give up?"   Angelina
searched the room for someplace to hide Diana.

"John's got an ax."   Doc Jenkins winked at
Angelina over his shoulder. "Looks like their going to
bust it open. If it's that Olympia, she'll fry before she
reaches us."

"Lucian..." Diana whispered and sighed.

The doctor frowned.

"Oh, my God, he's in the coffin!"   Angelina
glanced down at Diana than back at the doctor.
"Lucian!"

"Cover the windows," Doc Jenkins yelled and
flung open the door.

Angelina squeezed Diana's hand as she watched
the doctor race outside, heard his frantic demands
that the coffin remain intact.

The orderlies closed the blinds and curtains. The two wearing extra layers of clothing darted from the room. Katie took a step to follow them then turned and, raising her chin, returned to Diana's bed.

Angelina brought her lips to Diana's ear. "Your Lucian's here, isn't he, honey? Diana? Is it Lucian?"

But Diana didn't answer, didn't move no matter how hard Angelina and Katie nudged her. She looked so content, a soft smile curving her pale lips.

Angelina's throat constricted. "He's here, Diana. You have to hold on."

A lone tear escaped from the outer corner of one of Diana's eyes. A long, barely audible breath was the last sound Angelina heard before her own screams filled the room.

When the doctor and the men carrying the coffin entered the room, they found Angelina sobbing on her knees beside the bed as Katie, tears pouring down her cheeks, frantically searched Diana's neck and wrists for a pulse.

The men dropped the coffin and quickly left, slamming the door behind them. Doc Jenkins patted Angelina's shoulder.

"He's too late. She's gone." Katie whispered.

An enraged, ear-splitting roar erupted from within the coffin.

*****

Hearing Angelina's sobs and an unfamiliar voice say that he'd arrived too late to save Diana, Lucian roared in denial and burst free from the coffin. Splinters shot out in every direction as the wooden box shattered.

Standing amidst the remains of the coffin, he

searched the room for Diana. His gaze swept past a man in a white, threadbare doctor's jacket, past a desk, past empty beds, then came to an abrupt halt at a curtain partially obstructing his view of the only patient. He took a step closer. Flung the curtain aside.

Angelina rocked on her knees beside the bed. Shaking from the sobs wracking her body, she didn't even acknowledge his presence. The sweet scent of Diana's blood was so faint, he had to strain to separate it from the stench of medicines and antiseptics and fear permeating the air. Straining his ears, he sought some sign of life from the frail body lying in the bed. Heard not a wisp of a breath over Angelina's blubbering.

He glowered at her until she stood, then brought his face close to hers and growled. "Stop crying. You hear me? Don't you dare give up on her."

A whimper drew his attention to the nurse standing on the other side of Diana's bed. Her hand trembled, making the sheet clutched in it flutter above Diana's face.

"What the hell are you doing?" he snarled.

The woman reeked of fear, a foul, pungent odor that made his stomach roil. Her hand twitched. Her wide eyes darted from him to the doctor then back to him.

"I-I..." Crimson tears pooled in her eyes. She blinked until they spilled over her cheeks. "N-no pulse."

"Drop it." He flexed his fingers against the pain of his nails growing. Before she could cover Diana's face, before she could utter those two words again, he bellowed, "Now!"

The sheet fluttered from her hands as she crumpled to the floor in a dead faint. Tossing a chair out of his way, Lucian leapt across the room and caught the sheet a hairsbreadth away from Diana's face.

"She's gone, Lucian." Angelina sobbed and buried her face in her hands. "I heard her take her last breath. Our Diana's dead."

"She is *not* dead," he stated, his voice, burning glare, and clenched fists daring anyone to disagree.

"Then save her. Bring her back to me." Angelina pried open one of his fists and pressed Diana's wrist in his hand. "Like Mina brought back Dracula, you bring her back to me."

Lucian refused to acknowledge that his soul mate's heart no longer beat. How could it not when his own pounded in his ears? He leaned over and kissed her lips. "Come back to me, Diana."

When her breath failed to touch his lips, he howled in denial. "She has so little blood," he breathed. They were one; their hearts would either beat as one or he would join her in death. A tear burned a path down his cheek. Swiping it away, he licked the blood from the back of his hand and vowed he would not shed one more bloody tear. Diana needed every drop he had to give. "Mina help us, it's the only way."

Yanking the sheet from her body, he hissed. Gaping wounds marred nearly every inch of Diana's arms and legs. After he eased her out of the grey hospital gown, he discovered that more covered her torso. Thick, black thread sealed some, but others oozed with puss.

He tossed the sheet to Angelina. "Rip off a long strip." After shedding his clothes, he gingerly climbed onto the bed and lifted Diana's left wrist to his mouth. Sinking his teeth into her pale skin, he tore open her artery. Seeing through a crimson haze of tears, he hesitated when a miniscule drop of blood slid down her arm. When he opened the artery on his right wrist, his blood spurt out onto the pristine sheets. Moving so quickly, his hands blurred before his eyes, he pressed his open vein to hers then, using his mouth and other hand, bound their wrists together. Then waited.

And prayed to God, the angels, Mina, Dracula, and all who might hear. He focused on her lungs, her heart, their connected wrists. The tale of Mina's miracle rang in his ears. How she'd bound herself to her fallen love and begged the angels above for mercy. How a light brighter than that of the sun shone down upon them, filling her with warmth, peace, and hope. How Dracula's vein had felt as if it were suckling on hers, drawing in more and more of her blood to replenish his.

"Please," he whispered, gazing down on the face that had bewitched him from that first night by the lake. "Don't leave me."

Lucian saw no light, felt no warmth or peace. Diana's cold, limp wrist pressed against his. His lungs seized. He'd lost her. When he opened his mouth to curse the angels and anyone else responsible for taking Diana, he felt her vein adhere to his, felt her heart stutter. His blood surged through his veins to his wrist, left his body with every beat of his heart and flowed into Diana's. He allowed his tears free reign when Diana's blue lips turned pink.

"When I pass out, you must keep us together. And don't touch the bindings. Do you hear me? No matter what happens, we must stay together," he said, never taking his eyes from those lips.

He slid beneath the sheets and drew Diana into his arms. They had to be united. Completely. But his fear that he still might fail left him impotent. Closing his eyes he envisioned her naked, teasing him as he undressed in the cottage, moaning as she watched him wash her in the shower, and drawing his hips down to hers as she accepted him for what he was. Nothing worked. And then he saw her as he did that first night, dancing naked in the moonlight, running into his arms. Recalling the feel of her body slamming into him then melting against his chest when he captured her lips, desire stirred.

With a relieved sigh, he nudged the head of his cock between her nether lips. His breath hitched when instead of being engulfed in her heat, he felt as if he'd just dipped himself into a cool pool of stagnant water. He thrust deeper. A wave of dizziness from his blood loss hit him. Lowering his lips to Diana's, he struggled to remain conscious.

They were together again. Nothing else mattered. If this failed, they would at least die together. Bound as they were always meant to be.

*****

"You want me to what?" Frank sputtered, spraying the ancient map and Damien's face with coffee.

Damien scowled and grabbed the lace doily on

the arm of the chair. He gently blotted the drops off the already bleeding ink. "Do you have any idea how old this map is?"

"No, but I do know that my mother will have your head for ruining her great-grandmother's doily." Frank leaned back in the chair and crossed his arms over his chest. "Ink and coffee. Ruined."

"Your mother and daughter need this map more than some wisp of lace." Damien tossed the doily across the table.

"I won't do it."

Damien ran his hands through his hair. "It's the only way, Frank."

"It's suicide. From what you've told me, if I drop you into the center of the city, they'll have you bled dry before you hit the ground." He swiped his hand across the table, sending the map and doily to the floor.

"Frank!" Damien leapt up, tossed the map back onto the table then bent to retrieve the doily. He turned the delicate strip of lace over and over in his hand, then tenderly folded it and stuck it in the pocket over his heart. He turned to Frank. "I know it's risky, but if we do this right, if you dangle me out of reach until every damn one of them is there, then by the time I hit the ground, you'll have Angelina and Diana out of there."

Frank hung his head and dropped back down into the chair. "I never believed until today that you loved my mother, you know? All these years, all those executions, simply because I refused to believe a vampire could have any reason to want my mother except as a blood bank. My God, I even killed my own brother."

Damien shook his head. "You didn't know."

"What have I done? How many children are orphans because of my own jealousy?" Frank rubbed the back of his neck then stilled. "Did my brother have children?"

Damien hung his head. "He had a little girl."

Frank pounded the table with his fist. "I should be the one dropped. I deserve to die, not you."

Grasping Frank's shoulder, Damien squeezed. "Thanks for offering, but they don't want human blood, Frank. They want vampire blood."

"Then transform me." He raised his head, his eyes wide. "Give me your blood."

"It wouldn't work. Your scent wouldn't be strong enough to draw them all, if any. Even if it could work, I could never do that to Angelina. How could I look her in the eyes knowing that I'd sacrificed her only living son rather than myself?" He went back to his seat and smoothed out the map. "No, Frank, this is the only way."

Frank leaned across the table and grabbed Damien's arm. "A bag. We could fill a bag with some of your blood."

"No, Frank."

"We'll poke a hole, let some drip down."

"Frank!"

"What? It could work. They'd definitely smell it." He dug his fingers into Damien's arm. "Goddamnit, at least consider it!"

Damien scowled. "They'd know, Frank. They may be mad, but they're not stupid. Some wouldn't even bother to show up for a small bag of blood. The first bite and the ground would get more than them."

Frank slumped back in his chair. "Ironic, isn't it Damien? I spent my whole life trying to kill you and failing. And now? All I want to do is find a way to keep you alive, and I can't do that."

"But you can save your mother and daughter, Frank. Now, let's get this rescue on the road. Get me some more coffee. We have a long day ahead of us and I'm not used to being up at this hour." He watched the man he'd once feared drag his feet as he left the room.

"Damien?"

Damien turned. Tomas, his wounds already healing, sat on the couch glaring at him.

"Are you crazy? You're going to let him drop you on Fentmore, in the middle of the city?"

Damien shrugged. "Angelina's my soul mate, Tomas. Her life is more important to me than my own."

"But if you're dead—"

"If I'm dead there's at least some chance we will meet again in another lifetime. Go back to sleep, Tomas. We'll need your help tonight."

"Lucian's already there, you know." Tomas mumbled as he snuggled back down into the cushions.

"He's on Fentmore?" Damien strode over to the couch.

"Yup. The fool thought I was dead." He yawned and rolled over. "They're bonding the ancient way."

Damien grabbed Tomas' shoulder and rolled him onto his back. "The ancient way? Why the hell would he do that?"

"What's the big deal? All of the ancient one's bonded with their human mates that way."

"And most of them died, Tomas. Most of them bled to death and were buried still tied to each other. You know that." Damien shut his eyes, searching for Lucian but Tomas' finger poking his chest broke his concentration.

"I think the two thousand years you've lived since your days in school have fogged your memory, Damien. They died because both their bodies didn't really need to take in the other's blood. Not so with Lucian and Diana. She was already dead, bled nearly dry—"

Grabbing Tomas' arms, Damien raised him until their eyes were level.

Tomas' eyes flew open. "Put me down, Damien."

"Explain what the hell you're talking about," he uttered, his voice deadly.

"Well, I didn't get all of it, because Lucian kinda vanished from my mind in the middle." He watched Damien's rage escalate and rushed on. "But I'm sure he's okay. He's in some sort of hospital. Outside the city."

Damien dropped Tomas back down to the couch and strode to the table. He returned to couch, the map crushed in his fist. "There is no hospital outside of the city. There's nothing but wilderness around it."

"Ah, well, it seems that an awful lot has gone on over there you elders don't know about." Tomas leapt over the back of the couch when Damien advanced. "Okay. Shit! Get a grip."

"I'll get a grip on your neck if you don't tell me what the hell you're talking about." Damien soared over the couch and pinned his nephew against the wall. "Talk Tomas. And don't stop until you've told me everything you know about Fentmore."

"Okay. Okay. You elders all blocked that place from your minds. Sure, you had the Slashers dropped down in the center of the city, but you always had us young ones fly the helicopters. And never more than a few times, warning us to wipe the memory from our minds and block out the maddening cries for blood. We had to promise when we returned not to talk about it, so that we wouldn't open any vampire's mind to the cries. Well, some went when there was a full moon, some saw a different place than the—"

"Different?"

"Yeah. Marek told me right before *he*," he nodded towards the kitchen, "killed him. Marek said a wall surrounded the city. Olympia used to tell him frightening bedtime stories about the island. So, when he returned he said she'd lied, because it wasn't all that bad. He'd seen a town on the other side of the wall, so it couldn't be like she'd said."

"A town? You mean the Slashers built a wall and a town? That's impossible." Damien started to turn away chuckling. "Marek was pulling your leg."

Tomas grabbed his arm and jerked him around. "Marek didn't lie. He said the Slashers were in the city. This town had others in it. It was night, but he saw women with babies, kids playing in a park, and even farms."

"Did Lucian know about this?" Damien couldn't believe word of these changes hadn't leaked out.

"If he did, he didn't hear about it from me. I swore to Marek I wouldn't tell anyone that he'd talked. He was afraid you and the elders would punish him. Can you imagine if Tobias heard someone talked?" He let out a long whistle.

"Go on, Tomas. What else do you know?"

"Well, I did tell Diego, you know, because he's been my best friend for, oh, years and—"

"Just get to the point, Tomas."

"Diego flew Lucian in this morning, so I guess he went right to the town instead of the city. Well, Lucian yelled some sort of good-bye to me, like I was already dead. I set him straight and gave him a piece of my mind about not coming to save me. Then, bam! He floods me with info. Diana's dead. Ancient bonding. Hospital. Doctor. Nurse. Diana dead. He shouted that about twenty times."

"Diana's dead?"

They both turned. Frank stood on the other side of the couch. The cup of black coffee tilted forward in his loosening grip, its steaming contents pouring onto the cushion below.

Damien rushed to him. "No, Frank. She can't be. Angelina would have sent me some kind of word." He grabbed the cup and looked down at the dark stain on the couch. "When she gets back here, we're going to have a lot of explaining to do."

"Maybe she didn't send word because she's dead, too." Frank mumbled, turning away.

"Oh, no. I definitely picked up that Angelina was fine. Just freaked out about Diana being dead and all—" Tomas clamped his mouth shut, when

Damien bared his fangs. "But Lucian's giving her his blood."

"And probably killing himself in the process," Damien muttered draping his arm across Frank's slumped shoulders. "Frank, Lucian won't let her die. He'll give her his last drop, before he let's that happen."

Frank shuddered. "If she's already dead, how could she suck—?"

"Ancient bonding, man." Tomas leapt across the couch and flung his arm over Damien's from the other side of Frank.

Frank looked at the vampires standing on either side of him. "You're both consoling me as if I've never killed your kind. You're better men than I could ever hope to be. So how does this bonding help Diana suck?"

"Lucian tied his open vein to hers," Tomas said, making the motion of biting into one of his wrists then holding it to the other.

"Tied?"

"This way, when he passes out from loss of blood, his vein remains on hers," Damien answered, a chill at the implications running down his spine. "The old ones believed their blood would pass back and forth until it had completely merged, making them one with their mates."

"Right. We're talking big time romance, Frank." Tomas grinned.

"Except Diana supposedly has hardly any blood. Which means it will all flow into her, probably take all day. We heal during the day. By dusk, Lucian's vein will have closed." Damien stared at the two men and waited for what he said to sink in.

Frank grasped his meaning first. "Before enough flows back into his body?"

Tomas' grin vanished.

"Then she would live and he would die," Frank mumbled.

"It doesn't quite work that way." Damien explained, "If he dies, then his blood will be useless to her. Ancient Bondings are where you humans got all those fallacies about vampires only living as long as the one that transformed them lives. The Ancient Bonding created one entity of two people. Each couple's blood is unique. Ancient Bonding is no longer acceptable because, for some reason, when one of the bonded mates died, the other quickly followed."

"And Lucian knows this?" Frank asked.

Damien raised a brow and looked at Tomas.

Tomas grimaced. "I guess that's what he meant by their hearts would either beat as one or he would join her in death."

"Do you all commit suicide so casually?" Frank gasped.

"Only for our soul mates, Frank." Damien tried to smile, but failed.

"He's counting on us getting there in time," Tomas said. "He said you knew what to do."

"Then let's get moving. If I understand you two," Frank moved out from under their arms, "I don't have to use Damien as bait."

Damien nodded.

Frank glanced at the clock. "Well, we've got three hours till dusk."

Damien handed his cell phone over to Tomas. "Call your friend, Diego. Tell him to pick us up by the lake at dusk."

When Tomas had finished, the three gathered around the map. Damien grabbed a pen and drew a circle around the city.

Tomas once again let out a long whistle. "I bet the Slashers can smell Lucian's blood a mile away. They must be freaking out."

Two grim faces turned his way.

Tomas laughed. "They couldn't get over that wall. Marek said it was really tall."

Damien scowled.

Tomas shook his head and looked at Frank then back to Damien. "They couldn't possibly get over it. Could they?"

*****

Olympia huddled against a boulder. Unable to stop shivering since she'd taken refuge in the dank cave when dawn had approached, she wished she had the courage to get closer to the band of fading light at the entrance. The remains of the rats she'd drained during the day were sprawled at her feet, along with the swarm of insects drawn to the blood surrounding them. She saw them, heard them, felt them crawling up her legs.

She tenderly ran her fingers along her left arm. The gash from the helicopter blade striking her when they crashed had already healed completely but still throbbed relentlessly. She had stitched the wound that had extended from her shoulder to her elbow with the suture kit she had retrieved from the wreckage. Now, she wished she'd taken the time to wash out the muck that had been imbedded deep within her wound before closing it. The throbbing could only mean an infection brewed. But she didn't dare reopen the wound out here.

Her second mistake had been to toss the kit to her pilot as he struggled to release his seat belt moments before the helicopter tumbled off the cliff and fell onto the rocky coast below.

Now, with nothing to seal her wound, reopening it was not an option. She'd just have to deal with the pain until she found a way off this island.

The screams from the city made their way into the cave and kept her from moving toward the entrance when dusk finally arrived.

She jumped up as some unseen pest pierced the tender skin of her inner thigh. "Ugh, they're in my damn pants!"

Flying out of the cave, her pants half down, Olympia screeched and started swatting at the red ants covering her legs. Trembling, she searched the shadows surrounding her.

Slashers inhabited this island. She'd dropped enough off herself to know.

She jumped from the rock and fled when a twig snapped. Branches whipped at her face, animals, catching scent of her weakened state, lurched from the darkness and nipped at her ankles. For the first time in her life, Olympia was terrified.

Father! Father!

She'd been trying to reach him all night, but to no avail. She refused to believe he would block her from his mind, decided instead that something on this wretched island, something the elders must have installed to protect their kind from hearing the constant calls of the Slashers, blocked her own cries for help.

Taking a deep fortifying breath, she slowed to a walk. She had no idea how she'd get off the island, if ever, but sitting on a rock all night wouldn't get her any closer to home and running in circles would only wear her out. If she could make it to the ocean without bumping into a group of Slashers, she would figure something out.

If only there weren't so many creatures scurrying around in the shadows. When the cries of the Slashers grew more frenzied, her pace quickened. She stumbled, cutting open her knees, releasing more of her scent.

*****

Doc Jenkins paced back and forth between the foot of Diana's bed and the window.

Angelina tore her gaze from Lucian and Diana and watched him peer into the darkness for the tenth time. "Doc, would you please sit down. You're driving me crazy."

They were the only two left in the makeshift hospital. The minute Katie, the nurse, had opened her eyes, she had taken in the scene on the bed, listened to the screams coming from the Slashers then fled to the safety of her house.

The remaining few hours of daylight had dragged on. Lucian's breathing grew shallower with each passing minute.

At one point, John, the man who had carried Diana out of the city, had returned to check on her. Seeing her cradled in Lucian's embrace, he had left and returned with a bowl of cool water. He'd wiped the faces of the couple with a wet cloth, declaring gruffly that Angelina and Doc Jenkins should take better care of them.

His wife had arrived with enough food for an army shortly before dusk. Angelina virtually drooled from the aromas rising from the steaming dishes. She avoided asking what animal they feasted on, preferring to enjoy the succulent meat ignorant of its origin. Corn, broccoli, and carrots melted in her mouth. But the food lodged in her throat each time a moan arose from the bed.

When John and his wife finally left, she and the doctor had nothing left to do but wait until sunset and pray that Damien had heard her calls.

An hour after the sky grayed, it sounded like all hell broke loose on the other side of the wall. While most of the Night-timers—too afraid to be near a full-blooded vampire again, too afraid that the scent of his blood would tempt them and awaken the beast they'd worked so hard to control—had stayed away from the doctor's, it soon became apparent the Slashers wanted nothing more than to storm the town in search of that same scent.

Screaming and snarling, they clustered at the base of the wall closest to the doctor's street. One by one, the residents of the town flew into the hospital with word from the lookouts.

"Every single Slasher in the city is clawing at the wall."

"They're killing each other!"

"The dead are stepping stones for the living!"

Then John charged in, his eyes filled with terror.

"The pile of dead is almost to the top of the wall!"

One hour after dusk, a crowd of terrified residents gathered on the doctor's front lawn and demanded he hand the vampires over to the Slashers.

"The Mayor's here. He'll calm them down." Doc Jenkins moved away from the window to unlock the door.

The Mayor charged into the room, his eyes wide and his hat twisted between his trembling hands. "They're going to reach the top!" he cried, his voice as shrill as a young girl's.

Angelina placed her hand on the Mayor's arm. "Calm down, Mayor. Lucian's stepfather is on his way. I can feel it."

"Another vampire? Oh, no! They'll get over for sure if they smell another one. We're doomed if they come over that wall. Doomed!" He crept over to the bed and peered down at the couple. "One might satisfy them."

"Don't even think about it, Mayor." Angelina ran up and slid between him and the bed. "If you separate them now, they'll both die."

The Mayor held out his hands. "What can I do? I can't sacrifice a whole town of innocents for one vampire!"

Doc Jenkins walked away from the window. When he spoke, his soft voice seemed to calm the Mayor. "If you take him, you'll kill the girl. Give them a little more time. The Slashers have never scaled the wall before."

"They've never had a full-blooded vampire on the other side before, either." He dropped into a chair by the window and resumed twisting his hat. "As if this one's scent weren't enough to drive them over the wall, we have reason to believe he's not the only vampire on the island."

Angelina's heart swelled at the thought of seeing Damien again. "You've seen him?"

He jumped as the demands outside suddenly surged. "No, but the field workers came in this morning with news that the helicopter that dropped off this young woman crashed. They were on their way to check it out when they saw the wreckage fall off the cliff."

Doc Jenkins looked up from taking Diana's pulse. "So what makes you think anyone survived?"

The Mayor smacked his hat down on his leg. "Vampire's don't die that easily, do they? And the Night-timers could smell it. The males said it was a female."

"Olympia." Angelina walked up to the Mayor. "Release the Slashers into the woods. Let them go after her."

He laughed nervously. "The only way from the city to the crash site is right through the middle of town, woman. They'd feed on every Night-timer they found on the way, not to mention these two."

"He's right," the doctor added, his hand now on Lucian's free wrist. "I just can't imagine how they could scale the wall. Do you realize how many of them would have to die to create a mound that high?"

The Mayor and Angelina shuddered in unison.

If Damien didn't get here soon, he'd arrive to find no one alive to rescue.

A soft whimper from the bed drew their attention. Diana's eyes opened for only a moment, but the smile on her face as she tucked her head under Lucian's chin gave Angelina more hope than she'd had since she watched Olympia lower her granddaughter from the helicopter.

"I hope your vampire gets here in time," the Mayor whispered. "I'd hate to see these two go through all this just to have to fall into the hands of the Slashers. It'd be a damn shame."

"He'll make it," Angelina stated, her voice sounding surer than she felt. Ever since she'd landed here, her abilities had weakened. Past visions had never gone further than their rescue from the city.

John burst into the room. "The beach lookout said a helicopter's coming this way."

"Damien." Angelina turned toward the door but halted and glanced at the Mayor then Diana and Lucian.

"Go on." Doc Jenkins wrapped his arm around her shoulders, "I'll keep them safe."

She ran to the door then with a weary sigh, turned away. "I haven't seen him in decades." Her hands flew to her hair as she glanced down at her blood-stained cloths.

John let out a bark of laughter. "You couldn't look awful if you tried."

The Mayor nodded and smiled. "You look fine."

"The man flew across an ocean to save you. Don't keep him waiting," Doc Jenkins said with a wink.

Her heart lodged in her throat. "I've waited so very long for this moment. And now I find I'm terrified he won't want me anymore."

The sound of the helicopter finally met their ears.

Doc Jenkins and the Mayor went to the window and peered out into the darkness.

"You'd better hur—"

Angelina ran out the door.

Chapter Sixteen

Damien stared down at the town in amazement. He had expected huts, not well built houses with electrical wires strung between them. It amazed him that this place had remained a secret for so long.

The crowd clustered around the town square parted as the runners of the helicopter touched the ground. He saw a figure charging down the path they'd created.

Angelina. Flinging open the door, he jumped out and ran to meet her. Her hair flew behind her as she sped towards him; her eyes shimmered with tears as she called out his name again and again.

When she finally reached him, he swept her into his embrace and crushed her lips with his. Years melted away. They were together and nothing, nothing would ever take her from him again.

"Angelina. My beautiful, Angelina," he murmured against her lips.

She clasped his face in her hands and pressed her body into his.

Their tears mingled as they continued to kiss each other passionately, the crowd surrounding them forgotten.

"Mother?"

Angelina peered around Damien. "Frank? What are you doing here?"

Damien laughed and swept her up into his arms. "You'd be surprised how much your son and I have in common, Angelina. Did you know he hates golf, too?"

Laughing at Angelina's confused face, he kissed a bruise on her cheekbone then carried her through the crowd.

Before they entered the doctor's front yard, Damien brought his lips to Angelina's ear and whispered. "Do you have any idea how much I want to dash off into the woods and tear off your clothes?"

She kissed her way up his neck.

"Unfortunately, we're running out of time." He raced into the house she pointed out then gently put her down. Not bothering to take the time to acknowledge the three men gaping at him, he went directly to the bed and placed his hand around Diana and Lucian's bound wrists.

"The blood is still flowing, but much slower than I hoped. Just as I thought the young fool only cut one vein. Get me sutures, quickly."

He tore open the veins on their unbound wrists with his fangs and, faster than normal eyes could follow, sewed the veins to each other then bound them with the strips of cloth he'd ripped from the clean sheet Angelina had handed him. Untying the strips binding their other wrists, he did the same.

By the time Frank and Tomas entered the room, Damien had cocooned Lucian and Diana in sheets.

"Did you look around, Damien? It's amazing!" Tomas moved around the room, checking out the crude instruments made from wood and clay and others that looked like antiques.

"There's no time, Tomas. For everyone's safety, we have to get out of here fast. Give me a hand." Damien draped another sheet around the couple as Frank and Tomas ran up to help him carry them out to the helicopter.

In the helicopter, they gently laid Diana and Lucian down on the floor. Angelina blushed when Damien wrapped his hands around her waist then lifted her into the helicopter and onto his lap. He stole a swift, deep kiss before leaning out and yelling to the crowd. "We'll draw the Slashers to the center of the city long enough for you to clear away the bodies. It didn't look like there were enough left alive to create another mound high enough to scale the wall."

Frank frowned. "Shouldn't we send help to get them all off the island?"

Angelina shook her head. "I mentioned that to Doc Jenkins. He said the Survivors had married and bore children with the Night-timers. Here they all accept each other. He fears their children will be considered freaks if they return to the mainland. They have no intention of ever leaving."

Damien couldn't stop staring at her, couldn't believe he held her in his arms. His fingers wove through her hair, brushed over her lips, her eyes, the line of her jaw. When they came to rest on either side of her neck, he felt her pulse leap. He rested his forehead on hers and gazed intently into her eyes. "I thought I would die on the way here. I could feel your growing fear that we'd be too late."

"I knew you'd find a way to save us, Damien." Angelina kissed his neck. "I've missed you so very much. Every single day we spent apart, I called for you."

His eyes burned. "Forgive me, Angelina. I'll face banishment rather than spend another moment

Doreen Orsini

without you."

"You won't have to if I have anything to say about it."

They both turned to Frank.

"What?" He nervously shifted beneath their gaze. "If you knew what this nut was willing to do for you, mother, you wouldn't look so shocked. Any man, I mean vampire, willing to offer himself to those animals for my mother and daughter is okay by me." Frank hung his head. "God, he forgave me for —"

"Not now, Frank," Damien cut in.

"Man, look at them," Tomas yelled as he looked out the window of the helicopter.

Below, the Slashers clambered down a massive pile of bodies to follow the path of the low flying helicopter. On the other side of the wall, the townspeople waited beside towering ladders already leaning against the wall.

Angelina shuddered then turned her face into Damien's chest. "Will Diana and Lucian be alright?"

"I hope so, Angel." He didn't tell her he could barely hear their hearts beating. Didn't dare reveal how close they both were to stopping.

*****

Carcasses of the sharks daring and hungry enough to approach floated behind Olympia's kicking feet. The log she clung to scraped her arms raw hours ago, but the stabbing pain as each rough edge cut deeper into her flesh was nothing compared to the pulsating agony of the infection deep in her bicep. She kicked faster, terrified that dawn would catch her in this vast ocean.

Earlier a helicopter, one of her father's, had

soared over her head as it left the island. She had run to the shoreline and screamed out to its inhabitants than tore at her own hair when it continued on its way. Within moments she had dived into the water, her upper body clasping the remains of the tree she had found.

She slammed her fist into the tender gills of another brave shark and cackled as its body soared into the air. Oh, life was good. The fools aboard the helicopter had to know she had been there and believed her trapped. No longer a threat. Fools.

Kicking even faster, she began to devise a plan that would make them all rue the day Damien chose that whore over her.

She had foolishly thought when she had snatched the whore's son from his dreams and mentally led him to the lake and his mother decades ago that she had succeeded.

Certain that his heart was then hers for the taking, she had convinced her father to order Damien to become her mate. It didn't matter that he had refused to mate. She had thought time would change his mind.

But it hadn't taken her long to realize that the woman still held Damien's heart in the palm of her hand. After a few, measly decades, she had known she would never win his love as long as that woman lived.

She should have killed Angelina long ago instead of giving into her need to make the bitch suffer, make her lose touch with sanity. But nothing she'd done, not killing her husband or grandchildren had driven the woman mad. And when she'd sent Angelina's daughter-in-law to Europe in search of a sister that never existed, wiping out all memories of her husband and daughter, she'd thought Diana's grief would shatter Angelina's heart, push her over the edge. Instead, she'd grown even stronger for her grandchild.

Olympia's eyes welled up.

How many nights had she lain beside Damien, praying he would touch her just once?

She might as well have been alone. Decades and not one kiss, not one caress. Oh, they would pay. Every last one of them.

Banishment meant nothing. She would gladly leave.

And her father? She had to be miles from Fentmore. She still received no response, still found his thoughts and actions blocking off her constant probes. He would pay, too.

But she mustn't forget her brother. Desmond had lowered his defenses just long enough to condemn her for her interference with Lucian's bonding and to declare she no longer had the right to call him brother.

They would all suffer.

A dark form took shape on the horizon. Land! Water sprayed into the air above her churning feet. When she realized why the buildings lining the shore looked so familiar, why the crowd watching her approach sent chills down her spine, it was too late. A current too strong to be natural dragged her in.

*****

Frank thought his lungs would burst. They'd already walked at least a mile into the woods. Even with Tomas and the pilot carrying Diana and Lucian, he found it nearly impossible to keep up. Damien and Angelina were far ahead.

He was just about to plead with them to stop and let him rest when a cottage came into view.

Leaning against the white picket gate, he stopped to catch his breath. When he finally entered the cottage, a fire already burned brightly in the fireplace and the four were tenderly gazing down at the bed.

Frank cleared his throat. Still bound together with sheets from shoulders to toes, their lips touching, their wrists wedged between their chests, the couple appeared to be sleeping. Frank noticed for the first time that evening that their shoulders were bare.

"Are they naked?" he asked hoarsely.

"As jay birds." Tomas grinned, and held up a pair of black jeans. "Found these under the sheets at the hospital. Gotta be naked for Ancient Bonding, dude. United. One."

Frank's grimace had Tomas smirking. "You do know that—" he began.

"Tomas!" Damien shook his head.

Angelina just smiled.

Frank went to the bed. No one had to tell him that Lucian's hips were nestled between his daughter's legs. The shape of their bodies made it quite obvious. "Thank God he's unconscious," he muttered, reining in the overpowering urge to tear the two apart.

Tomas chuckled.

Damien turned away when Frank's eyes met his.

"He's unconscious," Frank repeated as if they hadn't heard.

"He'd have to be dea—"

"Tomas! Use your head. He's her father." Damien spun around. "Now Frank, it's not what you're thinking."

"No?" Frank scowled. "Then why don't you explain what the hell young Tomas here is just bursting to tell me?"

Diana moaned.

Damien flung his arm over Frank's shoulder and gently but firmly led him away from the bed. "Their not actually doing what you're thinking, Frank. But they, well...help me out here, Angel."

Angelina joined them in front of the fireplace. "Now, Frank, don't get all righteous on us. If you try to separate them—"

"But he's unconscious," he repeated, and dropped onto the chair. "It's just not right."

"They are unconscious, dear" Angelina rested her hand on his shoulder. "Their just..."

"Bonding." Tomas' voice was filled with awe. "Their hearts beating as one, their blood united to give them life, and their bodies merged into one being. See the romance of it, dude."

Another moan came from the bed.

"Why the hell is she doing that if they're not actually doing anything?" Frank asked, wearily closing his eyes. "Don't any of you believe in the sanctity of marriage?"

"You can't get any more married than this. Once you're joined like this, you're bonded mates whether you go before the elders or not. Some believe their spirits will now be together for all eternity." Tomas rose and drew in a deep breath.

"Tomas, don't forget, only true soul mates can even hope to survive an Ancient Bonding." Damien warned.

"Yeah, I know. I know."

A cough from the doorway reminded them that Tomas's friend, Diego, was in the cottage. Frank groaned. "Must everyone watch my daughter bond?"

Tomas strode up to his friend. "What do you say we check out the bars? For all we know, our soul mates might be sitting in one right now. You don't need us anymore, do you, Damien?"

Damien shook his head. "Don't forget, Tomas. Ancient bonding is dangerous."

"Yeah, yeah. I hear ya."

*****

Angelina went over to the bed. "When will we know if they'll be alright?"

Damien sighed.   Diana's mouth suckled at Lucian's neck. Leaning down, he absorbed the sound of their combined hearts. While Diana's pounded in his ears, he had to strain to catch the soft thump of Lucian's. The sound of blood trickling from his veins into hers told him all he needed to know. The tables had turned.

"Well?" Frank asked, his hushed voice booming in the silent room.

Ignoring him, Damien strode to the kitchenette and filled two tumblers with Jack Daniels. Turning he held them out to Frank and Angelina. When they both shook their heads, he downed both drinks. "It's going to be long night."

Pillows flew off the couch onto the oak floor. Standing beside the couch, Frank gasped.

"Go to sleep, Frank," Damien commanded with his voice and mind.

When the hunter dropped down onto the pillows, Damien turned to Angelina and opened his arms. Capturing her mouth, he supped on her sweet taste like a man starved and entered her mind. Angelina pulled away.

"Don't you dare, Damien. I'll wait with yo..." her voice trailed off as she succumbed and, collapsing in his arms, fell into a deep sleep. The scent of her blood enflamed him. His fangs pierced his lip; his erection throbbed. For years he'd dreamt of holding her again, of sinking his teeth into her slender neck, his cock into her tight pussy. But Lucian and Diana needed him.

The elders had banned Ancient Bondings after they'd lost countless vampires. Too many had seen soul mates where there were none; too many had erred in the binding of their wrists.

Yes, Dracula and Mina had survived. But only because they'd had the angels on their side. They had told Mina to bind both wrists to her lover at the same time, had explained that she would not survive if their combined blood did not flow from Dracula back into her body and replenish every ounce she lost. Had explained that even if she succeeded in bringing him back to life, he'd succumb with her death. What Damien had feared most when he'd first entered Fentmore's hospital and discovered Lucian had erred was occurring. Diana's body, in its instinctive need to survive, had sucked the life from Lucian for too long. By the time Damien had bound their other wrists, Lucian had filled her mind with only one thought.

Drink.

Now, his blood flowed from both his wrists into her body.

He laid Angelina on the couch and brushed her lips with his. "Forgive me, Angel, but you wouldn't understand what I have to do. I couldn't chance you interfering and there's no time to explain."

Rising, he went to the side of the bed and knelt. "Diana."

When she didn't stir, he pressed his forehead to hers and merged their minds. *Diana.* *You must turn the tides of your blood. Send it back.*

Her fear and her will to survive took hold and strove to push him from her mind. He felt and heard her body suck in more of Lucian's blood, heard his stepson's heart falter.

Diana! He yelled into her mind. *Send it back. You're killing Lucian. If he dies, you die. Send it back.*

Bound this way, he knew she would balk at another's kiss and hoped it would snap her out of the feeding frenzy. He pulled her mouth from Lucian's neck and crushed her lips with his, felt her heart and mind explode with rage that he would dare take what belonged to her mate.

"Save him," he begged, his voice ragged. "Give him life."

The rush of her blood surging into Lucian released the tears searing Damien's eyes. Diana's melodic voice slipped into his mind, but she spoke to another.

A thousand nights, a thousand dances. Give me my wishes. Give me my stars.

Still merged with Diana, Damien saw a

multitude of memories rising in her mind like mist off a mid-summer lake. Memories of Diana as a child, a teen, a woman, memories of her dancing naked for the moon and saving the stars she bargained for, stars she'd hoped would someday grant her every wish. Her memories vanished in an explosion of light. Damien fell back, propelled away from the bed by some unknown force. Momentarily blinded, he rose up onto his knees and blinked into the white curtain surrounding the bed, blinked until he realized Diana's moon had come through for her. Millions of stars rained down upon her and Lucian. As each touched their bodies, it shattered then vanished. Seconds later, the last star landed where Diana's lips touched Lucian's. He couldn't be sure, but Damien thought this final star slipped between their lips.

At the sound of Lucian and Diana's hearts beating as one, he wiped the tears from his eyes and approached the bed. Not wasting a moment, he cut the sheets he'd tied around their bodies then set to work, separating their wrists and sealing the wounds that would always bear the scars of their bonding.

Diana's eyes fluttered open. Lucian's soon followed. Damien watched silently as without a word they brought their lips together. He drew in a deep breath then hit the switch that would lower the bed to his secret room before the sun rose.

He adjusted the cottage's security system. No one would be able to enter or exit without his help. He slid his hands beneath Angelina and lifted her from the floor. Her eyes flew open.

"Damien, you're really here. I thought it was another dream. That I'd wake to find I was still on that horrible island." Tears hovered over her lashes.

He pressed his lips to her forehead then laid her down on the bed. Angelina's eyes darted from the empty bed to the couch then to the floor. "Where's Diana and—"

"In our secret room. You do remember the nights we spent there, don't you?"

Holding her gaze, he slid the tip of his finger between her parted lips and felt himself grow hard as one of her fangs slit open his skin. Turning his finger over, he watched her eyes dilate, knew she remembered, then rested the cut on the center of her tongue.

Her first taste of his blood since their last night together thirty years ago.

His own hunger tore at him when her hot mouth enveloped his dripping finger and her tongue curled around it like a babe's to a nipple. His other hand removed her blood spattered sweater, the knowledge of her thirty year chill breaking his heart. "You won't need this any longer, Angelina."

She blinked when his fingers grazed her breasts as he moved to unbutton her shirt. "Frank—"

"Will not wake up until I want him to," he said, freeing a button with each word.

Angelina gasped as his hands swiftly removed her shirt and bra. "He said you and he spent all day yesterday going over the map and talking."

"We did." He pushed her shoulders until she fell back onto the pillows.

"So you haven't slept for—"

"Nearly thirty-six hours." Her pants slid off to reveal a scant lace thong. He frowned. "Tell me your psychic ability led you to dress for today."

"I've been dressing for you for thirty years," her voice cracked.

He slid his finger beneath the thin strap on her hip.

"I'd understand if you were tired," she whispered.

"I'm tired of waiting for this moment." His finger followed the line of the thong until it touched her soft curls. "So, you've been wearing sexy underwear for thirty years? For me?"

Her eyes welled up. Her hand flew to her mouth but failed to stifle her sob.

He waggled his brows. "Oh, Angel, you know I prefer you naked." He flicked his wrist then tossed the tattered thong over his shoulder. When she giggled, he let out a relieved sigh. That short sob had told him exactly how unbearable their time apart had been for her. "Do you want to see what I've been wearing while I waited for you?"

Angelina's eyes rounded. "You didn't. You said you'd never, not even for me."

She sat up and quickly unbuttoned his shirt. Pushing it off his shoulders she checked his arms, chest, and back then frowned.

Damien rose to stand beside the bed and popped open the snap on his jeans.

"No." She knelt, her eyes twinkling. She moved closer to the edge of the bed as he brought the zipper down. His hand stilled. Before her eyes the bulge in his pants grew.

He regretted the delay this little show would cause on his return into Angelina's heat, cursed himself for starting it. The firelight caressed her skin, danced across her breasts and inner thighs. He envied it.

He noticed her eyes darken with desire, her thigh muscles clench.

"Oh, damn!" He quickly stripped and stood naked before her, his hands on his hips.

Her wide eyed gaze first landed on his massive erection, jutting straight out from a bed of black curls, then darted to the tattoo to the right of them.

"Oh, Damien. My tattoo." A heart with her name scrawled across it and a silly lovebird atop it, just as she'd described when she'd thought they would spend eternity together. She leaned closer, ran her fingers over her name. His penis twitched.

"A man, Angelina, just as you asked. I let a man sit between my legs for hours. For you."

"But, Olympia."

"Never saw it. I haven't touched another woman since you, Angel. And no one has touched me." He cupped her chin in his palm and tilted her face up so she could look into his eyes. "As far as I'm concerned, we completed our bonding. Our failure to go before the elders didn't change the fact that we bonded. You have always been my bonded mate."

She rose up and wrapped her arms around his neck. "And you mine, Damien. I never doubted that you were mine."

A tear rolled down his cheek. His eyes closed. "But I betrayed your trust."

"No. I understand why you stayed away." She wiped the tear away but another soon took its place. She pressed her lips to it.

"Our baby, Angel. I took our baby."

Angelina's lips stilled.   "Our baby died, Damien." She squeezed her eyes shut.

The hissing and snapping of the fireplace was the only sound in the room.

"We had to take him. He was one of us." Damien cringed when Angelina wrenched free of his arms.

She scrambled back across the bed to the far wall, shaking her head. "You came to the hospital? You took my baby?"

"I—"

"But then you must have seen me. You must have seen I wasn't mad!"

"No, Angel, I never saw you. I didn't even know about it until the elders sent for me. They already had our baby and—"

"Why?" she cried, "Didn't they know how I longed to hold him, to look into his face and see you? Oh, God, why?"

"How could he have lived in your world? He would have been treated like a freak." He moved across the bed toward her but stopped when she held out her hand and violently shook her head.

"I was his mother. I would have protected him." She spat each word out, the pain of losing her baby as piercing as it had been that night.

"Olympia told me she'd seen you. That you were crazy from the hunger. If I had gone to you, I would have been bound by our laws to bring you to Fentmore. I couldn't take that chance. And I couldn't trust your husband to accept a vampire as his son with you not sane enough to help. So I brought him into my home and raised him—"

"Tell me where he is, Damien," she coldly demanded, "Tell me where my son is!"

*****

Before Angelina's eyes the face of the man who'd been willing to offer himself to the Slashers to save her life crumbled when he opened his mouth to answer. She wanted to sooth him, wanted to cover her ears with her hands and never hear what had happened to cause him such agony.

A torrent of tears flowed from his eyes. The more he tried to explain the more he sobbed. Her heart shattered for Damien, for the son she now knew no longer lived.

She sat back and drew the sheets up to her breasts. Unable to bear witness to Damien's raw grief, she stared out into the room and caught sight of her first born sleeping peacefully on the floor. He'd said he accepted Damien as her soul mate yet had not met her eyes the entire flight home. Her son, the vampire hunter. Avoiding her eyes just like he had as a child when he felt he'd done something unforgivable.

"Oh, God. Tell me it wasn't Frank. Please, Damien, tell me the vampire he's been insisting was you wasn't our son. Please!" For the first time since she'd watched Damien walk away from her and Frank at the lake, Angelina felt her sanity slip.

Damien wrapped his arms around her, pinning her arms when she struck out at him, again and again.

"No! You're lying!" she wailed, "Oh, dear God, not Frank!"

He held her, his tears falling upon her cheeks,

mingling with hers. "He didn't know. He didn't know, Angelina," he repeated, over and over in her ear. "He had no idea he had caught his own brother."

She buried her face in the crook of his neck and cried for what felt like hours.

After a while, Damien loosened his grip and let out a sigh of relief when she clung to him. He drew her onto his lap and ran his fingers through her hair.

"Forgive him, Angel," he said. "He was still that angry little boy believing in monsters. But he's changed these past hours. He's come to understand us, to see us as more than unfeeling monsters. And he's terrified you'll never forgive him."

"Did he have the name I chose?" she asked, her ragged breath cutting into her words. "You remember. I told you I wanted our first son to have your father's name."

Damien smiled. "Yes, my love. I insisted. And he had a happy youth, Angelina. He grew to be a good man, one you'd be proud of."

He cupped her cheeks in his hands and gazed intently into her eyes. "And he knew you were his mother. I had to tell him you'd died in childbirth, but I told him all about you, about how much we loved each other. Then one day he came to me and asked me to describe you while he painted."

"He was an artist?" Her breath hitched. "Like me?"

He leaned over and lifted his pants from the floor then took out his wallet. "He gave this to me. Kept a larger one for himself. I've carried it with me since."

He pressed a small portrait into her hand.

Angelina gasped. It was her. Every detail. Her eyes, her nose, even the shirt she'd worn their last night together.

"And this I had done by another artist."

She raised her eyes from her portrait.

Damien stared down at the one he clasped between trembling fingers.

"Marek?"

He held the portrait to his heart before placing it in her outstretched palm.

"Oh, he's beautiful!" She swiped at her tears before they could fall onto the face of her son. "He looks just like you."

"He had your nose."

"Poor thing." She giggled. "And my father's ears, unfortunately. I always felt, here," she placed her hand over her heart, "that he was still alive. Sometimes I would wake up and hear a baby crying, convinced it was him. But everyone said I was just a mother refusing to admit her child was gone."

He kissed the top of her head. "He once told me it broke his heart that I'd lost my soul mate. He said he'd give up his own life if it could bring you back. That's the way he was, Angelina. Always willing to sacrifice his own needs and desires for those he loved."

"Then he must be very happy because, in a way, he did bring me back to you, didn't he?"

"Forgive me, Angel. I left you with nothing." Damien stared at the two pictures silently.

"Oh, Damien. You stayed away because you loved me and wanted to protect me from Fentmore." She brought his face close to hers and brushed her cheek along his. "And then, you took our son because you loved him and wanted to protect him from my world. There's nothing to forgive. Nothing."

This time, his lips made sweet love to hers. He kissed the tears from her lashes, her cheeks, her lips. Her nails dug into his chest.

The years spent apart melted away. Hands instinctively caressed the most sensitive spots. Familiar tastes flowed past clinging lips. Molten heat surged through veins as the growing hunger they'd contained for three decades erupted into an undeniable force.

Angelina's nails scored Damien's back, her need to get closer, closer than nature would allow obliterating her desire to be tender. Her legs wrapped around his hips as she twisted and turned, attempting to impale herself on his rock hard erection again and again.

Damien's hips brushed against her nubbin as he shifted from side to side, refusing to give her what she wanted.

She let out a cry of rage. "Damien!"

"No," he groaned, "I've waited too many years. Believed too many dreams that ended all too soon."

"This time I will go mad, Damien. And it will be your fault."

The guilt that flashed across his face immediately brought her to her senses. "Oh, Damien. I'm so sorry." She caressed his lips with her fingers. One slid into his mouth.

This time she would tempt him.

She winced at the stab of pain but the corners of her lips rose as the hard ridge pressing into her leg jumped.

Taking her finger from his mouth just before he could taste her life's essence, she delved into his mind. Memories of their past, of her wild tendencies, incited him. The pain in his groin escalated; his imagination took flight. She dropped back on the bed and let a drop of blood fall upon each erect nipple.

While one hand, planted firmly on his chest, held him back, the other seemed to dance before his hungry eyes, smearing more and more blood around each rosy peak.

"You're killing me!" he growled.

"You wanted to take it slow," she said, then brought her finger to her mouth and licked it clean. "Want a taste?"

He was upon her before her words left her mouth. She screamed. Heat enveloped her aching nipples, tiny pricks of pain covered her breasts. She knew she'd brought him over the edge, knew by they way he stopped himself again and again from burying his fangs into her tender breasts. She arched her back, driving her breasts deeper into his mouth. He flicked his tongue over the sensitive peaks until they felt raw then sucked them between his fangs. Trill after trill of pleasure had her squeezing her thighs tightly together, increasing the jolts that lodged at her apex.

Suddenly her nipples grew cold. She lifted her head than tossed it back onto the pillow when she saw his head move lower. The hands he wrapped around her knees trembled as he spread her legs. Again, she entered his mind.

Damien knelt between her legs, torn. His eyes

fastened on the drops of moisture on her quivering flesh, his shaft twitching in anticipation of sliding between those moist nether lips. But he knew what she anticipated, what she longed for, and he could not deny her.

He brushed the tip of his finger along each lip then down the center from her hot nubbin. Her pleas urged him on, begged him to devour her.

But he was enjoying the show. The way her flesh trembled each time his fingers fluttered over it, the way her hips rose up to him whenever he withdrew his hand. What set his blood on fire, what had him bringing his mouth down to taste those sweet, sweet drops now covering her, was the way her legs spread wider when he let out a long hot breath.

Angelina dug her hands into his hair the moment his mouth touched her. When he flicked his tongue over her clit, she whimpered. When he ran his fangs along her length, she cried out. When his hot mouth enveloped her, she let out a long, guttural groan.

And when he pierced her and proceeded to draw her combined essences into his mouth, she screamed and tumbled deep into an abyss of sensation.

While she was still lost in her orgasm, Damien swiftly rose up and plunged his cock between those sweet, quivering lips, felt her internal muscles grasp and hold him firmly in place. The harder he drove into her, the higher she raised her hips. He let out a roar that sounded more animal than man then buried his fangs deep into the neck she instinctively offered. But he did not draw her life's essence into his mouth until he felt her much smaller fangs pierce his own neck.

They fed on each other as his hot seed filled her womb, both lost in the vortex of pleasure that immediately enveloped them. They continued to suckle at each other's necks long after they floated down to earth, exchanging blood for blood until they were completely merged.

*****

Lucian's blood surged through Diana's veins, heating every inch of her body. And as they kissed, as his tongue branded every inch of her mouth, the muscles deep within her took possession of his growing shaft.

Lucian raised his head and gazed down into her eyes. "We are one, Diana. We've bonded the ancient way. Now, we are truly soul mates. Do you understand? If you die, I die."

"And if you die, I die," she whispered against his lips. "As it was before, Lucian. I could have never lived in this world without you."

"Say you'll be mine, Diana. Say you'll be my light in the endless nights ahead." He shoved his hands beneath her and, cupping her buttocks, drove himself deeper.

"Always, my love." The fire in his eyes sent molten heat to the muscles drawing him deeper.

"Mine." He nipped her neck then raised his head and stared into her eyes, a mischievous grin lifting his lips. "To do with as I please."

She grinned. "This is the twenty-first century, Lucian. I have a say in what you do."

He drew back then slammed into her. Crying out from the impact of the burning head of his cock, Diana felt her fangs shoot out.

"So, exactly what may I do?" he asked in a sultry whisper against her mouth.

Diana ran her hands over the muscles flexing across his shoulders and slid her tongue over his lips. When he growled, baring his fangs, she wriggled her hips. "You can take me the way I like it."

He lowered her hips then gently lifted them up to his, giving her only half of his length. "Like that, my sweet Diana."

Her growl startled her.

He chuckled wickedly. "Ah, it seems I've bound myself to an animal."

"If you don't take me the way I want, you'll see an animal." She bared her growing fangs and brought them down onto his chest. Lucian gasped as the tips grazed his nipples.

"Two can play this game." He tore her mouth from his chest and pressed her shoulders into the mattress.

Beginning at her collarbone he slowly kissed and nipped his way down to her breasts. She writhed beneath him, needing to incite him, to drive him mad with need. He stared at her breasts. Arching her back, she offered them up to him. "Don't stop, Lucian. Don't ever stop."

He licked at the tiny dots of blood oozing from the spots where his fangs had just pierced her skin. She felt his cock grow deep within her when she dug her hands into his hair and held his head against her chest. He suckled greedily at one taut peak until her screams rent the air.

When he released her breast and continued on down, she cried, begged then let out a long guttural moan when he rose and withdrew himself from her. His tongue lazed around her quivering stomach, teasingly moved down then swept back up to her bellybutton. Unable to bear it any longer, she reached down and shoved his shoulders until his head rested between her legs.

"Beg me, Diana," he ordered, his voice cracking on her name.

"Please, Lucian. I can't...I can't...oh!" Expecting more teasing, she shattered when his lips clamped over her clit and drew it into his hot wet mouth.

Lucian held onto her bucking hips and lapped up her juices until she'd gone as high as she thought possible then buried his teeth into the soft flesh between her nether lips. Diana heard a deafening roar, felt it reverberate through her body.

He sucked relentlessly, until she begged for his cock, for one taste of his blood. Rising, he slid his tongue back up her body to her collarbone.

"Tell me how you like it, Diana." He slid the length of his cock along her cleft.

"You know how I like it, Lucian. Stop torturing me," she demanded on a ragged breath.

"Like this?" He surged into her so forcefully she screamed.

"Yes," she cried, rising up to meet the next with equal force.

Diana's nerves exploded. Streaks of exquisite pleasure splintered out from her breasts and stomach to where his cock battered her. Nearly lost in the depths of her orgasm, she felt his hot seed burst from him and fill her womb.

Flinging her head to the side, she offered up her

neck and waited for the initial pain of his fangs piercing her skin, waited for the inferno that always scorched her veins when he took possession of her life's essence. Her lungs burned and still she waited. The veins in her neck rose in anticipation, trembled when only his warm breath flowed over her skin. "Lucian," she pled, turning to see why he hesitated

Crimson tears filled his eyes. His hands caressed every inch of her body then cupped her face. "In the hospital...I would have sold my soul to see your vein like this. Quivering, pulsing with life. I love you, Diana. I was a fool to let you go. I just..."

Diana kissed each bloody tear that escaped. "I never doubted you'd come back to me. And I never stopped loving you, Lucian. Never."

He brought her mouth to his neck. Diana buried her fangs deep into his bulging vein. As she sucked ravenously on his warm, sweet blood, the jolt of his teeth sinking into her neck threw her into another whirlpool of rapture.

They screamed against each other's necks, lost in the merging of their souls. One mind, one heart. Forever.

Introducing the Triskelion Book Club - great reads come to you every month. You'll have them delivered right to your doorstep! At 30% off MSRP that's a huge savings off retail. This is a delightfully decadent way to get great reads by your favorite authors and meet some new ones along the way.

You'll receive 4 new titles each month. HOT heroes, exotic locales and heroines that will make you cheer. You'll find exciting new stories from all of Triskelion's lines including Paranormal, Science Fiction, Urban Gothic, Suspense and many more. All at deliciously tempting heat levels that are sure to please!

DEPT 57

Jewel of the Dragon

Lynne Connolly

A secret department in the CIA
Agents with extreme abilities
Dangerous assignments with deadly twists
Are you ready to enter Department 57?

Available in March